NIGHTOWL

By Stephen Rysor

Copyright © Stephen Rysor 2016
All rights reserved.

ISBN 978-1540511423

Cover Art by Stephen Rysor

Edited by: Ben Silberman
           Hannah Cartwright
           Patricia Lyons
           Robert Alfis
           Juliette Nieradzik
           Darren Gillen
           Stephen Rysor

Visit www.facebook.com/stephenrysorofficial/ for more information from the author.

To Josephine

Hope you enjoy the book!

NIGHTOWL

Thanks!

Prologue: November 3rd, Just After Midnight

... And from this moment on, my past doesn't matter.

No more history to drag along behind me.

No more people to let me down.

I am a new person.

It doesn't matter who I was. All that matters is who I am now. Who I will be. I have a blank page ahead of me. This city can give me that. I don't know anyone here anymore and, better still, no one knows me. Standing on the pavement, watching cars and bikes race past me, I feel like a spectator while others act out the scene. I'm not connected to it any more.

I want to hide in the dark for a while. Unburden myself from the responsibility and grievances of existing on the same plane as everyone else. From the calm and quiet corners, rich with history, to the modern, edgy boulevards full of life, I will live in between. In a city like this, it's hard to make friends. Maybe then, it will be easier to not make any at all. Those we meet at night, we rarely meet again during the day.

Two different worlds living side by side. The day, where everyone is living in the moment. Full of cute or worrying distractions, we never really get time to think. Rush to work, rush home. Rarely ever really going anywhere but always moving. This city is a paradox in the daylight. A place where everyone is Zen, and no one is at peace. We all mill around and mix into each other, but the night gives us space. This city, overall, becomes still at night. I can live in peace. Drift through the lonely streets with my thoughts. Only the odd, silent straggler wandering home after a loud night with friends. Cover myself in the tranquil nights of Paris.

The dull, frosty puddle on the street paints a poor picture of me. Dark, ragged hair with flecks of silver. Older than a young man like myself should look. Rough and dishevelled. Just worn out. A crumpled grey shirt under a brown jacket. Sad, blue eyes stare back through the ice. I seem to have lost my way a little.

I fumble around in my pocket for a cigarette. I'm exhausted. So apathetic. I've burdened myself with memories and thoughts for too long. Time to escape them. If I've finally cracked then maybe I can break out of this shell? Fly away. Never be part of the flock.

I'm making this my fresh start. Being lost is the best way to find myself. I can come back to the world when I'm ready. Build myself up from scratch. Burn through this cloud over my head. Be someone I only ever dreamed of. And what better way to dream than at night?

No need for me to have a name in the night. People come and go.

No more roots.

Just somewhere to perch from.

You can call me Nightowl.

Case 1 - Papers

He makes me want to strangle him, this boss of mine. I only started this job three weeks ago and I hate him already. He profits from the hard work of his employees, giving nothing back except maybe a bad wage and a stomach ulcer. It's fortunate that I don't see him too often, although had I seen him often it would indicate that he actually does something here.

When he does come in, his greasy, dyed-black hair shining more than his grim, brown eyes, he looks around and groans about anything that might look out of place. A painting hung slightly askew or dust on top of an unused shelf. Trivial things that won't break the place, yet he thinks needs immediate attention. But before it's done there's another thing lined up.

The work here wasn't too difficult at the beginning, only now I find myself working harder than I'm being paid for. Normally, a night porter simply lets guests in, gives them their keys, cleans and performs a few administrative duties. I'm able to do these things, but it's jarring to have a two minute break broken by Crow squawking down the phone at me with some new mundane task while he monitors the cameras.

How I hate him. The way his crooked spine, by the ravages of time, gives him the excuse to peer into my face each time he whispers his displeasure. He flies around the city, enjoying himself, while his cameras circle around me. Several small, black, beady eyes constantly surveilling my every move. I work and he watches. My sweat, his savings. This bastard, Crow...

Maybe I can't complain, a job is a job. They're hard to come by these days and this hotel isn't a terrible place to be stranded. I do enjoy the solitude. A thick silence hangs over me, only faint rumours of people milling around above. I can tune out those speaking foreign languages, even French, to background noise and ignore them all, be alone.

I rarely have any real conversations with the few guests I meet. Most of them say nothing at all. Others just make small talk. No words spoken too big to chew on later. These people I like. I find there's a certain sense of peace in talking without really saying anything.

The hotel itself exhibits a faded elegance that's not often seen. Scratched mahogany on the floor in an open foyer. Leather chairs in the middle, just to the right of the door as you enter. Beside the elevator, the stairs are made of a smooth limestone that echoes of history, lined with red carpet and wood. The sides of the steps have slight blemishes of red wine spills, near impossible to remove, which have mysteriously turned green.

Crumpled, cherry-coloured, satin curtains hang over the windows, their creases reflecting the light. The front doors are heavier than most, being made of strong wood and rich brass. The glass windows on the doors seem almost unbreakable being so thick. White marble walls with ornate engravings on the outside. The room where the guests eat their breakfast is, without sounding sarcastic, quite cosy. Although, the dark green carpet that gives the room its homeliness can only get darker as more food is dropped onto it.

Even the concierge desk where I work is comfortable. I'm bestowed with a new chair and an old desk. I have comfort and reliability. The sturdy counter seems like it has lasted a long time and, when one contrasts the computer on top of such a vintage worktop, it will last for a long time to come. Polished, steel chandeliers dot the ceiling every fifteen steps, their electric bulbs showing off the flawless metal. This place was once a palace.

Once...

****

At 3am, she walks in. Long, blonde hair under a dark, brimmed hat. The shadow cast over her face by the lights slightly veils her appearance, although she seems to be quite attractive and youthful for a woman I'm assuming is in her early thirties. Her left hand fidgets in the pocket of her white long-coat as she pauses in the lobby. A sparkly, charcoal band under her coat suggests she's wearing a black cocktail dress or skirt. She turns quickly in the other direction. The wood squeaks and clacks as her high-heels march away. Bold steps for a woman so slight of figure.

She makes her way over to the chairs in the foyer and sits down. Picking up a newspaper, she opens it right down the middle and leans her head into the pages. Occasionally, she glances over the paper and around the room, often catching my quizzical glances, before retreating back in.

She's forced to keep shaking the paper to keep it from drooping over. It's curious behaviour. So hissy and precious. I'll leave her be. I mean, I could ask her what she's waiting for or offer her assistance, but this chair is comfy and I really don't care.

Half an hour is filled with her flapping, peeping and shuffling in her seat. I'm starting to get annoyed. It's the tearing of the pages that breaks me. The ripping noise alarming me the first time, only to see her take the square and fold it. I stride towards her, inhaling to soothe my agitation before I reach her.

"Good evening, Madame."

"Hello." Her voice is soft, spoken with a Received Pronunciation English accent.

"Can I help you with something?"

"No, thank you."

"Are you a guest here?"

"No..."

"Then I'm afraid I'm going-"

A thumping sound comes from the window. Outside, a homeless man stares at us with ominous intent and sips on a can of beer. He lingers there for a few moments before shuffling off. These random occurrences tend to happen every now and then. The significance of them is lost on me. Half the time, I barely give them any notice.

"I'm waiting for someone." She tells me, her hands putting a final crease on the paper to reveal an origami Swan.

"For a guest here?"

"Yes."

"May I ask which one? I can call the room for you."

"That won't be necessary."

"But-"

"- Nope."

"Miss-"

"- Look-"

"- Now-"

"- My husband is having an affair in this hotel!" She says with an air of indignant humility. I can't help but notice that there's no sadness in her voice.

"I'm- I'm sorry." What started off as me asking her to repeat herself comes out as a sympathetic response.

She sighs and looks down. "It's fine... But I could do with your help."

"My help? You want me to confirm that he's registered here?"

"I know he's here! I saw him walk in with some bitch!" She pauses, holding her hand up to her mouth. Now she's upset. Once again she takes a breath and composes herself while I stare timidly around her, only catching fleeting glances directly at her. She clears her throat.

"I want his room number."

My turn to be indignant. "I can't just give out room numbers to anyone!"

"Either you tell me, or I'll come the other side of that counter and check myself!"

Judging by her size, I'd like to think I could restrain her, but there's a look on her face that tells me I'd probably end up on the floor screaming if I did try and stop her.

"Ma'am, please... Control yourself."

She's starting to look embarrassed now. "Then I need *you* to take a photo of him... With her."

"Oh! I- I don't think I can do something like that. I'm not even supposed to leave my desk! I'm sorry it's just tha-"

"- I can't do it, he'll recognise me! It's either this or I go marching into each room in this hotel! Take your pick, either we do this discreetly or there's drama!"

I really hate drama.

"Well, Ma'am-"

"- I have money!" She blurts out and begins to rummage through her bag.

"It's not about the money, ma'am. I just can't do... *This*..."

She stares back at me, frustrated, and throws a wad of fifty Euro notes onto the coffee table. My eyes pop out of my head, just for a moment. It's a lot of money. But I can't take it. She's vulnerable and nothing in life is really free, is it? With a little self-resentment, I push the notes back to her.

"I can't take this... And... I can't do it... I really am sorry."

She starts to lose control, shaking her head and raising her hand to her eyes.

"No, please! You have to understand..." The words come out like leaves off a shaken branch, fluttery and frail.

"Ma'am, I-"

"- Please!"

She takes my hand and looks right into my eyes. So brown and weary. She's tearing up. It's not the first time a woman has grabbed my hand in this hotel, but they're usually four or five Gin and Tonics in before they do. Her grip becomes tighter, the cold gold around her finger digging its way into mine.

"I *need* you to do this. I need this to be *over*..."

She won't stop staring at me. I can see closer. The creases around her eyes and the grim bags underneath them. Familiar evidence of sleepless nights, tossing and turning in agony, the scalding neurons of dread flowing through her head. I feel awful. No one deserves what she's feeling. Through her welling eyes I can see glimpses of a mad desperation mixed with a horrible uncertainty.

Her other hand is still holding the paper Swan tightly. The only thing about her that doesn't seem damaged. Poor Mrs. Swan...

I should help her. After all, who am I to turn down help to someone that needs it? Although, that doesn't mean I have to be happy about it. I pull back my hand and sigh.

"Alright... I'll do it."

"Thank you!" She stands up and wipes her eyes. "Thank you so much."

"I don't have a camera though."

"I brought one!"

She rummages through her bag and pulls out a small, black digital camera. It occurs to me now that I could have used my phone, but it's better that I don't leave too many of my own fingerprints on this.

I need a minute to fully evaluate what it is I'm doing. This could get me in a lot of trouble. My boss would be furious. Maybe even more furious than usual? Also, the police could be called if I get caught. Spying on people is illegal, as far as I'm aware, and not knowing the penalty makes it a little bit more frightening. I better not get caught.

Her husband must want to cover his tracks, so even if I knew his name, it's unlikely that I'd find it. So, how do you find someone that doesn't want to be found?

Cash! He'd want to pay in cash so it wouldn't be on his credit card bill. I search through the log of all the people who paid in cash. Three people today. Only one of them is booked for just one night.

"Okay, that's-" I stop myself from reading the room number out loud. No need for this to get messier than it already is. "That's okay."

She looks at me, embarrassed, and hands me the camera. "I'll just wait here then..."

After glancing at her, and being quite aware that my facial expression wasn't exactly eager or keen, I make my way through the foyer to the stairs.

It dawns on me, while on my clandestine mission, that I too am being spied on right now. With his eyes on the walls my boss can see everything. I can appreciate the irony that I'm avoiding being spied on so I can spy on someone else. I reckon I'll need a valid excuse to leave the foyer. The excuse is quite easy to come up with. The good, old-fashioned "I heard a noise" usually goes without questions.

There aren't that many cameras aimed at the guests, it's not them he doesn't trust, so getting there undetected should be easy enough once I'm out of the foyer. Mr. Swan is on the first floor, Room One. Our cheapest room. The camera I need to get past is at the bottom of the stairs. Fortunately, it was knocked slightly to the side by one of my colleagues. This blunder happened when our boss asked him to polish the lens because he couldn't see properly. The irony builds.

Hugging the window, I awkwardly sneak my way over. From here I can climb over the bannister and onto the stairs without being seen. Now the fun part is over.

I walk slowly, my heavy feet climbing the stairs, yet I'm still there in seconds. I pause in front of the brass sign for the room numbers. One to fourteen on the left, fifteen to twenty-seven on the right. There's a camera watching the hall but the light is never on. Knowing my boss, it definitely doesn't work.

Outside Room Four, a cart loaded with towels is abandoned at a crooked angle. One of the maids obviously didn't stay a second longer than their shift. This could be useful though. Inside the cart there are fresh towels, some small bottles of shampoo and a grey, plain baseball cap that I presume was left behind by a guest.

I put the cap on, take off my jacket and move to one of the mirrors. With the white shirt and black waistcoat that I'm wearing, it could almost seem like it's part of the uniform. I just need to raise the pile of towels in front of my face and I have a disguise. I think if I hide the camera in the towels I can take the photos without them knowing. I turn the flash off on the camera and position it in a way that the lens peeks out. All I need now is a good excuse to go in.

At the door to Room One, I'm held up from knocking on the door by a cardboard *Do Not Disturb* sign. I put my ear up against the door to confirm that both husband and mistress are present. Judging by the muffled giggling, I'd say both are present and accounted for. I can see through the crack in the door that the light is on in their room. Surely if I knock the lights out, they'll leave to investigate. Then I'll take the incriminating photos of them together.

There's a silence and my heart stops. The muffled talking seems to be slower and more playful. I need to kill the lights before the sparks start flying. I race away from the door and head towards the fusebox. Fortunately, the fuses are properly numbered by room. I flick the switch down and creep my way back towards the cart. There's a cheer from inside the room followed by giggling, rummaging and squeaking. I'm probably the one that's going to have to fix that bed... I'll need to think of something else.

Five minutes go by and I've got nothing, but the moaning seems to have stopped. The door to Mr. Swan's room swings open. A middle-aged man with a receding hairline and a simple face plods out, wearing only a white bathrobe. His chest is laid bare, all flushed and scarlet, betraying him. He's been busy.

"Hey! Gimme one of those towels, yeah?" His Mancunian accent makes it a little difficult for me to understand right away.

I raise the towels to cover my face better and stare down at the pile on the cart, all folded by one of my co-workers, albeit rather poorly. "I can't really just give these out. They're for the empty rooms."

He marches towards me and grabs a towel off the trolley before he leans in close to my ear. "I'm the guest here, you do what I say!" He hisses.

I stare back at him over the pile. My fist clenches and my nails bite into the soft fabric. He looks me up and down quickly then turns away muttering to himself. "Fucking Frenchies."

Not an expert on accents it seems, not that I have much of an accent anyway. Still, the less he knows, the better.

Before he reaches the door, a young, moderately-attractive-but-not-exactly-stunning brunette steps out wrapped in a towel. "What's taking so long?" She whines.

She seems to be in her twenties, but the way she hangs off the door makes her look about sixteen.

"Nothin', babes." He grunts.

On further inspection, I realise that she's mistakenly taken one of our floor towels. While not exactly a tiny piece of cloth, it's a snug fit on her. Every curve being accentuated. The edge of the cloth pressed against her upper thigh. She *is* pretty attractive now that I think of it and if I don't focus on something else then I might have to lower these towels.

Mr. Swan clears his throat and I wake up from my daze. Fumbling around awkwardly under the towels, I start to take the photos. When he reaches the door, he kisses her deeply. Camera's rolling.

"Ooh! So manly!" She pulls her head back and looks at me. "Hellooo!"

"Miss." I nod back at her, courteously. I think I might be blushing.

Jesus...

"He's so shy hidin' behind them towels. Isn't he?" She muses. He gives me the blankest of stares.

Slowly and loudly, she asks "WHAAAT IIIS YOWOR NAAAME?"

I speak English, and I can barely understand her.

"Sorry?"

"YOOOR NAAAMUH!"

"It's-" Shit! "- Pierre."

Whatever disease that's causing her to talk like that seems to be contagious.

"Ooh la la! Very French!" She titters. "You say that here, don't you? Ooh la la?"

"Eh... Oui." I realise that I'm looking at a perfect opportunity.

"And your name, Mademoiselle?"

Her head leans at an angle, like one side is heavier than the other.

"My name is Robin. Robin with a Y!" Robyn says.

Maybe it's more likely that one side is lighter?

Mr. Swan grabs her by the arm. "Don't be telling him anything! It's none of his business!"

She giggles. "Ooh la la, someone is getting jealous, I think!" Turning to me again. "My name is Robyn and I'm from-"

"- Oi!"

"You are jealous, aren't you?!" She shouts, in the hallway full of sleeping people, and pokes him. These two are just the worst.

"'Course not babe." He grins. "I know you belong to me!" And with those romantic words that suffrage forgot, she touches his face and laughs. *Click, click*. He gives her a peck on the lips, *click*, turns to me, snorts and pushes her back into the room with a smack on her rear. The door clicks shut as the camera yields its last.

    They're gone. The silence seems to rush back into the air. My heart is pounding. I exhale pure relief before I pull the camera out of the towels with shaking hands. The pictures came out almost perfectly! Although the images are framed by the towels and aren't as close as I'd like, I can zoom in on their faces in viewer mode. It's clear enough for an identification. I feel great! There's a roguish sense of validation still lingering in my bones. Dare I say I'm smiling. The silence is broken by muffled cackling and cooing from the other side of the door. I think it's time I left.

****

    I make my way down the stairs slower than I made my way up. It's not the first time I've seen a marriage fall apart, but it is the first time I've felt like an agent in the mess; depending on perspective, I suppose. What if they had kids? Did I break a marriage to its end or did I end a broken marriage? These questions keep spinning in my head as I lean against the railing of the stairs. I know that her husband's in the wrong, so why protect a fiction?

    I guess I won't...

    I'll need to think of something to say to her, words of comfort or empathy. I'm drawing a complete blank here and I'm already at the bottom of the stairs. She's still sitting on one of the chairs in the lobby, only a few metres away from me.

    Her head is drooped down, her nose almost touching her chest. Yet still, she looks elegant. Her frayed nerves shown by the way her hands grasp the sides of the chair underneath her. What were once rosy cheeks of fiery passion are now pale and white as snow. She doesn't seem to notice that I'm here.

    With the few seconds I have, I gather my courage and walk purposefully towards her. Her neck cranes up slightly, but she still doesn't make eye contact with me. I can imagine that she's hurt, but her face is vacant, as if she left all the woes in her head and went out for a walk. I stand in front of her for a few seconds before I bend down to her level, placing my hands on my knees for support. She blinks a few times in rapid succession, then stops.

"You have the photos, don't you?" The empty stare has an empty voice.

"I do, ma'am." I try to keep my voice as soft and as apologetic as possible.

"I should take a look then, shouldn't I?"

"Only if you want. You don't have to look at them now."

"No... I should do this now."

She reaches out for the camera and I pass it to her gently. Her hands are shaking a little. I'm close enough to her to hear teeth grinding under lipstick lips. An irate respiration comes out of her nose as she scans each photo. With fleeting glimpses, I notice that she's looked at all the photos several times. I can almost smell the bile and rage evaporating out of her.

She eventually returns to the photo of her husband kissing his mistress for the fifth time and stops to stare at it. Every muscle in her body is tensing tighter and tighter. She looks like she's going to implode, but her flight into madness reaches its height and she settles down again. Not calm, but certain. She turns the camera off and puts it back in her bag.

"At least it's not my best friend. Or my sister." She sighs. "One cliché is enough. A private eye and an affair."

"Her name, if you want it?"

She hesitates for a moment. "Tell me."

"Robyn?"

"Robyn... Robyn with a Y?"

"Yeah..."

"That's his secretary... I guess I can't avoid another cliché!" She laughs manically for a moment then grimaces and looks down at her ring. "He was a good man once, you know? He used to make me these paper Swans. Told me he wasn't good enough to make a Crane."

Her eyes dart around the floor and I can see her playing the memories in her head. Seeing as I've come this far, I might as well hear the full story.

"Tell me about him?"

She speaks softly. Her story sounds tired but the articulation is fresh. She clearly hasn't been able to talk to many people about her circumstance. How she once loved a man with a kind spirit who devoted himself to her. He was a sensitive man. They were happily married for six years when they decided to add a child to their content coupling. She chokes on a laugh as she talks about how they imagined a child with his big ears and her long nose, how funny it would have looked. A pause and a watery eye lingers before she continues. Her voice quavers in agitated grief as she recounts the first month without result. This led on to the next month, to the next. She counted eight in total before they dragged themselves to a doctor, who referred them to a specialist.

A tear plummets from her eye and dashes her cheek. "He held my hand... And he looked at me... And he said: *No matter what happens we'll get through this together!*" Her voice breaks as my heart twinges. "I felt so *safe*... So *loved*... I didn't *care* what was going to happen next. I had *him*! *He* was enough!"

The pair took the tests and waited. There was a dark electricity in the air that bristled with anxiety. For those few weeks, they forgot each other and thought only of the tests. They wanted out from under that shadow, but the doctor called and in the office they sat. She describes to me the curtness, seemingly disinterested manner of the healer behind the desk. The doctor stated that the sperm count was too low and relatively immobile. He continued to talk about their limited options for a natural conception. He offered no solutions, but alternatives. No way forward, but around. Her husband's hand, so neatly fitted into hers, slipped away as the sterile man walked out into the sterile hall.

He spoke little after that. Stared into space alone or was distracted during conversations. He drifted further and further away, completely lost. Low and immobile like the doctor said he was. His interest in having children leaving with him.

Instead of moving forward, they moved apart. He became short with her. His loving face replaced by anger and guilt. The guilt. How he reeked of it. Every argument he started, he held an air of self-defence. She pleaded that she was never trying to hurt him, but he was deaf to it. A year passed with some good days and a lot of bad ones as he began to change. His slim frame grew bulkier and his hair shorter. He came home late, doused in whiskey and perfume. Just whiskey at the start, and, only recently, just perfume. Her story concludes on that, leaving me to fill in the gaps.

What can I say to a story like that? I settle for nodding my head in sympathy.

She looks up at me and pulls out the money she had before.

"Thank you for everything." She says as she tries to put the money in my hand.

"I can't accept this, ma'am." The self-resentment comes back in the form of me pinching my legs.

"Yes, you can. You've given me closure."

"You've had quite a bad night. I reckon I can chalk this up as a favour. Keep the money."

I need to stop talking.

"A tip, then." She pulls a fifty Euro note out and stuffs it into one of my pockets. "And I won't take no for an answer."

I give her a sad smile and nod my head. "I appreciate it."

She gets up off the chair and makes her way to the door, then turns to me with brimming eyes. "You've been kind to me. I am so very grateful for all your help!"

She reaches for the door handle and, as her left hand grabs it and pulls, her wedding band of gold clinks against the brass. "How much do you think I could get for this?" She asks rhetorically, a dry, smug undertone laced in her voice.

I smile back at her and shrug.

"There aren't many people out there like you!" She declares. "I did the only thing I had left... You did what was right."

With that parting phrase, Mrs. Swan swoops out and the door swings shut behind her. Her high-heels click on the pavement for a few steps before they fade out.

Her last words buzz electric in my mind. I think I did the right thing. If a marriage is falling apart then the least I could do is catch some of the pieces as they fall. Now that she has the evidence she needs, she can find better.

He's not so lucky. I wonder, when he stood at the alter with her, vowed to stand by her for richer and poorer, did he imagine himself to end up the poorer? I must admit, I wouldn't feel this good if he hadn't been so arrogant to me. Although, I'm pretty sure there's a correlation between being an adulterer and an asshole.

The evidence on the camera changed something in her. She started a clean sheet and threw out his dirty ones. Found a way out from the dreary life she lived before, tied at the finger to that horrible man. From the moment she walked out that door, she was born again. Baptised in tears.

For the first time in months, I feel good about myself. I have purpose. I want to keep doing this. I could keep doing this! Help strangers with their problems when they have no one else. Find solutions when all other routes are exhausted. I can make a difference. Plenty of things go bump in the night, so maybe it's time I start shining a light on them.

The lady that came in tonight was merely a coincidence though. I'll need to actively find people that need my help, preferably away from the hotel where I might risk getting too close to them. But how to go about that? I could maybe intervene when it seems suitable? Are there any other ways? There's something in the back of my mind. Something that happened a few nights ago...

I was on my way home from work when I saw the poster. It stood out to me because the word "Missing" was written in English in large, red print. Despite the rain pouring down on top of me, I couldn't help but wander over to take a closer look. Family and friends haven't heard from her in a week. The same age as me. She was last seen wearing a green shirt, denim jeans and a khaki overcoat. She looked happy in the photo; sweet, even. A smiling, pretty face. She had long, brown hair, and a short, slight figure. The darkest of eyes, black on poorly-pixelated paper.

There's a story untold there. One I could discover. Roam the streets in my spare time and ask if anyone has seen her. Do some digging, look for clues. A mystery. My greatest adventure yet – Mouse.

****

The phone rings out. There's a slight crackle as I pick up and I brace myself for the worst.

"Allo?"

"Hello, welcome to Hotel-" I reply, somehow believing that if I pretend to not recognise my boss' voice, he'll leave me alone. Instead, he cuts me off.

"- 'Ow are you doing?"

"Oh, hello, sir. I'm fine."

"I juss wanted to sank you for 'elping wiss dose towels for ze gue Good job."

"I- Yeah- It just came to me."

"Wat?"

"Thank you, yeah. Just thought I could help."

"Okey, okey. Well, bye."

I pause for a moment and breathe a sigh of relief. I've been lucky tonight. Lucky that most bad people are idiots. It did seem strange that he'd compliment me on anything I did. He never seems to thank me when I do all the other things I do. I guess I should just take my victories where I find them. On that note, I should get back to work.

I slowly begin the monotonous organising and shredding of the photocopies of people's passports. Now that they've left this place, we don't need any photos of them. No need for reminders or keepsakes. We bring people in and push people out. As each photo is torn apart, the next one goes in and I shuffle another bundle. It occurs to me now that, somewhere in this city, another person is tearing photos and someone else is starting to shuffle papers too.

Case 2 – Out of Order

I wake up to the slight sound of sleet tapping on the window. I can tell that it's still daylight even though the dark clouds are cheating the sun out of its show. I turn the light on to get my bearings in this dim room. A small sofa-bed against a wall underneath me, a kitchen across from me with a table and two chairs, all the same room. Beside the sofa is a door that leads to a large room currently occupied by my roommate. It's always left slightly ajar because that's the way he prefers it.

As far as I know, he pays the same amount of rent as me for this one bedroom apartment. Finders-keepers seems to be his motto. Speaking of whom, it seems there's a new note left for me on the fridge. The message reads: *I heard you come in last night.* Oh, joy... I was worried that I wouldn't get my passive aggressive fix for the day. Close the fucking door then, dickhead!

I crumple up the note in my hand and give it an extra squeeze, balling it up in my fist. I'd tell him how annoying it is but I never really see him in person. He's never here at the weekends. During the week, I arrive home when he's asleep and wake up after he's gone to work. I know for sure that he's gone because he keeps slamming the door on his way out.

It was never my intention to end up sharing an apartment with someone. I was trying to get away from people. But Paris is expensive and apartments are hard to come by. I was desperate when I took this place. In dire need of four walls, a roof and a bed. This serves its purpose for now.

On that note, with the daylight still lingering and time to waste, I make my way back to bed. I check my phone for messages, only out of habit, before switching the light off. I take a few deep breaths and close my eyes.

I wish I could stay sleeping forever. Never wake up to an

unpredictable reality. I long to be completely free in a world of my own. To only wander in that wonderful place in-between, where the pillow meets the sky.

****

My alarm goes off and I roll out of my sofa-bed. Literally. This bed isn't incredibly big and my phone is left underneath so the charger can reach the socket. This place is a mess of little irritations, even the architect seems to be out to get me. I'd linger on the thought if I wasn't already in a rush for work. I had apparently slept through two previous alarms.

I throw on my jacket and check the pockets for my cigarettes. Beside them is the folded up flyer that I tore down on my way home last night. I had forgotten about it in my drowsy awakening. It has all the details I need to identify this girl and who to contact when I do. I shove it deeper into my pocket and zip it closed.

I can't help but feel a little proud of myself for taking on such an endeavour, even somewhat excited for the adventure ahead. As I fly down the stairs of my building and gather speed, the giddiness rises. I've found a path to follow. A mission to complete.

A game afoot.

****

It's been two nights since Mr. Swan made his hasty flight from the hotel and I tore down the poster of Mouse. God, I'm bored. A little angst-ridden even. I take out my petty frustrations on as many inanimate objects that I can throw or slam onto the counter while no one is around to see. I need another distraction. Maybe I'll take a walk after work? Find someone to help rather than wait for the opportunity to open up to me. At the very least, I'll show the flyer to people again and ask them if they've seen Mouse.

The clock seems to be running at a brutally slow speed. With only a few minutes left to go, my replacement walks in. He's figured out by now that small talk isn't a popular choice with me. He seems to be relieved when I tell him that there's nothing at all to be done. I imagine he's going to spend the rest of the darkness on his phone texting people or listening to music, two things Crow hates, but some manage to get away with it. I'm just glad he showed up on time.

If I can't find anyone that needs help, then I can just buy some food for a homeless person. They tend to be quite active at these hours anyway. I'm sure I'll be able to find an épicerie or somewhere that sells food. I need something to take my mind off all this nothingness...

My colleague's indifferent goodbye is all I hear as I brush past the door. I don't think I could possibly walk faster. I scuttle past closed shops, their grey, metal shutters covered in graffiti. They're normally lined by beggars sleeping under the canopies, yet empty tonight. The only homeless person I see is passed out against a tree with an open can of beer nestled between his legs. Needless to say, I'm annoyed at my options.

Raindrops start to fall and I lean up against the door of a residential building for some shelter. I guess I'll have a cigarette then.

Just as I spark up, a young man gingerly approaches me. He seems fidgety and, considering the time of night, he's making me nervous. The one comfort is that he's on his own. It's rare that anyone here would try and mug someone unless they were in a group. He awkwardly raises his hand in a gesture of introduction before he stammers out a few words.

"H-Hey. What's up?"

I just nod and stare at him. He seems like he's struggling to speak.

"So... What kind of stuff do you have?"

"What?" I ask.

"Oh, nothing! Sorry!"

He looks up and down the street hopelessly. The rain has made it barren, any person that had been around would surely have found shelter too. His wringing hands are working themselves into a fit. He's still not walking away though. Judging by his edginess and evasiveness, I'm assuming he's looking for some pretty hardcore drugs.

"What are you looking for?" I ask.

"Um... I-It's-uh-well-"

"- Because I might have what you're looking for?"

It's a pretty safe gamble, I think. Whatever the drug, I can say I don't have it. Plus, I can find out what his deal is and maybe help him overcome his addiction someday by putting him on the right path. He doesn't seem particularly worried about my inquisitive nature. Or, at least, his anxious disposition seems to be more or less the same.

"I just need a Xanax or something to make me calm. Any kind of Benzodiazepine! I ran out and all the pharmacies are closed and I can't sleep and I have to work tomorrow and I just need something to calm me down!" He's trembling so much I think he might shatter.

"Why do you need a Xanax to calm down?"

"Why do I need a Xanax to calm down?! I need a Xanax to calm down because I don't have a Xanax to calm down! Because I've always had Xanaxes to calm me down and now I don't have a Xanax-"

"- Okay!" I raise my hands apologetically. I figure that roundabout conversation probably wouldn't have stopped until I either agreed with him or gave him a Xanax.

"Well?" He asks eagerly.

"Well, what?"

"Do you have any?! Anything?!" He blurts, his eyes welling up.

"I'm... All out."

"Oh, God!" He starts hyperventilating.

"Whoa! Shit! Calm down!" I'm obviously not helping by shouting at him. I'll try a different approach. I grab his arms and tell him firmly. "Look at me." He's not doing it. "Hey! Look at me." He looks up. "Everything is going to be okay. Tell me what you do for a living."

"I-I work in a factory."

"What do you make in the factory?"

"We make juice c-cartons."

"What colour are the juice cartons?"

"Eh, orange and white with a blue stripe. D-different colours, you know?" He exhales sharply.

"You're going to be fine, okay? You *are* okay." His breathing is slowing down.

"I'm f-fine."

"Yes, you are..." I smile at him to calm him down. He fakes one back at me before his twitching face falls back to agony. "Let's get you some Xanax, okay?"

"It doesn't *have* to be Xanax, either." He says.

"Right, just a benzodiapraline."

"It's benzodiaz-"

"- And we'll find it! Don't worry!" He's starting to annoy me now.

We set off together down the street and it dawns on me the moment he asks.

"Where are we going?"

He's following me, it seems. I'm going to call him Hummingbird. Ever fretful for that nectar. I'm struggling to think of ways to help him. Where does one buy drugs in Paris? I walk past some graffiti and a clue is written out for me. A white *A* in a circle.

Anarchists.

Sex, drugs and Rock n' Roll, right?

"We're going to Bastille."

****

In the taxi, I can't help but feel sorry for this guy. I know anxiety well. Living like you're walking on glass. You can see the fall below. You're just waiting for the floor to crack and send you tumbling down. Every challenge you face builds up on your back and makes you heavier. Every success brings you higher and threatens a greater fall.

I'll admit that I've never really had it as bad as this guy does. We're all born equipped differently. I know when I'm anxiously afflicted I tend to play out the scenarios in my head and come up with a solution. If I have a plan of action then I can do something and fix it.

It makes sense, right?

Only it never really works.

I worry until I can't any more. It consumes me. One scenario becomes countless and the right direction gets frayed into a million different threads, as do my nerves. The problem then isn't actually the problem, it's which path to take. It's the basest anxiety. Will I make the correct choice?

The truth is, the worst things that happen to you come out of nowhere. It's the thing that you never prepared for and is out of your control. I know this. I've experienced this. So, why do I worry so much about everything else?

We swing around the precarious roundabout at Bastille. The green pillar standing tall, topped with a golden statue. I can see crowds stumbling down streets, probably from Rue de Lappe; a cobblestone street that hosts bar after bar. It's a place where people of all walks of life tend to meet, bumping off each other with mixed results.

The taxi pulls up in front of the Bastille Opera building and I pay the driver as Hummingbird flutters out. I calmly exit the vehicle, into the chilly breeze, and walk towards him. He's pacing back and forth, looking around. His skin is shimmering under the street-lights, a garland of sweat around his brow. I survey the area while he scrapes a demonstration flyer off his shoe.

The Opera building in front of us shows off its black marble under flood-lights. Take the stairs up and I'm sure you would be met with divine music and people dressed luxuriously. But we're taking the darker, dirtier steps to the right, down to the metro entrance. There's shouting and howling emanating from the depths.

This is the right place.

I'm nervous on the way down, but my feet keep propelling me forward. It helps that I have Hummingbird on my heels as a constant reminder. A gang sit in a circle against a dank, graffiti-ridden background. Some of them sit on the steps, others on the ground. Most of them dress the same. Jackets of different colours with patches sown on to them, military-style pants and combat boots. Militant Anarchists.

I've never been a true advocate for Anarchy. I like Democracy because it seems like it works the best. I'll admit that there are better forms of the argument for Anarchy given by people much smarter than me. That we don't really need currency and we'd give each other whatever we need instead of taking it. But I think it's an idealistic belief. People aren't benevolent enough to trade fairly. Everyone wants more. Of course, this gets exacerbated by the fact that value is relative to perception. If I have a stick and you have a pile of stones, I could say that my stick is worth all of your stones. On the other hand, you could say my stick is worth one of your stones. We would argue about it. Words can never hurt us, but as this argument develops, a deal isn't brokered but bones broken. So, forgive the crude analogy, but I like having order.

The group take turns trading glances at us as we descend. I can hear Hummingbird gulp behind me. I nod my head in gesture of greeting. Two of them turn to each other and start whispering. I've got nothing to say and I'm about three steps away from being too close to these vagabonds.

I think, for the first time in my life, I need a Xanax. I root through my pockets for a cigarette to hopefully take the edge off this encounter. A small part of me also thinks it might make me look cooler.

My finger hits paper before cardboard and I immediately have an opening. Pulling out the Missing-Person's page, I raise my hand in greeting.

"What do you want, cop?" One asks. I can't really see who, it's pretty dark down here.

"Ehm- I'm not a cop! I'm just trying to find someone." Hummingbird starts to pull on my jacket, so I take a step down.

"You look like a cop!" Another mysterious person shouts as they all start murmuring.

Where are the fucking lights?! I'm a little flattered that they think I look like a police officer. To me, it makes me seem exciting or dangerous. Although, to them, it probably means I look like a dickhead.

"I'm really not a cop!" I'm not sure if steam is escaping from a nearby vent or if they're all making fun of me. "Has anyone seen this girl?" I ask, handing one of them the flyer.

She's kind enough to pass it along. A few of them simply hand it to the next person without looking at it. I hear a thump and some hissing. Some guy with a Mohawk haircut and a whiny voice is whispering to another guy with a completely shaved head. The conversation seems pretty intense and the Weasel with the haircut is holding the page.

"Hey! Do you know something about her?" I ask the Weasel.

"Fuck you, chicken!" This is an unsurprising response. Chicken, oddly, is the French slang for cop.

"She might need help!" I plead.

"She doesn't need help! She's fine!" Weasel exclaims. Another thump comes from the Bald Vulture followed by more hissing and snapping.

"You've seen her? That's how you know she's fine?" I'm feeling pretty good about myself right now.

"Fuck off!" Vulture says, now taking over the conversation. His voice is gravely and coarse, almost as rough as he looks. I don't feel as good as I did before.

"I'm only-"

"- Fuck off!" Feeling pretty shit now, actually.

"It's-"

"- Fuck..." Waiting for it. "Off!"

"Fine, I'll stop asking about her. Have a nice night and thanks for your help!" I turn around and walk straight into Hummingbird. I completely forgot he was there!

"One more thing before I go!"

"Fuck-" Vulture starts. I'm not waiting this time.

"- We have money!"

He leaps up onto his feet and walks crookedly towards us. "And? You want to give it to us?"

"I want to make a trade. I need some pills for my friend." Hummingbird buzzes in my ear reminding me to make sure I get the right one. "We need Benzodio- Ben- fucking Xanax! We need fucking Xanax!"

"Well, we don't sell to cops." Weasel feels like contributing to the conversation again. Perhaps to redeem himself for his earlier blunder.

"Again, I'm not a cop. I'm not even French! What do I have to do to prove I'm not a cop?" You can't prove a negative, after all.

Vulture starts chuckling and drags his feet backwards towards one of his buddies. A less raggedy-looking guy that lets himself down by being completely stoned off his head. He pulls what appears to be a joint out of the man's fingers, with very little resistance, and hands it to me. The previous owner of the joint reaches out slowly and then his hand flops down in defeat. He reminds me of a Sloth.

"Take a drag. Cops can't do drugs!" Vulture states.

There are worse ways of proving your lack of connection to authority than smoking some hash. I'm quick to start pulling. This guy is pretty frightening. The group starts laughing and then some of them start cheering. Am I cool yet?

I thought three puffs would be enough, but the death stare from Vulture and his lack of interest in taking the joint back seems to imply that I'm to finish the whole thing myself. I guess I better soldier on then. I start taking drags, slowly at first, then pick up the pace as the awkwardness sets in. The group isn't cheering any more and it doesn't seem like I'll get any more applause for a while as they start shoving each other throughout the circle.

It occurs to me that the best idea would be to keep myself in check instead of losing control of the situation. This is about as safe as juggling snakes. But, fuck it, I'm starting to feel it.

****

Hummingbird seems to have calmed down after a few tugs on a joint. He even seems to be enjoying himself now that he's talking to a girl with a shaved head. I've moved on to a plastic bottle of cider that's being passed around, probably not very hygienic. The hard ground is made even more uncomfortable by its icy coldness.

Vulture has been talking to me for a while now. Some of it is hard to hear. He was beaten by his alcoholic father from a very early age. When he was sixteen, he ran away from home and lived on the street. No one ever tried to find him. He told me his father wouldn't bother and his mother would probably think he's better off. His one regret is leaving her behind. After telling me this he started to go on about how Anarchy is the way forward. That it's the natural order for humans to live in. I'm a little high now and it's easier to listen to than the darker stuff I heard earlier.

They definitely lay the tracks for earning my sympathy. He's telling me about how the world is always in a state of disorder. How control is just an illusion. It's nothing I haven't heard before but now it makes a bit more sense. Power is something you give to people. They, the government, can't have it unless we give it away. All these people want, after their various struggles in the past, is to keep their power. Boyfriends, girlfriends, family members, teachers, priests... When you've seen what horrors power and control can do to one person, why would you elect someone for a nation? They've seen the tyrant from a front row seat.

As he talks and quotes various intellectuals, I catch something in the corner of my eye. Just a flash of blue. My heart freezes over and my stomach sinks. Is she back in Paris? Her, a memory in passing. I take a harder look but it's gone now. Probably impossible anyway. A blue dress from a time gone by. Nothing but an echo.

Focus...

I could never control how I feel. The one thing in my being that's in a total state of anarchy. My emotions get the best of me sometimes. Anxiety is probably the worst of them. Dread and conversations unsaid. Its prickly hands twist knots in me. Most of the time I can't even do anything about what I'm worrying about. The rare times I can, I'm not brave enough...

Well, tonight, I'm going to be braver. Someone needs help and someone has to help him.

Someone has the drugs.

I look at my two main suspects. Vulture stands at number one, being the most intimidating and, therefore, the most likely to be committing some illicit narcotic dealings. Sloth stands in as my second, but ideal, suspect. I say ideal because in his state it won't be too difficult to initiate a trade. I might even be able to get a good price for it. He's already been smoking a joint which means he definitely has drugs on him, although maybe not the kind I'm looking for. Either way, I'd like to start with him. Vulture is still talking to me though. A call from nature gives me the inspiration I need.

"The government is just in the pocket of these corporations and-"

"- I have to take a piss." I pat him on the shoulder and stumble towards the closed metro entrance.

I'm too drunk to really care who's watching, it's normal in Paris anyway, and they're probably too wasted to care. A bottle explodes behind me after one of them hurled it at the wall almost as if to prove my point. Besides, pissing on the streets of Paris is a cultural norm as soon as the sun sets. Bars are the only places that are open and most have a strict *customers only* policy. The public toilets provided by the city shut down automatically at ten at night. This has led to some drunk, impromptu irony as people drolly urinate against a closed toilet booth.

I slide down beside Sloth, the frosty ground biting into me again, after dodging two guys having a wrestling match. The two seem to really be going at it as punches fly into each other's torsos. It isn't until one pushes the other away and starts laughing that I realise they just like to play rough. Sloth seems oblivious to it all. He's bobbing his head up and down with his eyes closed to whatever tune he's mumbling.

I lean into him, feigning a lack of sobriety. Well, maybe I'm not faking too much at this point. My legs are a little uncoordinated, but I've always been good at keeping my mind sharp when drunk. It's a little voice inside that cuts through the blurry thoughts. Sloth doesn't seem to have noticed my presence yet. I guess I'll just have to talk to him.

"Hey. What song are you singing?"

"*This* song..." He laughs dryly and mumbles on.

"Cool. That's pretty cool... So, listen, I'm trying to help my friend out. He's having a rough time with his nerves and I was hoping you could give me something to calm him down?"

"He seems fine to me..." Sloth says with his eyes closed, still mumbling his Anarchist A-Cappella.

"Well, he might not be later on. I just want to look out for him, you know?"

"Shit, man... Give him some hash and... That should mellow him out." Sloth interrupts his tune now and looks right at me.

"I think he's going to need something a bit stronger than that. He's got this disposition... We could do with some Xanax if you have some?"

"Xanax? Uhm... No, ain't got Xanax... Why would I?" He starts laughing again. "Uhm... It slows me down... You know?"

"Who has Xanax then?"

"Uhm... Who has Xanax?" His eyelids droop along with his head.

"Yeah. Who has Xanax?!"

"I... Hang on... If you're looking for Xanax... You gotta pay him, then get it off the other guy..."

"Pay who? What other guy?"

"That..." He flops his arm in the air. "What?"

"Okay... Just point me in the right direction and I'll let you get back to it."

"The right direction..." Now he's starting to fall asleep. He wraps his arms around himself and buries his head in his chest.

"Who do I talk to?!"

"Who?" His body is leaning on me so I gently push him back upright. He probably doesn't have it. This leaves me with only one suspect and two options; buy the drugs or steal the drugs.

Scanning Vulture, there's no real indication that he has anything on him. His tight leather jacket with a fur collar doesn't seem to show any bulges. Maybe he only has a few pills? If he had a bottle, I'm sure I would have seen the elongated outline of it. His stained cargo pants are baggy on his wiry frame, but as he moves they don't seem to reveal any movement other than the cloth they're made of. Perhaps he keeps them in a plastic bag somewhere. Or maybe he doesn't have any at all. Either way, I have to check. I stagger towards him. He looks up at me mischievously from the ground as I approach and tilts his head to the side inquisitively.

"Can we talk over here for a bit?" I jerk my head to the left towards a corner previously used by myself to urinate. Vulture looks to his buddies, who give him indifferent looks, and he gets up. We shuffle our way into the corner as he intimidatingly wraps his arm around my neck. The smell of urine rises as we step over tiny streams emerging from the point where the two walls meet directly opposite the metro entrance.

"What's up?" He asks, his arm snugly squeezing me.

There's a butterfly flickering around in my stomach that I swat with a faux-machismo that even I'm starting to believe. The kind of primal, me-man-you-man brotherhood that I've never particularly subscribed to, but adopted for this scenario so I don't somehow end up getting the shit kicked out of me.

"I'm trying to help my friend out. He could do with some Xanax. He's not looking for a good time or anything. He really needs it."

"I could help you out... But it's probably going to cost a lot." He looks serious, like he means business. He glances over his shoulder briefly before squeezing my neck a little harder and gently rocks it side to side. "How much money do you have?"

"I don't really have a lot. I don't think my friend does either. You'd be helping him out. Even if you just had one for him to last him the night." I realise as I'm talking to him that I'm appealing to the kindness of a man who has seen very little of it come back to him in his life.

"I could give you one for seventy Euro." He says, deadpan.

"Seventy Euro... Kind of sounds like a lot..." The pauses in my voice, I'm already aware, betray an ignorance and a timidness.

"You won't find one for less. That shit's hard to come by. It's medical grade stuff. It's not like anyone can get it, you see? A guy can get in a lot of trouble for having it!" For the words he uses, he doesn't sound apologetic or patient. He's not teaching me the ways of the street, he's telling me to give him money and not talk to anyone else.

I can hear laughter to my left now. Hummingbird and his new friend are sitting on the bottom step. They seem to be getting pretty close. His movements are becoming more animated, but not in the same nervous fashion they were before.

"It's that simple!" He exclaims joyfully.

"Yeah!" She gives him a slap on the shoulder.

"Bad shit is going to happen!"

"Bad shit is *always* going to happen!" She seems just as revved up as he is.

"Fuck it!"

"Fuck it! Let it go!"

"Just let it fucking go!" At this they both start laughing manically.

I tap Vulture on the hand and tell him I'm going to go talk to Hummingbird with his offer.

"Yeah, sure. No worries! But you come back to me, yeah?" He drops his cool-breeze charade and gives me a dark look.

I smile at him and nod as he releases me from the *friendly* headlock.

I pick up more on the conversation Hummingbird and this Hummingbirdette are having as I get closer, their voices having died down after their initial jovial reaction. Hummingbirdette has her hand on his lap and is talking quite close to him as I light up another cigarette. I hover near them, not wanting to interrupt them.

"There's shit in life that you can control and there's shit you can't. You can't make the sun shine, man. You can't make yourself fly. You can't breathe underwater. You can't- You can't-" She flutters.

They both laugh for a bit as he moves his hand on to hers. "I get the idea."

"Okay then! So... When you can't control stuff, I mean when it's really impossible to control stuff, what can you control?" She grins at him sweetly.

"Well, nothing." He shrugs back, shyly.

"No, that's not true!" She gives him a slight, affectionate slap on the arm followed by a you-still-don't-get-it smile. She sighs and starts again. "You can control how you *deal* with it. How you *feel* about it. Govern yourself, man! You're your own boss! No one and nothing can tell you how or what to feel except for you! Everything is always falling apart. We're always just scurrying around, picking up the pieces and putting them back, pretending there's an order to it. The natural order is chaos. Things break down all the time. They're supposed to break down. We just have to stay true to ourselves and what we are. Hold the line, man!"

Hummingbird has this perplexed, almost surprised, grin on his face as he listens on.

"It's your mind, man. You decide what's cool and what's not. No one can tell you differently. You can't control the world, just yourself!" She laughs and I watch her thumb stroke his palm. Hummingbird raises his eyebrows at her.

"Maybe I can't control myself?" He blurts out and kisses her. I cringe a little at the sight, not only because of the notoriously cheesy line, but also because they really seem to be going at it. I can't watch this any longer.

Turning away from the love birds, I see Vulture stooped over Weasel. He has him caught by the lapel of his coat and is talking intensely in his ear. Weasel seems reluctant to whatever Vulture is saying to him. Eventually, I see Vulture's prey give up. I can just make out Weasel reach into his coat pocket followed by Vulture stuffing his right pocket a second later. Vulture looks around and I turn back to the love birds. It's clear that I wasn't supposed to see what just happened. Staring at the couple in front of me, their hands roaming, I probably shouldn't see this either. I'm stuck between a rock and an awkward place until Vulture slaps his hand on my shoulder.

"We good?" He asks with shifty eyes.

"He's a bit busy now. I'll ask him in a little while." I throw out a laugh and point at the couple to put my new, gruff friend at ease. He returns the laugh and rolls his eyes as one of his party calls out to him.

"Come to me when you're both ready." And with that he hobbles back over to his friends, shouting obscenities at them.

  I should probably have seen it sooner. Weasel had been holding the drugs, and the risk of being caught with them, all this time. It's survival of the scariest. I'm a little disappointed with myself for not cluing myself in. Red-handed isn't a victory. But if the objective was to calm Hummingbird down then I suppose I'd call this a win. I look down at the couple and, after the initial discomfort of feeling like a pervert, find myself proud of what I've accomplished. Unfortunately, it's as I'm smiling and staring at the two that his lover opens her eyes, then stares directly at me. She pulls back and squints at me.

"Who's your friend?" She asks Hummingbird.

"He's- Ehm-"

"- Leaving! It was nice meeting you. Take care of him for me!" I know I sound as smug as I feel.

"I will. Don't you worry." She laughs and pulls him back in for another tongue fight.

  On my way out, I pass by Weasel. He's rolling himself a cigarette, keeping to himself. I get down on my haunches to talk to him.

"Hey, man. I'm leaving. Take care of yourself, okay?"

"Yeah, okay." He says indifferently, his dirty thumbs giving a solid form to the tobacco in the paper skin.

"I mean... Take care of *yourself*, okay?" I give him an apologetic nod as my eyes shift towards his pocket. He looks up at me, a little confused at first and then somewhat surprised. The filter falls out of his cigarette without him noticing as his fingers pause their motion.

"Yeah... Yeah..." He says pensively, looking down. I get up and start to walk away when he calls back to me. "She was on the Seine last time I saw her!"

"Her? Who?"

"The girl you're looking for. She had been by the Seine, near the Louvre, about a week ago, alone. Gave me a sandwich."

He picks the filter up off the ground and begins rolling again, this time more attentively. I take it that he's not so much focusing on rolling as much as he is on ignoring me. I probably wouldn't get more information out of him if I asked, which is fair enough.

****

I make my way up the stairs, away from the pandemonium below. Bedlam is replaced with soft engines revolving around the roundabout, boisterous cackles swapped for drowsy drunks hailing cabs. The sky has gone from black to a dark shade of blue as I walk towards the green light of a free taxi. The sun will rise soon. I can't control that, I've heard.

We spin around and set off. I stare out the window with contentment. For all the worrying I did in the beginning, I did my best in the moment and it paid off. Everything worked out better than I thought it would.

I'm optimistic for Hummingbird. I couldn't get him his Xanax, but he seemed to have found his own way. He's sitting on the bottom of the stairs, but it's still the first step on the way up. Plenty of people need medication for their moods, it's biochemical, but I think he was looking for the wrong drug all this time. Not one to calm him down, but one to lift him up. He needed just a little, delicate taste of the strongest drug we know. The same one that once calmed my nerves.

Love, complete.

The secret pill.

Case 3 – Wandering Roots

Snow gently falls from the sky, each frosty kiss burning my skin. I needed a walk. My original plan to cook myself some dinner was foiled by the ceramic tower of dirty dishes that my roommate has accumulated over the last week. Considering I'm pretty annoyed at him for doing that, and that I don't really feel like cooking anyway, I've decided to treat myself to a meal out. I'm going to fill my stomach and clear my head. Just one stop to make first.

There's no one here. It's a Friday night but the weather is too unforgiving for anyone to sit along the Seine and drink. Even a bottle of whiskey couldn't take the sting out of this chill. I was stupid enough to forget my fingerless gloves and now my hands are stuck in my pockets for the rest of the night.

I'm not entirely sure why I'm still hanging around. There's no evidence of Mouse ever having been here and, to make a terrible pun, the trail has gone cold. I can't even canvas the area and ask people if they recognise her from the flyer because there's no one to ask. The flashlight that I naively brought with me to search for clues is now useless. There's nothing here for me.

In the back of my mind, I hear groanings and mumblings as I look up towards Pont Neuf. Dirty marble that's been polished for centuries by passing hands. Its ornate wreathes and shadowy lines running along the sides. There was a time when I sat on that bridge. Back in the days when things were magical and this city shone at night. In beautiful eyes, for the first and only time, I saw the brightest spark... I believed it meant something... I need to leave...

I'm not in a very good place right now. I keep telling myself that I'm working my way out of it, yet I look towards the future and I see a long road to recovery. I can't seem to find a way to speed this up, to jump start my life. With this weighing on me constantly, a defeat like tonight doesn't help much for my mood.

I decide, out of sheer boredom, that I'll make my way to find food by cutting through the street between the Tuileries Gardens and the Louvre. I can't help but bury my chin into my chest, half to comfort myself from my most recent failure and also to provide some kind of warmth. The rushing sound of the Seine grows fainter as I cross the street over to the Louvre.

This place has always been special to me. When I first arrived in Paris I would spend all my spare time just walking around the museum. It was so easy to immerse myself in the crowd back then. With no friends to speak of at the time, I would amble through the rooms and take in the magnitude of what I was looking at. Everything was fresh to my eyes, a new experience. Each exhibition, a new adventure to lose myself in. History within history. Works of art within a work of art.

Later on, I would return to the Louvre to play my guitar and sing in the arches, hoping tourists would toss a few coins in my guitar bag, which I found out later was against the rules. I managed to stay ahead of security most of the time though. Their presence was usually preceded by several men carrying hundreds of Eiffel Tower key-chains sprinting past me. This jingling alarm usually gave me plenty of time to snatch my bag up and race after my employment-challenged colleagues.

Of course, there were times when I didn't manage to escape the men in orange vests. Fortunately, not being native to the country and, frankly, because I'm white, I always pleaded that I didn't know it was against the rules and they'd simply usher me away.

Those archways brought me great peace. The acoustics resonated back to me with a soft and warm clarity that few other places are able to emulate. I was expressing myself to the world. Sharing myself. Stone angels looked down on me as I sang, even when the tourists didn't pause a moment.

Every now and then, some ignorant tourist would stop and take a photo of me or record me before walking off without leaving a single penny. My smiles met with sour looks that I'd be insolent enough to expect money from them. I know it seems unnecessarily callous to be like this, they aren't obliged to give me anything. But if they liked the music enough to record it, did they not have twenty cents?

Regardless, they were happy times for me and perhaps when the winter cold is gone I'll return to them again.

I walk past a row of undecorated Christmas trees. Several of them have little, white fences bordering them, with the others having only partially completed fences. I can see something of a commotion ahead, two men having a heated discussion under the apathetic supervision of two police officers.

Both of the men are wearing the park caretaker uniform. The man on the left is waving his arms furiously at the police officers while the one on the right is trying to comfort him. The calmer man is older, dark hair with a white band struck through it like a Badger. The incredulous man with a thorn in his side is younger, let's call him Hedgehog.

My French is quite good but it's difficult for me sometimes to understand when I'm thrown into a conversation without context. I light a cigarette and linger out of curiosity, turning my back on them to face the large, glass pyramid of the Louvre so they don't suspect me of eavesdropping.

It's a funny thing to see the Louvre at night. The throngs of tourists that usually flurry around the place have gone. All that's left are a few people scattered around taking photos, a snow-covered van on the south side of the square and some scaffolding covering the illuminated glass and stone.

During the summer, the whole building seems to be made of sand under the floodlights. Something about seeing it in the winter makes it seem greyer. Like the cold has taken all notions of warmth out of the light and even the building itself.

I'm starting to pick up on the conversation. Hedgehog is saying that someone has stolen one of the Christmas trees that they were setting up for the holidays. He's complaining that his boss is going to fire him for letting it happen. His colleague is less worried about the situation. He's even going so far as to tell him that it's one less tree to decorate tomorrow and that they should be glad someone stole it.

One of the police officers is saying that he'll see what he can do, which is a popular way of saying that he'll do nothing. I can't see his face, he's wearing a ski-mask. His gruff voice and curt way of speaking gives the impression that a missing Christmas tree, especially one paid for by city hall, is the last thing on his list of priorities. Maybe I can help?

The police officers walk away and talk casually to each other. The fretful gardener continues his minor tirade before being dragged off by his colleague. I turn around to make sure they're gone before I go to examine the pit. The air is still and quiet as I make my approach. I peer down into the hole and turn on my flashlight to get a proper look.

The uprooted tree left black mud and grey stones, but there's something else inside. Flecks of a light coloured powder. I dismiss my first thought that it could be cocaine. It's unlikely that a coked up man running around with a Christmas tree under his arm would escape unnoticed. Not to say that something like that would be uncommon in Paris.

It's probably just sand from the neighbouring Tuileries Gardens. One of the irritable things about living in Paris is the sand that they use in every park for the footpaths. With the wind blowing in your face in dry weather, you'll usually end up spitting and crying your way through the park with your arms flailing around like a mad man on coke.

I'm confounded as to how someone could have gotten away with this. There's nothing out of the ordinary that I can see, aside from some scaffolding on the left wing of the Louvre. Undoubtedly, they're cleaning down the walls, scrubbing away at the smog marks to reveal the limestone beneath.

Even more bizarre is the lack of a trail. There are no drag marks, tyre tracks or foot prints. This is probably due to the steady fall of snow throughout the night. That means either this would have happened some time ago or I'm looking for a giant, festive Eagle.

Without any witnesses to the theft or a trail to follow, no twigs to track, I appear to be stumped...

The only thing I can think of is that whoever took this tree came from the Tuileries Gardens side before making off with it. The caretakers must be around here somewhere. I wonder if there's a building that they operate out of that I can locate. I cautiously hop over the fence and set off into the gardens to find them.

∗∗∗∗∗∗∗∗∗∗∗∗

It's eerie walking around here at night. The open space provides little comfort in the dark. The shadows of the trees are cast off even longer from the faraway street-lights, their barren branches seem hideously disfigured. Charcoal clouds silently chug their way on an invisible track and not even a glimmer of the moon's silver can peek out through.

Despite this slight blindness, I can still see the path in front of me and I carry on. I'm pretty nervous so I start humming to myself. This is what I used to do back in Ireland when I would walk down sombre country roads. It's a song to keep me company, the irrational fears in my head pushed out by symphony and lyrics.

Halfway through the garden, I catch a glimpse of someone. It appears to be the distraught Hedgehog. It's one of those moments where I can't just shout or run up to him, especially given his temperament and the fact that I'm not supposed to be here. So, I begin my slow walk towards him as he turns around a corner into the black.

I reach the corner, but he's vanished and I'm alone in the dark again. I suppose I'll follow my common instincts and step back into the light of the streets. As I trudge through the park snow to the exit, I make out an odd shape in the frost-laden grass. It seems to be a pile of several, small planks of wood. There's no work being done in the park itself and the *Keep Off The Grass* sign would indicate that it wasn't left there by the groundskeepers.

Under the sterile glow of the street-lights, I make my way up the street as a man cycles past me bleating like a sheep for no obvious reason. I bob and weave in between the cream-coloured pillars that support the overhanging buildings. Thinking through the facts, I start to dream of cranes and rockets plucking the tree away without being seen. My mind tends to wander. I think I need to take breaks from reality, step outside my body for a while and let my imagination take me somewhere softer.

Turning right after the golden statue of Jean D'Arc, I reach the small arch that stands between the gardens and the Louvre. The placated Badger emerges from behind it with his hands in his pockets, whistling to himself, his feet idly kick at the ground, unearthing snow and sand.

I make my way over to him with a gentle wave and say "Good evening!" in French.

He smiles back "Good Evening!"

"I hear you've lost a tree?"

He shrugs "Oh, never mind that."

"You won't get into trouble?"

"Maybe, but who cares really? I'm not going to get fired for this. It's just a tree and it's paid for by the city. Someone could take ten of them and we'd still have more trees to plant." There's a slight trace of an Eastern-European accent.

"Aren't you curious what happened to it?"

"Not at all. There are more important things to worry about in life than a tree that will be replaced tomorrow and it's one less thing for me to do now." His worn face and shaggy appearance is enough to convince me that he has seen some hard times.

Although I slightly resent the implication that my intentions were completely frivolous, I tell him to have a nice evening at work. He nods at me, smiling, while he scratches his scruffy stubble.

As I walk off, the silence makes me look back. I can see him staring at me. I stop for a moment.

"Oh, I found a light-coloured powder in the hole. That might be a clue as to who did it?" I tell him.

He shrugs in response and I continue on my way, looking back every now and then. His calm demeanour seems a bit fidgety now. He glances off into the distance and pulls out his phone. His voice carries across the silent air, but he's speaking in a language I don't understand. It doesn't matter, I'm done for the night anyway. I head towards the Louvre square to leave through an arch and walk down a memory lane.

****

On the way out, I look at the van that I saw before. On top of the roof, buried in snow, lie some planks the exact same size as those I found in the park. My first reflex is to find the owner and tell him about the planks but, given the state of the van, I decide that they almost definitely aren't around to tell. I walk a few more steps until my conscience tugs at me. I should leave a note.

Pulling out a pen and a piece of paper that I stole from work, I scribble down "*Some of your planks are in the park.*" Maybe I'm being stupid, for all I know they probably left them there themselves. But you never know, do you?

I go to stick the note under the windscreen wiper when my foot steps on something uneven under the snow. I bend down and brush away the snowflakes to see a tiny sprig of green, the same kind one would find on a Christmas tree.

I look around to make sure no one is watching before I creep to the back of the truck and scrape against the frost on a rear window so I can peer in. Inside, I can make out a canvas sheet laid over an unknown object until, towards the front of the van, I see a tuft of Spruce sticking out. I found my tree!

On the back door, I see an address and the name of a company. I scribble it down on a piece of paper and jog away. I make it six paces before I double back and start kicking away at my footprints in the snow. I don't want anyone to know that I've been here.

As I head out the northern archway, I duck into the shadows to check that no one saw me leave. Almost instantly, a man comes slinking around the corner. His tan skin contrasts against the white hair of his balding head. He jumps into the van and drives off. There's my Eagle. I manage to sprint to the other side of the passage to see him drive off north towards Opéra.

My stomach is growling. I may as well call it a night and get something to eat.

****

I've been waiting in the cold so long my nose is starting to hurt. It's the kind of cold that makes you feel like your muscles are sticking out at odd angles. My efforts to stay casual and unassuming are foiled by the fact that I have to move around to stay warm. I showed up at around seven in the evening, expecting him to leave his office, but the light has been on since and it's now ten at night.

This isn't particularly an area I want to be in. This street is quite nice, but those surrounding it tend to be a bit shadier. It's a weird part of Paris, some streets are rich, some are poor, but that's Marcadet-Poissonniers.

Looking up at the second floor, I can only see that his office light is on. I can't see inside from the street. My eyes stray further to the black sky above. It seems void of everything. No stars to be seen... I know they're up there though. We just drowned them out. We made our own light. Twice as effective and half as beautiful. Bare trees that inhale the darkness and exhale a dull, gloomy yellow. Thousands of them across this city, all with one root.

A shadow is cast down on me. His office light has gone out. After about two minutes the same man that I saw jump into the van comes out. A scarf covers his face but I can tell it's him by his receding hairline. Despite his hair, he doesn't seem to be that old, only weary. Keys jingle in the pocket of his shabby wool-coat. The back of his pants have some white paint stains scarring them. With his head held low as he walks, it's apparent to me that he's quite troubled. Whatever it is on his mind, it's stopping him from paying any attention to me.

He doesn't travel too far. With a shake of his head and a sigh, he bashes in the code to an apartment building and enters. I sprint forward as the door closes. I just about manage to jam my fingers into the crack before it shuts, causing a moderate amount of pain even though my hands are almost completely numb at this stage. I listen intently to the other side of the door in case he heard me and turned back to investigate. I hear a door close, followed by silence, so I make my way in.

The foyer to the building is worn. The plaster on the wall has cracked and is tinged with mould. A wooden staircase leads up to apartments on the right hand side. Directly in front of me lies a door with large, fogged panes of glass.

Just to be sure, I give the stairs a try with my foot. As I lean down, the wood squeaks for mercy. The same with the second step. I would have heard him climb the stairs, he definitely went through the door.

Pushing the door open gently, I peek through the gap to see a small, concrete patio. It's dark save for the lights coming out between the slats on the windows of a ground floor apartment. Four stripy rectangles of yellow decorate the floor in front of me, save for the last column of light, the furthest away from me. This one seems to have a rough triangle cutting it in half. I can hear pots and pans clinking inside. I creep past the front door to the apartment, over to the obstructed window and peer in through the slats.

The tree stands obscenely tall inside the small apartment, from the roots to the roof. The very top is adorned with a crooked, cardboard star, the ceiling not allowing it to stand upright. Paper chains of various colours envelope the tree. A few baubles hang off some of the branches, although these are not as prominent or as numerous as the chains. Still, not a single branch is left undecorated.

There are no presents stuffed under the tree and, glancing at the bottom, I suddenly remember how stupid I had been. Christmas trees don't have roots...

In the other corner I can see a woman, working away at a fatigued kitchenette, talking to Eagle. It's a very basic looking place. The décor inside is reminiscent of the eighties. The ugly green wallpaper with fleur-des-lis decorating them has patches missing. A pipe protruding out of the wall above Eagle seems to have a watermark stain beneath it and the wallpaper has bubbled around it. He doesn't seem like a rich person by any means. The one exception to the rule is the wall by the tree, which has no wallpaper and seems to be a gleaming white. That explains a few things. He's rubbing his eyes and nodding his head wearily. He raises his hands, lets them drop to his side and walks exhaustedly towards the door.

I start to panic, the kind where information comes in flashes. He's leaving his apartment. The door to his apartment is in between me and the exit. Go the other way.

I spin around and make a start-stop jolt in the other direction. There's nowhere to go and in the few seconds I've already wasted, I realise there's nowhere to hide either. Eagle comes out and, a little startled, faces me.

"Good evening?" He asks. He's speaking French but his accent also smacks of Eastern European.

"Good evening!" I reply awkwardly.

"Can I help you with something?" He asks, now in English. Probably picking up on my own accent.

"No, I'm just leaving."

"Leaving? But why are you here?"

"I got a little lost. I thought my friend lived here, but I think they live somewhere else."

I glance over at the tree and Eagle's face darkens.

"I was told about you... That someone was trying to look into the missing tree. You don't look like a police officer to me. So, why are you trying so hard to find it?"

"Because you should give it back." I confess.

"Who's going to miss it?"

"I don't know?! But people could get in trouble because of it!"

"There's no trouble in taking home a tree that I paid for with my taxes. Why should I constantly give and get nothing back? You don't know what it's like to live like I do!"

"The tree is for the people of Paris. It's not just for you! You can't just steal it!"

His face softens. His once intimidating frame sags and his eyes move away from mine melancholically.

"You think I am proud to have to steal tree for my family? I was architect over twenty years ago. We did not have much money really, but we were well off in my country. We had to escape the war. We had to run, you see? Leave everything... The things you leave behind. The most precious things. They are not objects or items. They are people. But we had no choice. Our land was not safe any more. We seek asylum here. We arrived with nothing. I became a carpenter. I used to draw houses, not build them! After many, many years of rough trade, I finally opened up my own company. Almost the moment I did, this recession began. I've been struggling for seven years now, begging people for small contracts, all to keep food on our table... We have four children to take care of, the eldest is in university and the youngest is only three... You see how small it is in there? We are like fish in a can. But we are family. I would do anything for them..." His gaze meets mine once more as he rubs his arm. "Yes, yes... A crime... Just not justice..."

On that note, the Eagle lands. I can tell he isn't faking it and his logic isn't alien to me. Few people are aware of the reality of his plight. These battles against bills are held behind closed doors. Debts trapped in people's heads. He's simply trying to get above the gravitational pull of dues to give his family something unique. Something they only ever dreamed of.

They were forced to run when others uproot themselves

willingly. Pull themselves out of the dirt to live in the air. Rarely ever standing on solid ground, but never smothered in it either. In the air, your roots grow out further. They try to find what they need when it's always just slightly out of reach. Touching just enough to sustain you. It's difficult and it's perilous, but it's liberating. It's through these experiences that we grow. I would know just as well as anyone. I had wandering roots myself, once.

When I was fifteen years old, I found myself in toxic soil while dark, thunderous clouds loomed above me on the horizon. Waiting for the storm to break is almost worse than when it does. Caught in misery from above and below, I packed a bag. I had my eyes on what I thought would be greener pastures. I was gone for two days before the police found me and brought me home. When I did, the storm broke, the soil washed away to become less acidic and the situation seemed more tolerable. So, I tolerated it. I was always in a hurry to grow up and head out. Now, I'm giving rootless a try. Leave everything in passing and everything behind. Focusing only on what's in front of me.

My past pales in comparison to theirs...

So, what am I doing here?

Was I really trying to help anyone with this escapade or was I simply bored?

He shouldn't be distressed just so I can feed my ego. There was no malice in this crime. No victim but the perpetrator himself. He went above and beyond to give what his family deserved. Love brings out the best in people. I know for a fact that it does.

I peek back through the window to see that green triangle pointing upwards to a inelegant, but earnest, star. What's one tree anyway? Especially one without roots. It has no place to call home until someone is inclined to give it one. It seems like it would be better served here than ignored by the throngs of people walking through the rows of other trees. It would be appreciated.

I'm looking down at the ground now as he stares at me intently.

"Will you call the police?" He asks timidly.

"No! No... You should keep it. No one's going to look for it. It was stupid of me to try and find it."

A couple seconds go by until I realise he's awkwardly waiting for me to leave.

"I'm sorry, I'm holding you up!"

"It's okay. My wife just wants me to buy milk."

"I'll walk out with you."

I follow him out through the doors as he holds them open for me until we stand outside the front door to his apartment building.

"I'm going this way." He gestures with his thumb.

I have no intention of prolonging our awkwardness so I tell him I'm going the other direction.

As we separate on the street, he calls out to me. "Tell me something, stranger... Did you know which war I was talking about?"

I tell him I know exactly which one he was referring to and make my lonely way back through the snow.

I can feel the tiny tendrils of memory brushing at the cracks in the walls I put up. Memories of joy that follow to those of sadness and rage. I push them out to the dark corners of my mind. It's been over two months since we stopped talking to each other and I'm still healing, so I'll keep the stitches in it a little longer.

There's no need to follow those branches of neurons tonight. Following them leads only to an old tree and the fall of a paradise. I'll find more fertile places to rest my wandering mind.

After all, I'll never forgive her for all the things she did to me. For burning me down and salting the earth. All the pain I suffered when she broke my heart...

I wish she'd call me...

Case 4 – A New Man

    I called both of my parents and told them I wouldn't be home for Christmas. They protested, obviously, but I was firm with them. I explained that, because I'm the new guy at work, I had to make the sacrifice and that maybe next year there'll be someone else to cover for me. They gave up after each of them made me promise to Skype them on Christmas Day, which I did. I know I shouldn't have been that blunt with them, but sometimes it's difficult to talk to them. Letting them get close.

    Christmas when you're alone is almost the same as every other day, although there was an emptiness that hung around the streets. Everyone was indoors with friends or family. All the businesses were shut. There was even a void that I felt lingering inside myself, one I had to suppress.

    I had the apartment to myself for a few days and it was nice to have some freedom. The fact that most of the shops were closed in the area meant that Christmas dinner was pasta and pesto. Although, to be honest with myself, it was going to be pasta anyway.

    I spent my free time showing the flyer of Mouse to the few people loitering around and came up empty handed. I'll need a new approach if I'm going to find her quickly. Especially seeing as I'm juggling this with a full-time job.

    When Crow told me himself that I was to stay working over the holidays, I wasn't disappointed or outraged. I had no desire to go home to a Cold War and I welcomed the excuse. I remember the way he tilted his head to the side as I gave him a curt "That's fine." Even after he made the odd effort of sitting down beside me and putting his hand on my forearm. He never had anyone agree to it outright before. This was apparent to me because he started rationalising the importance of having someone here at all times to keep things running. I just raised my eyebrows and agreed with him.

Crow then reminded me that he gave me a job without having any hotel experience, probably to imply that I owe him something for it. His belief seems to be that you can still flog a horse with a carrot, you just need to try harder. Still, I was complacent about working through the holidays. He looked at me with dark, cold eyes that tried to mask his confusion until a smirk appeared on his face and he crinkled his nose.

"Of cowerse, you will nowt be able to attend Honukka eizer."

"Right." I nodded, not minding the idea that he has to keep guessing about who I am.

On this, he looked away, shrugged and walked off without so much as a goodbye. He had given up on why I wasn't trying to get out of it. Probably because he didn't really care that much anyway.

****

We're quite busy tonight, even if most people weren't on holiday we only have a skeleton staff but now we have to work even harder. There's a lot of people coming in for the New Year's celebration weekend and the hotel is fully booked. It being a Thursday, most people have gotten off work and travelled here the same day. Our clients are usually people on something of a budget. They're by no means poor, but they don't have a lot of disposable income. The money they do have, they'd prefer to spend on shopping or drinking rather than on a nicer hotel.

A couple of mid-twenty year old, American girls come in at around nine at night. They're clutching each other's arms and giggling excitedly. I'm guessing they had a few in-flight drinks on their way here. When they reach my desk, their eyes confirm my theory. Glazed over and unfocused like that of newborn babies.

"Hi, we're checking in!" One squeals.

"Paris! Woo!" The other one shouts.

I take their names, checking them in as quickly and as quietly as possible while they murmur to each other in between outbursts of laughter. I give them their keys and point them towards the elevator.

"Thank you! Hey! Do you like American girls?" One asks.

I feel a twinge in my heart. A sore memory.

With a tired smile, I say "Love them!"

They turn to each other and burst out laughing again. "Woo! We're in Paris, motherfuckah's! French guys dig Americans!"

I give them another insincere smile. A fake smile always seems to make me a little sadder. Pretending to feel what I can't command. Showing something that's not there.

I rummage around the desk for my cigarettes as they hobble towards the elevator like a pair of confused ducks. On a good night, I might have flirted with them a little bit. There was just something too familiar about them. Something that hit a little too close to home. I pull on my jacket and stride towards the door with a cigarette in hand. As I pull at the handle, another new arrival comes in.

It's going to be a long night.

****

Only ten minutes to go until midnight. All the guests have cleared out to make their way to various parties and events. A few asked me for my advice as to where they should celebrate it. Rather than send them to the Eiffel tower or the Arc de Triomphe, where the fireworks and celebrations are usually held, I sent them to a bar I used to go to. I promised them a good ambiance and that they could run out to see the firework display then pop back in again.

I watch the clock on my computer screen tick over midnight anticlimactically, as the new year rings itself in silently in the hotel. Nothing has changed, just the calendar. I wonder, though, will things be better this year?

At half four in the morning, Crow comes in and flaps snow off his jacket. He seems to be in excellent form. He hangs his coat up on the rack and makes his way over to me, humming to himself. He's the kind of man that will acknowledge your presence when he requires it, and simple manners to an employee should never get in the way of a mindless tune. He knocks twice on my desk and beams at me.

"'Appy New Year-uh!"

"Happy New Year, sir."

"Eet ees! Eet ees!" Smirking to himself "But, ay few details beforuh you leave at five. We are changing ow-er ze seestem of running buziness. From now on, only I will take ze reservations for ze guests."

This is odd. Normally it's Reception's job to take reservations, regardless of who's on. If someone called or emailed us, we'd simply let them book it and take their details. Why is he taking on this much work for himself?

"Okay, sir. You want all reservations to come to you and you alone?"

"To me alowen. *Oui*. I will change ze number on ze websites."

"Okay?"

"Okay! Good-uh!"

He turns around and inhales deeply "Eet ees a beautiful 'otel, izent eet?"

I nod my appreciation as he turns his head back to look at me. There are times when I do feel bad for him. This hotel was his life. Pre-recession, he was supposed to be a relatively happy man from what I've overheard from the older-serving members of staff. Stern, but composed. His emotional baseline seems to have fallen with the economy. He started to take his bad turns out on other people. He lost a lot of good staff to it too.

Crow claps his hands loudly "*Bon*! I go to my office and zen I come back!"

Crow, despite his bad back and the fact that we have an elevator, always takes the stairs up to the sixth floor where his office is situated. He circles his way up higher and higher until I can no longer hear the soft squeak of the stairs. Instead, I hear the dull thump of someone hitting their head off glass. Peering in the window, using his hand as a visor, my colleague stands with his hood up, trying to ascertain who's inside, and he's shitfaced drunk.

I better get my coat.

I start hissing at him outside, telling him that Crow is upstairs and he needs to either hide or invent the solution to immediate sobriety. He's trying to calm me down, saying he's lied his way through worse situations before. He's stumbling all over the place, laughing.

"He's right upstairs! If he sees you like this, you're fucked!" I whisper urgently.

"It's fine! I just need some gum. Do you have gum?"

"Nope."

"What do you have?"

"Cigarettes?"

"Shit! That won't help... But there's no harm in trying, right?" He chuckles and sticks out his palm.

Just as I reluctantly, and irately, give him a cigarette from my pack, Crow comes outside. I freeze completely. My colleague freezes, sways a little, coughs, and then freezes again.

Crow approaches with a maniacal look in his eye.

"Are-uh we feeling okay, Monsieur...?" He croons as his eyes scan my co-worker's chest for a name tag that isn't there yet.

"Yup! Fine! Great!"

"Not a leetle under ze weazzer, no?"

"Nope! A-okay! Happy New Year!"

Crow looks him up and down then, much to both our surprise, starts laughing. He's slapping the young man's shoulder and shaking his head.

"Go-uh. Get eenside. Yew will feel yower shift become longer and-uh longer as ze night goes on. Yew will be just like ze guests, no?"

Crow gives us a solid minute of cackling again before he bids us good night and walks away. I'm increasingly suspicious of his new behaviour. Old Crow would have had a fucking conniption. Seeing as I've had no luck tracking down Mouse, I might as well investigate this.

With everything I need in my coat, I hand my co-worker the keys, tell him good luck and make my way after Crow.

****

I follow him down jubilant and raucous streets, into the metro. The metro stays open all night on New Year's Eve. I'm keen to stay out of his sight. It wouldn't be terribly hard to explain why I was in the metro with him as I had just finished my shift, but I would prefer to avoid any interaction with him at all. I put on my fingerless gloves, pull the scarf out of my pocket and wrap it around my face. I'm still wearing the same clothes he saw me in at the hotel though, so it's probably not going to do much.

As I go through the turnstile I'm met with two tunnels adorned with dirty white tiles. I might have lost him already. I stop and look at my two options for a moment, both leading to trains in opposite directions. Just before I panic, a soft, familiar hum emanates from one of the tunnels.

I slowly make my way down the concrete stairs and listen for the sound of the approaching train. I can hear the dull rumble coming through as I pretend to seem interested in one of the many large advertising posters that you can find plastered to the walls. I briskly walk onto the platform as I hear the brakes squealing, keeping an eye out for Crow. He's about eight metres ahead on the platform, staring at the train. I make my way to the carriage before his, careful to stay close to the wall and not attract too much attention.

We're on Metro Line 1, heading towards La Défense. I'm a bit more wary now, as this train has nothing separating the carriages, but

I'm fortunate to see him sitting in a direction facing away from me.

As pipes whizz by methodically through the window, my fatigue starts to set in and I find myself depressed. It's a brand new year and I'm following my boss for lack of better things to do. I feel old-souled and weary. It's exhausting going nowhere.

Groups fall into the carriages laughing as they end their celebrations. I can barely remember what they're feeling right now. When I see misery, I can empathise with it. Joy seems so foreign to me now. Mournful, too familiar. It seems I have stock in sadness.

I've been like this for most of my life. Always melancholic and self-pitiful. Not to say that I didn't have reasonable excuses to be so at the time. It seemed like something bad was always going to be around the corner. A life in constant state of decay. Don't get me wrong, there's no one on this Earth that I'd rather be than me. I just wish being me was easier sometimes.

****

We're two stops away from the end of the line. I'm still no closer to figuring out what has him in such odd humour. The only plausible conclusion I can come to, and it's barely plausible, is that Crow has found himself a mate... Perhaps it's not impossible to believe that someone could love him. No one is unworthy of love.

Love can change people. It changed me once, quite recently. I'm too tired tonight to fight the tide of memories flooding in. All I can do is channel it towards the best moments.

The day we moved in together, she was wearing a headband with cute, little tiger-ears attached on. They peaked out of her long blonde hair that fell over her lightly tanned face. She was purring manically, her hands clawing at me playfully as I laughed uncontrollably. I couldn't believe that this was my life. That I was so lucky to have this goofy American girl and that she was going to live with me in this tiny apartment with a fold-out sofa for a bed, even if it was only going to be for a month.

All of her stuff came in suitcases and plastic containers. Mine came in backpacks and an oversized cardboard box. We took a taxi from her place but my apartment at the time was close enough for us to walk to our new home. From Pyrenées to Parmentier we carried that stupid white box. Our dead arms and sore backs in the sweltering July heat, her piloting us as I walked backwards down the street. We made flags out of traffic lights and bins for places to rest before struggling on. Dodging pedestrians and cars, we might even have had fun.

I loved everything about her. She was so different to any other girl I'd ever met. She was quirky in so many ways. She'd make faces at me, crossing her eyes and sticking out her tongue. We had staring contests and thumb wars. She'd lick my face and pinch me. I felt young with her. Like I was catching up on a youth that was lost to me. There was an innocence there, in that love.

She was my weird and wonderful. Her voice was music to me. A celebration of life itself instilled in someone. My favourite person. My darling, Cat...

"Can you stop?!" I protested, laughing after another purring fit.

"No! This is who I am *meow*."

"I kinda preferred you when you were human."

"Why?"

"Conversation was a little more stimulating."

"Meow?"

"Although not by much."

"Asshole!" She yelled and threw her head back laughing, her perfectly white teeth gleaming in the dim light. She had a beautiful laugh. The kind that forcefully came out from her diaphragm and slowly waned in a soprano.

"I'm joking!"

"Are ya *joking*?! You want to sleep on the couch tonight?!"

"Babe, the couch is our bed."

"Well, you better get me another drink then... If you're *lucky*, I'll let you sleep here!"

"I am lucky..."

"Shush, babe..."

The hungover morning after our night of partying and dancing around our new apartment, I was greeted with a messy bandit as her mascara smudged around those gorgeous, pale-blue eyes. A sapphire shade only the sky itself could create. I could lose myself in them for hours.

I remember that night as one of the best nights I've ever had. It was the first time in my life that it seemed like everything was good and things were shining on the horizon. I had changed by being with her. Before her, I was living through a haze of sunrise and sunset without ever really going anywhere or having anything to look forward to. Kicking myself to sleep. Then, all of a sudden, tomorrow there would be her. I woke up early to see her and went to bed late thinking about her.

I changed on the outside too. Back then I was all awkward angles and ends, growing into myself. A shit haircut and a sad smile. Only with her I took better care of myself. She would run her fingers through my hair and sweep my fringe to one side because it looked better. I traded in my hoodies and jeans that were hiding my body for button down shirts and fitted pants. I followed her example on hygiene, discovered what floss was for and showered more than once a week.

I wanted to be the very best version of myself for her, and at that moment in our apartment I had produced the final result. The apex of my arc. Me at my most complete. I was a new man because of her...

It hurts to think about it...

The doors to the train close at the last stop before La Défense. Crow stays put which means he can only be getting off at the terminus. I stand up and make my way to the doors in preparation.

Yes, I remember being full of life and joy.

Now, staring at my reflection in the window, all I see is a ghost in the glass.

****

Paris in the snow, at night, can be pristine. A fresh blanket has been lain down and an immaculate sheet lies before me on a small walkway as I follow Crow. The only blemishes to be seen are his footprints followed by mine. It seems I'm to walk a mile in the man's shoes.

This new Crow intrigues me. He seems nothing like himself, yet he plays the part convincingly. Perhaps he truly has turned over a new leaf?

I wonder if we ever get that fresh start with other people. That blank slate that states the present is more important than the past. That who you are now is more important than who you were. Perhaps not... Forgiveness is earned, isn't it?

As different as he may be acting now, there are still memories of who he was. Footprints that he left behind on the pages of everyone that he's ever met. Some of them will take more than one winter to erase. Scars on the inside always take longer to heal.

Out of sight, I follow the shadows of his shoes carefully until I reach the square of La Défense. Tall, futuristic skyscrapers tower above me. The edgy, grandiose brilliance isn't lost on me. It provides a nice contrast to the rest of Paris which, although holding an elegant, ancient beauty, can seem a little uniform when you stop looking too closely. Here, each tower seems to have its own identity.

He's further ahead, across the square, climbing up the stairs to La Grand Arche – an Arc de Triomphe inspired building. He makes his way inside the building and disappears. I'm left with very little cover to hide behind so I decide to stay put.

Ten minutes go by without him coming out. Public cleaners come to shovel away at the snow. One of them catches my eye particularly. An African man with hair as white as the snow that lands on it.

He must have be doing this job for quite some time to be working at that age. How could someone stay doing the same thing for so long? I don't think I could ever decide on one thing to be in my life. To pinpoint something that defines such a large part of me and dominates most of my time. I don't understand how everyone else seems to do it and I'm clueless as to when I'm going to be forced to choose myself.

I would often muse at the fact that people always see city cleaners or bin men as dirty, when they're the only people keeping this place clean. We're the ones making all the mess. I'll never understand how a Marketing Executive makes more money than him. Businessmen rush in and out of this place until they rush into their graves. If only they could see that keeping everything looking like it always does requires a lot of work. This man is fighting against entropy.

After twenty-five minutes of waiting, Crow exits La Grand Arche. I can see him smiling, even from here. I think I'll give up trailing him tonight. I'm pretty tired and it'll be morning in a few hours. Instead, I'll pop in to La Grande Arche and see what he was up to.

The young woman at reception seems surprised, if not a little bit troubled. It seems I'm not the only one that was working through the new year.

"Law, Accounts or Insurance?" She asks.

"Sorry?"

"Which one? There's only three offices open right now, a law firm, an accountants office and an insurance company."

"Uh..."

She tilts her head sideways at me. "Did you get lost from the rave? Go back downstairs, take a left, you'll find the party soon enough. If it's still on at seven, I'll be there too!"

A little startled, I nod, mumble my thanks and leave. I wonder which office Crow had been to and did it have anything to do with his mood?

Maybe he was at the rave?

****

I arrive home to find two of my roommate's friends passed out on the couch, also known as my bed. Two others are slumped, unconscious, in chairs and one more is lying on the floor. Music is playing from the stereo and an electronic disco-ball is throwing lights around the apartment. I tear the plugs out of the walls and shake one of those on the sofa to wake him up. He starts drunkenly and blindly pushing back at me. I try the other one but she's essentially comatose. I really hope they didn't have sex in my bed.

I go into the bathroom to brush my teeth, only to find someone has vomited in the sink. An orange and brown, chunky soup. A blurry streak on the wall leads to the toilet bowl. I really can't deal with any of this tonight.

I rip my blanket off the couple and climb upstairs to the sixth floor of the building where there's a little corridor that leads nowhere. Using my jacket as a pillow and the blanket as a sleeping bag, I lie down on the floor and roll over. Blue light is coming in through the window above. I'm reminded that for the new year, I've still inherited the same problems that I had before.

I know I could have gone downstairs and screamed at everyone to get out. I could have torn my stupid roommate, who never had any real problems to overcome in life, out of his bed for being so stupidly selfish. Only, I don't want this particular problem to effect who I am or who I'm becoming. I want to rise above to resilience.

I don't understand people sometimes. There are people out there who have suffered so much, yet they come out happy and kind. They fight for the life they have, meagre as it may seem to others, and they don't let this inner war spill out on anyone else. They're careful not to hurt anyone. I've been through things myself. Things that seemed bigger than me.

I dwell on this for a while. The street-sweeper who does his job well, thanklessly. What has kept him so devout to his work when others have it better? Crow and his assumed favourable circumstances that have him in a good mood, compared to his usual vitriolic behaviour. My roommate, who has had everything easy his whole life, and his total lack of consideration. It seems to me that we're all cast our lot, it's how we deal with it that matters...

As the wall of the corridor turns a shade of purple, I'm left wondering about what kind of person I'll be this year. Now that I've shed my past, what will the future bring?

So far, it seems to only be a test in temperament and a lesson in loneliness.

Case 5 – The Accidental Predator

    It's my first weekend off in a very long time. I'm not sure what caused the change in the rota but, because it's given me three nights off in a row, I didn't stop anyone to ask. Things are tense in my apartment now. My roommate gave me, what I can only call a defiant apology for his behaviour on New Year's and, while agreeing he was wrong to do what he did, argued that everyone in the world was the same that night. Tensions have been building since, but it doesn't matter to me now. My night of liberation must be celebrated! I'm going to find a bar.

    I can only hope that tonight I might fare better for myself. The last time I had a night out was on Valentine's night and the closest thing I got to any action was a drunk girl accidentally punching me in the dick when she fell on the stairs.

    I'm not in dire need of a lay. I'm usually content to work that urge out at home alone, but the real thing is always better and my roommate is away for the weekend. If there's ever a night to try and give the tissues a break, it's tonight.

    There's still a chill in the air as I leave my apartment, even though winter has come to an end. It's an effect of global warming, as far as I know. The seasons are becoming a bit askew. The program is starting to get a bit buggy, like you'd see in a computer that's overheating. That being said, things are pretty okay in this part of the world. The weather is milder. There are no hurricanes or typhoons to sweep us away, just a bite in the wind, is all.

    I'm a little unsure as to what kind of place I'm in the mood for and I venture towards Les Halles so I have a broader choice. The Tour de Saint-Jacques stands tall as I walk down Rue de Rivoli. I always thought it was a funny tower. An intricately ornate building, its height originally seemed unnecessary to me given the fact that it was surrounded by an open park. Then I found out that it's the last surviving part of what they once called the Butcher's church, named so for the people that came in. The last piece of a missing puzzle. An island of antiquity.

I turn right on Rue Saint-Denis. It's a mongrel street. A litter of sex-shops, grocery stores, hot-food stands, restaurants, cafés and bars. A few people are already a little buzzed and bopping around even though it's only ten o'clock. I stroll through them until a café catches my eye.

I have no intention to go in. I'm not really in the mood for sitting at a table alone, surrounded by groups eating and drinking. I'd prefer a place where I can drink at the bar, watch the people around me and maybe find an idle conversation. But I'm stuck on this place because I came here once with Cat, during the day, a long time ago.

She had just started working in the same bar as me. I went to the bar with the excuse of visiting a co-worker, when really I had just wanted to see who the new girl was. I was so shy around her. I didn't dare look at her or talk to her too much, she was so pretty. I left after an idle conversation, leaving behind some chocolates given to me by a hostel receptionist because she had made a mistake with my room. I'd almost think it was clever if it wasn't an accident, to have given her chocolates the first time we'd ever met.

The next night we ended up working together, it was just the two of us behind the bar. We contrasted quite well. She was smiling at customers, while I was sourly drifting through my shift. It wasn't long before she took notice of my ill-humour.

"I'm just having a bit of trouble finding an apartment at the moment."

"Where are you staying?"

"In a youth hostel."

"I'm sorry." She said and rubbed my arm sympathetically, then popped her thumb in her mouth.

"You cut yourself?" I asked.

"It's nothing."

"Let me see."

I held her hand in mine and examined the tiny scar. "I'll get a plaster."

"A what?! No, it's fine! I chew my thumbs like crazy all the time!"

    I raced down to the First-Aid kit and got a band-aid, almost as if the cut on her thumb would change its mind. She protested that it wasn't a fresh cut, but I insisted. She seemed to think it an unusually nice gesture as I forced it on her. Seeing as I thought I had scored some points, I invited her for coffee the next day.

    I took her to this café right here. We were chatting and laughing. She always looked right into my eyes as we spoke, giving me her full attention. She told me that she had to drop out of college two years ago when her parents ran into some financial difficulties, then came to Paris to simply do something different with her life. She'd been living here ever since.

    Another coffee came and I knew I really liked her. When we went outside for a cigarette, she started telling me about how broke she was.

"Right here!" She said, showing me a tear on the back of her pants. I really tried to focus on the tear.

"Well, you're talking to someone who's homeless, so I think I win the poverty game."

"You're not homeless! Stop being such a Debbie Downer!"

"I don't have an apartment!"

"Yeah, but you've never had to sleep on the streets, have you?"

"Not this time, no."

"You mean you did *before*?!"

"I slept in a car park lift once."

"In an elevator?! Why?!"

"It was warmer than the stairs..."

"You're insane!"

"No, I amn't!"

"What?"

"I said - *No, I amn't*."

"*Amn't* isn't a word, dingbat!"

"Sure it is! It's the abbreviation of Am Not."

"That is just not true... You're going to have to learn how to speak like a real human being if you ever want to not be homeless! Y'know what I mean, Jelly bean?"

At the end of our coffee, I walked her back to the metro. Under an unusually clear, bright February sun, I gave her the traditional French goodbye of a kiss on each cheek and then began a slow, pensive walk back to the bar. My head was spinning. All I could feel was a low hum in my chest. Neurons resonating in new paths. My body electric and rising spirits.

I was falling in love with her and my soul was singing...

I pull my attention away from the café and continue on down the street. Eventually, I find a small, Scottish pub. There's a good number of people inside, but it doesn't seem too crowded and there's a few stools free at the bar. May as well give it a try.

****

I climb up on a stool at the bar and take a look at the menu that's peeking out under a partially-completed crossword puzzle. There's no Guinness on tap so I opt out for another favourite of mine, an Amaretto Sour.

It's a cosy bar. Bottles of spirits line the shelves, flanked on both sides by two barmaids. English and American judging by their accents. Frank Sinatra is singing "New York, New York" in the background. Groups of relaxed people sit at tables while a few lonely stragglers like myself sit at the bar, some of whom talk periodically with the barmaids. I figure I might spend a quiet night here.

After finishing my first cocktail, I amble outside for a cigarette. The chill seems to keep most of the other smokers indoors so I don't have anyone to chat to, only a continuous train of drunks walking past me on their way to the next stage of their night out. My head goes right to left in a repetitive motion as I watch each group all head in the same direction.

There's always very few old people in Les Halles. At least, those that aren't crazy. You mostly get the teenagers coming in from the suburbs, bouncing off each other. It's a place dominated by youth and obnoxious freedom. A loud cheer for a moment that will soon be behind them forever. A few groups go by when I notice a static figure in the background that doesn't seem to be going anywhere.

Across the street, with his back up against the wall, there's a man with folded arms. He's wearing white runners, jeans and a dark hoodie with the hood up. A shadow casts itself over most of his face. I can still make out his eyes through the darkness. In them, there is a long, smouldering stare. The intensity of it seems eternal, like time could slow down inside the portal of his gaze. Almost everything gets drawn out of the world. The light only highlighting him, the sounds of the street numbing themselves to silence.

Crowds of people stumble between us, breaking his line of sight, but not his focus or discipline. It takes me a few moments to realise he's staring more at the bar than he is at me. I turn around to see exactly what he's looking at. The two front doors each have relatively large panes of glass on them, accounting for maybe a third of the size of the door. Through them, I can see the bar counter, the American barmaid and the people sitting on the stools. Him being further away, the field of vision being narrower, I reckon he can only see the barmaid.

I take a few steps towards him, hoping to fake a drunken conversation with him and see what he's up to. As soon as I do, his attention switches to me and he walks off at a swift pace against the current of the crowds. He throws a look over his shoulder at me before he disappears around a corner. It seems like I've scared him off, but it doesn't answer why he was spying on the barmaid.

I throw my cigarette-butt on the street and head back inside. I'm not going to tell her about it because either she already knows, and I'd be getting involved, or she doesn't, which could frighten her. Regardless, I'll keep an eye on how this plays out tonight.

****

I've had a few. I dutifully stayed in the bar to keep watch on the barmaid, during which it was encouraged that I keep drinking. They politely asked me to leave at 2am, which I did and I decided to hang around to make sure the mystery man wasn't back. On the street I see a couple staggering home, holding on to each other for support.

Cat and I were about as drunk as that when we first slept together. I was staying in a hotel at the time. The reception closed at 2am so I couldn't really stay out long, but all of the bar staff ended up in this small bar near where we worked. I kept glancing at my watch nervously about when to leave. I really didn't want to go. We were all having so much fun and I was getting to spend more time with her.

She told me I could stay at her place if I wanted to stay out with them. It was pretty kind of her, considering I had spent about a week ignoring her in a vain attempt to regain control of how I felt about her. With my cripplingly low self-esteem, I told myself that she would never settle for someone like me. I dismissed the thought of being with her as a fantasy. But the hope and the feeling dug itself under my skin.

She and I left the bar at around 3am to go back to her apartment.

"Do you like to dance?" I asked.

"Sure. I mean, I'm not good at it, but I like doing it."

"I can show you!"

"You can?"

"Not really... But I know a move or two!"

I took her hands into mine as she asked. "How are we supposed to dance without any music?"

She giggled to the sound of me drunkenly singing as we danced a simple waltz. I spun her around a few times to break it up a bit. Each time I dipped her she would burst out laughing.

The pavement was our stage. The streetlight, our spot-light. It was the very beginning of something wonderful. Either hand in hand or arm in arm, we danced our way home, merry and mysterious to all...

****

The metal shutter comes down as the two barmaids stand outside. They bid each other good night and separate. As the American barmaid walks down the street, a shadowy figure emerges out from a doorway. His pace is slow but determined. Each step he takes seems deliberate. He's following her.

I stagger after them, veering slightly in different directions every now and then. Walking in a straight line seems to be a problem at this hour. My vision isn't exactly in top form either. The dark stranger seems to keep duplicating himself on the street and merging back with himself. I'm not sure I can stay on him.

I stifle a laugh to myself when I realise that I'm stalking a stalker. The two turn a corner on a main street and I have to jog to catch up with them. I make the corner just as she crosses the street and walks down an alley with him trailing behind.

I take a step forward on the edge of the footpath when a car comes hurtling out of nowhere, cutting across in front of me at high speed, followed by another and another. They're both out of my sight now. Seconds that feel like minutes go by until the flurry of cars cease. I throw my foot down onto the road to sprint across but it slides on something and I'm sent flying back on to the pavement.

My back hurts, or at least I think it does. The alcohol is helping to numb the pain. I roll over and pick myself up. What the hell did I slip on? It's not cold enough anymore for ice!

To my absolute disgust, I realise I just slipped on a dead pigeon. A very flat and circular plume of grey mottled with red blotches. The yellow entrails coming out of its chest eked out and elongated, no doubt helped by the sole of my shoe. A reminder that somehow the car has ended up as king of the concrete jungle.

I hurry over to the alley and look down to see that I've lost them. I'm too drunk for this. I'll come back tomorrow night and make sure everything is okay. If it isn't, then I'll pass on the guy's description to whoever needs it.

Looks like I'm going home pissed in every sense of the word.

****

I'm relieved to see she's back at work. Her joyful demeanour is one that would definitely contradict the notion that any evil had come to her the night before. I take a seat and order a Coke, having learnt from my mistake last night. To avoid the obvious suspicion that would come from not drinking alcohol in a Scottish bar, I ask the English barmaid for a pen and get to work on a fresh crossword lying on the bar.

I keep casting occasional glances out the window of the front door. It's not a great angle to see from though. I lean across the bar to get a better look when the English barmaid jumps to attention.

"Can I get you something?" She asks.

"Oh, no, sorry! It's nothing."

"Don't be shy! If you need something, I'll do my best."

"Uh..."

"Yeah?"

"A six letter word for 'Dig'?"

"A six letter wo- Shovel!"

"Thanks."

"No problem!"

A customer waves her down and she skips over to him. I take another sip of my Coke and head out the front door with my pack of cigarettes demonstratively on show in my hand.

Sure as it's Saturday, he's there. He's even wearing the same clothes as the night before. The same intense stare, like that of a Tiger, drawing the reality thin around it. When he notices me he seems to fidget a little. He stares down at his shoes and potters around. I pretend to ignore his presence but I keep an eye on him in my peripheral vision.

Out of the corner of my eye, it looks like he keeps putting his fingers in his mouth. It's only as he turns away to the side and I sneak a look at him that I realise he's eating. Judging by the minute tinkering he does with the objects, and the size of the things, I guess that he's eating pistachio nuts. He fiddles with another nut, dropping the shells on the ground, as I return to the warmth of the pub.

My crossword buddy seems to be the most exuberant of them. She's flying up and down the bar chatting with everyone animatedly. Somehow she seems to manage holding two, or sometimes three, conversations at any given time before she'd introduce the conversationalists to each other. Running out of people to talk to, and probably knowing better than to talk to me, she slides up beside her co-worker.

I can't really make out their conversation, but it seems innocuous enough. I keep cracking on with the crossword. Some of them I know I'll never get, others are just on the edge of my memory. Either way, I know I'm not going to be able to finish it. Futility is a frustrating thing.

My crossword buddy beams out to her co-worker "See! This is why you're the coolest Chick I know!" She makes her way up the bar singing "I got next Thursday off!" to herself. She interrupts her chorus to ask me if I want another Coke, which I accept.

My third Coke has me feeling a bit jittery and the crossword is about as complete as it'll ever be. I'm not sure if I can feasibly stay here much longer, but I know this stalker will be out there at the end of the night, waiting for his prey. I'll have to compromise.

I pay my tab and retrace my steps back to where I lost them the first time. The pigeon-turned-pancake makes a decent landmark for me. Down the alley, I find a small bar with a little terrace that seems like a good place to wait for them. They should be passing by in an hour and a half. A beer won't matter now.

I sip away on my pint as couples chatter around me. I'm sure there's a story for each of them. How they met, their first kiss, the times they spent together. I guess the one thing I'd never be able to figure out is why they're attracted to each other. How did they pick one out of all the others? It's something I never really understood with Cat either...

I was a miserable mess of a man when she met me. Hollowed out and homeless. Out of shape and introverted. Just lost in the wild. But she saw something attractive when it seemed completely alien to me. It still moves me that at my very worst, when I had nothing good to give, she *chose* me.

A week after we first slept together, I had found an apartment. Cat was my first call.

"Oh my God! I'm so happy for you! What's it like?"

"It's nice! I mean, it's pretty small but I'm grateful to take anything now. Get this, she doesn't even want a deposit!"

"Who doesn't want a deposit?"

"The Austrian woman renting the place. She's leaving for Vienna for part of her medical studies. She said she just trusted me!"

"Wow! Are you happy finally?"

"Yeah, I am!" I said, having gotten used to the idea.

We went out a few nights later to celebrate, which would later prove to be a typical outing for us. We went to a piano bar with friends. Her laugh filled the air in between the times I drunkenly bashed on the piano and serenaded her. It seemed like I was a hoot when we went out. We threw back beers and bounced off other people. I felt comfortable around strangers because I had the validation of her company. I didn't want to hide anymore, but for everyone to see me with my trophy.

The night carried on as we drew closer to each other. I picked her up from the bar stool and spun her around, kissing her. I put her back down as her hands wandered my body and I started drinking faster. I slid her giant, white, faux-fur coat on her back as we stumbled out. We walked three feet before we started making out on someone's car. I just couldn't keep myself off her.

Sheer force of will brought us to a taxi. She propped her feet on my lap and leaned back. I'd always hold on to her ankles because she'd refuse to wear a seat-belt. It would have done nothing, but it made me feel better. With no loop around her waist, I'd lace myself into her.

Every day, I built bridges to get close to her. I was crazy about her and I chased that girl like no other. I liked her and she liked me. Everything in my life seemed to be going right. But all I could think at the time was that there were so many ways that I could screw it up and that the only reason I hadn't so far is because the wheel of choice was still spinning...

And so it spun...

****

I waited for three hours, or the equivalent of four pints, without them showing up. Neither Tiger nor Chick. I kept my eyes on the street the whole time. They definitely didn't walk by. Now I know why he always follows her directly from the bar each night.

It occurs to me that I can't keep coming into the bar or she'll start to think I'm a stalker. I'll have to show up as they close the bar and follow them both from the beginning. I've only got one night off left, afterwards I'll finish work too late to pick up their trail.

It's quieter on a Sunday so I show up about four hours before their weekend closing time just to be safe. I pass the time by listening to music on my phone and taking brief walks around until the metal shutter comes down at midnight. She looks down on the ground in concern and uses her foot to sweep something invisible to me. Just like the first night, she walks the same direction and he strolls out of the doorway in pursuit. He's now donned a fedora hat, sunglasses, a black jacket and brown chords. I know it's him though, he's still wearing the same pair of shoes. I pull out my headphones and follow suit.

Together a trio, with two incognito, we make our way back to the alley. Careful not to slip on any roadkill, I manage to follow them all the way this time. The barmaid appears to be texting on her phone while Tiger slinks in and out of shadows. From light to dark and light to dark again.

She arrives outside a bar and kisses a solid, well-built guy on the lips. I can see Tiger's fist clench. I pull my hood up and peer down at my phone as I walk past him to within earshot of the couple. I just manage to catch the ending.

"I'll come by again after work tomorrow and I'll stay till you're done like we did on Friday." Chick says.

Her boyfriend replies with an English accent. "Are you sure? We'll be closing late tomorrow because of that private party I told you about. I could just give you the keys and you could crash at mine for a bit?"

"Nah, I'd just get bored at your place alone. I'll swing by and have a few drinks. It'll only be three hours or so to wait and I'll get to talk to you. Besides, my place is better."

"Okay. Get home safe?"

The couple kiss goodbye and she makes her way back out of the alley the same way she came in. Tiger seems to be closing his distance now, he's only a few metres away. I'm worried that he might do something but he seems to be maintaining the current pace. I should still keep him close, just in case.

We walk for about four minutes, she pulls her phone out of her bag and looks at it. Suddenly, she starts sprinting. Tiger starts to walk as quickly as he can, breaking into a jog occasionally. Chick plummets down the metro stairs and disappears.

I'm losing Tiger. The second he goes down the stairs after her I sprint down it. I just manage to catch a glimpse of him going left as I tear around the corner. I stride forward and try my best to regulate my breathing so it seems normal. Running isn't my strong suit, I'm much better at smoking, and this would be obvious to anyone right now.

I can see him go down the stairs. He pushes through behind some woman to get past the metro turnstile. I beep my way through using my Navigo pass. Tiger takes four steps forward when he looks across the tracks. Chick is on the other side.

He spins on his feet and briskly walks out through the exit. I move to follow him then stop myself and glance over at the metro clock across the way. It's late, that means the trains are running slower than usual. The next one is in six minutes. I can hear his legs rub off each other as he sprints up the stairs. The abrasive sound of denim on denim. I wait until I imagine he's in the connecting tunnel before I slowly make my way back. I also sprint up the stairs but it's only due to impatience and a chance to exercise.

As I get to the turnstile I swipe my pass and move forward. A dull, monotonous squawk, the kind you get when you get answers wrong on game shows, comes out of the pillar as my right hip meets an unmoving rod. I swipe it again and look down at the panel on top. It tells me that I've already gone through. They don't allow you to use it more than once, otherwise people would just scan themselves through and give it to a friend. I remember someone saying once that you'd have to wait ten minutes for it to work again. With only around three minutes to spare, I have to jump the turnstile.

It's not the first time I've done it, and technically I've paid for it, but I'm nervous anyway. I make sure no one is watching me from either side of the platform before I place my right foot on the top turnstile bar and hoist myself up on the metal-sheet barrier in front.

As soon as I'm up, I place my left foot up on the pillar and squeeze through the barrier. I land down silently on the balls of my feet and start walking casually towards some seats. No one seems to have noticed, aside from a drunken man mysteriously balancing a stick on his head.

We hop on the metro, a carriage each, and ride it out as far as Bastille where a ten minute walk takes us to a small side-street. Chick holds her keys up to a keypad and enters a building. Tiger looks up at the number on top of the door and crosses the street to get a better look. I find an adjacent alley to spy on him from.

My eyes flit between him and the building. He looks decidedly hipster given his outfit. The king of scene and stalking. He's eating the nuts again and suddenly smiles to himself. I look over at the building and realise that a light on the third floor has just come on. I start to panic when he walks away. I'm not entirely sure what I should do.

Should I chase him?

Confront him?

Beat him up?

I don't think I really prepared for anything and he disappears before I can decide. I really need to do my homework on this kind of stuff. I can't fix a problem unless I have a solution. With no end in sight, I'm left no end of an idiot.

****

When asked by my co-worker what I did over the weekend, I simply told him I had a few drinks and he stopped asking. He had made the rare mistake of coming in fifteen minutes early, at a quarter to five in the morning. I grabbed my coat and started yammering about the new Scottish bar that I like, all the while deliberately avoiding looking at the clock he was shifting his eyes to with concern. As a result I left fifteen minutes early and took a taxi here, outside Chick's boyfriend's bar, just in time to see them leave.

They loiter around the metro for half an hour until it opens.

They seem like a nice, loving couple from what I can gather. On the carriage, he has one of his barrel arms wrapped around her and promises to make her the pasta that she likes while she protests at his generosity. He speaks to her gently and she nestles into him. They clearly love each other.

Outside her apartment, there's no sign of Tiger. He must not have heard the conversation Chick and her boyfriend had outside his bar last night. I'm more than relieved to say the least. I had decided that an encounter was inevitable, if I really wanted to help, and I brought my flashlight with me in case things got physical. I'm not that good of a fighter. Even though I know for a fact I can take a punch, or a headbutt, returning one has never particularly appealed to me. Not to say that receiving one ever did...

It's comforting to have the flashlight in my pocket, nonetheless. It's small, sleek and concealable. Only about four inches long. The steel construction gives it a bit of heft and it's black coating means it only emits light when I want it to. Even better is that, as a night porter, I have every legal reason to carry one with me at all times without it being considered a weapon. I can always make the excuse that it comes in handy at work and that's why I carry it on my person. A knife, pepperspray, or even a corkscrew would be harder to explain.

As they enter the building, they look down and around themselves in confusion. I stand over at a door and start punching in some bullshit numbers into the keypad to make it seem like I'm just going home. Their confusion subsides and they giggle to each other as they slip in the door. With them gone, and nothing else to do, I might as well test the defence of the door to make sure Tiger can't do anything sinister when I'm away from this watch.

Just before the door, I hear a cracking sound under my foot. I pull out my flashlight and shine it over pistachio nut-shells that are littered everywhere. A few minutes of following the trail left behind reveals that he had been beside the bin across the street, the neighbouring doorways and in the nearby park beside a relatively tall tree.

The tree stands out to me because the surrounding mud also gave me an impression of his foot, should I ever need it. I also notice that one of the lower branches was twisted and some mud was grazed on the front. He must have tried to climb it for some reason.

This guy is starting to seem more dangerous than I had imagined. His oddness is escalating.

****

For the first time in my new job, I called in sick. It was my usual and, ashamedly well-practised voice, that portrayed a tone of fatigue, worry and self-disappointment. Crow didn't seem to mind too much and told me that he'd even cover for me. His generosity is increasingly worrying, but I'll take what I can get. I get down to the Scottish pub at around ten to find Tiger waiting smugly outside.

He's wearing the same hipster attire. Granted, it makes him less intimidating, but I'm still wary of his slyness and wiry physique. I pull a cigarette out of my pocket and light it for the small courage it can give me. I'm really nervous and I don't want to do this. A guy like this is probably imbalanced and I have no idea how this is going to play out.

All of a sudden I start to get angry. Who the fuck is this asshole who thinks he can just stalk people?! What gives him the fucking right to invade someone's privacy like that?! I'm half-way through the cigarette when I storm over to him, slowing down just as I approach.

"I've seen you around here a few times."

Tiger almost jumps out of his skin when I say this and I can finally see his face properly. He's not a bad looking guy, but there's a weirdness with him in the way that he carries himself and expresses himself. He shuffles his feet uncomfortably and his eyes, motionless, never seem to meet mine.

"Yeah! Well, not really! I just like to hang out here..."

I fix my tone on firm and hostile, it'll keep him on the edge while I'm in control.

"Why?!"

"It's a nice place... There's people... I really don't have time for this..."

"You have somewhere to be?"

"No- Yes! I-I have to meet some friends soon... I'm just waiting here for them..."

"So, you're waiting for them here?"

"No. I'm- Look, I don't know who you are but-"

"- Because if I didn't know better, I'd say you were stalking that barmaid in there. You know... Following her home, to where her boyfriend works, through the metro..."

"I-What?! I mean... I don't know this girl..."

"Cut the shit! You stop following her from this moment on!"

"Look, I don't know why you're asking me-"

"- I'm not asking. Either you stop following her or the next time I see you, I'm telling her to call the cops and get a restraining order."

"I think you've made some kind of-"

"- Fine. I'll do it now!"

    I storm defiantly towards the front door of the pub when I feel a thin, tight grip on my arm. I reach into my pocket for the flashlight, but I keep it in there.

"Get your fucking hands off me!" I yank my arm free.

"You can't tell her! Please!"

"Why the fuck shouldn't I?"

"She'll never be with me if she finds out! She'll think I'm a weirdo!"

    I look at him properly now. His face is white. The band of black sunglasses across his face slips down to reveal a fiercely desperate expression. The kind that portrays an outcast from society.

Doomed to hunt alone due to his odd nature. Too rare a person to find a friend. He continues to beg me.

"I just wanted to find out what she likes so I could swoop in some day and be what she wanted to be. She's the only person I know that really gets me. She doesn't hate me. She talks to me every time I go in and she's always nice to me. I wasn't going to try and break her up with her boyfriend or anything like that. I just wanted to get to know her better so I'd be ready for when she's single."

"You can't do it like that! That's not how it works!"

"You don't understand! I love her! I know she's perfect for me and I'd be perfect for her! I'd treat her like she's the most important person in the world! I would never do anything to hurt her. I really do love her!"

"This isn't love, kid."

"What would you know about it? You're the same age as me."

"And I've been in love. This isn't it. This is an infatuation."

      I won't deny that a lot of times that's exactly how love begins. That there's a connection and all of a sudden you find inner parts of yourself moving to destinations unknown to you. It's enthralling and the rules are fuzzy, but you always know what's right. You have to let that person driving you crazy either choose you or crush you.

"We can end up together!" He argues.

"No, you can't! What are you going to tell her? That you followed her for nights all the way back to her home without her knowing? I've got news for you. If you're perfect for her then you don't need to do that shit. Or were you just not going to tell her and lie to her for the rest of your life? That's not a relationship, buddy, that's a farce. Things don't work like that in relationships."

He starts beating his head. "You don't understand! She's the one!"

"No, buddy, she's not the one. There's no such thing as the one. There's lots of *ones* in this life. The truth is, you have to let some things go, no matter how hard it is, so something else can come along. Let something unhealthy end so something better can begin. It's not easy, but it is worth it. It's necessary." I think I might be lying to him for his own good.

He pulls his hands over his face. "No. She's- You-You don't understand- It's-No."

"It's time to end this. Leave her in peace. If ye find each other then it's meant to be, and if it's not then it's not. That's life..." I'm running out of things to say and give it one last desperate attempt. "If you love something, set it free?"

On this he composes himself a little and looks up at me to reveal the bare, intense stare that I always felt. This stare goes on for three seconds that feel like a lifetime until he breaks it and looks down. He starts to shake his head.

"You're right... I'm going to stop... It's time... I should go..." He rubs his arm and gives me a sideways look before he slinks away.

I wait until he's gone for a few seconds, looking behind me just to be on the safe side, and then I loosen the grip on my flashlight. I pull out another smoke and light it. My throat feels raw but it's helping with the wave of nerves that's just hit me. I look into the window to see the barmaid going about her usual business.

I think I did well.

****

I'm back to being assigned my mid-week days off and, it being about a week since I've been there, I head over to the Scottish bar to stick my head in. I have my hoodie up and my head down as I listen to music. Just as I roll up to the front door, I see a pair of familiar feet on the other side of the street. The same shoes as before. I enter the pub without looking directly at him.

They're busy tonight. In the corner I see two girls setting up musical equipment. I lose myself in the crowd and angle myself so I can see outside through the windows on the front doors. It's Tiger. He's a little bit further in the shadows this time, but it's definitely him.

I can't let this go on anymore. I call Chick over.

"What can I get you?"

"I'm actually fine for the moment, thanks. I just wanted to ask you who that guy is across the street?"

"What guy?"

"Just there in the doorway. I've seen him outside a few times since I've been coming here. I was just wondering if he's security or if he's not allowed in or something?"

"I think I see the guy you're talking about? I'm not sure. I've never noticed him before."

"Oh, really? Strange looking guy. Always eating pistachio nuts."

Poor Chick turns sick. "Did you say pistachio nuts?"

"Yeah. Look, he's even eating them now." I nod discreetly over to him and she gazes over.

"I've been seeing those shells everywhere I go. This is really weird..."

"Do you have security here?"

"We usually have a guy on the weekends but he's been sick lately. The regulars usually help us out... I... I am going to call my boyfriend... Hang on."

She pulls out her phone and steps off into the corner of the bar. She talks for a few minutes, one hand on the phone and the other on her shoulder in a kind of embrace. She seems to make two calls. As she walks back, she talks to her English colleague. I hear her co-worker's voice break through the hustle and bustle of the crowd first.

"Yeah, that is fucking weird. Paris is a really shit city for that. There's all these fucking weirdos that keep following girls home. You can't be too careful. Even look at that girl that's gone missing recently. I think she was working in some cocktail bar."

I takes me a second to make the connection in my mind and

when I do, I call out.

"What's this?"

"There's a girl that's gone missing, like... Three or four months ago?.. No one has seen her. There were flyers up everywhere. A friend of mine said she used to work in a cocktail bar down near Maubert-Mutualité... Who knows what happened to her?!"

My mind is racing. It sounds like she's talking about Mouse! The flyer didn't mention where she worked. I lean against the bar to get her attention again and push her for some more information when Chick chips in.

"My boyfriend is coming now. He told me to call the police, so I did."

This is poor timing. I really need more information about Mouse but I don't want to get involved with the police or her boyfriend should Tiger start to rattle on about our previous encounter. I casually wish them luck with the stalker situation and leave the pub with my hood covering my face again.

Watching from the corner, I can see Chick's boyfriend march down the street and call after Tiger. Some other guys come out of the bar to join him. The boyfriend stands in front as their leader. I can see his teeth gritted even from here. An angry Wolf with his pack. Wolf extends his arms, speaks a few words to the gang behind him and approaches Tiger on his own. Tiger immediately pounces in the opposite direction, right into the arms of two police officers. They grab him firmly and lead him over to the wall as he roars out. It seems like Tiger is captured and, with a strange guy like him, everyone in the pub will probably stick around to watch the circus.

Tiger hid his malignancy from everyone, maybe even himself. He didn't have to end up a creep. All he had to do was start the next chapter in his life instead of dwelling on the one that lead nowhere. Close the door on his darkness and allow himself to begin again better. I guess I should feel a little sorry for him, he just couldn't change his stripes.

On the other hand, I have a new lead on Mouse. I'll start by showing the photo of her around all the cocktail bars in that area. There can't be too many.

I am left with some reservations about my quest after this incident though. I know I have the best intentions at heart. I'm trying to find Mouse to make sure that she's okay and that she's safe. Although, this does feel like a hunt at times. I know, if she's out there, that she'll know people are looking for her. But in that scenario, it's likely that she doesn't want to be found. I have to wonder, in my own way, if I haven't turned into an accidental predator like Tiger. His intentions, though perverted and creepy, weren't dishonourable in his eyes...

My mind eventually settles on the plan to continue with my pursuit, although I need to check myself and my ethics as I go along. I have every intention of helping this girl any way I can. My main mission is her safety.

Still, the doubt remains.

That nagging reminder of the best laid plans of mice and men...

Case 6 - Missing Time

I'm checking a young couple in to their room. My first guests of the evening, they're smiling and holding hands, getting lost in each other's eyes, kissing, generally ignoring me. Normally, I'd be cynical to the whole affair. Irritated even, at how lovely-dovey the two seem to be, but I've been there before once. On a romantic holiday, being alone with the one person in the world you care the most about. I'm trying not to think about that though, I'll just do my best to concentrate on the two giggling idiots in front me.

I'm in a particularly bad mood because I've been covering for the other night porter who has gone on holiday. It explains my long weekend two weeks ago. It was both a silent peace offering to me and an exploitation of him. As a result, I'm working a single shift tonight from 6pm until 2am, which is earlier than usual, and double shifts for the next six nights. I've been too busy or exhausted to look into Mouse... I'm growing incredibly sick of this place and how it's run.

The hairs on the back of my neck bristle up. The room temperature drops about twenty degrees, the air drawn out, the couple take a break from their cooing and the general hum of the hotel lobby dies down. My boss must be here.

Some people are known to have an effect that when they enter a room, all eyes turn to them. If ever a man could strut with his back hunched over, it was this man. He shoots me a smile and takes my hand firmly, far too firmly, without shaking it. With his death grip crushing my fingers, he makes small talk with me for a few moments.

"'Ow are you?"

"I'm fine, thank you."

"You 'ave found some place for you to live?"

"Four months ago, yes."

"Good! Zis ees good!"

>He's nodding at me.

>I nod back at him.

>We're both nodding at each other.

>This is incredibly awkward.

    My guests are waiting a little impatiently, but my boss never really cared about what the guests thought anyway, or his staff... or people in general, for that matter. His behaviour now isn't new to me anymore. I'm assuming he had read about talking to staff in some business article that taught the importances of *building rapport*. He probably heard it made us work harder.

"Well, you 'ave work to do, no?" Finally relinquishing my hand.

"Yes, of course." I turn back to do my job, which I was doing before he interrupted me and vaguely insinuated that I was lazy. I check them into their rooms and whisper an apology on my boss' behalf towards them. They raise their eye-brows and laugh. I let out a sigh as they skip off to the elevator. Enjoy it while it lasts, kids.

    The elevator rings out a ding and the doors open. The couple's hands, gaily joined, are torn apart by a dishevelled and clearly disgruntled man who marches his way towards me barefooted. His light blue shirt is open, revealing a hairy chest, and flaps along over his tan pants. He throws his hands on the counter and gives me a death-stare with blood-shot eyes.

    Why am I always the first person to get screamed at when something goes wrong? And why do so many fucking things go wrong here?

"Yew see this?" His English is pretty understandable, even with his Hispanic accent, but he's pointing to his wrist so I don't really understand. There are no marks or anything out of the ordinary. His breath though, it wreaks of stale alcohol.

"I'm not sure what you mean."

"My watch. Do yew see my watch?"

"No, I do not, sir." I really wish he'd get to the fucking point.

"Exactly! Where ees the owner?! I would like to speak to the owner! Or if not, the owner, then someone in charge!" He's shouting towards the end and spinning around, looking for said owner or person in charge.

I know my boss, I know he hates talking to guests and I know he loathes talking to angry guests. His only love in life is money, seven million reasons to own a hotel in Paris. There is nothing in the world he hates more than other people, seven billion reasons to be angry. With this in mind, I shall do my best. I hope I can take advantage of his recent good mood.

"The owner may be a little indisposed at the moment, but I will go and look for him now to see if he is available."

"Yes, well you tell him who it is who's looking for him." The man shouts after me.

I have absolutely no idea who it is looking for him, I didn't check him in. I don't really care either but, because of his fiery passion and Latin spirit, I shall call him Salamander.

Mr. Crow is in his office surveying the cameras when I knock on the door and step in. He quickly exits out of the program, as if his espionage is a secret to the humble slaves he calls his staff.

"Yes? Wat ees eet I can do for you?" He gives me another crooked smile, but if I was to lift my thumb to cover his mouth, I could see the anger in his eyes.

"We have a guest complaining about a watch. He wants to speak to you. He seems to be quite an important client."

He grumbles to himself, drags the chair across the wooden floor and pulls himself up off the desk. He jerks his hand out at me to lead the way and I comply.

Crow's jagged breathing behind me nips at my heels like a terrier. I couldn't walk faster if I tried. We wind our way down the stairs. I take a few steps at a time to gain some distance. Crow seems to glide down just as fast. With his bad back, his speed is a mystery to me.

Señor Salamander has his arms crossed when we hit the foyer. He's hissing through his teeth.

"Yew are thee owner of this eystablishment?"

"Yess. What can ay-"

"One of yewer maids has stolen my watch!"

"I am sure zat zere ees a rationa-"

"Which maid wass own my floor?!"

Salamander's voice is booming again. Crow, on the verge of snapping, looks at his watch and turns to me.

"You can get ze guest whatever ee desires-uh... I shall review ze camera footage... Excuse me."

Crow, having made his excuse, proceeds directly back up the way he came as a few guests dodge out of his path. Salamander drums his fingers on his arm dramatically. I sigh and make my way over to the binder that holds our rosters. I shuffle through it until I get to the cleaning staff's section and find out who was working last night. My finger pauses over the name.

The maid accused is someone I've seen quasi-regularly in my time here. Every now and then she would swing by the main foyer, no doubt on special assignment from Crow himself, to do some dusting, clean the floors or wipe the mirrors.

She was always friendly to me, every time. I always kept my answers curt but polite. Part of this was to avoid attachments, but I'd be lying if I said I wasn't timid around her. To be honest, I was a little enamoured with her at first, even though I thought she hated me. Her pale face in neutral always seemed to be angry until an easy smile breaks out. She told me it was her *resting bitch face* and that she couldn't help it but she promised she was a nice person. Her grey-blue eyes assured me of this.

I found out later, from her, that she had a boyfriend. I've always been quite good at locking down my desires in those instances. Nipping it in the bud. I'm lucky in that respect because it's rare that I pine over girls any more. When it's not going to happen, I usually accept my draw and move on.

Auburn hair and slight of stature, she sings as she cleans. The songs are always foreign to me, despite the fact that they're all in English. Her voice is always sweet and lyrical. A sweeping Songbird.

I can't say I know her very well, but I highly doubt she stole anything. There are some people out there that you can just tell wouldn't do something like that, and she was one of them. Too self-deprecating to be dishonest.

"The maid will be in later. Why don't you tell me what has happened exactly?" I ask him.

"My watch was stolen!"

"Yes, but when did you notice it went missing?"

His face is reddening, although this time I can see that there's more in this hue than just rage.

"It must haffe gone missing when the maid came in. The watch was een the room. I take it off every night I go to sleep. Me and my girlfriend, we lie in bed. The maid comes in, walks around a little and leaves when she sees that we are awake."

"What time did the maid come into your room?"

"Twelve."

I check the clock behind me. He's been in bed for over six hours apparently. Turning back to him I can see the newer shade of red get brighter.

"And you're sure you didn't lose it last night... In a restaurant... Or maybe... A bar?"

"We only went to one barr and I caalled them, they did not find nothing. I go there tonight and I will ask them again!"

"How did you get back to the hotel last night?"

"We take a taxi... I think..."

"You think?"

"I'm not sure, I don't rreally rremember how we got home."

"You might have lost it in the taxi?"

"No, we leave the bar. Eh..." He starts rubbing his temples.

"And?..."

"I'm in my room. My girrlfriend leaves to order more Champagne... Eh... I wake up!"

"But you're sure in the bar, or the taxi that-"

"- I rremember taking it off beforre going to sleep! I will give yew the name of the barr if yew want to call them?!"

Pen in hand, Salamander snatches a piece of paper off the counter then scribbles down the name, along with the address and phone number, of the bar. He seems angry again so I'll give him a solution where we both win and I can be rid of him.

"There's nothing we can do until the maid comes in, however, I'm going to bump you and your girlfriend up to a private suite and-" He raises his hands in protest but I speak through it. "- AND we're going to continue to look for this watch until it is found."

Salamander hisses in defiant submission and disappears after I hand him the keys to his new room. There are some serious gaps in his story that aren't helping with the retrieval of this watch. Checking the database, it seems I have a few more arrivals expected in the next hour but it'll be quiet after that. Songbird should show up at around eight. Meanwhile, I guess I'll try and take a look in the room to see if I can find it first.

****

It's just like almost every other room in the hotel. The door follows into a small corridor which leads to the main room. There's a bed in the centre, flanked by two nightstands, two windows to the left of it and the door to the bathroom on the right. This room, however, is a total disaster. Aside from the typical crumpled bedsheets, there are glasses knocked over on their sides. There's something chaotic about a glass on its side, even when it's empty. Champagne bottles are strewn across the room, some of them even on the bed. There's a faint smell of tobacco, sweat and alcohol.

The window closest to the bed is open. There's a crooked cigarette-butt stubbed out on the sill, impressively still standing like some kind of modern art piece. Ash is scattered around next to it, smudges on the floor and streaks on the curtains. There are even some marks of ash on the bedsheets, amongst other dubious stains.

In the bathroom, towels carpet the floor. The mirror is freckled with mysterious white dots. A small pile of cotton buds lie beside the sink covered in diluted-black blots. With these first impressions in mind, I get to work on the finer details. I reluctantly start with the bed. The left pillow has a faint trace of cologne on it with short, dark hairs. The right pillow is decorated with black streaks and one long strand of black hair curled up on the edge. I grimace at the sight of a used condom I find buried under the sheets and I'm incredibly glad that it's not my job to clean the rooms.

All the champagne bottles are empty. I count five in total. One of them, by the window, appears to have been knocked over, judging by the stain on the carpet. Under the bed, I find an empty carton of orange juice and an earring. Lifting up the mattress, I find nothing out of the ordinary.

I look everywhere for the watch. I shake down the curtains, check behind the nightstands, under the pillows, look at the bed sheet for bulges, in the toilet cistern, everywhere. I even go so far as to turn the water off in the sink and take out the U-bend pipe to see if there might be broken pieces of it thrown down there.

The watch isn't here. The maid will be in soon enough and I'll be able to ask her if she's seen anything out of the ordinary in the room.

Although, I might have some trouble defining ordinary...

****

On my way back to my desk, I run into Crow. He seems to be on his way out. He nods at me and moves to the door.

"Sorry, sir. Did you happen to find anything on the cameras?" I ask.

"Oh... No, I did not... I see that zey enter ze room wit ze watch at fower in ze morning and zen zey leave wissout it at six-sirty in ze eveneeng. Only ze maid haz entereduh and exited ze room een between zat time."

"So, what should I do?"

"I am sure you weel figure zis out!" Crow pats me on the shoulder and scurries off into the night, leaving me pretty perplexed.

I get the feeling I'm not entitled to see the footage and the office door is locked, as always, so there's no chance of me sneaking in to use it. I return to my desk to give the whole thing some thought.

The maid comes in for her shift a few minutes after Crow's departure. She seems untroubled, despite her face resting in the usual troubled position. I catch her halfway through the lobby.

"Hi. Ehm... Did you go into a room with people still inside?"

"I did, yeah... Why, are they complaining? The *Do Not Disturb* signs are provided, you know? All they have to do is hang them up!"

She's smirking at me. I can't help but give a slight grin back at her cheekiness. I shake my head to get my mind back on focus. She seems like a nice person, and I don't want to outright accuse her of anything or mention that the guest has.

"Did you happen to see a watch when you were in there? It seems to have gone missing."

"Well, I didn't clean the room yet. I'm hoping someone *else* has?"

I shake my head back at her apologetically.

"Ah, shit! The smell alone in that room would knock you out! I thought it was empty anyway. I was too distracted by the state of it. It was only when I saw someone move in the bed that I realised there were still people there. Nearly gave me a heart attack!"

"Right... You didn't see anything on the nightstand to the left, did you?"

"I don't think so... I'm not sure, though."

"Okay, then. Keep an eye out for it?"

"Ugh, fine! I'm not looking forward to cleaning that room though... You night porters have it so easy! Just staying up watching films on the computer. Sure, I do that when I'm *not* at work!"

With a sly grin, she ventures off to change into her uniform. Meanwhile, I'm left wondering why, after four months, I've never tried watching films here?

****

Salamander passes by for an update on his watch at around eleven. He seems to have calmed down a little and his spirits are higher with his girlfriend draped on his arm, a gorgeous, dark, sleek woman. A model if I ever saw one. Everything about her seems to be put together by a team of professionals. Her black hair shines, thick black lashes hood olive eyes. The dress she's wearing is so tight, I have to wonder if someone had painted it on. She's stunning.

He states that he will be going to the same bar as last night to check and see if his watch was found there.

"We're also looking here." I assure him.

His girlfriend chimes in "Ooh, honeey. Yew worry too much about thees watch. Ze maid stole it so they will get it back off her. If not, thehn it is gone in the wind!" He's about to say something but she cuts him off. "And to think that it is from a woman who brroke your hearrt long ago."

"It has nothing to do with my ex-wife, my darrling. It's just a nice watch! I promise!" He keeps his voice earnest but I see a nervous tick in his left eye.

"Ah, but you prromeesed you would not fall asleep last night and yew did!"

As he begins to protest, she cuts him off again.

"Yew were out like a baby. I come back with champagne and yew were dead to the worrld. Yew deedn't even hear me slam the window shut! Some men can't handle alcohol."

"Ey! I had more than yew to drrink and-"

"- Do not fret, my love! I will buy you nine of them to replace the one yew had! All different colours and styles! Yes, my love. All will be well. Now, we must go!"

  Her last words are given with the ferocity of a Panther and shuts his tongue back in his mouth. Salamander leaves with this Amazonian princess dragging him impatiently and playfully for a night on the town. He seems keen to oblige, probably because it will lead him back here.

  I'm a little envious. It's been a long time since I've been intimate with anyone.

  Longer still with someone I love...

****

  The clock hits one in the morning as Songbird spirals down the stairs singing in notes so high I truly didn't know they existed. She interrupts her melodic entrance to speak with me.

"Two things: It's finally – FINALLY – safe to go back into the room, and I didn't find any watch."

"Oh, right... I'll pass that on."

She stares at me pensively. "You've been here a while now haven't you?"

"Eh, yeah! I started about three or four months ago?"

"You don't really hang out with the rest of us though... But, I suppose that's because you're here when we're finished?"

"Sure, I guess... I mean, well, yeah." I shrug at her.

"You're finished at two tonight though, aren't you?"

"I... Am. Yes."

"Do you fancy having a drink with me and another one of the maids? I'm broke as a joke, but what harm anyway? I reckon a few people will want to buy you pints for working over the Christmas holidays for us."

"I... Well..."

"I should warn you- Oh, but I already told you I have a boyfriend. Never mind! Oh, but she doesn't... So, maybe... Well, you know?"

"I actually have plans already, sorry."

"Oh, right! Another time, though! All this not going out can't be good for you!"

"Another time. Sure."

She gives me a smile in response and waits outside texting on her phone.

I'm starting to feel conflicted. I really want to follow up on my lead on Mouse, but I feel like I should help Songbird. That means I'll have to figure it out tonight, which is the only night for the next week that I can look into where Mouse used to work.

The decision, although grating, is already made for me. Mouse has been missing for months now and a week won't change much. Songbird needs to be exonerated either before Salamander gets back, or before he wakes up hungover again. Maybe Crow was wrong about them coming back with the watch? I could try and follow them to get a better idea of their movements?

The small hand eventually hits two and I grab the address that Salamander left behind. I'm on the clock and I don't have a second to lose.

****

I get a stroke of good luck on the way to Salamander's bar. Looking out the window, I see the metro sign for Maubert-Mutualité. The barmaid mentioned that Mouse worked in a cocktail bar near here. There's a chance I'll be able to hit two birds with one stone tonight. Less than a minute later, the taxi driver pulls onto the street.

I arrive at the bar the couple have come to, a Mexican cocktail bar. Gazing in the window, I scan the tables for Salamander. I'm not too worried about being seen by them on the street. I know enough about lighting to be confident that the glare on the window inside will be enough to shield me from sight. I spot Salamander with his hand covering his wrist. He's looking around himself with quite a bit of enthusiasm. Perhaps he found his watch after all?

My hopes are dashed when he removes his hand to reveal a bare arm. His enthusiasm is explained by the very pretty waitress that comes down and chats with him. She's laughing and touching his arm as he leans in close to her while he speaks. The waitress pulls away from the table, letting her smile drop as she moves to the next table before she puts it back on again.

Panther seems to have less of an interest in putting on appearances. Her genial face tightening as Salamander turns his head to check out the waitress as she walks away before he turns back to her and gives her a quizzical look. The two argue inside for a few minutes and his girlfriend storms out the door.

I step into a shadowy doorway to avoid being detected. Panther pulls out a cigarette and Salamander steps out just as she lights it. They start to argue in Spanish with each other. I don't understand a word that they're saying but the context seems pretty clear to me. She's furious with him for being as leery as he is. Occasionally she jabs at him with the lit cigarette in her hand. It looks like she's going to stab him with it and it's obvious that she'd only love to. He pulls his head back and fans the air around his face in disgust.

They argue like this for five minutes before she lashes out her arm to a taxi and gets inside. Salamander just manages to slither his way in before the taxi shoots off into the night. There's no way that I can follow them now. With the way that they're behaving, I can only imagine that they're going back to the hotel anyway.

I'm assuming he already asked the staff there if they've found a watch. With that in mind, I guess I'll follow up on Mouse and head into the bar the couple just exited.

I approach one of the bartenders who is counting receipts and shaking his head with an air of irritation. I'm guessing it's Salamander's tab which he walked out on. I wait politely until he's finished. He lets out a long sigh, looks up at me and puts on a smile.

"How can I help you, sir?"

"Good evening. I'm looking for a girl that's gone missing a little while back who was working around here."

I pull out the slightly worn flyer that I keep in my jacket pocket.

"Baah, no, I don't know her. She didn't work here anyway."

"Okay. Well, maybe you could tell me if there are any other cocktail bars in the area?"

The bartender bursts out laughing.

"Thanks! Truly... There are many, *many* cocktails bars in this area!"

"Oh, I see..."

"Okay, I'm going to give you a list of the bars that are still open now and you can check them. There are not that many because it's quite late, you see?"

He scribbles down a list of three cocktail bars with their addresses on a notepad, tears off the paper and hands it to me. I thank him and walk back onto the street. The addresses seem to be scattered out in a radius. I'll have to be quick about this if I plan on getting there before they close. The last one on the list seems to be the closest to me. I may as well work the three backwards.

While my legs run, my mind strolls. Salamander and Panther didn't seem to be too happy together. If I'm being frank, it looks like the beginning of the end for those two. It's funny that it's not their troubles that tell me this as much as the absence of joy does.

I remember joyful times with the person I loved. Just two people in a bed. I could have spent an eternity there with her. The two of us caught up in our own lazy mania as we chatted to each other about everything and nothing. No distractions but each other. No need for anything else. I would stare deep into those incredible eyes as my thumb stroked her cheek.

"For the last time, you're not fat, you're gorgeous!" I pleaded and reached out to her over the sheets.

"Yes, I am! Just look at me!"

"I am looking at you, dummy."

"Well, obviously not hard enough, *fucker*!"

"Is that my new pet name, huh?! Fucker?"

"Yeah!" She laughed and grabbed my wrist.

"I've been called worse."

"Like?"

"A customer called me a dickhead yesterday."

"You want some cheese with that *whine*?"

"Whine?"

"Wine, idiot!"

"Excuse me if not everything is about alcohol for me!"

"I thought you said you were Irish?!"

"I'm the other kind of Irish... The kind that represses all his anger and guilt, not an alcoholic."

"Oh, good... For a second there, I thought you were fun..."

What did we say to each other all those other times that made us laugh so much? We would spend lifetimes in that bed, each day, just talking to each other. The tangential and never-ending conversations are lost to me now. I can only remember flashing images of the laughing, the kissing, the caressing. For hours and hours. Where did all that time go?

****

The first bar yields no results. A mad-house full of students, loud music and weary bartenders who are so stressed that they seem to get more of the cocktail on them than in the glass. The haggard bartender looks at me confused when I show him the photo. I shout over the music as he shakes his head. I know he's trying to get rid of me so I poke at him again. He shouts back that he's never seen her before and gets back into the fray. I push my way through the crowd, my feet peeling off the sticky floor. I scrape my shoes off the pavement outside to get the adhesive shards of glass off my feet. Both bars will be closed in two hours so I turn left and start to sprint towards the second one.

At the second bar, where everyone seems a bit more relaxed, the bartender's eyes light up when I show him the photo. He taps the page with a fierce certainty, mumbling to himself and then looks back at me.

"She never worked here." He tells me in French.

"So... You don't know her?"

"No, I do know her!"

I decide at this point to stay silent so his annoying way of revealing information can work its way back to a normal rhythm.

"Yes! She was a waitress at a cocktail bar not too far from here. Lovely girl. I used to pop in after I finished my shifts and practise my English with her. She was always smiling. One does not forget someone so beautiful!"

I produce the list of bars and once more the bartender reinvigorates himself by tapping on the third bar. His excitement is contagious now and I thank him endlessly. There's a spring in my step as I turn left out the door and break into another run.

The third bar has a heavy looking green door on the outside. It almost seems like it's fortified. The security guard looks me up and down critically. He asks me what it is I'm doing here. I tell him, not completely insincerely, that I'm looking for a friend. He asks me to open up my jacket to see what I'm wearing underneath. I show him my work clothes which, although not terribly stylish, do appear quite smart. He nods his head and opens the door for me.

It seems she worked in a curious place. It's very dark inside, although not altogether gloomy. Stuffed, dead animals are propped up everywhere. A fox by the window, a stag's head on the wall, a badger by one of the tables and so on. The bathroom door is only a curtain. It's by no means a large venue. Behind the bar seems to be about two metres squared and to the right of it are bottles stacked so high that they seem like they're perpetually about to fall over.

I'm surrounded, uncomfortably, by a hip and trendy clientèle. Dressed up and trimmed. I make my way over to a bartender that looks like he fist-fights bears for a living to ask him about Mouse. The second I get to the bar, he places a glass of water in front of me and hands me a menu.

"I'm actually okay for the moment. I was just hoping to ask you a few questions about a girl that worked here." I produce the poster and hand him my flashlight so he can take a better look.

"Yes, she used to work here."

"What can you tell me about her?"

"It's been a while. I remember a few days after she was paid she just disappeared. I wasn't too surprised. She'd been complaining that she needed something different in life. I tried calling her but her phone plan was cancelled."

"Anything else?"

"She was amiable, bubbly. Did her job well."

"Did she have any friends? Maybe a boyfriend?"

"She had friends. I think most of them moved away. I don't think she had a boyfriend but she was seeing someone for a while."

"Does he have a name?"

"I can't remember. She told me they weren't serious though."

"Okay. Do you know where she used to spend most of her time outside work? Any hobbies or things like that?"

"I didn't really know her that well. We'd talk after work about stuff, but nothing serious."

"Anything at all?"

"Eh... She liked to party. She always loved discovering new music... She liked to read, I think. Used to spend her time down in the public library near Montmartre, if I remember correctly."

"Can you think of anything else?"

"Not really. It's been many months since I've seen her. I believed she moved back home." Handing the flyer back to me, he asks "Do you want a drink?"

"I'll take a look at the menu."

    He rotates to serve a few customers as I browse the cocktail list. They have some interesting choices here. All of them seem to be original. My palms start to sweat when I see the price of each. They're way too rich for my blood. I steal away from the bar while he's distracted and emerge onto the street.

    I have a new lead on Mouse. This one seems quite promising. It's also a relief to hear that she disappeared just after pay day. The odds are that she bolted from the job. I might try look into this guy that she was seeing too. Maybe they're still together despite keeping it casual? It wouldn't be the first time it's happened...

    Cat was clear cut and spoke her mind at the start. About two weeks after we first started seeing each other we were sitting on a train in the metro and words started to fall out.

"I like you. I really do! You have good taste in music and you're funny and I'm comfortable around you... And I *extremely* like hanging out with you..." She said.

"I feel like there's a but coming up?"

"But... I was seeing someone for a year here in Paris and we just broke up two months ago... And I don't know how I feel about that only... I'm pretty sure I don't want a relationship right now, and I feel like you do..."

"Well, I'd be lying if I said I didn't. I mean, that is what I would like... But I don't mind spending time with you doing whatever it is that we're doing."

It was disappointing to hear at the time. I was always worried that I wasn't good enough for her. Her beauty and intelligence compared to my blandness. But in a way it was reassuring to hear her tell me things I didn't like, a confirmation that she was being honest. That I knew exactly where I stood with her and what was around the bend.

"But if you don't shower every day, we can't even be friends!" She teased. "I don't want to spend my time with a smelly, Irish boy."

It seemed simple. I'd try and keep my distance, as would she. We'd keep things casual between us. But as the months went past, we ended up spending most of our free time together. Things ticked over and our two hands drew closer to each other...

I check the time on my phone. It's four in the morning. I'm no closer to finding this watch and it's too late to really do anything about it. I feel bad for the maid. I've done my best to keep the accusations of theft from her to spare her feelings, but I'm pretty certain that they're going to come out by the time the morning comes.

Suddenly, there's a small explosion right in front of me. I use my hands to shield my face and stagger back. Looking down, I see broken glass. I shoot glances all around the street to see who's throwing bottles at me but I find no one until I look above me. Music is playing from an apartment upstairs and two hipsters are smoking cigarettes on the balcony. One of them is drinking beer from a bottle.

I start hurling abuse up at them. How the fuck can they be so fucking irresponsible?! A bottle from a sixth floor window could do a lot of fucking damage! They start hurling abuse back at me. Telling me to calm down and that everything is fine. That I'm being ridiculous about the whole thing. They stub their cigarettes on the window and disappear from view.

And then it hits me! Not the second bottle that they throw down at me - the fuckers - but the solution to this mystery of the missing timepiece. All along, it was hidden in the minute details.

****

I circle around the hotel until I find the window to the room that had previously belonged to Salamander. There's some large, potted shrubbery lining the walls and sure enough, nestled in the leaves, I see some cigarette-butts.

I pull out my flashlight and peek in through the foliage. A silver disk shines back at me. I reach in and pull out Salamander's watch. A satisfied relief gives way to a smugness. Everything will be fine now. As the expression goes, one in the bush saves nine.

I hand it over to my colleague and simply explain that it belongs to a guest. He seems a little concerned to see me. I imagine none of us would like to spend any more time working or being here than we have to. I leave him to his mystery, content that I've solved my own.

****

The next night, Salamander approaches the front desk to speak with me.

"Waz it the maid that stole it?" He asks.

"The maid did not steal it and I'd appreciate it greatly if you didn't mention the suspicion to her."

"Then what happened? Yewer co-worker said yew were the one to find it!"

"I did find it. It was in the bush outside your window."

"What?! So you're saying it magically fell out the window?"

"I'm saying that there's a good chance whoever was beside the window might have dropped it..."

It takes him a few moments to realise what I'm really saying to him.

"Yew think my girlfriend did this?"

"She seems to have quite a temper on her when she wants to. I wouldn't be surprised if she decided to throw your ex-wife's gift out the window to replace it with her own. Especially if you two are having difficulties lately."

Salamander seems troubled, but not completely surprised. I can see the cogs working behind his eyes, trying to piece together the events of the night it went missing. He abruptly gives me his thanks and walks away.

It's quite obvious now that I think about of it. Salamander was probably just as leery with the waitress the night the watch went missing. Him passing out prematurely was just the detonator to her wrath. I should have picked up on their troubles when Panther mentioned she slammed the window shut. You only slam things in a rage. Even more obvious was the lie she was telling. Who slams a window shut and opens it again? She was also incredibly quick and certain to accuse the maid. Eager to push a well established cliché as the truth.

What's more is the subtle hints that liars often like to leave. She mentioned the window and that the watch was gone to the wind. There's a game to be played in lies. Subtle hints that are supposed to go undetected but reveal themselves in the end. It provides a thrill for them, I'm sure. The only drawback to this game is that the truth will always, *always*, come out. The lie can only go around and around until it unravels. You cannot make something real that isn't.

Their relationship is likely over at this point. It's probably for the best. Salamander has a bit too much restlessness in his eyes when it comes to the opposite sex. It's something I don't quite understand anymore. I used to think it was hard to commit to one person. The endless waves of other people flirting with you, promising something new and different. But, after finding someone special, I've found that it's about devoting yourself to them. And the waves roll on, but you turn into them and let them pass. And maybe it's a biological urge even the times can't change? A need that fulfils all others...

Cat worked the day shift usually and I worked the night. At the end of my shift, if she was working the next day, I'd draw on band-aids and leave them for her to put on her torn thumb, along with a note to make her laugh. A cute and constant communication of companionship.

The wonderful nights where I finished work early, we'd sleep together. She would twitch in bed, no doubt caused by that active brain of hers not giving her rest. Each time she did, I'd stroke her arm or gently kiss her shoulder to pull her out of it. Those nights would lead to an early morning for a Nightowl like me so I could help her bring the terrace tables out. For once, it wasn't hard for me to resist drifting back to sleep. What dream could rival her? She was bringing light into my life for the first time ever. There wasn't a girl alive that I would rather have been with as I lay in bed watching her get dressed in the morning.

I did all these things because I loved her, and I wanted to show her how much I loved her every day that she'd let me. I did it because I liked that person I became. Kind and caring. Generous and gentle. A good boyfriend...

I hear a sweet song echo out from around the corner. The delicate notes are sung to the percussion of what sounds like a mop hitting a floor. Songbird is back again. She shouts across the hall to me as she comes into view.

"Hello!"

"Hey. How are you?"

"Ah sure, I'm alright. Tell me something, are you Irish?!" She asks.

"I am."

"I was wondering, alright. I could kinda tell from your accent but it's pretty neutral. Not like that's a bad thing though!"

"Yeah, it's pretty soft."

"Funny how we're both Irish and we never really hang out. You working a double tonight?"

"For the rest of the week."

"That's a load of bollocks giving you them hours. Tell you what though, next night you have off you should pop your head in and we'll go out with whoever else is free."

"Ehm... Sure. We'll see how it goes."

"Anyway, see you later!"

"Grand!"

Grand is a funny little Irish expression. Something that generally means large, magnificent, awe-inspiring or majestic simply means fine or well to us Irish folk. I guess we just like making big things out of little things.

Songbird returns to mopping the floor and, gratefully, not a single guest returns to interrupt her performance.

****

It's an average 5am experience for me. I'm cooking pasta again and ignoring my body's feeble cries for something more substantial. After eating, I head over to my sofa-bed only to find a coffee stain on one of the pillows. I prod it with my index finger to discover it's still quite wet. The bastard spilled coffee on my pillow and not only did he not wash the pillow cover, he didn't even dry the fucking thing.

I veer towards the door to his room in a fit of rage and somehow manage to stop myself just as I raise my hand to start banging on it. I take a few deep breaths to calm down and edge away from the threshold. There's no good to be had in blind rage.

Lying in bed, after flipping the pillow, I start to think about Songbird's invitation. People will let you down if you give them a chance to. I've had first-hand experiences of this more times than I'd care to mention. I'm trying to avoid these kinds of attachments. They'll all end up leaving anyway.

So, I'm not going to hang out with my colleagues. I'll make up a decent excuse the first couple of nights I'm free, after that I'm sure they'll stop asking. It's not like a night out with them would be any different than others I've had with friends. I'm probably saving myself another round of misery in the long run by doing this...

Even though I might be missing the time of my life...

Case 7 – The Sacking

    I'm finally free from the longest work week I've ever had, although my sheer exhaustion caused me to miss all my alarms to wake up early and get to Mouse's library before it closed. I think I'll go to the library anyway, as I have no way of tracking down the guy she was seeing, just to know where it is for the next time.

    I take the metro up to Barbès-Rochechouart. I'm aware that this isn't the best area to be walking around in at night. I exit out of the metro to see the tracks of the other lines looming overhead. A mess of sprawling iron, providing shadows for those who wish hide in them. At least it provides some shelter from the light rain falling down. It's just a drizzle but it's nice to be out of it.

    Groups of young men hang around drinking at the corners. It's a good thing I know exactly where I'm going because I doubt I should ask anyone for directions if I get lost. I know part of this anxiety comes from racial bias. I don't want to be racist, very few do, but I can't deny that it's there. I try to work against it, to some success, but it often just ends up being reverse racism. I hope that I get over it eventually, that I can push my perception past my privilege.

    The local population is mostly comprised of immigrants or their descendants from Africa and the Middle-East, with some Bangladeshis and Sri Lankans. Many of whom work in low-skilled jobs, despite whatever skills they may actually be qualified for. Doctors running delis, disenfranchised to be constantly stuck in second place so the French and other Europeans like me get first pick without trying at all.

    Most of the shops are closed for the evening. Their heavily-graffitied, steel shutters pulled over the front doors. The streets are littered with fast-food wrappers and plastic bags. The wet pavement only adding to the general gloominess of it. You're immediately overcome with an edgy sensation that everything is dirty. The residential buildings, equally as ornate as the rest of Paris, have a certain foreboding nature about them, like each one is a haunted house. Not much attention can be paid to them though. Tacky, plastic shop fronts catch the eye quicker at street level, offering phone accessories, cheap clothes or kebabs.

I walk briskly and with purpose. My hands stay in my pockets and one hand stays firmly on my flashlight. I learned early on in this city that it's best to keep your head up, avoid eye contact and to move with confidence. The Bible says that heaven loves the meek, but so do muggers and the like.

It's not a particularly far walk. There's a group of young men that I have to walk through, but they're caught up in their own boisterous conversation so I don't feel like I have to cross the street to avoid them. I veer clear of one homeless man drinking a bottle of wine, shouting abuse up and down the street. Two other men stand, bent over with a couch resting on their backs giving the middle finger to another person taking a photo.

I turn right past a derelict shop covered in posters for several concerts long since performed and end up on the street I've been looking for. To my surprise, I can see light coming out from the front door of the library. I walk a little bit faster and peer in through the glass door. The first thing I read is "POLICE" written on the back of an officer. He's talking to a firefighter, in full gear, wearing one of those silver helmets that makes them look like space villains. As I lean in to get a better look at what's going on, the door opens a little bit and the police officer turns around.

"The library is closed!"

"What's going on?"

"I need you to step away from the door, sir, and move along."

He moves towards me and I step back before trundling off slowly in a random direction with my head down in obedient submission. I get a few metres away when I see a white jacket decorated stylishly with a spotted pattern, like that of a Snow

Leopard, draped over someone's legs. A young man, around my age, seems quite distressed about something. I start speaking to him in French which startles him a little bit.

"Is everything okay?" I ask.

"What? Yes, I'm fine. Thanks." He then mumbles something to himself. His accent is very soft, I can't place it, but he appears to be saying something in English about a door.

"English better?"

"I can speak both, but yeah..." And so, we speak in English.

"Were you hurt in there?" I ask.

"Hurt? No... I work there. I locked the door tonight, but they're saying I didn't. I'm sure I locked it though! Every night I check the door after I lock it. But maybe... I don't know... Who remembers something like that?!"

    He has a point. When you search for the memory of such a monotonous task, the file isn't there any more. It's discarded with all the other useless information.

    A detective comes out. He's followed by a blonde woman wearing a business suit, a well-built, bald guy in a long coat and an old man. They're heading towards us. Leopard stands up to meet them. He's a lot taller than I thought he was, now that he's not bunched up on the ground. His sleek frame is revealed when the jacket is removed from his legs. He steps into the light to reveal sandy hair and a charming face.

    I step away to give them the appearance of some privacy and listen in on their conversation, of which I can only get snippets. I gather that the detective and the woman are asking him some questions to which Leopard shakes his head as he protests. They say it appears that there was no sign of forced entry. The place was ransacked, with a few shelves set on fire and two computers stolen. I inch a little closer at this point.

    The detective says it was clearly an inside job given the

leisurely time the robbers took and that an eye-witness described the event in full, at which point he turns to the old man. The detective tells Leopard that he believes the fire was originally started to hide the theft and that, if he could prove it, he would arrest Leopard as an accomplice to both. Leopard has a clear spasm of shock and starts shouting at them.

"There's no way I set this up! There's none! Why would I do this?! How can-"

The woman interjects. "- There's no way around this. Even if you're not part of the theft, you left the door wide open for them! You're fired!"

     Leopard roars at her as she walks away. The bald man keeps his hand on Leopard's chest to make sure he can't give chase. They appear to know each other. The old man shifts uncomfortably on his feet and gives himself a little distance. Poor Leopard has just been sacked.

     With the three in the middle of a dramatic moment I venture over to the old man to ask him a few questions. I find him instantly easy to talk to. Age, and the neglect it often brings, makes conversation an eager thing.

"You saw what happened here?"

"I saw everything! The scum started yelling on the street so I look out over my balcony. Then I saw them run into the library there. They must have been in there a good ten minutes before I saw them tear out of there with big bags on their shoulders. About five minutes after that I heard the fire alarm go off and then, maybe two minutes later, I saw smoke billowing out of the place."

"Why didn't you call the police when they ran in? Surely they would have caught them in time."

"I did call the police! The second that I saw that rabble run in there, in fact! But around here, the police take a little longer to respond to calls such as these. They like to wait until the crime is over before they catch them."

"What happened after they left?"

"I called the head librarian over there." He says as he points to the businesswoman, "I have her number because we'd gone to a protest together that we helped organise. She showed up about five minutes later. The firefighters came a few minutes after that, then the police. That young man arrived around the same time as that big guy."

I'm struck with a strange thought. "Where are all the police cars and firetrucks?"

"Hmm... They must be around the back entrance. This is a small street and you can get through to the library from the main street. Strange that it's the back door though. You'd have thought it'd be the other way around!"

I wish the old man a good night, glad with the wealth of information he's given me. Didn't we once rely on elders to teach us what they knew of the world? All of that had been made obsolete by the library. Now, with the internet and various portable devices used to access it, libraries are becoming obsolete too.

The head librarian has a frighteningly thin frame made even more absurd by the round thick-rimmed glasses that she wears. A Bookworm if I ever saw one. She's speaking to the detective and describing what was damaged in the library while Leopard retreats back to where I found him.

"I live near Les Halles. As soon as I got the call, I jumped in my car and raced over here. The shelves that were damaged were the international books. We have - or had, rather - a broad selection of books in various foreign languages. It's for all the foreigners in this area. It's not too much of a loss, to be honest. Not many of those people came in here anyway... I should never have given that fool the keys. Bumbling idiot!"

The detective, turning to the large, hairless Ox of a man, questions him on his whereabouts.

"I was on the metro at Simplon when I got her call. Was going to meet some friends for dinner. Who would do something like this?"

Ox laments, shaking his head sadly.

"We'll look into this gang that our witness has seen and we'll call you with any updates. The odds are, your former employee is probably getting a cut of the takings. We'll need his address?" He asks Bookworm.

She scribbles it down on a notepad provided by the detective and he leaves her nodding her head solemnly. Leopard leaps up to get a word in but she sticks her hand up to his face and marches away. He calls after her as she gets back into her car.

Leopard stands dejected as the car pulls away. He makes a false start forwards as it hits a red-light before giving up. He buries his face in his hand and paces around, groaning to himself. I don't think he's a master criminal like the detective said. It's altogether possible that he simply forgot to lock the door. He removes his hand and looks over at me. I realise, and I know this is selfish, that there's a chance he could help me with finding Mouse. I'll have to approach it gently.

"I'm really sorry to bother you... I know this is a terrible time-"

"- I know I locked the door... I'm sure now." He says with a tone of disbelief.

"They might have picked the lock? I'm currently looking for-"

"- I pulled at it. I always do..."

He seems to be in a state of shock. His grey eyes glazed over and fixed. I'll need to lure him out of it if he's ever going to help me find Mouse.

"Any idea who stole the computers?"

His eyes start shifting now. "There's a gang of guys that hang out around here. Every now and then they'd come in to use the computers for a while – to use the internet, I mean. They're rough enough, but they were always pretty decent to me. They even asked me if I wanted to smoke a joint with them down by Sacré-Coeur... But... They'd still be my prime suspects... I didn't want to mention it to the detective after he accused me of working with whoever stole the computers. He might think I know too much to be innocent if they are the culprits."

"You'd recognise them if you saw them?"

"Yeah... Wait, why?"

"Because we're going to find them and ask them what happened."

It takes a few minutes of protesting and tugging at his jacket to get him to follow me. We devolve into expletives, return to polite protestations and finally he agrees. Sacré-Coeur isn't too far a walk from here. I can ask him some more questions on the way.

****

The walk is a little jittery for both of us. We're two strangers walking through a rough part of Paris. Neither of us are particularly inclined to look out for the other, never mind fight for each other should it come to that. I try to defuse the tension with some small talk.

"So... What brought you here? Follow a girl over?" I ask.

"No, I just really like the city. Thought I could do with a break from life for a bit. I have a degree in finance and all those numbers can give you a headache. It's much nicer to get buried in a book. Also, I thought it was obvious, but I don't bat for that team."

"What team?"

"I prefer the team that bats to the team that catches, if you catch my drift?"

"I think both teams take turns batting and catching in baseball, so-"

"- Jesus Christ... I'm telling you I'm gay!"

"I know, buddy. I'm just fucking with you." I smirk at him and he lets out a laugh.

"So, are you a raging homophobe leading me down a dark alley to beat me up?"

"I'm not leading you down a dark alley, we're going to Sacré-Coeur to meet a potentially violent and dangerous gang of youths to- That doesn't sound better."

"No, it doesn't!" He laughs.

"I have nothing against gay people. The nicest guy I know back home is gay."

"That's how we get you, alright. First we're nice to you, then BAM! We ruin marriage for all you straight folk."

I burst out laughing down the quiet street. This guy seems pretty okay and I'm glad he's not as upset as he was before. We arrive at the foot of the hill leading up to Sacré-Coeur. It's a long walk up. With everything closed, and some sketchy characters menacingly slinking around, we hurry our way up.

I used to count steps in my head when I first arrived in Paris, but the hill to Sacré-Coeur has so many that I've given up. Glances over my shoulder reveal a splendid view of shrubbery and stone that grows more exquisite the higher I ascend. The climb is still arduous though.

I hear roars of laughter up ahead and put my hand on Leopard to stop him going any further. There's something trying to pry itself out of the back of my mind. *Shouting*. Who shouts before they rob a place? Especially if they're going to stick around for ten minutes...

We sneak up the stairs inch by inch to see a group of five youths the far side of the church entrance. Two of them are sitting on the wall, two more are standing. The fifth is sitting on one of the large canvas bags at their feet. The bags are marked to be used for recycling paper. A rectangular outline can be seen from the way the cloth hangs. The group is passing a joint around the circle.

"That's them." Leopard whispers.

"You wait here, I'll go talk to them..."

I look at the gang of youths and stay frozen.

"You don't have to go, you know?" He adds.

"No, no... It'll be fine..."

I'm not a huge fan of getting the shit kicked out of me. Realistically, it's unlikely that I'll be able to apprehend one of them, never mind five. However, sometimes you just have to bite the bullet.

I'll have to rely on my intellect and Irish charm to get me through this...

God help me.

****

I'm terrified as the first youth turns around, looks at me and spits in my direction. I will always attest to this, I'm not afraid of being dead, just of dying. It's something that I've thought of at great length one time. I came to the conclusion that, despite not knowing for sure if there was an afterlife, that I believed in one. After all, if my body is going to go cold, the warmth has to go somewhere.

I raise my hands as I approach. They all stand up and form a ring around me. My mind is melting and I can't really translate what they're saying. I can feel the blood rushing out of my head, my ears getting warmer. I definitely shouldn't have come alone. They laugh maliciously as one of them starts going through my pockets. I pull his hand out firmly and face him. I can't read anything behind his eyes. It's like reading ripples on the surface of the water, trying to see what leviathan lies beneath those gloomy depths.

"You don't touch me and I don't touch you." I tell him.

"Who the fuck are you?"

"You robbed those computers from a library about an hour or two ago-"

"- We didn't-"

"- I don't give a fuck about the computers! I just want to know one simple question."

"What?"

"Was the door unlocked?"

"Was the door unlocked?! You hear this?!"

The pack of Hyenas start laughing again. As confused as I am, I'm relieved to see that they're enjoying themselves rather than getting aggressive. Some of them even take a few steps back away from me, allowing me to breathe again and focus.

"What's funny?" I ask.

"The door was open! Some fucking crazy person started throwing stones at us and ran inside. We ran after the fucker to kick the shit out of them but they disappeared. Dunno where. We said, fuck it, grab a few computers while we're here."

"What did this person look like?"

"Not sure. Big jacket, you know the kind that security wear at night clubs. Had a scarf wrapped over their head like they were a fucking terrorist or something."

"And then disappeared?"

"Poof! Gone!"

"So... Did you set the fire to burn them out?"

"What fire?! Why the fuck are you talking about fire? We didn't start a fire!"

He starts pushing me and his friends tighten their noose around me. They're not taking this accusation lightly. Beating me up would mean nothing to them, it's only a form of expression to convey their anger by painting their knuckles with blood.

One of them punches me in the nose while another one shoves me to the ground. My eyes well up and my nose smarts. My elbow grazes against the cobbled ground. I lift my free hand up with the other one stemming the blood flowing out of my nostrils as Leopard comes bounding over.

"Guys! Calm down!"

"Hey! You're the library guy! You know him?"

"Yeah, he's- He's a friend."

"Then take him the fuck out of here before we kick his head in!"

Leopard helps me up and leads me by the arm as we walk back. I'm still a little shaken and some tears are running slowly down my face.

After we get some distance away, Leopard places me on a wooden bench.

"Are you alright?" He asks.

It's not fun being beaten by burglars. "Yeah, I'm fine... Just a little shook, is all."

"You would be. Had I known that little bollocks would go easy on me then I would've gone with you."

"It's okay. This shit happens every now and then."

"Hopefully not too often... Because if you tend to go out looking for guys to beat you up then you might be playing for my team after all!"

I burst out laughing again. Halfway through my outburst, I snort out a little blood which has the two of us erupting into a fit. It takes us a couple of minutes to calm down before we decide to get more distance between us and the Hyenas should they decide to pursue us.

****

I take a cigarette break at the bottom of the hill by the merry carousel that's almost as famous as the church. I look up at the domed building on top, illuminated against the dark sky. One might think that they're in some faraway country like Turkey or India. Apparently it's reminiscent of ancient Roman architecture, but it always seemed like an eccentric shape to me. An exotic echo of a foreign land.

We move on again back the way we came. Familiar ground is a

pleasant thing after being attacked, even with the nagging frustration lingering in the air. There's still some information incomplete about this case. I don't think I'll be able to get much by going back to the library. Maybe Leopard has forgotten something that could help?

"Who else has a set of keys to the library?" I ask him.

"No one... The head librarian gave them to me herself and said not to lose them because there weren't any spares."

"When did you get the keys?"

"Only two weeks ago. That's the kicker! If it was months ago, I might have been sloppy, but I've been pretty careful since I got them."

"You must have been working there a while before though?"

"About seven months? It's a bit embarrassing, actually. I got promoted over someone that's been there a year. You saw him earlier. The big, muscular fellah with a shaved head. He's useless anyway, but it put me in an awkward spot."

"Useless?"

"Doesn't know a thing about books! He's only good for the heavy lifting. He's nice, though. Always very friendly. Just a few pennies short of a pound, you know?"

"Sounds like a funny crowd in there."

"You'd have to be a bit funny to work in a library, I think. All that silence makes you a bit strange..."

His last words ring true in my ears as we walk down the street. As a teenager, I used to take long walks away from home when my parents argued. My house, once a place of peace, turned into a den of turmoil. All I could do was escape it.

As the hatred set in, so did the quiet. This was equally unbearable to me. Sick, electric razors in my stomach every time there was a suffering in the silence. All that vitriol being internalised, eating at us all.

Leopard hands me a tissue for my nose that's still bleeding a little bit. I hold it delicately against my nostrils. Along with the pain, there's a certain shame in being assaulted. It's a sense of defeat. You deal with the desire to exact revenge and hurt back. Your pride tells you that they deserve utter punishment for fighting cowardly in numbers.

Violence is a terrible thing to happen to anyone. Especially to those who don't deserve it. I can't justify their nature but, in this case, I understand it to an extent. It helps that I placed myself in the situation. I'm feeling quite okay about the whole thing. It's apparent to me that the attack wasn't exactly personal. No hurt feelings, only a hurt face. In fact, I'm glad with myself. My pride came after the fall.

A car speeds by and splashes us with a puddle. They must have been going eighty kilometres an hour! On any street in Paris, with its narrow paths and tight corners, this is lunacy. Not to say that to drive at all in Paris isn't lunacy itself. The car slows down a little at a red light and powers through again. Information is churning around in my head that leads to a sudden spark, albeit a bit of a stretch.

"You live near here? Near the library, I mean?" I ask.

"Yeah, about two minutes away from here and a five minute walk from the library. Why?"

"I think I know what's going on..."

****

We return to the scene of the crime. There's only one thing to check to see if everyone else's alibi checks out. I scan the ground on the street with my flashlight. The rain actually provides some aid as it gives the objects lying there a shine under the street-lights, but I still can't find what I'm looking for.

I reluctantly make my way over to the tiny stream on one side of the street and plunge my hands in, feeling around blindly. My fingers run over small bumps on the tarmac like I'm reading Braille. Indeed, it's a story I'm trying to ascertain. I cross the street and repeat my motions. A few minutes of this and I begin to find what

I'm looking for.

     I chuck the stones up onto the pavement as I go down the street. Leopard is watching me with some confusion, perhaps even with concern. It's not much proof but it's enough to assure me. I wipe my wet hands off my pants smugly and make my way over to the library door. Police tape covers the entrance, but the lights are off and there doesn't seem to be any activity in the area. The door has been locked again.

"What are you doing?" Leopard asks.

"Tell me something... When did the head librarian figure out you're gay?"

"About three weeks ago."

"And there was nothing suspicious about it?"

"Not really. I mean, she was pretty surprised. But aside from that, nothing..."

     I force myself to hide the smug feeling coming over me. Leopard seems oblivious still to the whole thing and I'm enjoying keeping him in suspense.

"Do you still have keys to the library?"

"I- Fuck! I do, actually! They never took them off me."

"Then how did they lock the door?"

"I don't know..."

"Let's take a look inside then."

"What?! No! I'm not breaking into a place I've been accused of breaking into. I'm not completely brain-dead!"

"Trust me. This should set things right."

     He looks at me and sighs. For some strange reason, my word is enough and the keys come out. I keep an eye on the balconies in case our eager old man is still watching for another dose of excitement, but there's nothing to be seen on any of the slabs jutting out. A bit of fiddling with the keys and we're inside.

I get Leopard to bring me to the head librarians office. A perfectly organised place with large volumes of binders filling the shelves to the left and right of the cheap-looking desk that supports a computer screen. It's daunting to be in a room as pristine as this one, although its cleanliness serves to remind me of something.

"Keep your hands in your pockets," I whisper, "We don't want to leave any prints in her office."

"Right! Should I wipe the door handle?"

"You- I guess not, actually. Your prints would have been on it anyway, seeing as you worked here."

Attached to the desk are two drawers with locks on them. I grab a letter-opener off the desk, sleeve pulled over my hand, and gently pry each of them open. The first one is full of mundane papers and new books on a variety of different, innocuous subjects. The second drawer holds classical, hard-back books that look a little worn. I get up and start rifling through the binders. Still, nothing of use to me.

"What are you looking for?"

"I have a good reason to believe that your boss may be a Neo-Nazi."

"A Neo-Nazi?! What makes you say that?"

"All will be revealed! I just need to find the evidence first. It's probably at her house. If you know where she lives, we should check it out?"

"Hang on..."

"We should go now. I don't really have that much time to-"

"- It's something we used to do in school..." Leopard mutters to himself and makes his way back over to the drawers of the desk.

He pulls out one of the newer books, removes the cover and looks at it perplexed. He then throws a stack of them on the table and quickly pulls off their covers. Each book that he uncovers and discards on the desk reveals exactly what I was looking for. Studies in Eugenics, positive effects of colonialism, white superiority and other racist literature lie sprawled in a pile on the laminated wood.

"How the hell did you know?!" He asks me.

"An air of self-righteousness... And a certain thing that she said. It got under my skin..."

"But what would make you think she did this?"

"Her alibi doesn't add up. It wouldn't take you five minutes to drive from Les Halles to Barbès, even if there was no traffic and you were speeding. There's too many traffic lights. It's just not possible! The other guy's alibi checks out. He got here when you did and he wasn't too far away. Although, I'll admit, his appearance didn't help with suspicions..."

"He's definitely not a racist. Yet... Why burn the place down?"

"Simple. She lured the gang in by throwing stones at them, knowing she could blame them for whatever happened inside. I couldn't help but feel something was off about her. She wasn't wearing a coat, even in this rain. I reckon she was wearing the jacket that those kids described, she probably ran out the back door and took it off. When they left, she burnt the books to stop foreigners from coming in, the gang would have been arrested, keeping them out of the way and, of course, there's you..."

"Me?"

"Well, you're gay... She probably thought you were a nice, blonde, Irishman. Now she can fire you with cause. France is a nightmare for firing people. Firing someone for being gay is impossible. She managed to kill three birds with one stone."

"This is fucking unbelievable... We should take this to the detective!"

"You- You might leave me out of this... Just take the information that I've given you and pass it on. I reckon that's the best way that this will work without anything getting messed up."

"Would you not come with me and explain it?"

"I'd rather not. To be honest, I'm only here because-" I suddenly remember the whole point of my trip to the library and pull out the flyer of Mouse. "Have you seen this girl come around here?"

"Ehm- Yeah, actually! It's been maybe four or five months since I've seen her last?"

"Anything you can tell me about her?"

"Not really... I think I remember her reading pretty much anything. She went through those books pretty fast too. I saw her start and finish one book in about three hours once. I was pretty impressed. I didn't talk to her much though."

"Try and think. If there's anything at all! Who she was with, what she was wearing, any-"

"- A bag!"

"What bag?"

"She used to come in with this knock-off designer bag. I told her I liked it and she said she bought it off a guy on the street down near Gare De L'Est... That's all I remember about her. I'm sorry. Do you know her?"

"No, I'm just trying to help out."

"If I think of anything, I'll give you a call. Give me your number, there."

  I'm hesitant about this. I've been doing pretty well without people in my life. Every relationship takes a bit of compromise. You take parts of yourself and parts of the other person. Ideas and idioms get swapped around. A small piece of you disappears to make room for them...

"I promise I'm not hitting on you!" Leopard adds with a smirk.

  I give in. I need all the information on Mouse that I can get. Gare de L'Est isn't the best part of Paris either and I'm starting to worry about her. It's entirely possible that she would drop off the radar of work and friends, it's what I'm doing, but people keep the things they like in their lives if they can help it. Her disappearing around pay-day might have just been a coincidence. Also, given the proximity between here and Gare de L'Est, it's entirely possible that she lived somewhere nearby. It wouldn't hurt to have someone in the area keep an eye out. I scribble my number down on a piece of paper and hand it over on the condition that he doesn't mention me to the police.

"Thanks for your help. I'll let you know how it pans out... I never got your name?" Leopard asks.

"It's better that way, buddy. Best of luck with this!"

    I give him a warm handshake and search for a taxi. A flood of them roll by, all with the burning, red light on top to declare that they're occupied. I walk a little further through the tense and torrid streets. My nose still hurts, but I'm proud of myself. You see, we all have dark thoughts that linger in our minds. Daring us to do wrong. We fear ourselves, or we fear everyone else for what they might think of us for thinking such horrible things. But, we think good thoughts too. Thoughts of joy and charity. Thoughts of compassion, being completely vulnerable to love and loss alike. Only, we're too scared to act out these thoughts too. Often times, fear holds us back from the best part of us.

    Overcoming fear is a part of growth. Why do fighters spar when they could easily run from every fight? It's the same reason why lovers love when they are not loved fairly in return. We all have goals, desires to be stronger. We fight to do battle better. We do it so we can win our own wars. So we can take the cost upon ourselves and the spoils for our own.

****

    I approach work with a new sense of purpose. It's one thing to hate your job, but if you hate your job and you're bad at it then what's the point? If I'm going to spend my time here, I may as well give it some effort. So, for the first time, I clean my work area without being asked to.

Songbird approaches my desk with a tall, red-haired man. They're both in animated conversation about a guest, from what I can gather, when she focuses her attention on me.

"Have you two met yet?" She asks, pointing between me and this Fox.

"Don't think we have." He says as he introduces himself, speaking with a Northern-English accent.

"Well, we were all going to head out for a drink some night and I figured we'd try and plan it for a night you're off?" Songbird asks me. A dawning realisation comes over me.

"Yeah, I suppose we can. Ehm... Also, I'm sorry I didn't pop my head in the last night I was free like I said I would. Something came up."

"Oh, don't worry about that! Sure, we'll see you the next night?"

"Yeah, sure."

"Anyway, we'll let you get back to your porn- I mean movies!" She says with her signature smile.

"Nice to meet you, mate!" Fox says as he shakes my hand.

The two wander off and resume their previous conversation when my phone vibrates in my pocket. I have a text from a number I don't recognise.

"Boss has just been arrested after they found video footage of her car by the back entrance. Nothing on the girl you're looking for, sorry! Thanks again for your help!"

That must be Leopard. I'm glad that she's going to jail. The realisation that came over me before is that if you have to justify something to yourself, then it can't be all that good. I justified lying to Songbird about popping my head in under the pretence that it was better for everyone, but I know it was a rude thing to do. It's important to own up to your actions.

Bookworm wanted her savagery to mean something so she justified it the best way she could. Pseudo-intellectual books on why white people are better to counter-balance the volumes upon volumes of books that stated otherwise, that a truly superior human-being couldn't be racist or bigoted. Those books didn't exist in her world and she didn't care for them in her library.

How could she be so bitter to entire races? I've had reasons to lash out at everyone. Hold a hate that's twisted my perception of the world. Focused on the narrowest parts that burned the most in my mind. But I know, with this sadness and anger, I'm only hurting myself, and that I could never hurt anyone else.

The whole thing was an ugly affair, but one good achievement did come from it.

I just bagged my first criminal.

Case 8 – Round and Around

"Yes, you are!" He insists with a grin, his Irish accent getting stronger. The other night porter's shaggy demeanour is offset by the brightest glint in his brown eyes. His jet black hair seems messy but trimmed at the same time, as does his beard. He has an air of contradiction about him. Half-wild, half-tame.

"I really, really can't go out after work. I have plans." I implore. It's been ten minutes of this.

"What plans? Are you going out, meeting people, drinking, getting laid?"

"Not exac- No."

"Then you don't have any plans then, do you?"

I'm starting to wish Crow fired him on New Year's Eve. He's not taking my refusal at all. He's a strange one, this guy. I keep giving everyone the impression that I just want to be left alone but here he is, oblivious to me spurning his friendliness, trying to get closer to me.

"It'll be fun! Do you remember what fun feels like?" He jokes as he starts doing a jiggly dance.

"Hang on! If you want me to head out with you, who's going to watch the counter? Aren't you working tonight?"

"Nope! I handed in my notice before going on holiday. Only here now to pick up my cheque."

"Then who's working after my shift ends?"

"The fuck if I know. Who the fuck cares?! You finish at midnight and if there isn't someone here then it's not your problem! Leave the keys in the drawer and write a note for whoever's coming next. I gave that fool plenty of time to find a replacement. If he doesn't have someone to cover my shifts then tough titties... Come out!... If you do, I'll kill you last!"

I mull it over in my head. It doesn't seem like this argument is ever going to end unless I agree. My protestations are beginning to sound like a broken record against his waves of intended thrills. I'm a little worried about what Crow will say when I abandon my watch, but it really isn't my fault, there's no one else here so he can't say anything to me. I'm too exhausted to argue with this guy anyway. I'm unsure where he gets his boundless energy. Either way, I only have to hang out with him until the first metro and I can swing home to sleep again. Better to just let this one lie and give in to his dogged demands.

"Alright, alright! I'll go..." I acquiesce.

"Good!... Because I already told everyone you were coming anyway..."

This sly Dog...

****

Dog and I begin our walk to a nearby Irish pub called Cole's. He's wheeling his bike alongside. On the rear-mudflap, there's a sticker that says: *This Is Where The Shit Ends!* The whole thing is covered in stickers of varying ages. I can just about make out that the frame is red underneath. He's clearly had it a while. As we stroll along, I find him surprisingly easy to talk to given that we seem to be of a completely opposite temperaments.

"Never thought I'd have a choice of jobs over here! You know what it's like starting off in Paris. To get a job you need an apartment, to get an apartment you need a job and to get either of them, you need a bank account, which they'll only give you if you have a job and an apartment. It's a vicious cycle." Matt tells me.

"It's not easy here. I think you just have to think outside the box for one of them so the others fall into place. Like, get someone to say you live with them for an address. Crack one, you can crack the rest."

"That's the one..."

"What's this new job, then?"

"I'm working as a bike tour guide. Every year they cut down their staff over the Winter because there's not enough tourists. Now that it's Spring, they're hiring again."

"But what happens when you get fired in Winter again?"

"Then I'll find another job for a few months and go back again in Spring like I did this time. Easy!"

  I wish I was working somewhere I liked. The hotel is gruelling at times. The monotony of showing up there every day to do the most menial of things can grate at you over time. Even the surprise tasks that Crow has us perform usually end with a dullness. But what else can I do for a living with no experience in anything better?

  A girl waves at us from a distance as she sits on the terrace of the bar. I can make out brown hair and some freckles. She swirls her drink and says something to her companion, pointing to us. The other girl that this mystery woman is with turns around to reveal herself. To my surprise, it's Songbird!

  The girl waving at us is introduced to me as Dog's girlfriend, who is also Irish. Sitting down with them feels almost like I've gone back home. She has the same spark in her eye as he does. Her energy equal to his but somewhat measured. More docile. She's instantly friendly and welcoming with me, telling me that she's heard a lot about me. For the first thirty minutes, I spend my time answering the questions of this darling Doe. Or at least, the one's I can't evade.

"What brought you to the hotel then?" Doe asks.

"Well, I needed a change from the bar I was working in so I had to find something new."

"Oh, right. What made you move over to Paris then? Fall in love with a French lady?"

"A French lady? No- I- Well, I moved here because I couldn't find work back home and I speak French so, it made sense."

"Sounds like there was a girl in there somewhere though?"

"An American."

"You break up with that girl?"

"We broke up, yeah."

"Well, from what I've heard from the other two, she's missing out. You can have your pick of them now. Am I right, ladies?!" Doe raises her hands, smiling, and looks over each shoulder to no one.

"Some day I'll have a group of ladies to agree with me... What happened with your American, do you mind me asking?"

"It's- Well-"

Dog starts shouting and leaps out of his chair as something whizzes past us on the street. His bike has an unwelcome rider and he's sprinting after it.

"Come on!" He barks at me.

I manage to catch up to Dog and we give chase to the bike. He's shouting abuse at the rider, a grey-hooded, gangly figure with a small satchel slung around his shoulder. His feet pumping at the pedals. Dog's tirade turns into brief yelps of obscenities as he begins to run out of breath. He tries to grab at the wheels but the bike is going too fast.

"You keep on him, I'm going to try and cut him off down this street. Try and make him turn right!" Dog shouts under panting breath.

I veer off to the left side of the street hoping the thief will instinctively cut right. He's gaining some considerable distance on me. He careens off to the left just as he hits the main boulevard. Dog's gone the wrong way and with no way of contacting him, the retrieval of the bike is up to me. I pivot left in time to see this guy bolt left again down a side street, faster than a Rabbit down a hole.

I swoop after him. He glides for a bit before he glances over his shoulder and starts pedalling again. He's not going to ease up until I either run him ragged or stop chasing him. Almost as if he's going in for his victory lap, he takes another left. My legs start to flap around uselessly. My smoke-corrupted lungs are burning. I push myself to the corner in time to see him continue on down the street before I'm forced to break into a light jog. My eyes are streaming from running into the wind, my heart thumping and groaning. An acidic tightness sinks into my calf muscles. Rabbit disappears as he dives down another left hand street. I think he's taunting me.

I run into a group in my pursuit. I shout at them and ask where the bike went. They point straight ahead and to the right. I start to gather my wind and hurl myself back into the chase. He's breaking his pattern at least. The next turn takes me to another group that look at me terrified. I can only whisper out "Where?" and they tell me he turned down a small pedestrian street. One large gulp of oxygen and I'm gone again.

I really need to give up smoking. Those cancerous cylinders are what's making me fail at this. I should have given them up years ago. Let myself get healthy again. I'd probably have more energy. Besides, it's not like I need another reason to give them up.

Something's odd about this new direction that I'm running in. I have company ahead. For a moment, I believe that it's Dog, but it seems to be another hooded individual with a funny run. His head is down and his arms are up, held close to his chest. For a moment I think he's just doing some intense form of workout until I see him toss something over his shoulder and sprint faster.

I'm finally out of breath and I collapse down to where my jogging partner jettisoned his cargo. A brown handbag lies crumpled a few feet away from a wallet. I extrapolate what happened in my mind until I come back full circle. I pick up both items and achingly trudge back to the group.

"The wallet's empty of cash and credit cards but your Identity Card is still in there." I tell them in French.

A young woman tearfully takes the bag out of my hands and nods gratefully. There's slim chance of me catching up to this cyclist now. My accidental intervention has my head turned around. I can't give up yet though. Not until I've exhausted all my options.

"Have any of you seen a guy on a bike?" I ask, expired and exasperated.

The group look amongst themselves shrugging and shaking their heads. They start talking about what had happened with the mugging that had just passed and how they were distracted by it. The mugging victim interrupts the group by asking me why I'm looking for a bike.

"One of my frie- Ehm - Friends had his bike stolen and I was chasing it until I ran into you." I try my best to not sound bitter, but there's no honey in my words.

"If it's stolen you could try Canal Saint-Martin? A lot of people that steal bikes go there and either sell them or throw them into the canal. The same thing happened to my pal."

The others chime in with their own stories of friends who have had their bikes stolen. It's not a rare phenomenon in this city. Sometimes the thieves would only steal the wheels, leaving a useless husk of a frame behind to rust and wither away. While they chatter on, I realise that Canal Saint-Martin isn't very far away from here. It's definitely feasible to get there quickly enough on a bike. I interrupt the group's endless mouthing with a thank you and begin my slow, lonely trot towards the canal.

****

It's been a while since I've been active. The last time I did any sort of physical activity was when I did a bit of swimming in the ocean last July. I was on holiday in Croatia with Cat. That whole trip, I was in love with life.

I packed my clothes into my red rucksack. It's always spelled adventure for me. It was the same one I used when I ran away from home all those years ago and I've been using it ever since. I think its consistency gives me comfort. Travelling can be stressful, so it's nice to have something that stays constant when everything is changing around you. This bag, my blankie.

It was the two of us together, away from everyone else and everything. We arrived in the town of Split to a torrent of rain, but the sun eventually burned its way through the clouds as we strolled to the Old City.

Climbing up the hill, chirping birds flickered in and out of holes in the old, pale, ruined walls. Their songs that filled the air ushered the mortals below to keep their voices down. Ornate and marbled, their housing held fantasy in its antiquity, like that of some Roman myth. Odours of spices and flowers wafted with the wind. The smiling faces of tourists turned from market-stands looking for the best souvenirs to bring back home. Airborne melodies and the most marvellous of sights were everywhere as we continued our intrepid exploration into this new, incredible world. The girl I loved by my side. I knew I was in paradise.

A few days later, we took the last ferry to Sumartin, on the island of Brâc, only to find that the buses were no longer running. All our hope was placed in an abandoned taxi by the pier. Someone in the tourist office rang the driver's wife, who didn't have any idea where he was. So, we both took turns waiting in the tourist office for a call back and by the taxi should the absent driver return. The barrel-moustached man eventually appeared and, after handing over some moonshine to a friend, dropped us off at our rented apartment in Bol.

Bol gave us rainfall again. It was no torrent, but the grim clouds were enough to steal our sunshine. We argued for the first day. She really wanted to just lie in the sun and on the sand. Instead, she got pebbles and droplets. Still, we soldiered on and partied throughout the night. Bartenders juggled fluorescent bottles and blew flames from mouths filled with spirits.

In the later hours, the storm grew worse. A firework display of thunder and lightning attacked the ocean. Gnarled, electric forks struck at the sea before disappearing in a flash, only their voices lingering. The whole night rung out black and blue, but we loved our way through it all.

When night fell on the second day in Bol, the storm cleared.

All the celestial beauty was reflected on the water. A quiet, rippling portrait of a million stars and a single moon tore across the sea as the clouds fled. Their static revolution was interrupted by the occasional streak of a shooting star. We were standing on a beach as we watched them. My arms wrapped around her, my chin nestled on her shoulder.

"This... I think this is probably the closest I've ever come to a perfect moment..." I told her.

Her face lit up. "You're such a sap!" She exclaimed, slapping me, before giving me a kiss.

We talked on the way home about what the future held for us. She was leaving soon after our holiday and we were too young for anything life-changing. I had told her I would like to be with more people before settling down with just one person. The conversation continued though, as we looked back on our day and then even further to the obstacles that we had overcome, to all the time that we had spent together.

"I think... I mean, if you really want to, we could try it?" She asked gingerly.

"I want to."

"Let's try it then... You could come to New York and we could just see how it goes..."

And that's what I decided to do...

We basked in the sun the next day. I was filming fish underwater and exploring the coast before she joined me in the ocean. The sun above, pulling the chill from our bodies. The water below draining away at gravity. She climbed onto my back and we took off, taking photos of ourselves. One of them captures the moment perfectly. My head turned around so my lips could meet hers, the corners upturned. She always smiled when I kissed her...

There we were. Surrounded by nature's absolute beauty mixed with the oldest, most vibrant buildings of humanity. A reminder that the constantly occurring force of nature can make the most beautiful things and that humans can build something from that to last forever. That her beauty could stay with me forever if I built on it.

In that warm water, I knew I had finally found what I'd spent my whole life looking for. That I was finally afloat.

I'll never forget her eyes as the sun met them. Each iris a well of Adriatic ocean. In the long sunset of a Croatian sun with her wrapped up under my wings, a feeling came over me. It's one I'm familiar with. Most of us are, in fact. It's that moment when you realise you're just dreaming a wonderful dream and you're savouring every second before you wake up. Because we know eventually, undoubtedly, we will always wake up.

But, that day, our sun only grew brighter...

Blinding headlights cause me to leap out of the way as an electric-car streaks past like a shark in the water. The red circles grow smaller in the distance and its bright lights are replaced by the dull, gloomy streetlights. I calm myself down in the darkness it leaves behind. You get used to crossing the street without looking at night. There's rarely any cars roaming the small streets in the wee hours and you develop a habit of being absent minded about them after a while.

Gare de l'Est looms ahead. There are flocks of people from the suburbs, many young and unemployed, congregated after their nights out to take their buses home. They rustle around the shelters. There's too much happening in too many places to keep track of what's going on. Shouts and cries come squawking out from all over.

It's a perilous walk through this crowd. Rough men step in and out of my path. Dominating the space that they have. Snide remarks and threats follow the back of my head when I make eye contact with one of them. I'm pretty edgy about walking through such an unkindness.

I see an old American woman alone with her daughter looking around anxiously. I ask them what they're doing, being so out of place in this area, and they tell me they're looking for their hotel which isn't terribly far from here. I opt instead, without argument from either of them, to bundle them into a taxi and send them flying away. That's the second group that I've helped tonight and I still haven't found Dog's bike.

It occurs to me that lately, when I help people, it always revolves around me following or chasing people. I could probably end all this brutal leg work by simply asking the right questions from now on. See the story rather than the trail. Look harder and sweat less. I could stop all this fruitless meandering for Mouse by interpreting the facts.

Before I venture further towards Canal Saint-Martin, I need to ask around to make sure that the bike has come through this way. No point in wasting my time and energy going in the wrong direction. I can even follow up on that lead from Leopard on Mouse.

I do a circuit around the area asking if anyone has seen the bike. After questioning a few shady individuals selling bags if they recognise the photo of Mouse, I find that none of them say they recognise her and most of them won't even speak to me. Why would they? I have nothing to give them. My questioning makes me look like police and no one here wants to talk to them. I'm probably not going to find Mouse this way.

It's a difficult thing to find someone in a city this big. We're two moving parts. I could walk on the same street as her and miss her by a second, only for her to never return to that place again. For all I know, I could be a step behind her wherever I look.

I eventually head along a wrought iron gate where a few groups of youths have huddled around the front entrance. I spot the grey hoody first. It's draped over the handlebars of a bike that's propped up against the fence, without any locks. I casually orbit my way around the group and check the back mud-flap. *This Is Where The Shit Ends!*

I'm sure to give these guys a wide berth. The memory of the last time I confronted a group of youths is still present in my mind and I have no intention of repeating that mistake. If I go in straight, they'll only end up circling me. I'll need to draw them away from the bike. A lightbulb goes off in my head. Every problem can be circumnavigated...

I do a bit of preparation beforehand. Building up my momentum. I walk the whole perimeter of Gare de l'Est before returning to the group again. I don't know why I'm doing this. I could easily go back to Dog with my tail between my legs and tell him I lost it. It wouldn't be my fault at all. It's not like I'd even care much if he disapproved of me afterwards or was disappointed in me. I don't want any friends. I don't want to be pulled along social circles or wrung around people.

Maybe it's not about making friends or impressing them though? Maybe it's about repaying the kindness that he's shown me so far. That good intentions come back to you in the end. That we can keep good things going around indefinitely.

I gulp as I brace myself for this smash and grab. I stretch out my muscles. I fucking hope to God that I'm faster than these bastards.

I'll use a trick I've learned, from first-hand experience, that is sure to provoke a reaction. I pick up a bottle and hurl it at them. Their heads snap back to me in shock as I raise my twitching, middle finger to them, terrified. I feel like a fucking lunatic. They tap each other with the back of their hands and start a slow walk towards me. I bolt in the other direction.

Glancing over my shoulder, I can see the angry mob tearing after me. Death threats scald my already burning ears. I still have a head start on them at least. So long as I don't trip up and fall, there's a good chance I won't be eating from a tube for the rest of my life. My right leg springs me left around the corner and I dodge the bin that I'd reconned before. The fastest of the flock runs straight into it, distracting the others enough for me to gain back some of the distance they closed.

Heart heaving and lungs wheezing, I fling the hoody off the handlebars. I lose precious seconds turning the bike away from my pursuers and throw my leg over the bar. Why is the seat so fucking high? I hobble along with the bike, desperately trying to push down on the pedal that keeps scratching my ankle as I miss it. My fellow bicycle enthusiasts swing around the corner just as I manage to get enough momentum to hike myself on the saddle and peddle my fucking ass off. Rabbit manages to keep up with me. I look forward and send my legs into a wild flurry. Don't look back, it'll only slow you down.

 I soar over the streets as I leave Rabbit and the Ravens in my dust. I manage to calm my anxiety and enjoy the brief moment of victory that I've earned. These moments of elation are short lived, although sweeter when they're unexpected...

 I wonder why these glories don't stick in my head as much as my disappointments? I try my best to forget those maddening memories, but I'm not great at switching my mind off when I get a thought on track. I tend to spiral out of control with my own thoughts. They bury themselves into me and leave my head spinning. It was the same when I was with Cat.

 It was just a few words. An idle thing said, but still stuck somewhere in my head. In Croatia, when we spoke of our future, I had asked her if I would be cut out of her life should things end between us. She thought on it briefly before she answered.

"I feel like we'll never *really* be done with each other... because we're special..."

 Because we're special...

****

I end up back at the bar just as it's closing. Songbird is standing outside as the terrace is being brought in. She tells me that Dog followed the bike as far as he could after seeing it turn left. His girlfriend, Doe, ran off on a one-woman patrol in search of me. It's been two hours and they were worried sick. They've gone off again to look for me. Songbird sends them a text and they hurry back after a few minutes.

"Holy shit! You have my bike!" Dog exclaims with his now familiar exuberance. "I don't know how to thank you!" He pulls me in to him and lands a big, slobbery kiss on my cheek.

"We're just glad you're safe!" Doe says, rubbing my shoulder.

"I never thought I'd see this thing in one piece ever again! You're a fucking legend!" He says spinning the wheels.

"How the hell did you find it anyway?" Songbird asks.

I shrug back at them. I'm unsure of what to say. I see faces looking at me with an intense gratitude, an affection even. This is going to have repercussions. Ripples in the water. I'm starting to fall into their orbit and I'm not sure how I'm going to be able to pull away from them. I don't want to go through this again.

They force me into telling them the story of how I got the bike back. I try to give them the abridged version because I want to go home but they keep asking questions. This, coupled with their brief interruptions of laughter make for a long story. As the words come pouring out, my energy picks up. I have a warm audience in front of me.

My story comes back to the moment I arrived and I'm met with their astonishment. Their disbelief makes me feel a little uncomfortable. I know they don't doubt that anything I say actually happened, but there's a strangeness to what I've done. I don't mind being the strange person I am, but I prefer it without spectators. There's a security in only being strange to strangers.

My exhausted limbs ache as we linger outside the bar, chatting. I'm in dire need of a stretch and a lie down. This is complicated by the fact that the bar is closed and the metro isn't open yet. I really just want to go home and voice this to the others.

"We're all headed home anyway. The wife and herself are going to split a taxi home, I'm going to cycle. I'll give you a lift! C'mere!"

Dog instructs me to stand on the spokes of the back tire. I profusely object to the idea until he asks me if it's any more dangerous balancing on the back of a bike than stealing it from a gang of thieves. There's a perverse logic to what he says and, knowing his powers of persuasion, I reluctantly agree.

"Remember, this is where the shit ends! If you start swaying and shit, then we're both going to eat shit. Got it?"

I nod and we pedal off.

I feel the cool wind on my face as we whir down streets. Dog holds up his hand for a high-five from a business man getting into a car only to slap him on the shoulder when he spurned him of it. We laugh as we roll down the street exhilarated. At each red light, Dog warns me to get ready to jump off. I continue to bounce off the bike, hit the ground running and get ready for the green light to hop back on. My final leap comes just before my front door.

"Thanks for your help, sweetheart." Dog says. "If you ever need a favour, just ask, okay? Seriously, tell me if you need a body buried and I'll do that for you. Later, dickhead!"

I watch that odd rascal cycle away from me. I'm finding it hard to dislike the guy. He has a charm that seems infectious. Like all you want to do is enjoy the randomness of his company.

The last thing I see is an obscene, but endearing, mark on the bike as Dog disappears.

****

I get in to my apartment and hear a dull, whirring sound. My roommate must have put his laundry in and gone to bed. How the fuck am I supposed to get any sleep with that thing clanking away for the next hour?

I lie down, plug my earphones into my phone and start listening to some music. My eyes closed, I can feel some vibrations coming from the floor, out of sync with the mechanical grinding of the washing machine. I raise my head to see my roommate hovering above me.

"Try and be a bit quieter when you come in. I could hear you. Also, when that's done," He says, pointing towards the washing machine, "can you hang it up for me? Otherwise the place will smell damp."

Fuck the neighbours, fuck this apartment and fuck him. I start roaring at him. The cliffnotes being: I'm not a fucking slave. You'll hear me come in if you're fucking awake. Close the fucking door if you have a fucking problem with that. You keep your fucking noise down so I can fucking sleep.

His sole response as I shout is: *Who's apartment is this?* I tell him to fuck off as he storms back into his room. I seriously can't put up with this shit any longer. He's wearing me thin. I start punching the pillow beneath me until I calm down.

Maybe it's time to leave this place? I had gotten so used to this life of constant abrasiveness that I forgot I shouldn't have to live like this. I need a break. Only, finding an apartment in Paris is difficult and I would be homeless again. Looking for the right one that you can afford and that they are willing to rent to you feels like an endless search. I guess I'm stuck here for now.

I wonder how others manage to co-exist with each other for as long as they do? Many flatmates spend years with each other. Take married couples for example too. I'm sure sex helps considerably, but in the twilight years when things stop rising and start falling there must be some form of diplomacy involved.

I think of my grandparents and how they've been together for so long. I'm not naïve enough to think that they have a perfect marriage by any means. But they stood by each other. I wonder how so many descendants of mine have followed this ritual? This continuous cycle of connection.

It's a story that repeats itself a thousand times, a thousand different ways. How love transcends the mortal coil, so much older and more powerful than any of us. We're not doomed to follow the exact motions, but blessed to continue on in its likeness. Where life and death is a closed loop, the natural order of love and eternity itself is us spiralling outwards. Fibonacci's story is our story. Maybe it's even my story too? Maybe there's something beautiful waiting for me around the bend as I swing upwards from the lowest point?

It's time for me to sleep. I need my rest for work tomorrow and it's harder to fall asleep when the sun rises. My night has been a little too interesting to say the least. It's an experience I don't hope to repeat again in the future. My burnt out body goes limp and cools down its muscles at last.

I'll need to avoid some people tomorrow.

No point getting closer for no good reason.

Only, it was nice to take a break from the usual with something impromptu.

Case 9 – On the Wire

I'm chained to my desk, as usual. I've been working double shifts, five nights a week ever since Dog left. Crow seems to have intensified his intent to discipline his staff by throwing out as many tasks and trials as he can. Essentially, when I'm not checking in a guest, I'm supposed to be cleaning. However, with all my hours over the past few weeks spent cleaning due to a reduction in clients, all the important things are done and I've given myself a bit of a break. I can't keep doing the maximum for minimum wage.

Fox has changed out of his work clothes and is outside smoking. I can see him idly pace back and forth as he repeatedly checks his phone. I find it strange that he hasn't gone home yet. He goes through two more cigarettes which he rolls patiently and skilfully before he comes back inside. He looks down at his phone one more time, scrolling down with his thumb before he approaches my desk.

"Alright, mate? How are you getting on?" He asks.

"Yeah, I'm okay. You?"

"Ah, I'm fine... Can I ask a favour off you?"

"Eh... Sure?"

"There's been a bit of talk 'round the hotel that you're the guy to go to if someone needs a bit of help with things, like with the watch-" I try to cut him off and tell him I just found the thing, but he cuts me off sooner. "- Or the cheating husband, the bike, some rumours of other stuff too. Well, I had a guest chat to me today. Good man. Comes down every now and then from London for business. Brings his daughter along with him. Always stays here. Anyway, he was worried about his daughter and I said I'd come talk to you."

It must be pretty important for Fox to break from his usual behaviour. He's quite stoic from what I gathered. It's not the same kind of stoicism that I employ in conversation. He's searching for the answer inside himself, I'm searching for the exit out.

"Why, what's wrong?"

"He told me she met some lad online – fair enough, it's the twenty-first century – but he mentioned that she couldn't go out last night because she gave him a loan of some cash. She's never actually met the guy. He's worried she might be getting scammed."

"Has he talked to her about it?"

"He did. She thinks she loves him though."

"What age is she?"

"Just turned nineteen, I reckon."

"Why haven't they met in person?"

"The fellah lives in Lyon, apparently."

"So... What can I do about it?"

Fox sighs and scratches his chin. "The dad gave me the password to her email account. Says he won't go through it and I don't feel comfortable with it either. I know her well enough by now. Nice, shy. There's not much else I can do to help... He asked me to ask you to look into it..."

Fox moves in behind my desk and opens up an internet browser on the computer. He loads an email page and types in an email address. I catch the word Butterfly before his shoulder covers the screen again. He rattles off the password on the keyboard and hits enter, then turns to face me.

"I'd appreciate it if you kept it between me and you. The dad's a decent bloke, but he's desperate. This seems like more your area than mine. I told him I trust you." He says as he begins to roll himself another cigarette.

"What makes you think you can trust me?"

Fox remains silent in deep reflection. As he licks the skin of the paper, rolling the cigarette shut, he gives me a toothy smile and shrugs. "You just seem like that kind of guy... You didn't say anything about the watch, so I know you're discreet. Have a look through it and tell him if he should be worried."

The door swings shut as Fox leaves quietly. I'm left feeling pretty uncomfortable about the whole encounter. It should take a lot to have trust in someone. Why does he trust me, then? How, when I don't trust anyone anymore? I barely trust myself.

Crow has given me a few things to do, but I figure I could forget some of them to give me time to do this. I start to pore over the emails in front of me. The most recent email states that she wired him the money. He thanked her for it and assured her that she'll be paid back soon while apologising with some humble embarrassment for having to ask. I decide to start my investigation with the oldest email and work my way forwards.

They met on a dating site. There was some charm to her meeting him because she had accidentally changed her distance filter from twenty kilometres to two thousand and twenty kilometres by entering it twice. A meeting by mishap.

She's sweet and modest in her introduction, describing herself as timid while laughing at her own blunder. She doesn't feel like she's that attractive or interesting. He admonished her for saying she's not interesting and tells her the photo he saw on her profile was beautiful. For a laugh, she sent him a photo of her that had been taken a few years beforehand. It was far from enchanting, but he simply made a light joke about how Butterflies used to be Caterpillars.

The next few emails are similar in the respect that she would try to hide some details about herself because she doesn't feel like it's fascinating enough and he would pry them out of her with flattery. He's got some pretty smooth lines.

"If I had to ask you one question and you had to answer honestly, would you do it?" She asks.

"Yes?"

"Do you really find me attractive and interesting?"

"I think I've met people who are attractive and interesting, yet none of them are a special as you are. You have won me completely."

Eventually, the conversation accelerates to her bursting out with information about herself. They both talk about their friends, their secret desires, their ambitions and goals. Every crevice uncovered and exposed to each other. All of them met with compliments and enthusiasm.

It's a familiar sight. Cat and I exploded into each other like these people too. Equally self-involved, like nothing else exists. It's remarkable that other people can have this effect on us. With Cat, there was that instant connection. Talking with her was easy. Making her laugh, I could initiate almost accidentally. We just clicked...

It's still too early to tell if this guy is genuinely nice or just a Snake in the grass. The timestamps on the emails reveal that they spent about a month getting to know each other before they escalated things.

He sent her a photo of himself topless under the heading: *You be the meat, I'll be the bone*. It's the first time I'm seeing his face. The photo is quite blurry, but I can tell that he has a beard at least. His body seems quite in shape too, skinny rather than athletic. The photos that follow leave me glancing around the hotel foyer nervously.

The two traded photos back and forth for weeks. The subject headings turned to a flurry of fantasies of what would happen should they be in the same room together. I click on an attached file of her reply. The first image I see of her is explicit enough that I avoid all the emails with a file attached to it. This is someone's daughter who I might meet at some point. I'm already violating her privacy by going through these emails without her knowledge. It was naïve of the father not to expect this, but I suppose maybe it's difficult to keep up with the times.

Deep inside I can hear a whispering, nagging voice telling me that no one would know if I looked. A dark impulse, that there is power in my hands. Voyeuristic pleasure to be entertained. I dismiss it as quickly as I can, dwelling on temptation only fuels it, and instead I scroll up until I find one that does not have an attachment.

"Are you objectifying me as a woman? ;)" She wrote.

"Baby, with an ass like that, I'm objecting to nothing!" He replied.

  Her next email brushes over his linguistic mistake and begins the whining pining from both of them. Both of them wish they could be together and that they didn't live so far apart.

"What if I came to London?" He asked.

"You can't just do that! It's too expensive for you!"

"We can meet the next time you're in Paris! Tell me when you're father is taking you there next and I'll meet you there."

"I'd love that! Email me later?"

"I always do!"

  They traded relatively mundane details for the following weeks. He asked her about college, she asked him about work. These emails I skim over. The details of which don't seem terribly relevant to what I'm trying to find out and they're all quite lengthy.

"Send me another naughty photo of you!" He wrote.

"I can't right now. I'm just running out the door!"

He didn't reply to this email and it was another two days before she wrote back to him. She described what she'd done for the past two days and the various interactions with her friends.

"Yeah, I've been busy at work." He replied.

She wrote back with another paragraph of stories.

"Cool" is all he had to say.

  For about three days they carried on like this. Her pouring herself into the emails and him replying with the same apathetic disinterest. Then, she sent him an email with a photo attached entitled "A present for you!" I don't need to click on it to know exactly what it meant. His reply was the same affable responses as the beginning of their relationship. Full of interest and empathy.

My gut feeling tells me that he's manipulating her, but there's always the chance that he could simply be petulant and over-sensitive. In my own neurotic messages with Cat, I'd often read too much into what she replied. Trying to find what she wrote in between those squiggly lines to understand what she was *really* saying. I'd question the very foundation of everything we had. What little we had, as I over-thought about it. Each new violent imagining in my head turned into a thorn in my side. An insecure barb that stayed there until she pulled it out. A never ending cycle where I'd blush and pester.

The couple buzz on about themselves. The usual photos were traded with the subject headings of: *Wish you were here* or *When I see you*. The messages without photos attached were still jubilant, manic even. As the dates get closer and closer to the present, the frequency got more frenzied. Then, she wrote to him excitedly. "Get ready! I'm coming to Paris!"

"When?"

"The second of April until the sixth!"

"Oh, I'll be working then."

"Can't you get a few days off?

"I don't have that much money right now. I can't just buy a train ticket to Paris and not work those days. I'd be losing money."

"But I really want to see you and I don't know when I'll be in Paris again?!"

"I don't know what to tell you, I'm broke."

"What if I paid for your ticket?"

"That would help, but I can't ask you to do that!"

"You're not asking! I'll buy it for you tonight if you'll come!"

"I'd need some money for a place to stay too though."

"I can book you a hotel room?"

"It would be cheaper if I look on a French site."

"I could send you the money by bank transfer?"

"I'm not sure I'd like you to loan me money though. Even if I did pay you back soon afterwards."

"Please! Let me do this for you! Let me do it for us!"

"Okay. And thank you! I can't wait to see you!"

"Done! Can't wait to see you too!"

There, the messages return to the present day. I don't know what to make of all of it. If I give Snake the benefit of the doubt then I could come to the conclusion that his original reluctance to meet Butterfly was based on nervousness. Perhaps his financial reasons were really an excuse. They'd be meeting for the first time in real life and that would add a new dimension to their relationship.

It's also possible that he's just unsure about how he wants to proceed with the relationship. His level of interest seems to rise and fall continuously. Like a man walking a tight-rope, he leans to the left and right for balance so he can take a few steps forward. Indecisive until the equilibrium favours him. I have a bit of experience in this.

Cat was never sure what she wanted from me. At the beginning, she didn't want a relationship, but she didn't want to stop seeing me either. We fell into a vagueness where the rules weren't clear, the balance always tipped in her favour. She knew exactly where I stood on how I felt, but with her it seemed like it depended on the day.

It was a time rife with anxiety for me. I loved her with everything I had. I threw myself into our relationship as eagerly as I could, frayed nerves and all. All my eggs in her basket. So, after Croatia, I tried to straighten it all out.

"C'mere!" I pleaded and pulled at her under the bed sheets. I was trying to get her to turn around and face me.

"I am here! What do you want from me?!"

"How about a kiss?"

"Kiss yourself! I'm hungover!"

"Or we could go further and-"

"- Fuck yourself!"

"Fair enough... Do you remember what you said last night?"

"What did I say last night?"

"That we should be boyfriend and girlfriend."

Cat remained perfectly still.

"You were pretty drunk..." I offered.

She rolled over and looked at me.

"I just want to know what we are?" I asked.

"Geez! What does it matter? Why do you have to be so maudlin about it?"

I stared back at her quizzically.

"I take it back... You're not maudlin... But you *are* a little too needy..."

I have to admit that I was needy. I had thought it was just me proving how strongly I felt about her. Also, I didn't really know at the time what the word *maudlin* meant and I was impressed that she did. She was wrong to take it back.

"You know I'm not intentionally trying to hurt you." She continued.

"I know... But what do you want out of us?"

"I don't know."

"Well, where are we going with this?"

"I told you, I don't *know*! I *cannot* keep having this conversation with you!"

"I just want an answer..."

"*I don't* – I mean – You know my visa is expiring and I have to go back to America! I don't want to, I love Paris... But I need to sort my life out, and I'm not sure if I can do that here... I don't want to be in my late twenties and be some college drop-out *slash* waitress..."

"Yeah, but I'm not sure I can just move across the Atlantic if I don't know what I am to you."

"Of course you'd be my boyfriend if you moved over!"

"But, if I didn't?"

"We'd stay in touch... I mean, I'd be like: If you're ever in America... Hit me up..."

I was conflicted. I knew she had to go back at some point to finish her studies. I had to summon all of my energy to resist begging her to stay. Our relationship would have been easier in Paris and I would have done anything to keep her here, if only I thought that was what was best for her.

I'm not sure I could have convinced her to stay, I just know I never did. Her future versus my selfish needs didn't allow me to. So I kept my silence. I only ever pushed her to make her own choices, about us and America, but her indecision turned my brain haywire.

I remember what it felt like to be with her through that. I really thought I was going to lose my mind. I was stretched thin by being pulled between what she said and what she did. Strung out, wondering why she was spending her time with me, loving me, living with me, when she wouldn't call me a boyfriend. Throughout the time we spent together, she would flip-flop in between whether we'd get serious or just keep it undefined and, each argument, my heart was on the line.

She rested her head on my chest and mumbled "It'd be shitty if you stayed here though... Coz you're gonna be here and cute, and some girl is gonna find you, and she's gonna be like *wow*!"

I kissed the top of her head and held her tighter. And, for that moment, I left it at that...

The computer beeps. A new email has just come in from Snake. Grateful to see that there's no attachments, I open the message.

"I'll pay you back the money I owe you by buying you drinks and dinner. Meet me tomorrow night at nine in that place I told you I'd love to-" Reading on, I'm not entirely sure how one could do that with a champagne cork and some string. I shudder to think someone would enjoy it...

I start to panic. There's no address of this place! I have no idea where he wants to meet her. If she reads this then she could disappear and maybe put herself in a dangerous position. Not just with the champagne cork either. This guy could be a con artist for all I know. Reeling her in. Hook, line and sinker.

Like with the champagne cork...

He must have mentioned it somewhere in one of the emails I haven't read. I scroll down and check the subject headings. I click on one entitled *Dinner for two* but instead of an address I'm left with the image of his penis seared into my mind.

I open the next likely candidate entitled *Big Fish* but it's the same thing. Men really aren't that imaginative when it comes to sending dirty photos. It's always just a photo of that one thing we value more than our other appendages, or anything else for that matter.

I hear the door to the foyer open and Songbird walks through waving at me with a smile. I have the cursor hovering over the close-window button. It's a deep-seated reflex, well-practised. Suddenly, I'm fourteen again.

Thankfully, she rolls on to the escalator. I dredge through a plethora of penises before I find what I'm looking for.

"There's a bar in Pigalle that I'd love to take you to. We can do whatever we want to each other there. Me and you making passionate love." He adds a link to the website at the very bottom.

The link brings me to their website. Their tag-line promises a night of debauchery and sin to all of their deviant customers. The prices seem quite steep too. After scrolling through the various booths they have available, I find the address written at the very bottom of the page. I rapidly write it down on a piece of paper and stuff it into my pocket.

The browser suddenly opens a new page promising sexy singles in my area. I click to close the page but a new window pops up, asking me if I'm sure I want to exit the page. The two options are written *Close* or *Enter*. I instinctively hit *Close*. A woman's voice is heard moaning through the speakers and the page stays intact. I hit it again, this time hitting *Enter* and, after twenty seconds of rapture-ridden wailing, silence resumes.

How apt.

"I fucking knew it! Porn!" Songbird shouts out from the stairs.

"It was a pop-up ad!" I protest, blushing.

"Yeah, yeah!" She chuckles as she gets back to cleaning.

Well, that was fucking embarrassing. At least I know where the debaucherous duo are going and I can find out if he's as duplicitous as her father suspects.

****

Walking down the streets in Pigalle at night is an uncomfortable experience for me. Bold, burning neon signs overhang cheap posters of topless women. The main street itself is poorly-lit. A seedy atmosphere hangs over the entire area. More disconcerting for me than this are the people I see here. As two women walk by a man starts heckling them, making obscene remarks of what he'll do when they take him home with them. As they ignore him, he turns sour and hurls abuse at them. To be honest, this can be seen anywhere in Paris. However, it's only in Pigalle where it seems like almost every man is like this. A boorish mass of misogynists congregate here.

It's the cheapness of life that unnerves me. They offer spectacles. Illusions of lust. The idea that a body is just an object for entertainment. A human being, a plaything. That the beautiful mind and soul of a person that takes decades of development is of little importance to another person against the brief thrill their flesh can bring. In my opinion, it's the people who look for these indulgences that are sadder than those who give it to them. There must be a horrible emptiness in them that they can't find beauty in their own lives...

Just outside their meeting place a woman comes over in an effort to entice me into her strip club. I tell her I can't speak French to get her to leave me alone, to which she begins speaking in English. A little irritated, I tell her I can't speak English by using the one sentence I know in Russian. She then starts speaking at me in Russian. Alternating between startled and annoyed, I give her a firm "No". She drags one finger down my body that feels like a full body massage and says something else in Russian. I start blushing as the blood flows to my face and... elsewhere... I give my excuses and cross the street before she can do any more tempting.

The couple arrive at their intended meeting place only to have the bouncer turn them away after looking Butterfly up and down. She seems dejected and apologetic, but Snake makes jokes as they walk down the street, cheering her up. He stops walking during their conversation and pulls her back into him as she walks ahead. The couple kiss passionately for a few minutes. Snake then looks to his left and nods towards a classy restaurant.

****

I feel just as out of place in here than I did out there. With everyone else in groups or couples, me sitting on my own feels like I'm expressly going against the current. This is a place where people spend time with those they connect with. Defiantly a loner outside and reluctantly a loner inside, it seems I somehow managed to fall through the cracks of both societies.

The waiters flow around me between the tables until one of them gets to me. I give my order as politely and directly as possible to keep the whole experience brief while I spy on the two. Snake seems positively animated. Butterfly is soaking up every second of it. They seem like a pretty good couple to me. The banter between them goes back and forth, effortlessly energizing each other. It's obvious that it's a thrill from them to have that extra dimension that technology could never bring to them as their hands reach across the table.

The food here is actually pretty good. It's probably the first proper meal I've eaten in a very long time. After their dessert, Snake signals her to wait outside while he looks over the bill. He wraps the coat around her snugly and gives her a gentle push towards the door then reaches into his wallet to stuff notes into the leather book. I throw whatever cash I have in my wallet on the table, certain that it's more than enough, and make my way after him.

Outside, he's holding on to her intensely and she's giving him a stunned look as I walk out the door. I casually light up a cigarette, pretending to ignore them. They start whispering as Snake accidentally makes eye contact with me. I can sense a hint of malice in them.

They embrace each other. He sticks his hand up and a taxi zips to the pavement. I jolt and try to catch another taxi, before I do she starts to plead with him.

"Won't you come with me? You can meet my father!"

"I cannot, my love. My 'otel is not far from 'ere and I must go back zere. But we shall be togezer again soon. I promise."

"Soon..." She says, with warmth.

He places her in the taxi and closes the door, waving goodbye.

Snake looks nervously back into the restaurant. The waiter is holding a twenty Euro note up against the light. When I glance back at Snake, I can see him slinking away in the shadows. I set off in casual pursuit.

We walk for a good ten minutes. I'm careful to stick behind corners and I cross the street a few times to stay under the relative cover of parked cars. He's seen me before and there's a good chance he'll be taking precautions after his hasty escape from the restaurant. He keeps his head down to the ground as a police car quietly rolls past.

Just outside an apartment building, Snake starts pulling at his beard. For a few moments, I watch with horror as the hair comes peeling off. I calm down, admonishing myself, when I realise it was just a fake all along. Snake has shed his skin to reveal a smooth, child-like face. The evidence is too much to support. He has to be hiding something. Fake money, now a fake beard?

Opening the lid of a large bin left in front of the building, he tosses the beard inside. I creep forward to get closer as he enters the complex. This is no hotel. The door is shut by the time I reach it. Trapped outside, I'm scratching my head as to what it is I'm able to do. There are no trees to climb like Tiger tried and I don't see any lights come on that weren't already on. I'm out of tricks and Snake has me tripped up.

I could take the beard for a DNA sample? Only I'd need a lab... And someone that knows how to get DNA samples... I pace up and down the street looking for a way in. The door is too solid to force and even if it wasn't, I don't know where to start looking for him. On the wall beside the door is an intercom with nine different last names on it.

I don't have any choice. I've heard his voice at this point and I've only got one more play to make. I start by pushing the buttons of all the names on the list. The first two that answer are pretty annoyed at me when I tell them I've made a mistake. I try calling three more apartments until I hear his voice. His name is listed differently to the one he's been using online and it seems he's living with someone else. I make my apologies to him and step away from the intercom. The father will probably want proof to show his daughter. I take photos of his name on the intercom then move over to the bin.

It smells terrible. My hand hesitatingly pulls at the beard but the adhesive seems to be stuck to a cheap and thin bin-bag. I peel it off as it tears the lining of the bag away to reveal a piece of paper with Snake's real name on it. It's a bank statement for a joint account that he has with what appears to be a girl that he lives with.

I have all the evidence I need. This piece of shit already has a girlfriend. I'm not sure if he's using Butterfly for money, sex, the distraction or the power, but I know he's a user. I gather as much paperwork as I can before heading back to my apartment.

****

Sitting at my desk in work, I have the papers I'd found the night before tucked into a folder. I thought it would give it a semi-professional feel and make presenting rubbish to a man a little more palatable. I leave the folder in a dark bag with the beard and hide it in the cabinet behind me.

It's a sad thing to see this girl get strung along like this. She seems too sweet to be deserving of such things, although that is what people tend to take advantage of. Giving makes ripe for the taking.

Love is sharing. The darkest thoughts, the faintest hopes, the dreams, the fears, the vulnerable parts. You share a kiss. You share two bodies. You share a life. You give, in the hope that you'll get as much back. That they're willing to give as much as you are. Sharing turns two things into one thing. Two people into one love.

These wires that connect us across great distances are stronger than people think. Thousands of messages from me to Cat are tucked away on my phone and online, the product of being in contact every single day. Either texts or emails or logs of 4am phone calls. A collection of online shrines.

Through these memories I'd feel faint lips meet mine, her ethereal embrace and a brief shadow of the joy I felt in that moment. How could you forget that feeling? That pure elation that you are the happiest man alive. Truly. Genuinely.

Enough about that... I need a distraction. The internet has always served me well with that in the past. A different world to connect to.

I type the name of the hotel into the search engine just to see what pops up. A torrent of abuse comes pouring over the screen. One star reviews abound, with only a few three or four star ratings.

One review popped out to me in particular. Not because it was a very poor rating, but because I recognised the person who posted it.

"Sneaky, nosy fuckers who don't know what fucking private means. One of their frog twats was peeking around, getting involved in shit he's not fucking supposed to."

The photo of this user? Our dear Mr. Swan. I flag the comment to be removed on the basis that the language was offensive. Honestly, if he was to rewrite a polite review advising all the cheating husbands in Paris to avoid this hotel, I'd be a happy man.

My phone vibrates on the desk. Leopard has just sent me a text.

"Hey. Still no luck on your missing person. Any luck on your end? I'll tell you now, this girl takes playing hard to get a little too far. You should be careful! Dating isn't what it used to be!"

I let a smile creak through. I send him a message back thanking him for his efforts and hoping that all is well with him. He's a good guy and I'm glad I have someone helping me in my search. I'm anxious to find her. Uncertain of what will happen if I do. For all I know, she could be dead... Or even a high-ranking member of the Swedish Mafia...

I debate whether or not I should contact the phone number on the poster. I reckon it's probably one of her parents. If I did, I'm sure I'd get more details or maybe even discover that she's been found. Although, there's also a chance that I'd get tangled up with other people in the search and if I failed to find her, the burden would be mine to share with them. I'm not sure I want to risk that kind of emotional attachment or complication.

A sudden realisation leaves me banging my head against the

palm of my hand. All this time, I've been ignoring my greatest resource! We're all wired up. All connected. I type Mouse's personal details into the search engine and start to flick through what I find. With no trace of her in real life, there's bound to be footprints left behind in the ones and zeroes.

****

Crow scares the living shit out of me as he squawks over the desk. I was fully immersed in the internet, but I couldn't find much useful information on Mouse. I deleted all my social media profiles months ago and it's hard to look into someone else's without one. He's asking me what I'm doing on the computer. For once, I have a deflection.

"Sir, have you any idea what our online presence is like?"

"Ower wot?"

"Online presence, sir. How people view the hotel on the internet? We don't have our own website and it's incredibly archaic to make a reservation by telephone these days."

"Ze phones work and zey 'ave always worked."

I let out a sigh. "Well, what about a website then?"

"Do zat."

"I don't have the skills necessary to do that, and it's also not my job."

"Yower job ees to work here, no?" He towers over the desk. There's a ruthlessness in his eyes.

"I still don't have the skills."

"Leave eet. I will 'andle eet." He says before storming off up the stairs. The man has the attention span of a caffeinated squirrel.

I can't wait for the day I leave this place. I'm tired of being pushed to work hard when nothing seems to improve. The rawness of it. Banging my head off an invisible ceiling. The fact that every time I see him I end up feeling angry. I have enough anger.

His interruption wasn't a complete inconvenience though. Looking back at the screen I can see a series of photos, from different times, where Mouse is in the same bar. The address is even tagged in them, placing it just beside the Centre Pompidou. While the people there might not have seen her in a long time, they will most likely remember her given the frequency of the photos. They might even know where she is. I have a new thread to pull on!

Fox comes hurtling towards the desk. Everyone is out to give me a heart attack tonight!

"Did you see her?!" He asks.

"See who?"

"His daughter?! She's gone!"

My brain starts firing up. There's a chance she got past me when I was researching Mouse or talking to Crow, but she would have had to have crept out. That means I don't know when she left or where she's going. I run my hands through my hair and then remember we still have access to her email. Fox rattles it in furiously and we both read a new message from Snake to Butterfly.

"Like we said. Gare de Lyon. By the shop in the main hall. Bring all the money you have. We'll leave together. See you at midnight."

They're meeting in less than ten minutes!

****

Fox said he'd cover for me after I grabbed the evidence and ran out the door. It's funny how it never occurred to me that I didn't have to bail on work. I could have told her father and he could have dealt with it. I think with the heat of the moment and the clock ticking down, me and Fox didn't give it much thought.

A painfully slow metro journey that saw me charging through tunnels takes me to the station fifteen minutes too late. I begin to look around for them frantically. To make things worse, I'm not entirely sure what they look like. He de-bearded himself when it was dark and the only photo of her that I remember was the one from her awkward youth.

Slow down.

They're a couple, that's a start.

He told her to bring all the money she had, so he probably plans on conning her. To do that he'll need to stick to his story about being from Lyon. That's probably where they're headed.

I race down to the tracks. At first glance I wouldn't have recognised him but he held my gaze by his slightly bizarre appearance. He traded his fake beard for a fake moustache and his eyes are wrapped with thick-rimmed glasses. He's a rubber nose away from being a caricature. They're walking along the train looking for their carriage. He signals her to hand him her backpack to carry. I bolt forward and manage to grab her before she hands it over.

"Don't do it! He's a fake!"

"Who the fuck are you? Get off me!"

"I'm-I'm a friend of your father's..."

"He knows I'm here?"

"He does, I think..."

I'm a little caught up in the moment. I'm not sure if I'm lying to her or not. I don't even know if these half-truths are the things I should be telling her. It's probably better than the absolute truth.

"We should go now!" Snake hisses at her.

"I-I'm not sure. My Dad-"

"- We'll call him when we're in Lyon!"

"I have proof he's a liar!" I interject.

I show her the bank statements, electricity bills and other documents I pulled out of the bin while telling her the story of what happened after she left.

"Those papers could be from anyone! There's no photo of me! This isn't proof!" He snaps.

The conductor calls out that the train will be leaving in two minutes. Snake wraps his hand around her arm, squeezing it tightly and starts to move her towards the carriage. She follows, bewildered.

I can't let her leave with him. I reach out and rip the fake moustache off his face. He stops cold and looks at me, positively shocked. Butterfly wrenches herself away from him in horror. I try to shake the moustache off my hand but it's stuck solid. He takes a step to the right when I grab him. He's surprisingly strong for such a thin guy! The cloth slides out of my fingers as he dashes away.

Tears stream down Butterfly's eyes. This whole thing must have been overwhelming for her. It's a good thing I caught them when I did. He could have disappeared anywhere if he had the money to do so. There are countless connections on the continent by train. I just barely managed to stop her getting robbed, right down to the wire.

It's still not entirely clear to me what he was really doing. Like he said, I don't have any definitive proof. I should feel better that I helped her, only instead I'm left with this raw feeling in my gut. She's a wreck because I broke her heart by proxy. To live through such a deceit is tough. I've learned that it's not what people say that counts, it's what they do. That's why trust should be built, not given.

We leave the station together, under the illumination of the tall clock-tower, and start our journey back to the hotel. She's quiet for the most part. I'm thrown an instant barrage of dirty looks as she weeps beside me in the metro. I'd like to tell them that not everything presented is as it seems. That you can't capture what's really going on behind this image. What would be the point, though?

"I really thought he loved me... I thought I *knew* it" She sniffs.

She remains silent again until we get back to the hotel. I can sense that she resents me a little. It's understandable. For her, I'm the reason she's in pain. None of it's my fault, but the sentiment would be there. This situation would leave anyone with some crossed wires.

Her father anxiously jumps forward when he sees her and she bursts into tears in his arms. Fox nods at me with a smile.

"Alright, then?"

"Yeah, I guess..." I sigh.

"Oh, come on! You did well! Never mind her. She'll thank you in a few years."

I give him a snort and a shrug. I think he can see my sardonic outlook on being rewarded for this.

"You like Sci-Fi, mate?" He asks.

"Sci-Fi?"

"Science-Fiction."

"Eh... Yeah, kind of... Why?"

"I got a show you can watch when you're not busy here."

Fox scribbles down the name of a show and passes the note over. I recognise the name and tell him I've already seen the whole series. We chat about it for a good twenty minutes. It's probably the first time I've ever talked with anyone about it. Most people I've met have an aversion to it as they find it too odd. I even find myself starting to enjoy our conversation. It's liberating to feel barriers being pulled down. A pleasure to connect with someone on a topic that isn't work, in both meanings.

Fox leaves me back to it and my stomach starts to rumble as my shift ends. For once, *just once*, I'm going to cook something when I get home. I didn't get anything to eat all day and all I had for breakfast this morning was two stale cookies and some whipped cream because I'm a terrible human-being. I'll be quiet and that riled-up roommate of mine will still be asleep. Eating is a basic human right anyway. There's nothing he can get mad about...

****

Well, aren't we fucking furious? He's waving the saucepan around and screaming like a housewife from the forties, only without the apron. Given how tight his underwear is, and the hostility of our current exchange, a frilly apron might actually lend a bit of gravity to the situation. To abbreviate what he's wailing at me in French is basically: Cooking makes noise and his superpower seems to be hearing pins fall. I would have picked invisibility, personally. Although, his power seems to suit him as an asshole.

I'm being relatively calm. Using my words. Some of them a little... colourful... He's pointing to the door and shouting "Leave" like I'm an animal to be thrown out. There's no way I'm walking out of this place and leaving all my stuff with him. I tell him firmly that I'll be leaving at the end of the month and that I'll call the landlord tomorrow. He seems a little stunned, then he just shrugs and drops the pan to the ground with a clang before he shuffles back into his room. The door swings half shut as usual. I really thought he'd bang it this time.

I never liked the man, but I expected some kind of common ground to be found on his part after all this time. Or maybe at least, on my part, some form of Stockholm syndrome.

It was a mistake moving in with him in the first place. There were doubts in my mind, but also a desperation. I needed a place badly at the time, I even had to take out a loan to move in, but I should have examined the evidence first. Thought ahead of how that story was going to end. What would happen a little further down the line. I guess I just took a leap of faith. Jumped into it without looking. For someone who worries as much as I do, I have a habit of doing exactly this.

It's unlikely that I'll find an apartment any time soon. I should have bought myself some more time, the end of the month only being six days away. It took me three weeks to find this poor place and I can't be sure that new shelter will be any sooner than that. Still, I've learned recently enough that I need to break free from this...

Living here isn't part of who I want to be.

So, why pretend to be something I'm not?

Case 10 – Seeds of Doubt

She's holding flowers, and not the cheap kind, while she approaches. This is a strange sight at night. All the florists are closed well beforehand and the thought alone of lugging such delicate things around with you all day is almost as cumbersome as the flowers themselves. Perhaps she's just a busy Bee.

She's maybe thirty years old with an athletic figure. Her short, earthy-brown hair overhangs her olive eyes. She starts our conversation by asking me if I'm the night porter that works in the hotel. I toss my dying cigarette on the ground and tell her that I am.

"I live in the building across from the hotel. I heard some of your work-friends talking in a boulangerie recently and they said that you were willing to help people?" Her Eastern-European lilt is more noticeable this time.

I'm a bit peeved by the fact that rumours of my endeavours are starting to spread. An invisible seed that plants itself, grows and reproduces, taking over the area around it. At this rate, the whole neighbourhood is going to be asking me for help with things. It makes me feel awkward to be seen in this way. A friend to people even though I don't really have friends. Still, there's no harm in hearing people out.

"What is it that's bothering you?"

"It's not me. It's a neighbour in fact. He's- He's not acting... himself..."

Even she seems slightly confused by what she's saying, her face is wearing a funny, twisted composition.

"In what way is he not himself?"

"I don't know... Every way... But only a little bit..."

"Can you give me an example?"

"Ehm... He doesn't water his flowers on the balcony as much as he used to. You have to understand, he loves those things! Lately, he seems more withdrawn. Even more so than his wife! He rarely leaves the apartment and he doesn't talk to me on the balcony. I worry there is something wrong with him."

"Has his wife said anything about his behaviour?"

"She said everything was fine. But she was very short. You know? Very curt. She's always cold, she and her husband are opposites like that, but this time it made me suspicious. It was defensive."

Either Bee's a clever chick or she's just imagining things. Regardless, I have very little interest in investigating the gardening habits of stranger. He's got a wife to take care of him, maybe even kids, so there's no urgency over his odd behaviour. Besides, some people just change with the seasons.

"Why is this so important to you?" I ask.

"Because you know what it's like in Paris. People rarely ever know their neighbours. No one really looks out for each other. It's very sad. We shouldn't be like this, we should all do what you do. This man, Daniel, is a very good man. Very friendly and kind. I want to be sure that he is okay."

It's true what she says. A city like this can be incredibly cold all year around. People often find themselves either isolated or insulated, by chance or by choice. We all mind our own business to the extremes that when we see someone in need of help, we ignore it. I've seen crowds rush past a man passed out on the ground without giving a glance to see if he was breathing or not. I never met any of my neighbours in the apartment that I left. I barely even knew my flatmate. This kind of apathy turns us into pebbles brushing against each other. Never feeling the connection. It's a barren thing, no growth to be had. Only, there's safety in a stone soul.

"It doesn't hurt for me to take a look. But if I don't find anything unusual, then I'm afraid there's nothing more I can do." I offer.

She thanks me and scribbles down the code to the apartment

building along with his door number, then I head back into the hotel.

****

Once again I find my feet getting heavier. This job is killing me. The food I eat sours in my stomach as the stress poisons my blood. Where's the release? I can let go of hate but I still don't know how to let go of this stress. Stress is a poor word for it. My body isn't stressed, it's toxic. Noxious vapours of worry fog up my stomach, too thin and weak to ever get a grasp on it, yet too strong to dissipate. How do you fight what has no form?

Crow keeps shouting down the phone with the most arbitrary of criticisms. The windows are to be wiped in order of left to right, apparently for aesthetics. Here we get our tests first and our lessons afterwards. Somehow, I doubt that the windows are going to bring in more customers than the poor online reviews are keeping out.

These diatribes, mixed with the long hours and the fact that I'm staying in a youth hostel have made me a very miserable man indeed. My hostel kicks me out at eleven in the morning. Considering I only get back there at around seven, this makes for quite a bit of sleep deprivation. My free time is spent looking for an apartment before work and, on my days off, catching up on sleep.

I wish I could afford somewhere that lets me sleep as I need to. I'd grab a spare room here, but I know if Crow ever found out, I'd be fired on the spot. Rumour has it he's had problems with staff staying in the hotel before. There's a sick torture in being between apartments and working in a hotel. Searching for a bed constantly, only stopping to work in a place full of empty beds.

I've discreetly left some of my stuff in the hotel. I can only leave some things in the youth hostel, the rucksack I've always had for example, but three Cacti that I have are too fragile to leave in a cloakroom. They were Cat's and she couldn't bring them with her due to an agricultural border law. She left them with me as a kind of a token. Something that she couldn't quite part with but couldn't bring with her. At least, that's how I looked at it.

I really blossomed under her light and I didn't waste a second with her before she left. I poured all of my love into us in the hope that we would grow into something more. She was my American girl, and she held all the promise of her promised land to a poor Mick like me.

We were ruined the first time just as we were blossoming. Now, three Cacti, that's all I have left of her. It's all I need to remind me too.

****

The first night of my new investigation isn't yielding any results. The door code and his address proves to be quite useless considering I can't really get into his apartment with it. However, the top floor of the hotel allows me to look onto their balcony, which is covered in various potted plants. Some of the flora hangs over the railing and other plants scale the wall on both sides of the door. There's very little that isn't covered with some kind of foliage or another, bar a terrace table and two chairs.

There's not much to report. The old man that I assume to be Daniel wanders out occasionally with a coffee to smoke a cigarette. A portly man, he sports a large, white beard that covers most of his face and his head is balding on the top, leaving only whiskers on the side. Thick-rimmed glasses shield his eyes. His dinner, in the warm evening air, consists of a boiled egg that rolls around the plate, some salad and a dried piece of toast. Overall, the man seems quite unremarkable. Dull, even. There's nothing to indicate where Bee's seeds of doubt are coming from.

It's my first and only night off this week, and I'm spending it in the hotel to spy on this bland man. As the lights to his apartment go off, I decide to give up entirely on the project. I've got my own things to sort out. I need to find a place to live, and I haven't had time to run down the lead on Mouse. It's frustrating enough to be here on my time off, to do so fruitlessly doubles the angst.

"Fancy seeing you here!" A voice exclaims as I turn around to find Songbird facing me.

"Yeah... I forgot something last night."

"Fair enough. Oh! While you're here, there's a few of us going out after work again if you fancy joining?"

"Ehm... I'm not su-"

"- We don't know where we're going yet though! Trying to find somewhere new to go just for something different, ya know?"

"There's actually a bar not too far from here- Well, by the Centre Pompidou. It's maybe a thirty minute walk?"

"Sounds good! We'll be done here in about forty minutes, then you can lead us to this new haunt of yours!"

"Sure!"

I guess I'll have company looking into Mouse's favourite bar. Perhaps it's not such a bad idea to have a crowd. Drinking alone is quite noticeable and having some people with me could provide some cover. People might also be a bit more willing to share any information they have about Mouse to someone that isn't a loner.

I head back down the stairs, curious to see who works the shifts when I'm not here. The usual day receptionist has clocked out and the changeover occurred while I was upstairs. I'm shocked to see Crow sitting behind the desk, glumly staring into space. Up until this point, I never asked myself who covered the extra shifts. I never would have thought it would be Crow himself.

"You are not workeeng, no?" He asks.

"No, just picking up something... You are?"

"For ze moment. Do you know of some person zat looks for work at ze moment? A friend, perhaps?"

"I'm not sure. I..."

"Yes?"

"I do know someone... He's lost his job at a library because it burned down. This was about three weeks ago though, so I don't know if he's found something yet or not."

"Burn-ed down?"

"It wasn't his fault though!"

"You 'ave ees number?"

"I do. I can text him if you'd-"

"-Text him. Tell him to come tomorrow evening."

"Again, I'm not sure if he's found something so I can't-"

"-Yes, yes. Text him. Hm?"

"Right..."

****

As Songbird and I trundle down the street, I tell her that Leopard leapt at the chance to work in the hotel after I texted him. I explained that, while offering him the job, I did my best to dissuade him at the same time.

"You gave him fair warning. Tell me, how is it you don't know his name?" She asks.

"It's kind of a long story... I'll get into it another time."

"Ooh, mysterious... You're just pretending to be interesting, aren't you? I bet you just forgot to ask him!"

"Maybe something like that." I grin.

The Centre Pompidou looms ahead of us in the distance, half of it peeking out from behind the buildings. Large, coloured pipes snake up and around the scaffold-like bars on the outside, giving the building an unfinished appearance. Small groups of people sit in the square just in front, illuminated by street lights that reflect aggressively off the glass sheets that comprise the walls of the museum. The bar is located across the street to the right of the museum.

We arrive to see Fox, Dog and Doe waiting for us. The bar itself is packed due to some kind of football match being on TV. Behind the bar are two people about the same age as myself, one male, the other female, and an older man. It takes us twenty minutes to get to the top of the queue. Fox takes our orders from us and politely asks the older bartender for our drinks while we all shove money into his pockets. We opt to go outside to accommodate the smokers of the group.

"Funny to see a man of that age working behind a bar. I mean, you get it back home in Ireland but they tend to be the owners. I don't reckon he owns the place for some reason." I say to my colleagues, maybe just a little in need of idle gossip to divert attention away from myself.

I'm met with murmurs of agreement from everyone except Fox who stares off into the distance for a few seconds before responding.

"Ah, I wouldn't be too quick to judge. I'm not a young man myself. I know a lot of people measure their life success by their careers. Fair enough. To each their own, I suppose. But me? Friends. Family. That's what matters. How you support that is up to you..."

"I guess I never really thought about it that way."

Fox shrugs as I allow my slight feelings of guilt and embarrassment to dissipate. I'm not incredibly close to any of these people, but they've proven their kindness and amiability enough to me that I don't wish to offend them, which I may very well have.

Our conversations grow outwards from the general grumblings of work to past experiences and stories. Most of them involve the various antics that we get up to when inebriated.

I remember nights like this one, a long time ago, when I'd be with some friends and Cat. We'd share our lives over emptying glasses. Each pint poured into us nourished another conversation. Her, binded in my arms and planted on my lap. Nights out of fun and frivolity. Of light heads and lighter hearts.

Those friends left one by one after she did and a distance grew between us. Perhaps they grew tired of me feeling sorry for myself after losing her. Tired of the same conversations over and over again. Or perhaps I had simply stopped being relevant in their lives? Their departure, in my mild sociopathy, had become an annoyance rather than a grief. Their absence an impediment to my own amusement. So, we lost touch and I lost the warm feeling they had brought me.

Instead I choose to tell my colleagues stories about my friends back in Ireland. The people I had in my life who I left behind. The people who didn't have that pesky fire under their feet because they were happy where, and as, they were. I never understood their way of thinking. I liked them, I really did, and they liked me... But I didn't like me...

The match is over as the crowd vanishes from inside the pub. Dog drags the group over for shots of whiskey, which I graciously accept, as he chats to the bar staff. As it happens, they turn out to all speak English. The older bartender regales us with stories of his experiences here in Paris. How he had difficulty believing that *etiquette* was a French word.

"No please or thank you, just *give me a beer*! So, you're a professional and ask them what beer they'd like and, right in front of the fucking taps, they ask you what kind of beer you have. Then you pass them a menu so you don't have to list off seven things forty times a day, but they don't read it and ask for a *biére normale*. Now, I'm not sure about ye, but to me *normal* can be pretty fucking relative when you have a choice of things. But, for these dipshits, it's the weakest beer on tap."

My workmates laugh aloud to the story while I commiserate with the bartender, having been in his position before.

"And that's not all! You ask them a simple question: *Do you want a pint or a demi?* And all they say is... Any guesses?... They ask for a *normal* one! Or worse, you ask: *Big or small?* And they say: *Yes*. Well done, lads! How can I help ye, if ye can't even fucking help yerselves?! Don't even get me started on the whole *order at the bar* fiasco!"

We laugh at his many stories as I idly watch the two younger bartenders randomly pulling off some gymnastic stunt out of sheer boredom. Another round of shots leads to a free round of shots and my head starts to take a heavier feeling. Dog and Doe promise me that I can sleep on their couch and get some proper sleep. I'm grateful considering my hostel would have me out by the morning.

Through the blurry vapour of intoxication I ask the younger barman if he's seen anyone fitting Mouse's description with the excuse of meeting her before.

"Yeah, she used to come here every now and then. Haven't seen her in ages though! It's a shame. She was a lot of fun."

He obliges me by asking the other two if they know what happened to her but, after talking to them, gives me an apologetic shake of the head and returns to serving customers.

We drink long into the night, moving to another bar near our hotel until the metro opens. Me, Dog and Doe skip, stumble and stagger our way to the station. We realise we had taken a wrong turn after finding ourselves at the Madeleine building. A large building that always reminded me of a temple you'd find in Athens. I popped in once to find a symphony harmonising under stained glass windows and concrete angels. It was a beautiful sight. I must remember to recommend it to Songbird.

Eventually, we reach Opéra. The beautiful golden statues above gaining radiance as the sun rises. I drunkenly mumble that I had played the guitar in front of the Palais Garnier once to a crowd sitting on the steps. Doe begins to joke that I had played in the Opera house and begins mocking me in an operatic soprano in an endearing way as we descend down into the metro.

I'm propped up against the wall as the incoming train creates a gust of wind that gently blows my hair back. The lights from inside the train cast yellows squares on the tracks that roll along with it like clouds. I find myself falling into its serenity.

After arising from the underground at their station, we crash into their apartment and the couple set up their sofa-bed for me. They have a nice apartment. Spacious, yet cosy. As I take off my pants in the dark, I hear some coins fall out. I listen to the direction they roll in and make a mental note to pick it up in the morning when I have the energy. I bury myself into the covers they've given me and allow my head to spin.

The murmuring through the wall to their room ceases after a few minutes. And when all the voices have gone, all but the ones in my head, sadness descends.

It's always been like this for me.

****

My phone is telling me that I've slept through all of my alarms and that if I leave right now, I'll still be ten minutes late for work. Even ten seconds late would be enough to land me in trouble with Crow. I throw my clothes on and charge out of the building, into the blinding light of the street. I arrive at the hotel fifteen minutes late for my shift to find Bee buzzing around the door.

"So?" She asks.

"I'm in a bit of a hurry, sorry. Can we talk later, please?"

"But did you find anything?"

"No. He was completely bland. Nothing out of the ordinary."

"But-"

"- Smoked a few cigarettes. Had dinner. Nothing."

"Daniel doesn't smoke, though."

"I'll look into it." I sigh in frustration and fly in the door.

It seems Fox is mysteriously working the day-time reception shift.

"Hello, then! How's the head feeling?" He asks smugly.

"Still attached, unfortunately."

"Don't you complain, now. You didn't get a call at nine in the bloody morning to cover the desk for whoever it is that has the flu!"

"You've been here since nine? Sorry I'm late. Metro problems."

"Ah, don't worry. You're not that late anyway."

"Still."

"Don't worry, mate. The world won't freeze over. Anyway, I'm out of here. Good luck!"

Fox pulls on his coat and slinks out the door.

Before I think I can get away with it, Crow calls to acknowledge that I was late and gives me my tasks. My blood starts to boil again but I concede to his demands. It's not the best time to start an argument with him.

I get to work, only to find that my hair keeps getting in the way as I bend down. The fringe, and the rest of it, I suppose, has grown out far too long. With no money for a barber, or time to get a hair cut, I make my way into the kitchen with a pair of scissors and begin snipping away over the bin. It looks absurd when held down straight but swept over to the side makes it seem somewhat normal. I sigh and look at the sad sight before me.

I've built so much anger and frustration here. I know I hate this place and this job. The only thing I really have going for myself is the knowledge that I'm quite good at it. That I'm tasked with the more arduous jobs because I'm the only one willing to do them. I'm a good worker, and there's some pride in that.

Albeit, not much else.

****

As I take a cigarette break, Bee comes back to me, having seen me from her balcony adjacent to Daniel's apartment, she explains. She hands me a key, telling me that Daniel is outside of Paris with his wife and they're unlikely to return until tomorrow.

"I still haven't found any reason to be suspicious. I'm not sure it's a great idea for me to just break into their apartment!" I protest.

"It's not breaking in! They asked me to water their plants and I told them I was busy but that I would get someone else to do it."

"So, you want me to water their plants?"

"And, if you see anything?..."

"*Fine*. I'll take another look... Why are they leaving anyway?"

"She did not say."

"I'll go in after I finish my shift."

"Thank you! I promise this is the last time I'll ask!"

    Bee leaves me alone with my thoughts. She is a particularly particular woman. I'm unsure if her persistence is admirable or unnecessary, but I suppose I'll find out tonight. I'll lose sleep for agreeing to this. Although maybe she would instead, should I not.

****

    Daniel and his wife live in a very large, ornately decorated apartment. I should have known by the area that they live in that they were wealthy. Still, the sheer scale of their wealth is something new to me. After having lived in the cramped conditions with my former roommate, to see an apartment with its own library comes as a shock. It's laid out as a wide place. The front door leads directly to the living room, with the library to the left, the kitchen to the right and doors leading to other rooms past the kitchen. All along the wall in front of me are doors that lead to the balcony.

    Anxious about being here, I lock the door behind me and set about searching the apartment in the dark. My hand cups the glare of the flashlight to reduce the chance of it being seen outside. The bulb inside is burning against the glass as I swing it over the desk in their library. I find some books on horticulture and botany, some fiction. Nothing surprising. In an apathetic attempt to be thorough I look around the library for some kind of secret switch before admonishing myself for my stupidity when I find nothing.

    The place is rather tidy for the most part, although I do find a few pairs of men's shoes to be strewn across the floor rather sloppily. The kitchen is exquisite. A marble counter-top in the centre for preparing food and silver taps on the sink. The cupboards are made of mahogany, of which there are many, along with some shelves. I root through them methodically, only to find a large range of foods that I assume none of them will ever find time to eat before it's expired.

The fridge is covered in photos. I glance over them to see the couple on holiday in different places. I'm slightly moved by one of them. Daniel is baring his brilliantly white teeth to the camera in the most joyous of all grins, his arms thrown around his wife. It's nice to see such a powerful display of affection after their many years of marriage.

Perhaps that's what's going on with him? A kink in the marriage that's left them both feeling alone. Or maybe it's Alzheimer's? That could explain his withdrawal from Bee and his new habits.

I open the fridge and see, once again, a plethora of food. It seems they keep the place well stocked. I'm sure to accommodate guests they would have over for dinner. Isn't that what old people do? Have people over for dinner and talk? One thing catches my eye, though. A faded sticker on the inside of the door that simply says: *No eggs, please.* Perhaps it was something placed there a time ago and long since forgotten, as there are most certainly eggs in the fridge.

I venture into their bedroom. The bed has been made perfectly. On one side of the bed, I find more of Daniel's shoes littered across like autumn leaves. Perhaps he has an aversion to them? The other side is kept relatively clean in comparison, with various ointments and tonics left on the night stand. To my left there's another door to the balcony.

I search the place high and low, including through their cupboards. I take a moment to myself when I find a large rifle in the closet before gently putting it back and wiping it for prints. One never knows, after all.

The last place I convince myself to check before giving up is under the bed. A cliché, I'm sure, but people like to hide things in places that never see light. We're discouraged to go to such places by natural instinct. Underneath, I find a small box with Daniel's name written on it. I sit on the bed and start rifling through it. What secrets are they hiding?

It's mostly comprised of photos with some aged love letters thrown into the mix. In contrast to the one's on the fridge, these photos have seen some wear as the owners pawed over them. Thin veins run along some of them, having been folded previously. They depict their younger selves on trips to the beach, on their wedding day, their honey moon. I leaf through them with some admiration. There's quite a lot of history in this box. Decades of the intertwined stories of two people. Of fresh bloom and graceful withering.

At the bottom of the box there is a single, clean sheet. It stands out against the faded love letters. I pull it out and, under the glowing light, translate the document. The title alone makes my face turn white.

All of a sudden I hear a key scratching at the front door. I hurl the photos back in the box, throwing the box under the bed, and, hearing frail voices coming from the living room, silently make my way to the balcony.

The door clicks shut and I look around. The plants are either too small or too thin to adequately hide me. I'm not left with much cover. I hear a clang coming from the kitchen. The frightening sound gives me a bleak inspiration.

I make my way to the floral partition between the balconies and grab hold of the railing. Swinging one leg over to the other side, I glance down below. The height is dizzying from here. Almost nauseating. And to think we descended from the trees all those years ago.

I desperately swing my second leg over and shimmy to the other side. I clamber over the railing and, with neither foot reaching the ground, fall sideways into the partition. I hear the door open from Daniel's balcony and he calls out.

"Who's there?"

"Hi! Sorry! I'm a friend of- of your neighbour's and I- I just slipped on a leaf."

"Well, be careful of the plants... Good night!"

"Good night!"

My hands are still shaking as Bee unlocks the balcony door, startled to see me at first, then anxious to hear my news.

"What's gotten you so scared?" She asks.

"I'm scared because I just spoke to a dead man." I tell her, holding the document in my fist that's entitled *Certificate of Death*.

****

Bee has a newborn baby named Rose. A lovely child, whose name matches her cheeks. A bright and cheerful kid, even at this late hour. Bee dotes over her for a bit, singing in what I think is Polish, before she returns to me with a stern look.

"What do you mean when you say he is dead?"

"This is the death certificate, signed and stamped..."

"But how?"

"Either they found a way to bring him back to life, or this guy is an imposter... You said he was acting unusual... What was his relationship like with his wife?"

"He was happy, she was cold, but they got along."

"It looks like they have a lot of money... Any chance that problems in their marriage could have resulted in him writing her out of the will?"

"It is... Possible... She is not that nice..."

"Perhaps she needs the imposter to change the details of the will in her favour?"

"It is a lot of money..."

We sit there in our own individual reflection. I can see that she's grieving for her neighbour, although she does a good job masking it.

"We have to confront her!" She says.

"I'm not sure that's a great idea. I don't really want to get involved in-"

"- You already are involved, aren't you? This is someone's life we're talking about. A whole life. She's covering up a death... Maybe even a murder?"

"I-"

"- You want to help, do you not?"

I sigh and shrug. Things were easier when I saw people as less than what they are. It's hard to capture the fullness of a person in an instant. Their past and future shot to death by their present until you get to know them. I only had people in passing until this one passed away.

After hearing their stories and ambitions, their lives, people grow on you. The same might be said for Daniel. It's hard to ignore his existence after rooting through his things.

Maybe it's time to start seeing people as people? Address that there is the weight of a lifetime behind them. A commonality to us. That I don't need to keep my distance from them in case they end up hurting me like so many others have. That we're all just folk...

"I'll help you confront her..." I submit.

"Then let's go!"

Daniel's wife looks angry when she sees us. Bee's crossed arms carry a baby monitor and I have my hands shoved on my pockets, one hand on my flashlight. After Bee explains that we have a few questions about Daniel, the old woman's face turns sad, then hurt, before she gazes back at us with brimming eyes.

"It's not what you think... You should come in..."

****

"Daniel had a heart attack... It was very sudden... I still- I still haven't come to terms with the fact that he's gone. I haven't even told our children. But he's buried. I even visited the grave today. I can't believe he's there... That that is what he is now..." Daniel's wife, who I now know to be named Priscilla, tells us. The man, formerly known as Daniel has taken to the bedroom and is hiding there.

"Tell me about the shoes?" I ask. "They're strewn everywhere."

"The shoes? Oh, yes!" She laughs. "Herbert's feet are slightly bigger than Daniel's."

"Herbert is the other man?"

"His twin brother... I was at a loss. Devastated by Daniel's death and Herbert stayed to comfort me... I know he's always had feelings for me..."

Priscilla breaks down into tears. The poor woman... In her denial over Daniel's death, she desperately tried to replace him, to ease her pain. A man is not easy to replace and the emptiness of one is hard to fill. Like throwing a handful of soil into a six foot hole. Bee hands Priscilla a tissue and the old lady composes herself.

Bee takes Priscilla's hand and looks at her earnestly. "I'm very sorry for your loss. Daniel was a good man and we will miss him deeply... If you need anything, I'm just next door." Paying her respect, as life has a cost.

Priscilla nods back at her gratefully. "His favourite were Tropaeolums you know? What am I supposed to do with that fact now?"

None of us have an answer for her.

The baby monitor beckons Bee back to her apartment. New life calling. I walk out with Bee as we leave Priscilla to her grief. No crime seems to have been committed and their bizarre arrangement seems to suit both dwellers of the apartment well enough for the moment. If that changes then I'm sure Bee would rise to help.

It's hard to tell if Herbert is taking advantage of Priscilla's grief or if Priscilla is taking advantage of Herbert. I suppose I may never know. I do have one question remaining though.

"One thing didn't make sense to me." I tell Bee.

"What?"

"Inside the fridge, there was a sticker that said: *No Eggs*... Why?"

"Oh, it was to remind the maid when they did the shopping... Daniel was allergic to eggs."

 I keep my embarrassment and my frustration to myself. I could have marked the man as an imposter on the first night had I followed up on that. Instead, I dragged the whole thing out. Digging, when the truth was waving itself at me on the balcony.

 I bid my farewell to Bee and Rose. She thanks me for my help and I begin my wandering walk back to the hostel that I'm staying in, reflecting on the way.

 I know that a person is only whoever they are in the moment. That in the grand scheme of things you are always only ever in the present and it is the present that defines you as you are. But that man wasn't Daniel, even with the shared DNA. He didn't have his past, his potential future. He didn't have Priscilla's love. With very little distinction physically between Herbert and Daniel, the only difference was their identity.

 A name, it seems, is a powerful thing for people to help them identify themselves and others. Something given to them out of the love of their parents like Bee gave to Rose. So maybe it's time I stop giving people names and start letting them give me theirs?

 My colleagues for a start.

 Who else?

 Mouse's name hasn't gotten me any closer to finding her, but maybe I could if I knew *who* she is. All I can gather about her is through stories and images. I know by now that an idea of a person is never the same as the person themselves. We change ourselves around our situation, when we're alone or with people. Only ever capable of showing one side of ourselves at a time as it's illuminated under the light. It is, indeed, a truly messy and mysterious affair to ask yourself about a person's identity. Who they really are...

I'm not sure I even know who I am...

There are people creeping into my life again. Good people who are starting to grow closer to me. I've been a wallflower for a while now and, even though I have no one to hurt me, I have no one to make me happy either...

I should let them in. Touch my heart and feel the light again. Plant seeds of friendship with them and reap the rewards while they are here. Nothing in this world lasts forever. Seasons change. The winds rise and fall. There is a birth and death of everything...

But the most beautiful things can grow in-between and blossom throughout the ages...

Case 11 – Little Green Men

Leopard introduces himself as Dylan to the rest of the staff. It's the first time I'm learning his name, despite our conversations through texts. He seems to get on particularly well with Amae, who I've always referred to as Songbird in my head. Crow creaks down the stairs to get us all to work and show Dylan that he's in charge of us.

"He's got us born in misery..." Fox, or Tom rather, says as the crew scatters and we all set about our various tasks.

I start by training Dylan to be a night porter.

"Is the boss always like this?" Dylan asks.

"Usually... He has his good days, though they're few and far between."

"You weren't kidding then?"

I pull a mock serious face and say to him "I never kid..."

"Any chance we'll ever be working together?"

"Not really. It's a lonely job. But... the way this place is headed, we might be looking for work together soon."

"Dare I inquire, is it really that bad?"

"Maybe not yet, but it's getting there."

"Yikes!"

"Ehm... You will be working with other people every now and then though, Son-Ehm- Amae often swings down to do some cleaning."

"Oh, that's not so bad! I won't die of boredom."

"Trust me, with *him* around, there's never any risk of that."

I show him the various things he needs to know on the

computer, what to say when answering the phone, the common answers to the common questions, and a few other things I thought to throw in. It's a new experience for him and I can tell that he's a little bit nervous so I try to be reassuring about everything. You see, when you work in the service industry, the most important thing is consideration. Consideration for the customer, for your co-workers, for your boss. You want to make their lives easier and they will often, although not always, do the same in return. It's not so incomprehensible a thought.

I'm showing him where we keep the spare keys when a grungy, young man opens the door and walks gingerly towards our desk.

"Which... Uh... Is one of you the private detective?"

Dylan glances over to me with an expression of bemusement mixed with expectation. I'm surprised to see strangers actually coming into the hotel looking for me now and I'm a bit uncomfortable having witnesses to it. If Crow found out he'd be furious.

Word must be spreading. It's out of my control now, as the stories about me go further out of reach. The result of these tales and rumours has given me a pretty unwelcome visitor.

"I'm not a private detective-"

"- But you investigate things for people who don't want to go to the police, right?"

"I-"

"- He does!" Dylan chips in, enjoying himself.

"My friend, he's gone missing. He's not picking up the phone. I've asked around and no one has seen him."

"When was the last time you heard from him?" I ask.

"About three weeks ago? He called me to hang out with him."

"You're sure he's not just on holiday or out of town?"

"He'd tell me if he was... We're friends..."

I feel a dig in my side from Dylan. He's obviously nudging me to look into it. Is this what I've become? An unlicensed, and amateur, private detective?

"Why don't you want to go to the police?" I ask.

"I... Well, it might be nothing, you see?"

"Okay..." I sigh. "I'll look into it."

A smile tears across the visitors face. This *is* getting out of hand, though. At some point I need to get my life together, or at least in focus.

I decide, for the first time in a very long time, to ask the simplest of questions. Maybe it's just to regain control, or maybe it's an effort to reach out into the unknown.

"What's your name?" I ask.

"François." He tells me.

****

François and I organise a meeting for tomorrow after work. I'm to visit the apartment and look for clues to his friend's disappearance. Our shift ends early at three in the morning as Crow comes down and offers to cover the rest of our hours. I'm sure he's only trying to win Dylan over early, knowing that the rest of the staff dislike Crow too much already. Even so, I'm grateful for it. I grab a taxi back to my hostel to catch up on some well-deserved sleep.

I check into my room to find a bleary eyed man coming out of the toilet to the left of the bunk-beds. I give him a nod and a hello which is the universal sign in hostels for: *I don't know you or want to know you but please don't steal any of my things or cut my throat as I sleep.* He gives me the nod back and climbs into the bottom bunk. I take off my pants and leave them at the end of the bed on the top bunk before awkwardly ascending the hard, steel ladder in my bare feet.

I close my eyes and try to force myself into a slumber, but that never works. I lie there for about twenty minutes silently, moving as little as possible to avoid annoying my bunk-mate, then I hear a whirring sound beneath me. A dim glow emanates from the bottom of the bunk. He must be on his laptop. Another minute passes before the bunk-bed starts shaking. I'm perplexed for a moment until it dawns on me. It's no quake, just a quickie.

He masturbates furiously to the images of porn beneath him. I can tell it's images because he interrupts his self-interference to click on the laptop, sometimes two or three times if he doesn't find something that does it for him.

Click, shake, shake, shake, click, click, shake, shake, shake. He rocks the bed for fifteen minutes as I lay above him feeling slightly violated. There's no lullaby to accompany this. As the sound of cheap steel squeaking in strain ceases, his snoring rises.

I paid money to sleep here and it seems I wasted it. What's worse is that, in a week or two, I won't be able to afford it anymore. I don't know what I'm going to do. With this on my mind and the dirty feeling lingering from my bunk-mate, it doesn't seem like I'll get much rest. I suppose it doesn't matter to someone like me.

I don't sleep much anyway.

****

I'm woken to the sound of Italian folk-rock music blaring from another room an hour before they kick us out. With my bunk-mate still snoozing and the opportunity open to leave without looking him in the eye, I slip into my clothes and leave. This is one of the many excursions I've had into the day-time lately, having been forced out of my bed by the hostel. I spend most of it in an internet café, looking for an apartment and, if I treat myself, watching a TV show, ever hiding from the new summer sun.

Very few people have replied to my emails and those that did, that weren't scams, made unreasonable demands. It is especially difficult and arduous to find an apartment in Paris. Most require that you must earn three times the rent. This makes it impossible to live in the city if you earn minimum wage. They also ask for a deposit which, during the winter months, can be three months rent. They do this as it's illegal to kick people out of their homes during the colder months, to avoid deaths from exposure. People take advantage by refusing to pay these months and move out at the end of winter, three months rent richer for their next apartment. The result of this has made many landlords paranoid. Others ask for bank statements, identification, work contracts and pay slips. The last thing they might ask from you is a guarantor, whose responsibility is to pay your rent should you be incapable. They cannot, however, live abroad as it makes things difficult should the landlord have to hunt them down.

Yes, as a foreigner, I give landlords butterflies in their stomachs. They're always terrified that our culture or character, whatever it may be, is to swindle or thieve. That we'll take off, without a moments notice, back to our home countries. That our restless feet make us troublesome.

I have two open house viewings so that's what I'll spend the rest of my day doing in between hyperventilating. You don't realise how much you need a home until you don't have one. And to think I ran away from mine all that time ago...

My parents were arguing a lot back then and even though I wasn't bullied at school, it wouldn't be fair to say that to the people who actually were, I wasn't the most popular kid. I was having a hard time dealing with my situation. There's not many places left to go in a teenager's life in-between school and home. And so I ran.

After getting caught and sent back, I escaped them in a different way. I put up walls and kept my distance from my parents the best I could. I let things get cold and numb inside. Sterile. Broke myself away from the feelings that you get in a broken home. It probably helped when they eventually got divorced.

I know that the only thing my parents were guilty of was simply being human. It's just jarring at that age to see parents become people.

****

Back in work, I scour the internet for apartments. The open

viewings both attracted fifteen other people each, all of them interested and eager. I don't know why it always seems to be exactly fifteen people, but it does.

Meanwhile, I keep spending money on sandwiches and drinks in cafés. Mostly because I don't have a kitchen but also simply to stay off my feet. It's difficult to bake in the sun all day when it's forced upon you. With all my money going towards snacks and nights in hostels adding up, it seems that being homeless is quite expensive. I only really have a two week window each month to find an apartment before I can't afford one. I know I could ask my parents for help, and they would help me, but I can't bring myself to rely on them.

My shift is rather uneventful. Dylan arrives at nine o'clock to replace me. He seems quite nervous now that he's on his own. I try to reassure him by convincing him that common sense will get you out of trouble and that it's not as mysterious or daunting as a new job can often be.

"It's not rocket science, just solitude!" I say to him with a smile as I leave.

A taxi ferries me to the Marais quarter. It's one of the nicest and most affluent areas of the city. Trendy bars and art galleries mixed with elegant architecture. Both the Gay and Jewish quarter, the streets always seem cleaner here than everywhere else, perhaps because it's more pedestrianised. Strange, considering its name translates to "The Marsh".

I arrive outside the address that François gave me. The apartment building is brilliantly white and stands above a chic vintage-clothing shop. The smell of falafel lingers in the air as I find my outsider hanging his head over the balcony.

"Wait! I'll drop down the keys!" He shouts down.

It's an uncommon sight in Paris, but this door doesn't seem to have a Digipad to open the door, just a lock and key system. A sparkling, bright circle hovers above me and erratically descends down slowly. I reach out and catch the key that François attached to a shopping bag as a cheap parachute. Six flights of stairs and one break to catch my breath later, I push open the door left ajar for me.

The apartment is spacious, luxurious even. An open living room comprised of only a couch, a coffee table, a large flatscreen television fixed to the wall and a table with a desktop computer in the corner. It's almost as though the less furniture present, the more modern the place is. The television is flanked by two doors that lead to the balcony which holds a single deck chair and a stout telescope. Off to the side, the kitchen is separated from the living room only by the wooden floor becoming ceramic tile. The bedroom features a king-size bed, two nightstands and a walk-in closet. This guy was living large.

I keep my hands in my pockets just in case this develops into anything more serious. Looking around, I find his phone, wallet and keys on the bedside stand. In his closet, I find three more phones, all of them are broken and won't turn on. They're old models anyway, he probably just upgraded and forgot to throw them out.

I grab two plastic bags to use as gloves and start going through the kitchen. The fridge and cabinets are full of food. The closet in his room are full of clothes. There doesn't seem to be any evidence of anything missing or of a struggle taking place in the apartment.

Few people leave their house without their phone or wallet and even less forget their keys. There's a chance he locked himself out by accident and sought refuge at a friend's place, although hardly for three weeks or without contacting François.

"I have a spare key. Miguel, my missing friend, gave it to me." François explains. "But there's only these two I think..."

I amble back into the living room, over to the computer that's been left on. I push the anxious voices in the back of my head away and start rooting through the emails. The third email stands out to me straight away, it's dated from today. The address of the sender appears to be a mess of garbled letters. The email itself, even stranger. Four sentences comprised of only strange symbols and characters, unknown to me. The message is undecipherable. The encryption requiring a password to crack.

I scan through the other emails, mostly subscription letters from various sites, until I find another encrypted email, dated a month before it, the first of April. I discover that they come once a month, on the first day of every month, for a year, without fail. The sender's address being different gibberish letters all the time, but the email service is the same. Every one is four enigmatic lines long.

One of the emails, from last month, is different to the others. It's encrypted like the one before it, only this one has two lines. The address is also randomised letters and numbers but it's from a different email service.

"What the hell is that?" François asks, leaning over my shoulder.

"I don't know..."

"That's crazy... It's like alien writing..."

"It's an encryption software."

"Yeah, like *alien* encryption."

"It's *not* alien."

"What, you don't believe in aliens?"

"No- Well- I don't know?! I just don't believe aliens abducted your friend!"

"Well... Just don't rule it out, okay?"

"Are you serious?"

"You're sceptical? The universe is infinitely large, man. We might, *maybe*, be the only life in the galaxy, but the whole universe?! *That's* crazy. If you think we're alone in this universe, you're wrong, man."

Judging by his slow speech, I assume that this guy likes to blaze. Although, perhaps he's right? Maybe there are other life forms out there? But other beings or people don't solve the problem of being alone. Sometimes it even makes it worse.

Loneliness isn't uncommon on earth, never mind the rest of the universe. I know because I've been lonely for a very long time now. I'm reaching a point where I'm getting tired of it. Hiding in a different dimension to everyone else. Drifting through empty space...

"I'd still like to find something I can follow up on." I tell him as he shrugs back at me.

To the left of the desk is a small bin. Rummaging through the litter, I find a clear bag full of small, green, toy soldiers. Maybe these are the little green men that François was talking about? Although an unusual sight in a grown man's apartment, there's nothing special about them. I examine them briefly before chucking them back in the bin. Aside from that I only find candy wrappers, shreds of paper and a crumpled note that reads: *9/04 10:15*. All in all, useless information.

The encrypted emails and cryptic notes are unsettling. There's absolutely no clue as to where or why Miguel disappeared. It's almost like he vanished into thin air. I tell François as much.

"But you'll keep looking, yes?"

"I'll come back and look again. In the meantime, you search this place while I'm away. Try and figure out the password to the encryption too."

"Okay. Keep his set of keys in case I'm busy."

I arrive at my hostel and clamber into bed. I'm lucky this time, no one checked into my room and I have my own space, even if it is as finite as this. As much as I hate loneliness, I need its peace just as much every now and then. An empty room to spill my thoughts into.

And maybe these moments that I spend with myself, I'm not so alone.

****

My day is once more spent travelling back and forth from the furthest ends of Paris to look at homes. I used to give each of them a detailed study. Checking for an electric shower, a heater, a comfortable bed and a Wi-Fi connection. Now, at this excruciating point, I'd take a shed with a hammock if it was cheap enough. There's the group of fifteen people again, maybe even the *same* fifteen people if I ever looked at them properly. One of them gets the apartment because they're better financed, better recommended or, simply, better liked than me.

I get a text from Amae offering to head out after she finishes work and, in desperate need of a drink, I accept.

We meet up outside the hotel five minutes after Amae's shift ended, as she had to change out of her uniform, when Dylan comes out for a chat.

"Ye going out, then?" He asks.

"Yup! You can join us when you're done if you want?" Amae offers.

"I finish at two though."

"It'll be grand, sure. You'll catch up!"

"I might... Do you mind if I invite some friends?"

"Sure!"

Amae and I head off to Cole's pub. We're later joined by Matt, the cyclist formerly known as Dog, and his girlfriend Marine, who I called Doe.

We drink for about two hours when Dylan shows up at ten past midnight. Crow let him off early again. He must be really trying hard to win him over.

"My friends should be here soon. Charlie is just picking up Leah from the bar she works in." He tells us.

It's funny to be part of this group. I've tried distancing myself from them but found myself inching towards them. I would have thought my cold shoulder and silence would have signalled to them that I wasn't interested in friendship, but they persisted. In this moment, I'm grateful for it. I need the distraction. People to take my mind far away from the problems that fester there. I like these people because, when I'm with them, I'm not really here.

We talk a little about work because it's a common language for all of us. We've developed a trench mentality where it's the guests giving us grief on one side and our boss giving us grief on the other. Camaraderie is a unique feeling.

Eventually we venture in to more personal stories about ourselves. I stay silent for most of these, although I'm entertained by listening to theirs. I open up a little and tell them about my college days. Self-deprecating tales of drinking before going drinking and the various antics that would follow.

"Here they are now! Charlie and Leah!" Dylan announces. To my surprise, I see Wolf and Chick walking towards us.

Leah, the barmaid of the Scottish bar I once frequented, gives me a quizzical look before Dylan moves in to introduce them. He starts with Amae and goes around the group until he gets to me.

"We've actually met before!" Leah says.

"Yeah?" Dylan asks.

"He popped in when we had that stalker incident. He was the one that pointed it out."

"Oh, right..." Dylan gives me a knowing look.

I'd be worried that he'd tell everyone about the episodes I've gotten into in Paris, but I trust Dylan's discretion. He doesn't seem like the type of person to risk embarrassing me for idle conversation.

Leah turns back to me and says "We haven't seen you since. You should come back sometime! There's a free drink in it for you!"

In my hesitation, Matt chips in, to my ultimate gratitude.

"That's probably my fault. I went on holiday for a bit and he had to cover for me. Then, I quit pretty suddenly and he was working crazy hours after that. The bossman took ages hiring someone else."

"And then they hired Dylan?"

"Exactly."

We all get comfortable as Matt, Marine, Amae and Dylan bring the new arrivals into the group. They have an inclusive way of talking and they're fearless in jumping right into a conversation. I've always been nervous that I'd say the wrong thing, but they create a safe space for me to drop in. A disagreement doesn't lead to dislike, just debate. An exploration of people. We're all friends here. I'm no longer on the outside looking in, and the thought of having friends in my life isn't so alien to me anymore.

We find another bar after our local closed. We'll probably only get another two hours of drinking in, but it's enough. Dylan and Leah strike up the most marvellously intelligent conversations. Matt and Marine, in their endearing ridiculousness, are a wealth of laughter. Amae and Charlie are incredibly sweet, yet still have a dry humour that comes unexpectedly.

I stumble back from the bathroom when I overhear my name being mentioned as Marine talks to Amae.

"He's a lovely guy! He should have been hanging out with us properly months ago... But I'd say he's a bit shy, is he?"

"Yeah... I think he's finally coming out of his shell."

I hang back for a few seconds before stomping up the stairs. I'm not mad at them, I'm just giving them a warning so we can resume our other conversations. A non-verbal communication on my part, unknown to them.

We decide to go to a place that's open twenty-four hours to end our night out with a bang. We're a miracle of messy co-ordination, with no one quite sure what's going on or if we're walking in the right direction, but the group is intact. I linger in the back chatting to Charlie. He's altogether a very nice guy. Moral, but not righteous. Handsome, and his body could only be fabricated in a gym, but there's not a single ounce of arrogance in him.

"I don't really go out too much." I tell him.

"Sometimes that's nice, mate. Stay in, play some video games, you know? Shooting zombies helps when you have to deal with drunken twats all the time."

"I don't have a console though."

"Mate, get a console. Save up, buy one, we'll play together online. Or you can always come over to mine sometime, if you'd like? I have some two player games."

"Yeah, I mean-"

"- Watch out, mate! We gotta run quick!"

Charlie sprints ahead as the early morning traffic cuts me off from everyone else. I squint through the buses and cars flying past to see the group still there. The little man in the traffic-light box holding an angry, red hue.

"C'mon!" Marine calls out. "We're waiting for you!"

I look at them in a moment of sober clarity. Some of them stare back at me smiling, others engaged in their own conversation. Odd and inexplicable as it is, I feel loved. And I welcome it.

The little man in the box turns green.

With my heart lighter than it has been in months, I cross the street, over the black and white void, to join them.

****

My head is pounding. I remember stumbling back to Miguel's apartment in the hopes of crashing at his place. It was an empty apartment and, being homeless, it seemed like a good idea. I got as far as the bedroom when my nerve ran out. There was too much unknown about what happened there and whether or not Miguel would come back for me to sleep comfortably. I didn't want to wake up with any nasty surprises, so I ended up paying a small fortune to sleep in a nice, budget hotel for the day.

The alarms on my phone and the strange location were enough to hoist me out of bed. I ran to work after calling the hostel I was originally supposed to stay in and asked them if they could hold on to my things for me for another day.

"Ugh. I am dying!" Amae moans.

"I know... I've been banging my head on the desk to try and lose consciousness so I don't feel this anymore."

"Why isn't it working?"

"I have a thick skull, it seems."

"Well... Keep trying!" She laughs "Ah no, I'm only messing with ya. Here, I have some paracetamol for you."

I swallow the small, white pill and, even though it doesn't really do anything to numb the pain, I'm grateful for the company. Misery loves it and, oh, how miserable we are.

I suffer through the shift until Dylan arrives, slightly fresher than the rest of us but still bedraggled. After grabbing some latex gloves out of the cleaning closet, I venture back to the Marais to take another look at the apartment. François arrives and takes a peek through the closet.

"I still haven't found anything." He states glumly.

"Maybe it's time to call the police?"

"No, we can't!"

"Why not? It's not like he's a drug dealer or anything."

"No, he's not a drug *dealer*."

"Why did you say it like that?"

"Like what?"

"You said drug *dealer*."

"I said drug dealer."

"François?"

"Bah, okay! He may... distribute... drugs."

"He's a drug distributor?!"

"It was hard for him to find a legal job here!"

"Why?"

"He's from Chile. He came here on a holiday visa and decided to stay just a bit longer."

"So, he's also an illegal immigrant?!"

"Kind of..."

"You should have told me this at the start!"

"I wasn't sure you'd look for him if I did!"

"That wasn't your decision to make!"

"You have a point... I'm sorry! I know it sounds bad but he's a good guy! He just took this job to get by. He didn't have much of a choice."

"Looks like he got by pretty well!" I argue, pointing around the apartment before continuing "He could also have just come back and done it the right way. Gotten a visa."

"I know. I agree... But he's my friend. I'm scared something bad has happened to him. Can you help me find him, please?"

I sigh and reluctantly resume my search. A dark thought enters my mind as I search the bathroom again. There's a chance, just a chance, that I might be looking for a body rather than a man. He was involved with drugs after all.

From top to bottom, I search the apartment. I haven't even found the shaving of a finger nail. There is absolutely no trace of him. No clues to his disappearance either. I need to start thinking outside the box.

I return to the bag of toy soldiers. There must be some significance to them. It's too odd a thing to overlook.

"Could it be some kind of new synthetic drug?" I ask François.

"I have no idea... Maybe?"

"Let's find out then."

I pluck one out of the bag, lick my thumb and rub it. It seems to just be plastic. Maybe there's something hidden inside? The plastic is too hard to break apart. I'll have to melt it.

I stick the mini-man into the microwave and set the timer for two minutes at its highest setting. François leans over my shoulder as we peer in expectantly through the glass on the door.

The soldier slowly melts and bubbles. The foul smell of burning plastic confirms that it's just a toy. There's nothing hidden inside the green puddle.

"That was fun." François shrugs.

"Didn't help us much..."

It was pretty fun though.

"Did you figure out the password to the encryption?" I ask.

"I wrote up a list. I was waiting for you."

"Let's give that a try then."

We go through half the list until one finally works.

"Pulsar?"

"He liked astronomy. It's why we became such good friends. Apparently, there's some great star gazing in Chile."

The emails reveal themselves as the decryption software turns the strange symbols into letters. The four sentences read "Bid on the toy soldiers from the usual account. Eight thousand Euros to receive product. Pick up at usual place on the 8th. Don't be late."

So, the toy soldiers were only a method of paying for the drugs discreetly. Seems clever enough. An inexpensive product, bought online at an unreasonable price. Money changes hands openly, it's purpose already assumed. They might even be paying taxes on it.

The other mysterious email from the month before, being only two lines long, reads "Forty thousand, agreed. Evening of April 8th."

I turn to François and ask him "What was Miguel's plan in the long run?"

"No idea."

"It looks like he might have sold his product on to another distributor for five times the value."

"That's good!"

"That can be dangerous! The dealers he usually supplies are probably looking for him!" I can't tell him this but it's starting to look like this deal went bad.

"Don't worry! He's always been careful. I don't think any of the dealers know how to find him."

"Either do we though..."

Light is pouring in through the window. Day is starting earlier and earlier now that the summer is here.

"I'm going to go and get some sleep. I'll work on this tomorrow, okay?" I tell him.

François, probably just grateful that I'm still helping him, nods his head and leaves with me.

Back at the hostel, I run through the various scenarios in my mind. I've uncovered most of the oddities that I've found, but still none for his disappearance. Now that I think of it, I never found out what the time and date on the piece of paper meant. His dealings were organised for the day before. I fall asleep, exhaustedly mulling it over.

****

My sleep is tortured with nightmares. In them, I'm being chased and I keep running, looking for a safe place, but there's nowhere safe. No walls or roof.

As I wake up, red eyed and fatigued, I ask myself what I was running from? I'm not sure exactly, I just somehow knew it was something dangerous chasing me. Dreams are like that. It's common to run from danger. I wonder, in Miguel's trade, why he never did?

Suddenly it hits me. I never found a passport. He would have had to have one coming from Chile. The crumpled note gives me an idea. I quickly search the internet on my smartphone for flights from Paris at the date and time written down. Sure enough, there was a flight to Santiago at exactly 10:15am on April 9th. He must have paid cash to avoid a trail. I guess he's gone back to where he came from.

I grab my things and rush over to the apartment, hoping to find François. Instead, I find the door kicked in, the place is ransacked, the computer gone. The sight of the apartment puts me in a mild state of shock. My ears are ringing. I can feel the blood drain out of my face. A tingling sensation comes over my skin. I could have been there when this happened...

I hear someone coming up the stairs. Panicking, I hide around the corner. Peeking out, I recognise François. I startle him when I call out his name.

"Thank God, it's just you! What happened?!" He asks.

"I don't know. I reckon his suppliers came looking for him. It's the fourth of May and he's late. I don't think he gave them a letter of resignation before he quit."

"Holy cow... If we were here..."

"Yeah..."

"I- Uh... Found a postcard today... It's from Miguel."

I take a look at it. It reads: *I'm going star gazing and I probably won't see you again. Thanks for the memories, my friend. Sorry I didn't get to give you a proper goodbye.*

That must have been why he called François to hang out, to enjoy his company one last time. I did the same before I ran away from home. I stayed up late with my mother, watching television. A quiet goodbye.

I look at the stamp and the date of the postcard. It's dated April 9th from Charles de Gaulle airport.

"When did you get this?"

"I don't know. I don't really check my mailbox anymore. It's always just bills."

"That's fine..." I sigh.

"Well, I guess we know he's okay!"

"Yeah, he'll probably be safer over there."

I guess it's impossible to disappear completely. Careful as he was, Miguel still left the tiniest of clues. I'm annoyed at myself now. I found Miguel even though he did his best, but I still can't find Mouse. I'll need to double my efforts to find her.

My hands are still shaking as I leave François at the door of the wrecked apartment. It's scary to think I had such a close encounter with real danger. Miguel was right to run.

I'm sure the money was good, but he should never have put himself in that position. He might have to look over his shoulder for the rest of his life as a result. It's dangerous out there, on the fringe of society. Maybe it's a sign for me to moderate who I keep in my life? Choose a bit more carefully that I find people who will only bring good things to me. I think I'm doing well so far.

I've discovered that completely alienating myself from people hasn't helped me much. Miguel left everyone behind, just like I did once. To see it from the outside is something different. To meet the abandoned. The care and concern that Miguel never got to see with his back turned. He never allowed himself that.

Did people try to reach out to me, I wonder? I know I didn't make it easy nor make an effort to contact them first. A lot goes on which we can't see. Knowing this, I might have made a few wrong assumptions in my life.

The friends I had, I abandoned them even before they left Paris because I wasn't happy with my life. I figured if they weren't going to make it better, why have them? And maybe they were concerned about me after Cat left me, maybe they wanted me to be happy? But maybe I didn't care...

I should care...

I return to the youth hostel. They've finished cleaning and I'm allowed to go back into my room. I'm alone again. This time it sinks in deeper within me. The absence of comfort in familiar faces.

I let my imagination distract me from the loneliness. Off in my own little world. The world I used to share with Cat...

The last week of May, she was in my apartment. Rooting through the place, we found some of my landlady's medical equipment. I pulled out a stethoscope and listened to her heart.

"Ooh, you wanna play doctor, honey?" She asked sweetly.

"Only if you let me give you a physical."

"Shut up, you pervert!" She giggled as she punched my arm.

"You are going to have to take off all your clothes though."

"Why is that?"

"Don't ask questions! Just trust me, I'm a doctor!"

Kissing me, she asked "Then why do you taste like a cigarette?"

With a husky voice, I replied "Because I'm also a cigarette!"

"Pfft! You're nuts... Doctor Cigarette, huh? Well, let me listen to your heartbeat, if you have one?!"

She listened to it and said it was beating pretty fast. It always did around her. I wish I could tense that muscle in my heart. Move that piece of me that makes me love so I could choose the ones who are good to me. But it doesn't work like that. It's never me moving the pieces...

She cooked dinner while I played the guitar and serenaded her. Us, isolated from everyone for the whole day. Self-sufficient in our little space as we climbed into bed.

Just before going to sleep, we started talking about what kind of animal we would be if we were one.

"You're definitely a Cat."

"Well, that's original!" She said sarcastically. "Why am I a Cat?"

I know it was because I found her selfish at times. Cold, even. She only ever accepted affection when she wanted it and was meagre in giving it back, but I didn't want to offend her by telling her this.

"I don't know... You have that kind of Cat-ness to you."

"Are you calling me catty?!"

"No!"

"Hmm... Well, babe... You'd be an owl, I think... Because you have bushy eyebrows..."

As we drifted off to sleep, I thought it was wonderful that I could have such a strange conversation with someone so comfortably. It was a sweet and soft lullaby for me. So, I thought about this in the dark and we were in bed and she was curled up on me and I had everything I'd ever wanted...

And that was the moment when I realised I loved her...

Case 12 – Anchorage

These days keep dragging on and I'm no closer to finding an apartment. My money has run out and I don't have anywhere to stay tonight. I need to talk to Crow about getting an advance on my pay this month. If I don't, then I'll be out on the streets for the next week. For the moment, he isn't here. Hopefully he'll come to the hotel soon enough.

"How's you?" Amae asks.

"Yeah, I'm fine!" I give her a reassuring smile. She probably saw the worried look on my face.

"Coming out tonight?"

"Maybe not... I have a few things to sort out."

"Is everything alright?"

"It will be soon enough, hopefully."

"Okay, well, if you ever need anything, I hope you know you only have to ask? We take care of each other here."

"Thanks... I will."

I know I could tell her that I have nowhere to stay. It's my pride that keeps these revelations from her. I don't like accepting help from people. It's a trust issue that I have. There's also a nagging doubt in my head that says people would look down on me. I guess I'm more worried about being in someone's pocket than I am about being in the gutter.

I can't help but think that it's my own fault that I can't find an apartment. I should have started looking sooner, my excuse being that no one looks for a tenant before they're supposed to move in.

Amae returns to her chores of cleaning the foyer. Her visits are becoming more frequent these days, her quota of rooms to clean being met before her shift ends. We're not as busy as we should be at this time of year. It's the beginning of the tourist season and hotels across the city are packed tight with people.

  Crow brushes past her as he walks in the door.

"Good evening. 'Ow are you?" He asks me.

"I'm fine, sir... Well, actually, I was hoping to talk to you about something."

His eyes turn dark. "Tawk abowet what?"

"Well, I'm looking for an apartment and I might need an advance on my pay."

"Yower looking for an apartaymawnt?"

"Yes, and I could do with being paid early."

"Why not ask zem to let you pay after you 'ave moved in?"

"I don't think it works like that, sir-"

"- Oh! So zey don't let you move in before you pay, but 'ere we pay you before you work, zat's eet?"

"I'm going to work the hours I've been given. I always work the hours I'm given!"

"You will be paid wen you are alwayz paid."

"I just need-"

"- No!"

  I can feel the pressure building inside me, like hot steam coming out of tiny cracks that you can't seem to keep closed shut. My mind is in a somersault. Half of me is furious and the other half is scared I might get myself fired. I've put up with his micro-managing misery, worked as hard as I can, and the total lack of respect I've gotten in return is maddening. I can't hold this in anymore.

"I've been working my ass off for months here! Non-stop sweeping, mopping, wiping windows and a multitude of other fucking things, and you won't give me a fucking advance on my pay?!"

Crow turns his nose up calmly. "If you don't like eet, leave-uh."

Before I can react, he spins around and saunters up the stairs. My hands are trembling fiercely and I can hear my own heartbeat. In my head I project images of me beating him on the floor. I clench my fists, pacing back and forth behind the counter. All I want to do is hit something. In an effort to release some of this anger, I pinch one of my knuckles. The pain is enough to distract me for a moment.

"What was that about?" Amae asks.

"That fucking bastard won't give me an advance on my pay!"

"Shite!"

"I felt like killing him..."

"I don't blame you... If you're stuck for cash, you can always ask me, like? How much do you need?"

"A months rent?"

"Maybe I can't help you there... Sorry... I can give you a loan of fifty Euro or something to get you through the week?"

"I'll be okay... Thanks, Amae..."

Through the anger, I check a guest out and Amae potters off to clean their room. Solitude doesn't do right by me when I'm in a bad mood. I work myself up. Anger turns to fury before subsiding to depression. It's a sadness that only gets deeper the more I explore it, and all I have left is time to do exactly that.

I grab my coat at the end of my shift and mumble some greeting to Dylan. I stare at the door, shake my head and sigh. Just before I move forward, Dylan puts his hand on my arm.

"Hey-"

"- I'll be grand." I tell him.

And so begins my night on the street.

****

I left my belongings at work and descended down into the metro. I figured it's warm down here and probably safer than the streets. Ambling down the tracks, I find a vent that provides a bit of warmth, making the hard ground a little more comfortable.

I take my phone and wallet out of my pockets and stuff them into an inside pocket in my jacket. It's a strange sensation to root through your pockets and not find a set of keys. Their delicate weight was a comfort, looking back. How a fixed address can give you peace. A focal point you can revolve your life around. A base. Without one, you're adrift and exposed.

I lie there for forty-five minutes before I give up. The announcements blaring out of the speakers and the thunderous rolling of the trains are too loud for me. Feeling as vulnerable as I do right now, the sounds are anxiety-inducing. The bright, fluorescent lights seep through my eyelids, scolding my circadian rhythm.

I get on a train and try to fall asleep on one of the seats, with my head propped on a little alcove between the carriages, but I fail at that too. I can't get comfortable enough physically or mentally to sleep here.

I idly glance at the next stop to find that it'll drop me off by Pont Neuf. I've heard that there are communities of homeless people that sleep under bridges and in parks, so I decide to get off here to look for a safe place to sleep. I skirt around a metro performers slightly-racist puppet show and return to the surface.

Crossing over the bridge, I see the place where I sat with friends. It was just before Cat uprooted herself to go back home. Her last night out in Paris. There was rainfall. We found some shelter on Île-de-Saint-Louis, under a canopy. She was delicate that night. Paris was a home to her in many different ways. I was eager to give her a night worth remembering.

I played the guitar with some friends who were there. As I sang, she looked at me with pure adoration. Her eyes centred on me, ignoring everything else. It's one of my best memories of her, wearing a stupid, plastic poncho and a sweet smile on her pretty face. I was so sure of us then. It was the last good moment in our relationship, where it was happily afloat and at full sail. The last night we'd be standing beside each other, linked together.

I think about sleeping in a garden nearby, but there seems to be dubious individuals lurking in the shadows so I decide to wander further down. I trudge along the river, tired and depressed, feeling the sweat-mottled socks cling to my feet. I've hit rock-bottom again.

My current predicament definitely isn't going to help my depressive issues. I'm stagnating in my immobility. I need to work my way out of this. Get unstuck. Rise up from this depth back to where I can breathe again.

I'm starting to realise that I have more power over my sadness than it does over me, but I've changed nothing. Life like a weight on my ankle, dragging me down, into the deepest of blues. I'm conditioned to view the world as *la vie en grise* ever since I was a teenager. I couldn't talk to my parents about it, they were part of the problem and, even if they weren't, they were often busy with work. As a result, I was raised on a television screen. This had its advantages and disadvantages. I learned what was good and right by popular, albeit fantastic, consensus. But, it led me to unrealistic expectations in life. That things would work out. I didn't want to face reality.

Part of me still doesn't...

My scanning eyes give me no reward for a place to sleep. I start to build walls in my head. Not those that shelter, but the kind of walls that keep you out. I see places I can't enter due to either futility or risk. There's nowhere accessible to me that isn't accessible to anyone else.

At Quai de Jussieu, I find a park. It seems like the perfect place to find shelter at first, but the closer I get, the louder the noise. Throngs of people sit along the river, most of them in these semi-circular steps that form tiny amphitheatres for the people playing music. Jambés and guitars fill the air. Bottles of wine sloppily being returned to the stone ground adding a gentle percussion.

They call these people Bobos, I hear. It stands for bohemian-bourgeois. All the money and security of a middle-class background coupled with a free spirit. A desire to make do with what little you have when you don't have so little. I find myself a little resentful of them. They're basically just hipsters.

Still, I listen to their music and watch them jeer as a tourist boat sails past. The bright lights of the boat blinding my view of the passengers but their enthusiastic reply to the Bobos carries well over the water. In the wake of the boat, I look across the water to see the lights from the other bank being reflected off the dirty Seine.

It's a warm night with a cool breeze. I could almost be content here, if I didn't need to focus on shelter. Searching through the park, I find a bench that suits my needs and lie down on it. It's not very comfortable so, with a plastic bag that I had saved after buying food earlier, I gather as much newspaper as I can out of a bin, stuffing the paper into the bag with the idea of fashioning a makeshift pillow. The bag is clean, to my understanding and the paper should be gentle enough on me.

Alas, I find that it doesn't give enough support and, not being able to find more suitable items to fill the bag, I opt to use my arm instead. I close my eyes and start counting in an effort to distract myself to sleep.

Drunken cheers followed by roars erupt off in the distance. Not close enough to warrant me getting up, but not far enough away for me to feel safe. Eventually, groups start to pass by me. I give up on sitting upright every time and just lie there. Their conversations, as I hear them pass, remain unbroken. Lying down on this park bench, I've found I've become invisible.

Jesus, this is bad. I have no idea why I'm still living in Paris. It was originally just a stepping stone for me. A start to travelling the world. There's nothing really keeping me here. No iron-clad links chaining me to the city. Maybe I should just move to Alaska and live in a log cabin or something?

If only I could afford to get there.

****

The rustling of leaves all around me and the sporadic shouts from the Seine keeps me sleepless. I'm simply just not tired enough. I need to wear myself out. Rid myself of the energy that's fuelling the anxiety inside me. Be too weary to care if someone robs me or attacks me as I drift into a deeper sleep.

I decide to reluctantly pick up my side-project while I'm here. All these people are supposed to be open and engaging. I'll see if any of them have seen Mouse on their travels.

All along the water, I'm met with shaking heads. Some misunderstand my intentions as I show them the photo and simply hand me cigarettes or coins before ushering me away. Perhaps I was recognised by some, sleeping on the bench?

One young woman spends a little longer looking at the photo before handing it over to the person beside her. She seems lost in thought. I broach her gently on the subject.

"Do you recognise her?"

"I'm not sure... Maybe..."

"Anything at all would help."

"Someone that looked like her was near the Odéon metro, I think. Again, I'm not sure..."

"Did she seem okay?"

"Truly, I'm not even sure it was her. I don't know anything." She says, somewhat troubled.

"Okay. Thank you anyway."

It's not the most solid lead, but it's something and it's enough to encourage me to continue asking people along the bank. Some stare quizzically back at me, others make jokes at my expense and none have any more information as I make my way further up the river.

Under the blaring sound of pop-music, I find a distraught, drunk, young man sitting on the quay. He's staring at the source of the music, a boat that's being used as a bar. People stagger along the deck with drinks in their hands, some resting their arms on the railings. My introduction seems to pull him out of a daze and into confusion.

"What?" He asks, in French.

"Have you seen this girl?"

"This girl? No." He returns his forlorn gaze to the boat.

"Why are you staring at the boat?"

"Huh?"

"Never mind…"

I have my own problems to deal with tonight. I'm sure he's well-equipped to deal with his. Judging by how expensive his clothes look, I'm sure his problems aren't as pressing as mine. I spot my next target to question further along the river when the rich kid calls out to me.

"I'm looking for a girl too!"

"Who are you looking for?"

"My girlfriend."

"Is she lost?"

"No… She's on the boat…"

"Then why are you looking for her?"

"Because they won't let me in. They said I'm too drunk."

"Call her?"

"She has my phone…"

"So what do you want me to do?"

"Ask her to come out to me? Please?… I can give you money!" He pleads.

"How much?"

"Fifty Euro?"

That's just about enough for a hotel at last minutes notice. I'm still cautious though. Either she's a really bad girlfriend for abandoning him outside or he's not what he says he is. Still, with nothing better to do, and the offer of fifty Euro, I might as well help him out.

"Fine... Give me both your names and tell me what she looks like?"

"My name is Jacques, her name is Tanya. She has black hair, green eyes and she's wearing a red dress, I think."

"You think?"

He shrugs back at me.

"Grand..."

Looking at my clothes, he gives me his jacket to ensure that I'll get in. There's a pin on it for some rock band so she can recognise that I'm an envoy of his. It's a pretty fancy brand of jacket. I've gone from rags to riches.

It's funny how fashion is a passport to different societies. That people recognise what you are by how you dress yourself. I'm sure if I wore a vintage T-shirt, I could probably have partied with the Bobos all night long. Expensive clothing is the flag for an expensive lifestyle, flown in the faces of those who can afford it. It's a uniform we wear to fit in.

I do believe labels are a good thing though. While we might resent the use of them in groups of people as it strips away from our individuality, it does help with keeping things organised. Putting things in perspective.

He also gives me twenty Euro for the entrance fee to get on the boat. I stuff it in the pocket of the jacket.

Time to walk the plank...

****

I tell the bouncer that I'm American and that European fashion is a bit ahead of us in the States. He wipes the quizzical look off his face, seeing my mismatched clothing, and lets me pass.

The music is deafening at this point. None of it is the kind of easy-listening music that I prefer. It's mostly just what's been in the charts the last year or so. It's not that I hate every song played or anything, just most of it. It all seems like a shopping list with a backing track to me.

People point over the railings to different buildings while others try their best to look bored by all the fun. The latter group of people seem to dominate the *in* crowd. It's obviously not a place I'd be made welcome if it wasn't for this shabby disguise, so I snatch an unattended drink off a table out of angst. A vagabond turned a pirate.

"It's like we're on the Titanic!" A random girl shouts at me before laughing hysterically.

I will never understand the French sense of humour. Once, I was up on a ladder changing a lightbulb in the breakfast room of the hotel when a young woman at a table with her friends started talking at me, but not quite *to me*, in English.

"Be Carefooool!" She crooned.

This was met with laughter and applause from her friends. I smiled politely back at her then turned around so she wouldn't see my eyes roll.

Her next punch line was "Dowen't fall!"

More laughter and applause followed. I still don't get what was funny about it to this day. I can only hope for their sake that, despite me being the one on the ladder, they were all much higher than me.

Another one was with a guest checking in at the desk with his girlfriend. In this case, he began with "I'm going to pay with my student card!"

His girlfriend tittered while I smiled back and raised my eyebrows.

"It's all I have, take it or leave it." He went on, humorously, as if I couldn't possibly have had anything better to do.

"No? Then I'm not paying!"

I shrugged back at them.

"Oh, come on, it's only a joke my friend. Here's my credit card. You should stop being so serious." He tutted back at me. It's about the same as telling me to smile, like anyone could know what it's like in my head.

I took a deep, *very deep*, breath and typed their details into the computer.

"That'll be twenty Euro each please." I said calmly.

"Twenty Euro for the two of us?" He winked at me.

"Twenty each." Firmer this time.

His girlfriend whispered quite audibly to him "He doesn't get it. Tell it to him again."

The second time got the same response from me, which led to him tutting at me again and reminding me that I should enjoy a good joke. I told him I only ever enjoyed *good* jokes, handed him his room key and walked out for a smoke.

We'll chalk it up to cultural differences...

I see my target sitting at a table with another man. She's hammered, laughing aloud and touching his arm. As it turns out, I can't actually tell if her dress is red or not. It seems kind of orange, but a bit darker. Is dark-orange a thing?

The guy that she's talking to seems to be relatively sober. The distance between them tells me that they're not boyfriend and girlfriend, just flirting with each other. I wonder then if that's what I'm really here for? To get her off the boat and into the arms of the other guy. Are Jacques and Tanya really boyfriend and girlfriend?

Definition is an important thing in a relationship. It creates a fixed point that holds you in one place. You can drift a little from it, but never too far. The further you go from that point, the greater the strain and the more likely you'll break that link you have.

About two months after the first time we slept together, Cat told me that her ex-boyfriend, Andy, was coming over from America to visit and that he'd be staying with her. I wasn't her boyfriend so I wasn't allowed to be angry at her, not that it stopped me anyway. On the other hand, I had gained enough confidence by being with her that I could meet other girls, although I kept these indiscretions a secret from her. I thought she'd find other people too and we'd drift apart.

I guess it would have all worked out casually but we grew closer in the month before he came. The night before he arrived, she told me that she had made a mistake. She didn't want to lose me and I was still angry about it all, but I promised her I would be there, waiting for her, after he left. In hindsight, I was a fucking idiot. I didn't even know what it was I was supposed to return to.

I stopped seeing other people, Andy left and we kept going. We argued a lot more in the few weeks after, I was always getting mad at her for trivial things. Obviously it was just the thin surface of a submerged anger. However, Cat had a knack for making me forget everything when I was with her and after a couple of weeks I thought the storm had passed.

Yet, looking back, some nights Cat would be asleep and I'd be smoking a cigarette out the window, thinking to myself. I'd look at my clothes on the floor and then to the door. A desire would come over me to get dressed and leave her there in the dark, only something in the silence always kept me there...

Is that what Jacques has waiting for him, I wonder? I watch as Tanya's suitor caresses her arm. She blinks and looks away. He leans back in his chair while she rummages through her bag. She pulls out a phone, gives it an odd look and leaves it on the table before pulling out another.

"Talent coming through!" A voice cries behind me in English.

Two large men escort a man up to the DJ set. He looks

familiar. I think I recognise him from an article about an up-and-coming musician. The man shouting at people to get out of the way seems to be English rather than French. I presume he's the DJ's personal secretary or agent. Someone to help the star rise above the rest of us. A man on an adventure, propelled by the success of others. I suppose people have been using stars to travel for centuries, so why not today?

I look back at the couple to find them missing. I pick up the phone she left on the table, which I assume was Jacques', and push through the crowd of drunks, searching for Tanya. Sliding past sober people with expensive drinks, down the side of the deck, I do an awkward dance to get by a man wearing nothing but shorts and a waistcoat.

This is Paris, I guess. Where you can rub shoulders with a fashionisto and a drug-dealer in the same place.

They might even be the same person.

I swindle a few more drinks and roam around looking at the people with disdain. I bet they think they're great people. They have their fancy clothes and their nice apartments. They've probably never had to deal with anything serious in their entire lives. While here I am, stealing drinks and crashing boats.

I wouldn't be able to start a conversation with any of these people. Our backgrounds are reflected to each other as clear as day by what we wear. They have more than I may ever have. The recession that caused me to leave my country left them unscathed. My worry is equal to their money and vice-versa... I'm lonely again...

I wish my friends were here. I'm starting to realise just how strong my connection is with them. There's a fondness there that's undefinable. With all my problems weighing down on me, being around them lightens the load. I'm at my most together when they're with me...

I find the couple again, leaning over the railing of the bow. He has his hand pressed against Tanya's lower back. They're getting closer, the wood creaking under their feet. He turns her around and runs his hand through her hair with a grin, then kisses her. A second after, Tanya pushes him away. He puts his hands on her shoulder while she shakes her head, waving her empty glass in his face. He nods and leaves as I walk up to her.

"Hi, I'm a friend of Jacques." I tell her, pointing to the pin.

"Oh, okay."

"He's waiting for you outside and he'd really like you to come out and talk to him."

"Yeah, in a few minutes, okay?"

"He's been waiting a while..."

"Okay... Just a few more minutes." She says, turning away from me.

Poor Jacques. This girl is in no hurry to see him. If only she knew what being on the outside looked like. I turn around to see Tanya's lover pull out his wallet to pay for the drinks. I don't have much time. I can't just grab her and drag her off. It's going to require a little more finesse...

With the second I have, I spend it on an apologetic look to the waiter as I gently shove the girl into a table full of drinks. She sends the glasses flying and the horrific shattering sound draws looks from everyone, including the security.

"No, it was the boat!" She shouts.

The bouncer grabs her gruffly and, in protest of his poor manners, I grab him. Another bouncer grabs my arm and twists it behind me. We're pushed quickly through the crowd, bumping off people, before we get marched off the boat.

I can see Jacques with his head between his legs. He seems to have passed out. I look at the swaying girl beside me and make a judgement call. I grab her arm and walk her up the stone stairs to the street, then put her in a taxi, taking a photo of the licence plate as a precaution.

I return to Jacques. Waking him up isn't easy. A lot of shaking, a bit of pinching and one dodge to avoid his swinging fist is needed before he's lucid.

"Tanya?" He asks as I hand him his phone.

"She took a taxi home."

"Was she with anyone?"

"Nope."

"Good."

"To be honest, buddy... I know she's attractive, but you can find better than her. Someone that's more interested in spending time with you."

"Maybe you're right..."

He rummages through his pockets and offers me fifty Euros for my help, and my advice. I hesitate for a moment, but only just. I'm a little resentful being at the mercy of generosity. Bought and sold. Like I have no value except what others give me.

I leave him, too exhausted and drunk to care where I sleep. I wander into a bush and slump down into the soil. There's a connection here, I feel. My depression ensures that I don't have the energy to take care of myself, which gets me into these situations, which makes me more depressed. It's a bad habit, but I crave experiences with a bit more gravity. If I don't feel the pressure, I'm scared I'll float away. I have no roots to tie me down... Do I?

It's finally starting to sink in for me. I wouldn't be here if I told the people at work that I'm homeless. At the very least, they'd offer me a loan for a hotel. They're the only relief that I have from all of this. They're the buoyancy fighting this gravity. They're the chains keeping me together. The links that bind me here.

It's a hard thing to stay in one place. Things shift around you. Push you. Erode you. We all need something to keep us tethered if we're ever to hold on to where we are, and they've become constant companions.

As I drift off to sleep in the mud, I see the twinkling lights of the city through the leaves. It's a sight to behold. The chattering and clamouring from all sides become fainter. All things considered, I'm glad I'm living here. I wouldn't find this kind of adventure back at home. I'd be bored out of my tree. A ship in port instead of out in the great blue.

After all, Paris isn't the worst place in the world to be completely – and utterly – fucked...

Case 13 – Cross My Heart

I pull on a crusty pair of socks, my only decent pair left, and leave the youth-hostel. With the apartment viewings, work, staking out the Odéon area without result and generally just living out of a suitcase, I haven't paid attention to doing my laundry. I give myself a brief scolding for my negligence.

The fifty Euro provided me with shelter for the last few days until pay day. Despite the fortune of fresh funds, I discover that this hostel is booked solid for tonight and I have to find somewhere else to stay. I trek off to view an apartment, with the intention of finding an affordable hotel afterwards that can host me for a night.

The apartment proves to be a waste of time. The owner asks me all the usual questions and I answer her as honestly as I can. I make minimum wage, I am an immigrant, I don't have anyone that can pay my rent if I'm not able to and my paperwork from the hotel is not exactly a guarantee that I won't be fired tomorrow. I tell myself that experiencing these interviews will make me better at them, that it'll help me get an apartment some day.

Every hotel and hostel that I enter tells me that they no longer have vacancies. It's the start of June and the tourists have taken over the city. I don't have any more time to look for a place to stay. I enter the stiflingly stuffy metro and march myself to work. I'll have to find somewhere after my shift has ended.

Tonight is the usual drudgery. I clean as much as I can. I'm growing a fondness for it. Getting things done, letting my mind wander now that it's become an almost automatic experience. My chores are interrupted sporadically with guests coming in. Some of them worse than others.

A guest comes down to my desk to complain about his room not being cleaned. Even though it's not my fault, I apologise and promise him that it will be cleaned the next time he leaves his room.

This isn't acceptable to him and he starts shouting. I plead with him to keep the noise down, but he shouts louder each time I do.

Eventually, pleased with himself, he storms back up to his room after picking up a notepad that was lying on the desk and flicking it at me.

I know it was because I was submissive that he got angrier. People feed on their own power. Had I been blunt with him and argued back, told him there's nothing I could do personally, he would have gone back to his room. You give some people an inch and they take a mile. I guess if people were easy then they wouldn't call it people skills.

My friends have dealt with guys like this. They tell me I shouldn't get upset about some nobody who thinks some small thing is actually a problem they can't fucking live with. I can't shake it off though. It's upsetting... I, unfortunately, now believe that everybody is somebody, and it's a thoroughly disappointing experience.

Dylan throws up his coat on the rack and shakes my hand.

"Hey! Are you doing anything tomorrow night?" He asks me.

"I don't think I have any plans. Why?"

"Big night out planned. We're going to get the whole gang out again."

"What's the occasion?"

"None, really. Just that our schedule works out. One of the receptionists traded me a day for a night. *Profitez*, as the French say! Are you joining us?"

"Yeah, sure."

"Brilliant! Anything I need to know tonight?"

"Some guy upstairs is complaining about his room being dirty. He got pretty aggressive."

I recount the story briefly to Dylan.

"God, what a tosser! If he takes that tone with me, I'll give him a sponge and he can fucking clean it himself!"

"Fair enough!" I laugh.

It dawns on me that I need to find a place to stay tonight. I spur myself into action and grab my coat.

"I gotta go. I'll chat to you soon!" I tell him and run out the door.

I hike down Boulevard Montmartre. Bars howl music at me as I jump into hotel after hotel. They all turn me away, even the ones with vacancies. They tell me that I have to make a reservation a day beforehand and that they don't take walk-ins. Maybe they're just following the rules for rules sake, I understand that, but deep down I think they might not like the look of me. A face of desperation often makes other people aversive to helping you. The more help we need, the less people want to give. It's like they think calamity can be contagious.

I reach Strasbourg-Saint Denis without any success for shelter. Standing at the crossroads, unable to make a decision which road to take, I find a short, concrete bollard to sit down on. The arch, one of two, looms above me like a golden rainbow.

I might have to go back to the park that I slept in a few nights ago. It won't be a pleasant experience, and I'll need to be careful not to get my clothes dirty, but at least it'll be a little familiar now.

Through the drowsy night air, I see a middle-aged man with his arms outstretched. His eyes are closed as he takes a step onto the edge of the pavement. I slowly stand up as a precaution and inch my way over to him, trying to do so as idly as possible to avoid attracting attention to myself.

He steps off the pavement and onto the road. A bus rings out. I sprint. With both hands I grab the back of his collar and pull him to the side. He trips on the curb. The fabric bites into my fingers as I drag him to the safety of the pavement. The bus veers off to the side, stops for a moment, then trundles off again. My heart is in overdrive.

"What are you doing?! Leave me alone!" The man shouts at me.

"I'm helping you!"

"I don't need your help! Mind your own business!"

"I saved your life!"

"Who asked you to?!"

"... You didn't have to ask..."

    I'm starting to get a feel for the situation as my senses focus. This man is under the influence of whiskey, anger and pain. I'm reluctant to hear his reasons for trying to kill himself. If the problems are too big for him to handle, I doubt I can do much to help. He seems pretty volatile too, like cracking him open would result in me being cracked open. I guess this is what it looks like on the other side of things.

    I have an idea of what he's going through. I've had suicidal ideations very few, but memorable, times in my life. Perhaps one of them was even quite recently. My most serious persuasion was a long time ago. I was facing something so much bigger than I thought could handle. A seemingly impossible task with no way out, only through. I didn't want to be myself at the time or even the person in the aftermath. Now that I'm here, it's simply who I am.

    His brown hair is bedraggled, his face covered in dirty stubble and his left eye is starting to swell, but there's more to him. His clothes, slightly stained, are trendy and high-quality. His frame seems more sleek than gaunt. Wrapped around a finger on his soft, left hand is a golden wedding ring. A man fallen from grace.

    I look into his tortured brown eyes and tell him "I'm sorry... I just don't want to see you die..."

    He whimpers and sits down on the curb, his hands covering his eyes. I offer him a cigarette and light it when he accepts.

"You... You didn't leave a note?" I pry.

"No one to leave it to..."

"What about your wife?"

"My wife has been dead for a year..."

"... Is today the anniversary?"

"No! Why would you ask that?!"

"I'm trying to figure out why you tried to kill yourself."

"It's- There- That bitch! She has her cross!"

    He breaks down into a miserable fury, screaming with his mouth closed. I rest my hand on his shoulder and squeeze gently. The poor man's gone mad. What demons must rattle around in that head.

"A cross?"

"A crucifix! The kind you wear around your neck."

"Who has it?"

    He starts laughing and looks at me. "The prostitute I just slept with!" He says, matter-of-factly. His menacing gaze and plastered smile is off-putting. It throws me for a moment.

"Why does she have it?"

"Because I dropped it. I went back to get it, but straight away the pimp asked for money. I told him I didn't have any. When I tried to explain what happened, the bastard punched me." His voice is sullen now as he points to his eye.

"Why is this crucifix so important to you?"

"... It belongs to my dead wife. She gave it to me."

    My sigh is more audible than I intend it to be. I've already agreed to help him by dragging him off the road. To be honest, I really don't see myself pulling this off. Still, for every hour I spend trying to get the crucifix back, I can ask him for the same amount of time to convince him against bringing about his own demise. He agrees to let me attempt to retrieve the cross and gives me the name of his prostitute and the street that I can find her on.

    Loved ones and gifts... Our attempt to show our affection with something tangible and lasting, to create symbols of love. Something new, should words become stale. A reminder of that invisible link between people. We've all done it for someone.

For Cat's birthday, in July, I was obsessed with being a great boyfriend. I got her a blue dress that she had wanted but had been sold out everywhere. She had seen it on a poster in the metro and had made a passing comment to me a few times about it. It was going to be the perfect surprise. The last thing she expected and the first thing she'd want. I tracked it down online and bought it at an inflated price. I took a cardboard box from work and covered it with the place mats we had for the bar-tables so it looked like a gift-box. I wanted it to have a personal touch, and I liked the idea of me doing more than the average for her.

I was over-enthused with myself. My ego encouraged me to do more. I went to an American shop in the morning and bought her the coveted Ranch dressing that she loved to add to her breakfast. I made her pick out a camera for me to buy for her, the same one we brought to Croatia.

I really tried to think of everything. I look back at all that and I'm still mad at myself for forgetting to buy her Sunflowers on the day. Still, I did my best.

And giving my best required a lot that day...

****

Prostitutes walk slower than everyone else. With no destination, they amble around, waiting for a man to come and take them somewhere they never wanted to go.

I question a few girls on the street until one of them points towards Rita, the one I'm looking for. Her body seems to gain dimensions the closer I get to her. She's gorgeous. This is contrasted by the thin, hardened man standing beside her. All of his features are sharp, from his jaw to his knees, and I doubt that's the only sharpness on his person.

A quick scan reveals that the cross probably isn't on her. None of her clothes have any pockets on them and it's not wrapped around her neck, which is exposed by an unbuttoned blouse.

Rita runs through the prices for me. Her eyes roll off to the side, not out of shame but out of boredom. It's fifty Euro for a blowjob and eighty for sex. I never really thought it would be that... Affordable...

My improvised plan running up to this was to pay her for one of her services and find the crucifix before anything actually happened. It's a pretty forgiveable betrayal. However, just now, I remember that I could pay her for a conversation. I heard somewhere that it's a common thing. That people really want company more than sex.

"A conversation costs sixty." She tells me.

It's a surprising figure in contrast to the others, but I suppose conversations can often last a lot longer in her line of work.

I hand over the cash to her pimp and she leads me by the wrist up the stairs of an apartment building. There's a new lock on an old door as we enter a small, dingy room. The only piece of furniture is a beat-up mattress on the floor. The linen looks clean, even though the colour has a bleakly faded appearance. It's better than the window. Black flecks of mould crawl up the plastic curtain. An ashtray sits in its own ash beside the mattress. I can't see the cross anywhere.

"So, what do you want to talk about handsome?"

That has me stuck from the start. It's not like we can talk about the weather for the next hour.

"Where are you from?" I ask.

"I'm from far, far away, my love. Where are you from?"

"I'm-" A lie forms in my throat, but gives way to the truth. "I'm from Ireland."

"Ooh, very nice. Irish men are sexy. You have nice accents, you know?"

"We do..."

The conversation dries up. I feel awkward. Her affectionate voice, a reminder of how fake this is. An act of fiction. A travesty.

"What do you do for a living?" She asks in desperate disinterest.

"I work in a hotel. A night porter. And you?- Right! Sorry! Never mind!"

"Don't be sorry, love. Is this your first time?"

"Yeah..."

"Well, you just relax and we'll be fine. I'll take care of you."

"Sure..."

I find a warmth to her that feels genuine. It takes the edge off. I don't feel so cornered anymore. I put my back up against the wall and start peeking around for the crucifix. It's not like there's much at all in this room but I still can't find any trace of the crucifix anywhere.

The mattress is mocking me as the exhaustion sets in. The only thing in the world I want right now is to sleep, and I'm sure this bed is used for anything but that. I slump down to the floor. She kneels down across from me.

"I'm pretty tired too! It's hard working nights isn't it? Like you're fighting what you know is normal. Sleeping during the day, waking up at night. It's backwards."

It's a surprising twist for me. We have something in common. That even though we couldn't be further apart from each other in all aspects of life, we're sharing a tiny part of ourselves that connect. I feel guilty that I thought of her as anything less than equal to me.

I have to ask. "How did you end up doing this?"

"I was *seduced* by the money!" She says flirtatiously and giggles. For the life of me, I can't tell if she's actually amused by herself or if it's just theatrics.

She wobbles a bit unsteadily as she laughs and, just behind her left leg, a glint of gold catches my eye. A tiny, bright dot under the mattress in my crosshairs.

"This bed looks old." I state as I make my excuse to get closer to it.

"It does what it needs to do, sweetheart."

To divert her attention, I run my right hand over the top of the sheet while my left hand pulls out the crucifix. My back is facing her, hiding my movements. The panic rises as I fumble around, trying to tug the rest of the limp chain out. There's a soft tinkling noise that I'm sure will give me away. I pull at it at a brutally slow pace.

"Love?" She asks, as I jump out of my skin.

"Yes?"

"You seem okay... If you want, I'll suck you off for an extra twenty.

I look back at her. She's not an unattractive woman, and it's been a very, very long time since I've been with one. Who would know if I did?

My fingertips touch cloth as the last bit of chain arrives to remind me of the task at hand. Snug in my fist, it's time to call it a night. I pick myself up off the floor and decline her offer.

On the way out, I turn back to her and tell her "I wish you didn't have to be here."

She shrugs "This is life..."

****

I find him huddled up beneath the arch, singing some French song I've never heard before. His face turns curious when he notices me.

"Here you go." I tell him.

His hand held out, I place it down. His heart seems heavy and he nods his head with a melancholic determination as he closes his fingers.

"I'll live for another day then..." Tears start welling up in his eyes. He shows me the cross and tells me "This brought her a lot of comfort towards the end. I don't know why... I lost my faith when I lost her."

His grim face shows his starving soul. He hasn't seen love in months. Malnourished of affection, even from himself.

"I loved her with everything I had! None of it meant anything in the end... She was so beautiful before that fucking cancer took her from me! And God didn't do anything! I know I fucking asked him to!... She didn't do anything..."

I can hear him whimper as he pulls his hands up to his temples.

"What was she like?" I ask.

"She... She was funny! I used to tease her about going to church but she'd tell me someone had to save me... She was loving... Her touch lit me up..."

He squeezes the cold metal in his hand. "This thing... It's heavy! I can't carry this any more! It only reminds me of her dying! I... I just want to die..."

"Give it time..." I suggest.

This gets an odd laugh out of him until his face grows low again.

I try again. "It's a lesson I learned a long time ago... Take it one day at a time until things get better..."

He remains silent after this until he looks up and asks "Do you think she's judging me?"

I reply, sincerely, "No..."

The man nods his head and stands up, after three attempts, before stumbling away.

****

It's been another hour since I left the stranger and I've come undone. A dull, hollow feeling consumes me. My very essence barren and void as I search deep inside myself for the energy to go on. I'm running on fumes now, and there's only one place I know I can go.

Dylan wipes away at the windows as I walk through the door of my workplace.

"Didn't expect to see you back?!"

"Yeah, just checking up on something..." I mumble.

"Right so. Chat to you in a bit then!"

Probably not... I'm hoping to tell him I slipped out the back unnoticed the next time I see him. I have the perfect hiding place picked out. A place where there is zero chance of me being disturbed. Any of the vacant rooms could be taken by walk-ins, but on the sixth floor, by Crow's office, there's a cleaning closet. It's never been used.

The old, wooden boards creak under my feet as I slip into the room. I damn near trip over a nail protruding from the floor. I calm myself down by reminding myself it's better than accidentally lying down on it.

There's dust everywhere. A brief glance over the products hail back to an era of the hotel when there were supplies for every aspect of cleaning as opposed to a few do-all products.

I lie down and a guilty feeling creeps in. I feel like I've betrayed Dylan. He's always been honest with me. There's also a chance the lie I told could get him fired and leave him in dire straits. If Crow was watching the cameras, it would look like he's helping me out. I should know better. Dishonesty can ruin many things...

I really believed that Cat would always be honest with me. After she moved in, she was going out a lot without me. I was working nights and she had quit her job in the run up to her departure, leaving her with a lot of free time to meet up with friends. She was evasive when I asked her where she went or what she did.

The night before her birthday, I managed to get off work early. I knew she was out celebrating with friends and, slightly jealous of the attention she was giving them, I wanted to join in. I sent her a few texts which she didn't reply to, then eventually returned to our apartment and waited for her, seeing as we only had the one key.

She staggered in at about 3am, falling about the apartment. I wished her a happy birthday and went down on her in bed, the first present I wanted to give her. After making love, she fell asleep and I lay in bed beside her when I heard her phone vibrate. I thought it might just be one of her friends sending a text to see if she got home okay, but there was always that creeping suspicion that something wasn't right. It was an asshole thing to do, I knew it at the time, but I took out her phone and opened the message.

All the horrible things came pouring out and I kept holding on to the hope that she'd make things right. The flirtatious messages between this guy, Jean, turned my blood to ice. The context of them revealed that he had bought her a bottle of champagne for her birthday and he was inviting her back to his place so he could cook for her.

I dropped her phone back into her handbag and sat in bed beside her, seething. I thought I could hold it down, but I couldn't carry that kind of anger for two days. I woke her up, shaking her, and confronted her.

We argued for hours after I asked her about Jean. She denied everything at first, like when I asked her who she went out with. She looked to the right and gave me a list of the friends I already knew she had.

"If I was to look through your phone, would I find anything?"

In her drunken, sleep-deprived state she started tapping away at her phone and said "No..."

"And if I went through it already?"

Her face dropped.

"*"Thanks for the champagne." "Yes, I love you!" "Shhh, you're a handsome guy!"*... Do you have anything to say for that, Cat?!"

"He's just some guy! It's not like I was fucking him in the nightclub! I didn't make out with him or anything!"

"How the fuck am I supposed to know that?!"

"You're ridiculous and you're over-reacting! What is your fucking problem?!"

I didn't understand how she could have been so angry at me when she was the one hurting me. I felt like she hated me.

"I don't deserve this..." I sighed.

We continued into the daylight, I needed the fight to end, only so it could be over. I hated being so weak with her.

We fell asleep again only because I believed she hadn't done anything with him yet, but there was a doubt lingering in the back of my mind. Something that said she wasn't telling me everything.

The day of her birthday, we barely spoke. I cooked her breakfast in bed, because I promised to, and I bought her gifts. I was giving away everything I could to her when my heart was breaking. I wanted it to be the best birthday she'd ever had, and instead it was the worst.

Maybe that's the struggle of living in a society? We've built a construct where things are given and taken. Debts are paid, services rendered and goods traded. We can get tricked into believing that we're owed things emotionally. It's a crossed-wire in the brain. When you give something, isn't something owed back to you? We forget that things can simply just be lost. That she promised me nothing in return for everything I gave her. That you shouldn't give to get.

I was supposed to be the person who could give her everything, but I couldn't, and she had no trouble getting what she wanted. I felt emasculated by the whole affair. I couldn't provide for her or keep her. It was heart-breaking that I was worth so little to her, and by proxy to myself.

I didn't break up with her, not so much out of cowardice but out of laziness. I figured she'd be gone in three weeks, so I bottled all my feelings up and carried on like it was over. I would have only had to say goodbye at the end, and she'd understand why.

Three days later we were on holiday. She apologised sincerely in Croatia for what she did, told me I deserved better and reiterated that she never did anything with him. I decided to give her another chance. After all, she didn't really break any rules... Although, there weren't any to break anyway...

Love is a lasting thing, vibrant and fluid, but trust is slower to build. I slept beside her in the dark. In return, she stole sleep from me. She tore my peace to pieces. In a single night all my trust for her was gone, which she never really got back.

And I still don't know how to forgive her for that...

****

I wake up lightly covered in dust. It takes me a moment to figure out where I am. I groan to myself. I have no idea what time it is. I brush down my clothes with my hands and put my ear up against the door. I don't hear anything, so I slip out.

The day receptionist, whom I rarely talk to, is sitting at his desk. The clock above him tells me it's the early evening. My shift starts in two hours. I smile at him and he nods back obliviously.

I grab some food and take a walk around. I'm a hair away from splitting in two. The couple of hours slip by instantly and I'm back at work again. At this point, I feel like a robot. I don't even have the energy to feel sorry for myself. I sit behind the desk, staring blankly at the empty room, watching the upcoming misery unfolding.

I find a sudden spark deep down inside me. Do something! I turn to the computer and start frantically searching for a hotel for the night. After five minutes of agitated clicking, I find something affordable. I book it immediately. As soon as I see it's gone through, a wave of relief flows through me. A weight has been lifted.

The map on the screen glows in the corner of my eye. Tiny, scattered dots showing the locations of various hotels in the city. A hotel by Odéon stands out to me. I wonder if Mouse is staying there? Of course, I'd have to check all the hotels in the other areas too...

That's it! If I mark down all the places that Mouse has been seen, I might be able to nail down a pattern and pinpoint where she is!

I open up another map online and start placing markers. By connecting the dots, I can see a narrow strip over the north and down to the centre of Paris. The giddiness rises as I take in how small the search area is. It seems to get wider the further south it goes. It's likely that's the best area to search in as they're clustered over a smaller distance.

I run through my shift with a new vigour. Mouse may finally be within reaching distance. I'm determined to find an apartment soon. Lift myself out of this mess. I might not know when I'll find a place, but I won't stop until I do.

I'll just grab a drink with friends first.

****

The hotel that's hosting me tonight has a 24 hour reception and an early-afternoon check-out, so I'm not in any rush. My shift ends early as the day receptionist covering Dylan accidentally comes in an hour before he's supposed to. I should tell him the truth, but at this moment I'm too worn out to care.

Our local bar, Cole's, provides us with the usual surplus of alcohol. The whole gang is there and turn around jubilantly when they see me. The ladies giving me the local kiss on each cheek and the men alternating between handshakes and hugs. I look at them smiling and, somewhat relieved, let out a sigh.

"What's wrong? Tell Aunt Marine!" Matt's girlfriend asks.

"Oh, it's nothing."

"Well, let's get a drink into you. Then you'll be telling us all your secrets!"

An hour passes before Marine and I get a chance to talk.

Sitting outside, smoking, I can see that she's sensitive to my suffering. It's spoken in tone of her voice and signalled by her gentle touch on my arm.

"What's going on with you then? You seem a bit down."

"I'm still looking for an apartment and... It's getting rough."

"Finding an apartment in Paris is a nightmare, isn't it? Have you tried looking on-"

"-Yes! I've tried! All the sites and papers and flyers and everything... Sorry, it's just been a long week for me... Christ, it's been a long year..."

"Why a long year?"

For the next hour, I speak of everything I've been through over the last twelve months. All the things I've just about managed to scrape through. My darkest hours and greatest moments. I share with her everything that makes me vulnerable. After it all, it seems more to me like she's going to cover my weaknesses. Protect them for me.

It's difficult when I tell her about Cat. Oddly though, the times she hurt me aren't the reason why. It's that I'm giving life back into her by talking about her. Sharing her existence with someone else. Finding the words to describe the essence of her. I'm aching because I miss her...

Marine throws her arms out and I fall into her embrace. I find my feet in the hold and regain control over my emotions. It pulls me out of my head.

"What was her name?" Marine asks.

"Catherine... Cat for short..."

"She doesn't know what she's missing..."

As the bar closes, the group traipse out and Marine explains to everyone my living situation, asking them to keep an eye out for an apartment.

"You okay for a place to stay tonight, mate?" Charlie asks.

"I have a hotel booked."

"And tomorrow?"

"Eh... Nothing yet..."

"You're staying with me, mate."

"I-"

"- I'm not asking. You're Irish, mate. If I ask you, you'll say no. So, I'm telling you. You're staying with me. You can crash for two weeks, after that we'll have to see. Alright?"

I don't know what to say to him. I'm overwhelmed by his generosity. I can feel a small, aching voice telling me to keep my pride and decline, that I can do this on my own. The rest of me, almost the entirety, is exhausted. I can't sleep on the streets or in a hotel closet anymore.

"Thank you. I don't want to put you out, but I really can't say no."

"Don't worry about it, bro. We got you. Text me tomorrow and we'll move your stuff in."

"Thanks, really!"

I shake his hand as we all go our separate ways. I've had friends in this city before, and I've been between apartments, but none of them had ever shown me the solidarity or support that Charlie and Marine just have.

I stroll back to the hotel that I booked for tonight. Tomorrow is going to be a better day. As I drift off to sleep, I make a vow to myself that I will always look out for my friends. I'll never betray them nor take advantage of them. And I'll always be grateful for them, because tonight I feel lucky to have them.

Problems crop up in life. They weigh us down and we're forced to drag these miseries with us, but eventually we'll find people to help carry the load. Things get better, even if it's only briefly. There are moments of rest in our pilgrimage.

So, I'll carry the weight with me and march forward.

After all, I only have to suffer until I survive.

Case 14 – Elation

    With my rucksack and plastic bags, I awkwardly hobble down the street looking for the address to Charlie's apartment. I had it in my head, but I suspect it might have been jumbled up in the bleary-eyed glance of an early-afternoon wake-up. I toss the bags down on the pavement and pull out my phone when I hear a shout coming from up high.

"You lost there, mate?"

"No!" I shout up to Charlie.

    Actually, for the first time in a long time, I think I might have found solid ground. He comes down to help me bring up my things and shows me the studio apartment that we'll be sharing. It's a small place, but there's a mezzanine bed that he's giving to me and a sofa-bed that he prefers sleeping on. Things will be intimate, but it's much better than a hostel.

    Charlie hands me a spare set of keys before leaving to go to work. I sit down on the sofa-bed and spend twenty minutes sending emails to organise some apartment viewings, then allow myself to watch a TV show. It's been a while since I let myself space out.

    A surge of relief flows through me. I feel like I finally have my strength back. Safe at last. Smoking at the window, looking out at the city, I wonder if Mouse is as fortunate as I am?

    I guess I'll just have to go and find out...

****

    There's still some sun, even at seven o'clock in the evening and the Luxembourg Gardens isn't the worst place to take a break from my search for Mouse. I spent the last three hours wandering around the sector I outlined on the map before deciding to head farther south in my pursuit.

I sit down on the lawn, flanked on both sides by trees, in front of the palatial building. Enveloped by warm greens and yellows, I slip into a slight daze as I idly inspect the other people around me.

A small group of students sit with cheese, bread and wine. Obnoxious music bleats at a low volume from one of their phones. A man sits up, arms laid back as his girlfriend rests her head on his thigh. A young man alternates between reading a book and sunbathing. A train of joggers flicker between the trees, a young woman in a khaki jacket dodges through them. A guitar plays softly- A khaki jacket... Why does that- Mouse!

I jump up off the grass and haul myself after her. Eyes glare at me as my pounding feet shatters the serenity of those in my proximity. I skim past the trees, frantically glancing in each direction that the sandy path in front of me has laid out. One leads to the exit, the other to another part of the garden. My pessimistic sensibility sends me towards the exit, as I imagine if she stays in the garden I can at least have a better chance of finding her.

I bob and weave around people, craning my neck for a better view ahead. Some muttering follows the back of my head as I push past an elderly man. Still no khaki jacket though... I head back to the gardens and follow the path in as many different directions as I can see, to no avail. It's been roughly fifteen minutes since I caught a glimpse of her and she's probably long gone by now. She simply slipped right through my fingers.

I sit down on a bench and stew in self-resentment by replaying the various courses of action that I should have done instead. Each of them leads up to finally meeting Mouse, which is where I get stuck... What would I even say to her?

I ease up on my angst and assure myself that there was no guarantee that it was her. A flash of khaki isn't enough proof to concede failure. The frustration wanes with the setting sun as a park attendant ushers people out of the garden.

The sky turns from amber to a deep blue and the city illuminates itself golden. There's still a steady stream of people strolling around with the tourists here. The look of wonder on their faces reminds me of a feeling I haven't had in a while. I forgot how much there is in this city. So big and so full.

I decide to use my new freedom to see some of it.

****

I never really thought it was much of a monument. It seemed jagged and unfinished. This moment, however, I arrive at the right time. The midnight strike of the clock lights up the Eiffel tower with a shower of sparks. Thousands of stars being born and dying in seconds. A tall festival.

I can feel myself becoming a child again. Dazzled by the glamour. Feeling small against something so large. It's a simple delight looking at the lights cascading and tumbling around randomly. Now that a new day is technically born, I acknowledge that today is a special day for me. It's my birthday.

The base of the tower is devoid of people, save for three soldiers patrolling around. It doesn't feel empty though. It's grandiosity keeps itself company. It stands solitary and strong. How I wish I could be like it.

In the distance, I see a small red orb disappear behind the north-west leg of the tower. It piques my curiosity, so I stroll forward to take a look.

On the way, a young woman, about my age, is consoling a wailing little boy beside a closed ticket booth. She seems young to be a mother, it's more likely that she's an au pair. There are a lot of them in Paris. A whole industry is based on it. Parents here are often too busy to raise their children, focusing more on their careers than their family, so they hire other people to take care of them.

I can't imagine being raised like this, that role models are replaceable. It also sets a bad example by giving the impression that people are there to cater to your every need, provided you are giving them money. I met these big brats when I worked in a bar. They expect you to clean up their messes, make decisions for them, read them the menu, basically coddle them.

The poor kid seems to be distraught. I always have sympathy for crying children. While I know a lot of people who see children crying as an annoying melodrama, I always see it as a minor tragedy. A tortured innocence.

"Let it go, my dear." She says firmly.

"But I want it back!" The child wails. His voice carries over the desolate square.

"It's gone. You should have held on to it!"

"I don't want it to be gone!"

"It wasn't going to last forever anyway. They burst."

"I want my balloon!" The child hollers and stamps.

"I'll get you another one tomorrow." The lady pleads.

"I don't want another one! I want my *red* one!"

Finally, it pops into my head. I swiftly, but gingerly approach the duo. The girl pulls the kid closer to her defensively. I can't say I blame her. It's late and there are strange people about. Myself included, I suppose.

"Good evening! I think I saw the balloon fly off that way!" I tell the au pair, a little excitedly.

"Oh, yeah? Too bad it's gone now."

"You can still catch it if you run now, I think?"

"I'm not running around Paris for a balloon."

"But if you run now-"

"- Please. Be realistic."

The boy pipes up. "We can still find it!"

"No, darling. You have to let it go."

"I can find it. But I'd need to go now." I offer, the slight guilt of maybe losing Mouse lingering still.

The expression on the girl's face is a mixture of pity and perplexed. "Mister... I'm sure you have better things to do than sort out our problems. I'm sure you even have problems of your own. I wouldn't ask anyone to ramble across the city for something that's already gone."

"He's not anyone! He's a balloon finder!" The child chuckles either endearingly or manically, I can't really decide. Although, it does warm my heart a little.

"I'll find it. Just wait here!" I tell the kid and sprint off.

Through the wind howling in my ears as I give chase to the balloon, I can still hear the child speak to the au pair.

"Everyone's a little bit different, aren't they?" He asks.

"Just a little..." She answers.

I careen around the leg of the tower and scan the open landscape of the Seine. There's no trace of red to be found. My eyes dart around from the trees of the Champ de Mars and I jog over to the intersection of the street to see if it's gone down there. It's nowhere to be seen.

Maybe it's a madness, my motivations for retrieving this red balloon? The au pair is starting to make sense to me, but the opportunity to do the impossible beckons me further. The balloon was hanging low enough when I saw it disappear which means it's semi-deflated. It's not going up, only across...

The wind!

I feel the cool breeze on my face, a gentle pressing against the sweat caused by exertion and the fresh, June heat. It must have gone down one of these streets. It would have gone down to the very end of them though, as I still can't see it. Hopefully they all join up with the one street to make my search quicker and not keep them waiting too long. I hurl myself down the one closest to me.

****

Still no joy. I let the breeze guide me down different streets as though I'm following the scent of something that isn't there. It's already been five minutes and I'm starting to lose hope. I'm completely winded, my tarred lungs heaving for air.

This isn't the first time I've ran around Paris looking for something lost. It reminds me of what could be described as my very first case, when I was with Cat. Late in the month of April, following a night of heavy drinking, she lost the keys to our bar along with a small purse with her driver's licence and bank card.

We had been fighting beforehand about something banal, but I know it was really about Andy's impending visit. I think this was her peace-offering. A fun night out after my shift ended. She brought her work-keys with her so she could stay at my place that night. I even checked to make sure they were there and I was positive that I saw them. The next day, I gave her my own keys to buy her some time to find them.

I must have trekked all over this city. I went back to the pub we were drinking in, the ATM we used, even the shops around the area to see if anyone handed it in. Eventually I asked two different taxi drivers, not having acknowledged the name of the one who took us home, where their Lost and Found office was. They both gave me the same address on the other side of the city.

After spending forty-five minutes on the metro, walking fifteen minutes and getting lost for ten minutes, I found the place. It was a police station that held on to the lost objects for the entire city. I wasn't hopeful, but I had to try at least. I asked the man at the desk to run her name through their database, in case they picked up her licence or bank card, but he found nothing.

And so, defeated, I met her at the end of her shift. They could only be either in her apartment or lost forever. On the way back though scurrying metros and bustling people, she worried. She talked about getting fired or paying for the locks to be changed, which would have cost about two-thousand Euro.

I couldn't find any words to comfort her, I didn't want to make false assurances. In my quiet reflection I prayed to God to take away this worry, fix this for her, put those keys in her apartment. I promised that if he did this for me, for all the doubt, sadness and hardship I knew would come from doing so, that I would love her with all my heart.

Even though I was worried we'd end in tears at the time, she opened the door to her apartment and they were there. She was jubilant in her relief. The burden lifted. I reminded her, in her elation, that I traipsed around the city looking for them.

"You're the best!" she said, kissing me.

Surely it was just our foggy memories telling us they were lost? The small purse was gone for sure and the ensuing panic linked it to the keys. A twisted perception of what was real... But there's always the ridiculous chance it was because I loved her already...

A small part of me still believes that maybe, against everything I know to be true, I moved time and space and the whole universe itself... All for a bit of peace in love...

Or for a set of keys...

****

I've been heading in the same direction too quickly and for too long. I should have found it by now. I peer up under sculpted balconies and behind bins, to no avail.

After searching high and low for it, I decide to circle back to the Eiffel tower. I might catch it on the way back, but assuming I don't, I may as well inform the kid.

As I drag my feet to break the bad news, I try to think about what to tell him. It was a long shot to begin with. There wasn't much hope I'd find it and I did my best. I wish I could have done more though. That I could show him the world wasn't always full of disappointment. That he doesn't have to be let down.

I'm a little envious of the kid. I was pretty happy for most of my childhood. Life was easier for me when I was his age. I miss the simplicity of things back then. When you're young there are just the big things. Play nice. Share. Be polite. As you get older, these things break down into little things and get complicated.

My mania disappears and my hope grounds itself again as I trudge on. I'm not destined to be a hero, just a greater fool.

Suddenly, out of the corner of my eye, I see a flash of red. It could be my eyes playing tricks on me. A mirage. But maybe, in the wildest of all possibilities, it could be the balloon? I sprint over towards it. Pivoting around the corner, I find an empty street in front of me.

I *am* losing my mind.

I let out a long, frustrated sigh before turning around and flinching.

There, bobbing right in front of me, floats a shiny, red balloon.

I rush towards it and snatch the twine lightly dragging itself off the ground. The balloon itself isn't as firm to the touch as I'd imagined. It'll be withered rubber soon. Trust time to take it out of you and bring you back to earth, whether you like it or not. This thing that the child held dear and that I've sought out desperately is losing its perfection. Although it was never filled with permanence anyway.

Still, this trophy is bound to make the child jubilant. It's done so for me. The impossible task completed. The hopeless case solved.

Magic in real life, held in my hands.

****

Landing on the Champ de Mars, I jog as quickly as I can to the Eiffel tower. I'm sure I look ridiculous. A twenty-three year old man – Twenty-four, rather – running with a red balloon past rows upon rows of trees. I'm sure it looks like I'm frolicking in the green, but I don't care. I'm ecstatic. A child's dream is about to come true.

Under the four iron legs, the area is deserted. Even the soldiers are gone. I'm alone under the tower. The disappointment and frustration sets in. They could have been here for this had they only waited a little bit longer. I feel low.

I'm sure the au pair dragged the poor kid away. Why waste time on something that's bound to be disposed of? But the balloon was something more to that child. It was a companion artefact. An object of joy. Not because it was special, but because the kid made it special by giving it importance. Something cherished that couldn't be kept, but experienced to its fullest. We all hold on to things we know don't last.

With no need for a balloon, I follow the advice of the au pair. Untying the string, I give the balloon a little push and watch it glide away from me, into the night. I tie the twine around my wrist as a keepsake, to remember the time I found something magical and had to let it go.

****

I'm woken up with a phone call from my mother. She's wishing me a happy birthday and asking me what my plans are. I can hear my own apathy as I reply to her. It's not that I'm not excited for my own birthday, just something lingering in the back of my mind that says anything I breathe out will be lost.

Her joyous tone seems a little absurd to me as she talks about how she can't believe it's been twenty-four years. The way she celebrates our relationship at me. She acts like we're all one, big, happy family. But we're not happy, not for a long time. Or big. Or even one family.

My father calls and gives me the usual polite interrogation of when I'm going to get an office job that he'd like me to have. It's an irritating insinuation that I'm doing nothing with my life. I know he does it unintentionally and he stops when my anger rises up.

They have the uncanny ability to return me to my adolescence. A sulky, surly teenager that's still full of angst for Mom and Dad. A petulant child. In equal parts, I'm as bothered by my own behaviour as I am with theirs.

I leave the phone down and take a shower. I have a clean set of nice clothes laid out for tonight. My friends are meeting me in Cole's for my birthday. I give myself a thorough preening to be as presentable as possible. Examining myself in the mirror, I notice I've lost a lot of weight. Probably from all this running around I've been doing. I look as good as I feel, and today that's pretty good.

Charlie comes back from work with Leah and we leave the apartment together. Amae is waiting for us outside the bar.

"Happy Birthday!" She smiles as she throws me a big hug.

"Thanks, dear."

"Do you feel any different now that you're an old man?"

"Well, my hair is already going grey so... No, not really."

"Silver fox! I bet the ladies throw themselves at you!"

"Only to get through me to the exit after I *try* to talk to them."

"Oh, would you stop?! Anyway, Tom is inside, Dylan is coming after work and I think Matt and Marine are drinking at home before they come here."

We sit down and begin the libations as the crew gathers one by one. Matt and Marine bring me a birthday card. I carefully pry open the envelope under the watch of their eager eyes.

"Read it out loud!" Matt cries.

"*On your very special day,*" I read, turning the page. "*Go fuck yourself!*"

"C'mere! Happy Birthday, Mr. Birthday Boy!" Marine says as she hugs me. Matt throws his arms around me from the other side. I'm squished, almost out of air, I can't help but laugh.

I'm introduced to Leona, the blonde waitress of Cole's who has the looks of an actress and an air about her that makes her seem older than twenty-two. Her Norwich accent is softened by four years of living in France.

"I hear it's your birthday. Sorry we couldn't get any balloons for you!" Leona apologises.

"They can be pretty hard to find!" I laugh.

"I guess?" She replies, perplexed.

I really can't talk to girls.

Dylan finally shows up just as the owner, Aidan, locks us in. The cigarettes come out and a plastic cup half filled with water is put down as an ashtray. Out of nowhere, a birthday cake appears, complete with twenty-four candles, and is placed down in front of me. The group start singing *Happy Birthday*.

"Make a wish then!" Charlie cheers.

I stare at the candles and, as I look into the flames, I feel the presence of the people around me. Each of them fantastic examples of human beings. I have nothing to really wish for. Right now, it seems like I have everything I could possibly want.

"I'd wish for a new apartment, if I were you." Matt offers.

"Right! Yeah!"

I blow them all out to the sound of an incredibly sarcastic rendition of *He's a Jolly Good Fellow*. Pints are dispensed while Aidan and I chat idly about owning a business.

"Ara, on cold days there's not that many people about. But we always have you'se hotel folks coming in and tearing up the place. It keeps the lights on." He says, his North-side Dublin accent shining through.

"Are we a bit of trouble for you?" I jest.

"Ye're the right kind of trouble." He winks.

I couldn't argue with him on that. There's a certain magic to my colleagues. Their joyous nature shapes the reality around them. Life itself conforms to their rules of freedom. They melt away the future and absolve you of your past.

"So, how does this compare to your birthday last year?" Dylan asks me.

"It's... Different... I mean, there's completely different people here now..."

"Of course, yeah. What were your friends like before?"

"They weren't the most reliable."

"So, it was pretty bad?"

"No, I mean... It was nice..."

"Oh, right. You were still with your ex, weren't you?"

"I was..."

I met Cat outside the restaurant in the dazzling summer sun. Her smile shone out when she saw me and she waved comically in the distance. She rooted through a shopping bag and, after kissing her hello, she pulled out a small, square box.

"I was with a friend and we were walking past a sex shop and I was like, I have got to get you something for your birthday, so I bought you these."

"You bought me furry handcuffs for my birthday?"

"Don't worry! It's a joke present! I'll get you your real present soonish. I just ran out of time today. I got you a card though."

The inscription was sarcastic and sweet as was her style.

"Happy Birthday, Fucker! You might not shower that much and you taste like a cigarette, but I love you anyway. Remember, nobody likes you when you're twenty-three! Je t'aime, Cat. X X X"

She paid for my bar tab later that night as we drank with friends. My hand was restlessly caressing her leg all night. My friends started applauding as a fruit trifle came out with two candles stuck into it, the best that she could do for a birthday cake with what the bar had. I had completely forgotten about a cake of any kind. I turned to Cat with joyous surprise. She looked deep into my eyes with the sweetest smile and squeezed my hand.

Her voice was sincere, moved even, and for the first time she said the words "I love you..."

    I can still feel that big, stupid grin spread across my face when I heard it. For twenty-three years, I never thought I could be that happy...

    The taxi home dropped us off at the top of my street and we almost made it to my apartment building without pausing. I couldn't stop kissing her. Touching her. The tight, grey dress that she wore, which I originally thought was ugly, showed off her perky breasts. She told me earlier that she wasn't wearing any underwear. I pushed her up against a wall and slid my fingers between her legs as she rolled her tongue against mine. Within seconds, I turned her around and lifted her dress, unbuttoning my fly. I slipped into her as she held on to a ground floor windowsill. We were still sliding into each other on the street when a car's headlights came beaming down and I briskly pulled her dress down.

    We hurried up the stairs of my apartment building and got as far as the kitchen table before starting again. My hands firmly grasping her waist. A disgruntled neighbour shrieked at us from below. I realised I had left the door to my apartment wide open and managed to shut it just as I heard the crazy lady storm up the stairs. As I turned the lock twice, I saw Cat climb up into my mezzanine bed. I threw off my shoes and scaled the ladder.

    I went down on her before entering her again. The poor girl banged her head off the ceiling a few times when she went on top. The laughter didn't interrupt our intimacy. If anything it elated it. It was the essence of it. In those beautiful moments with her, I was suspended in divine disbelief. A real magic in the world. Love exists...

    When she was there, the very best of me was there with her. The dull ache in my chest would lift. I let go of all her indiscretions. Like I chucked all the weight of the world on my shoulders to one side and picked up something lighter instead, something kinder. I just couldn't help taking off with her. A million miles an hour, up and up.

Wonderful events like these cast a light backwards, extinguishing the darkness of the things that she had done. Forward, also, as the frail future seemed brighter after these moments. A light that few things could eclipse. A delight in all directions. That despite anything that had happened before, better things were on the horizon.

And for all of her faults, on my birthday, she was perfect...

Why am I still too scared to let go of the memories? I look around the room at the beaming faces in this bar and I feel blessed. It's like these people came out of nowhere. Like their company is a surprise. How did I not know immediately how wonderful they all are?

Loved ones.

My family...

These people have taken such good care of me. Pulled me into their tribe. I'm going to finally show them my true colours. They've earned that from me.

I tell them about Mrs. Swan coming into the hotel that winter night, months ago. Their eager ears listen intently to every moment of it. Before I know it, I'm telling them about my run in with the anarchists and an hour passes until I arrive at the final story of finding the red balloon. They all look at me incredulously.

"It's true... That's how we met, actually..." Dylan says rather casually, a little smug that he was in on this before everyone else.

"Mate, that's fucking amazing. You've been running around Paris solving crimes?" Charlie asks.

"I – Eh – I'm not really solving crimes, just helping people."

"Jesus... You're madder than a bag of spiders... I love you, but you're a mad bastard!" Matt laughs.

"Well, I think what he's doing is really nice." Marine adds.

We talk more about my recent adventures until eventually, I don't know how, a new conversation takes off from there and all the revelations that I'd just made get lost in the distance.

The alcohol, and the confessions, frees me of all inhibitions as I bounce off the people around me. I guess maybe there's something to gain from letting things go?

My goofy, self-deprecating nature is met with laughter, love and affection. These people truly are magnificent to me and I'm so glad to have found them. There's a bond between us that's rarely felt. Because we're Nightowls! And birds of a feather flock together.

I forgot how it felt to feel so full. So complete. My beloved friends, my fellow Nightowls. They don't just accept who I am...

They celebrate it...

Case 15 – Mirrors

Tired eyes stare back at me as the cloth wipes across them. Crow has me doing the mirrors again. What's the point? The hotel is just as quiet as it was in February and it's now the height of the tourist season. Most of them have been walk-ins. One couple only came in because the holiday apartment they rented turned out to be a scam.

We should be packed to the rafters with people. Instead, we're barely filling a quarter of the hotel. If this keeps up, we'll all be out of jobs in a few months. I can't be homeless and jobless...

It's only nine in the evening and it's already quiet enough for me to be cleaning. Out of the maybe thirty guests we have, most of them are in their rooms. You'd think they'd go out and enjoy the city. The guests have become as boring as the hotel.

Halfway through one of the mirrors, the phone rings. I really hate being interrupted and leaving things half-done, even for a few minutes.

The voice on the other end of the line is slurred with an American accent. His sentences are punctuated with hiccups.

"I need help." He says.

"You need a room?"

"No – Hick – Fuck... Someone's – Hick – Someone's blackmailing me – Hick."

"Someone's blackmailing you?"

"Ye- Hick – Yes! Goddamn it! Put me on to the private – Hick – private detective."

I already don't like this guy. If there's one thing I know about blackmail, it's that there's rarely just one victim in it. Blackmail requires that you did something you're ashamed of.

"The private, private detective?" I dig.

"Yes! I – Hick – Fuck..."

"You, what?" I ask, a little sadistically.

"I just want to be able – Hick – Able to keep helping people..."

Goddamn it... I see myself for the asshole I am. Maybe it's the other pressures in my life? All the stress building up until I snap back at someone. I need to stop throwing my negativity back at people and start throwing my energy at my problems.

"You're speaking to him." I sigh. "How can I help?"

"Okay! Mee- Hick – Meet me at the Mental Health Clinic at – Hick – At – Hick – *Georges Cinq*. I'm – Hick – I'm Doctor Sandeman."

The last hick becomes a click as he abruptly hangs up. I had forgotten that Americans have different phone etiquette to Europeans.

I get back to cleaning the mirrors and reflect on what I'm becoming. At the moment, I'm leading a double life. Both at the service of other people, but with different degrees of willingness and attitude. I like helping people, I just prefer helping them with real problems rather than get them more towels. They seem like opposites of each other.

I don't want to be as angry with the world as I am, or as inconsistent. The duality of who I am when my mood changes makes me worry about its consequences and it's harder to define who I am to myself.

I believe I'm a kind person, only it'd be nice to feel like it too. That I'm a good person who's willing to help people that need it. It's just that I stop being that person when life's stresses bear down on me. It seems who I want to be, the person my friends see, defined and whole, will always be the man trapped behind the glass.

****

It's the early evening when I arrive at the clinic. There's a blue-haired girl looking up at me and, maybe due to a conservative upbringing, I require a few seconds to conclude that she's not a patient. She pushes her glasses back up, finishes scribbling something down and stands up straight. A red T-shirt and cargo pants don't do much to hide her athletic figure.

"Hello there. How can I help you?" She asks with a faint German accent.

"I'm here to see Doctor Sandeman."

"Do you have an appointment?"

"I don't. He- I think he's expecting me."

"Okay... He's with a patient now, but when he comes out I'll let him know that you're here, Mister...?"

"Ehm- I- I work in a hotel and uh... He'll know..."

She gives me a quizzical look but it fades as she shrugs her shoulders and guides me to some chairs outside the doctor's office. Someone hands her some papers and starts discussing medication with her. She notices the look of surprise on my face.

"Bet you thought I was just a receptionist, huh?"

"No! Well, I mean, I didn't really think about it."

"I'm an intern. Basically, that means I'm the only one who really works around here."

"Do you enjoy it though?"

"I do. It's interesting work. I get to talk to some really fucked-up people. It's great!" She laughs.

"You'd love talking to me then!" I remark, which is probably one of the worst flirtations in history.

"Maybe so, but my boyfriend is crazy enough to keep me entertained."

Disappointment kicks in. To be polite, I go to ask her how long she's been with her boyfriend but I only get to "How long-" before the door opens and Dr. Sandeman steps out. Thank God he did. I really didn't fancy prolonging that conversation.

"Who's this?" He asks the blue-haired girl.

"I'm from the hotel." I interject.

"Oh, yes! Yes! Indeed. The hotel. Please. Come in." He says with an almost comical suspiciousness.

His office is quite nice. Almost everything is white, save for a large, dark, wooden desk and matching bookshelves. To the left is the typical therapist couch made of white leather.

He offers me a seat across the desk as he sits down and pulls his attention to the computer. He types frantically and clicks nervously.

"How did you hear about me?" I ask.

"Hear about- Yes! Uh... I have a patient with some anxiety issues, mentioned meeting someone near a hotel that helped him out... I asked around the area, people heard about you and they told me the name of the hotel."

"So... Why am I here?"

"Someone sent me an email yesterday with a video attached. It's of me doing some... questionable things... He wants me to pay him six thousand and fifty Euro or he's going to send it to the director of the clinic."

"What does this video show you doing, exactly?"

"Nothing! That's not important!"

"It's probably very important! It's the reason why you're being blackmailed! Do you want my help or not?!"

The doctor sighs, looks down and wipes his hand across his forehead, then he turns the screen around to the side of the desk so we can both see. He looks intently at me for a moment before he presses play.

The setting appears to be the car park outside the clinic. Some foliage is present at the bottom of the screen. The footage is shaky and poor quality. It was probably recorded on a phone. The doctor is distinguishable though, by the tweed jacket that he wears and his floppy, blonde hair. He's unsteady on his feet. He zigzags over to a car mumbling to himself and starts pushing it as if he wants to provoke a fight with the inanimate object. Roaring drunkenly at the sad sedan, he spits on the windshield furiously. He goes on mumbling at it until, surprisingly, he stands up on the bonnet and urinates all over the car with broad strokes. The video ends there.

I suppress the laughter rising in me with a few choice coughs.

"Whose – Eh – Whose car is that?" I ask.

"It's my boss' car!" He moans.

"And, again, the amount demanded by the blackmailer is...?"

"Six thousand and fifty Euro."

"And fifty?"

"Yeah, why?"

"That seems oddly specific."

"It does, doesn't it?! I wonder..." The doctor's eyes light up as he rattles away on the computer. Different documents appear on the screen, each of them with photos attached.

"What's this?"

"These are all of my patients that have obsessive compulsive disorder."

"Should I be allowed to see these?!"

"I'm sure it's a grey area... Anyway! Take a look and find me someone!"

"I don't think the specific nature of the amount is an illness, I think it's more to do with you personally." I tell him, turning the screen away.

"What do you mean?"

"Well, have you had any disgruntled patients?"

"Lots! I'm a psychiatrist. You think people come here because they're so fucking happy with life?"

"I meant any people disgruntled with you..."

"Oh... A few..." His eyes wander the ceiling.

I find myself running out of patience for the man and the mystery. I want to solve the case, but I don't think I want to help him. I need to speed this along. No more long routes.

"Tell him you'll give in to his demands and arrange a meet."

"What?! I'm not paying thi-"

"- You'll give him the money, I'll follow him, find out who he is, confront him and get it back. It's just to help find the guy."

"Right! Like a sting operation! I'll set it up!"

I check my phone for the time. "I have to get to work."

"Yeah, no problem. Here, I'll walk you out." Dr. Sandeman offers.

The blue-haired girl walks past the office just as we step out.

"Joanna? Remember to be in bright and early tomorrow at eight, okay?"

"I'm always in at eight." She responds irately.

"Yes, good." He says, apathetically.

I feel guilty by association standing next to this guy. I like Joanna. She seems like an interesting and hard-working person. Here I am in the asshole camp.

We exit out into the car park and I reassess what I saw in the video. I light up a cigarette and head over to the bushes to search for clues. There's nothing left behind. There are no footprints, clothing fragments or even cigarette butts, which is strange for Paris. Maybe the guy cleaned up after himself? It's not the only strange thing I notice.

"Funny..."

"What?" Dr. Sandeman asks.

"The footage that he showed you, the images have been reversed. I mean, this is the place that he filmed it, there's no bushes over on the other side, but the video would have led to me believe otherwise."

"What does that mean?"

"Well, he probably made copies on his computer and the software flipped it. Copies means he has a back-up plan if things go badly."

"This fucking day..." The doctor sighs before unlocking his car with the fob and driving off.

Joanna comes out and lights a cigarette while she texts on her phone. She looks up to see me standing in the bush.

"Hello again! Did you boys enjoy your play date?" She teases.

"I'm not sure I did so much."

"Aww, poor thing... So... Why are you standing in a bush?"

"I- I'm just - It's a private matter..."

"Wow... So you really are crazy?"

For a moment I start to wonder if she's right.

"I'm just kidding with you! You don't seem that insane for a guy standing in a bush... We all do strange things sometimes. It keeps us interesting! Believe me, I have blue hair." She reassures me.

"Everyone has something, I suppose..."

****

I'm two minutes early for work which doesn't really allow me time to smoke. I'm already annoyed at myself for not spending my time earlier looking for apartments, but I decide to cheat a little and use the computer at work.

I pull up the various sites to look for an apartment. I find one I like and just as I'm about to send them an email, Crow appears before me. My muscles tense up and my gut tingles.

"Why are you nowt cleaneeng-uh?"

"I was planning on doing it later."

"Wat are you doeeng now, zen?"

I cross my arms. "I'm looking for an apartment."

"Ah, so I pay you to look-uh fower an apartaymawnt?"

"If it stays this quiet, I'll have to look for a job too."

"We 'ave a minor slump-"

"- It's the reviews online! Why haven't you done anything about them?!"

"Eet ees not yower job to ask zis. You are all in zis aystablishment - 'ow you say - *outils*?"

"Tools."

"Yess, you are all tools."

"Well, sir, we definitely learnt from the very best on being a tool." I tell him with pure venom.

Crow looks directly at me, gears turning behind his beady eyes, then shifts his attention to a bare wall and simply walks away.

My fists clench. The lust for closure and catharsis rising. An itchy curiosity left unscratched. I start looking into the reviews again.

There are a few new ones, all scathing and anonymous. There's no information provided about these people at all. The only thing I can dig up after I click on a few links is their IP addresses.

I look up how to trace the numbers online. Initially, I'm told to ping the address and let it send a message back, followed by some more things too complicated for me to bother with. A little more searching sends me to a site that will do that for me.

I start with the most recent anonymous reviewer. "The hotel is as filthy as it is expensive!" This is simply not true. All we do is clean now that there are fewer guests and the price is as reasonable as a hotel room in Paris could be.

To my surprise, the address given is the hotel. They must have been using our Wi-Fi. I guess it shouldn't come as a shock that guests would review our hotel while they're here, only that most wait until after their stay. It's almost a superstition.

I have my own complaints about this place too. If only these people knew what it was like to work here.

This thought leaves an uncomfortable doubt glimmering in the back of my mind. Crow's not a nice guy to work for. I'm not the only one who argues with him and even those that don't will still resent him. It's entirely possible that a member of staff is trying to sabotage the hotel.

I reluctantly start polishing the brass to distract myself from this. I wipe it down until it gleams again. Amae's voice flutters through the air as she comes closer with the broom.

"How does this place have so much fucking dust?!" She exclaims.

"No idea... It's not from other people anyway."

"Yeah... Jeaney-Mac, I've never seen it so quiet!"

"... Can I ask you something?"

"Sure?"

"We've been getting a lot of bad reviews online... Do you think they're being left by one of us?"

"What makes you think that?"

"I traced the IP address of the reviewers to the hotel."

"Oh, right... I don't think I know anyone that would do that. Like, none of us care about the hotel, but I don't think any of us would want to see it go. We like working here, with the people, like. D'you know what I mean?"

"I do... We're like family here..."

****

"We all set for the sting operation tonight?" Dr. Sandeman asks.

"Don't call it that."

"Why not?"

"Because it's silly!"

"Says the private dick."

"Guess that makes you the public dick."

"What?"

"There's someone coming."

A bulky, overweight man comes shuffling forward. His hands are shoved deep into the pockets of his long coat, the collars of which are turned up. I feel like I'm surrounded by people who have seen too many spy movies.

The doctor waits for my reassuring nod of approval before he emerges from the shadowy corner. He treads slowly towards the large figure. I observe the exchange from the cover of darkness.

Doctor Sandeman suddenly starts getting irate with the blackmailer. He's pointing his finger at him aggressively. I told him earlier to just hand the money over and leave. The large man shuffles on his feet for a few moments, looking down, before meeting the doctor's gaze. The mystery man then takes a step forward and holds out his hand.

Dr. Sandeman rubs his forehead then slaps the envelope into the blackmailers palm and stomps off. The large man trundles away in the opposite direction. I slink out of the shadows and follow him.

Walking down the Champs-Élysées at night is pretty surreal. Dressed-up folks stumble to taxis. The occasional shady character loiters outside closed shops under the massive LED screens that try to flog their wares to no-one. It's a long, straight and lonely stretch from the Arc de Triomphe to Concorde, an open-air tunnel of commerce and class.

The mystery man doesn't get far down the avenue before taking a side street. He doesn't seem too concerned about being followed seeing as he's not looking back.

As we turn the corner, the glamour of the Champs-Élysées is lost instantly to something dirtier and tackier. Restaurants and bars, imitations of luxury, laid out to trap those too drunk or too poor to care about the quality, only the price.

Shuffling over to a doorway, his fingers thump into the digipad in two successions before he enters the building. The door closes slowly enough for me to slide in a few moments later without interrupting its closure.

His heavy feet stomp up the stairs and mute my own as I follow him up two flights. Under panting breath, he fumbles with a set of keys and I approach him.

He pivots around, grabs me by the lapels of my jacket and shoves me against the wall. My hands try to pry his arms off, but he's too strong. There's a beam on the wall digging into my back. The two boulders that are his hands are crushing my shoulders. Pinned up against the wall, I'm staring at a face that's furious with the world.

"You think I didn't know I was being followed?! You think I'm an idiot?!" He shouts with a rough Australian accent.

"You led me to your apartment!" I retort, almost as if by proving he's an idiot then he won't tear me in half.

"This isn't my apartment!" He exclaims smugly.

"Whose apartment is it, then?"

"Wouldn't you like to know?!"

"...Yes?"

"Well, I'm not telling you!"

"Then tell me why you're blackmailing Doctor Sandeman?"

"I'm taking back what's mine!"

"Why six thousand and fifty Euro? What does that mean to you?"

"It's all the money I gave to him for his services. Fat lot of good that did me!"

"You were a patient of his?"

"I came to him for help... Everyone judges me because I'm big and after twenty sessions - Twenty sessions! - You know what he tells me?! Lose weight!... *Lose weight*! I fucking knew that already!"

He releases me before continuing to speak. "He was supposed to build my self-esteem. Give me a way to get through the day. Fix me on the inside so I could be happier. Something. Anything!... You think it's easy being surrounded by skinny, attractive people your whole life?"

"I imagine it's quite difficult..." I say without really needing to imagine.

"I just want to be okay with myself..."

"What's stopping you?"

"People. Everyone. Judging. Laughing."

"So what?"

"So what?! You try living with sneers every day! Sometimes I don't even know if people are laughing at me or something else... It's exhausting!"

"Fuck 'em"

"What?"

"Fuck 'em! Who gives a shit what they think about you?"

"I do..."

"Then change that..."

"How?"

"I don't know..."

"That's not much help to me, is it?! Every morning, I look in the mirror and I..." He shrugs sadly.

"Maybe you need to spend more time looking for the beauty there?"

"What beauty?!"

"There's some there! You just have to find it!"

"That's not true."

"What is truth?! Everything we see, hear, touch and feel in this world is reflected back to ourselves in our minds. Truth only exists in the mind of one person at a time. What is true changes! We create our own world around us!"

"So, I should lie to myself?!"

"Not lie! Just spend more time looking for things you find beautiful about yourself, and about other people, and other places, and other things... Practice looking for the beauty in things and you'll start to find it..."

    He's not saying anything, but he doesn't seem to be as explosive as he was before.

"Are you going to give the money back?" I ask.

"Not a chance! That's my refund!"

"Fair enough..."

    I'm more or less on his side now. He doesn't seem to be a bad guy, just an angry one. Part of my motivations stem from genuine sympathy for the man, but I know at least a small part of it is the fact that he would be able to beat the living shit out of me if I got self-righteous.

"Will you delete the videos?" I ask.

"I'm not deleting the original, but I won't send them either... I'm not a complete arsehole."

"Are you going to blackmail him again?"

"Nope... He learned his lesson, didn't he?"

****

"What do you mean you didn't get the fucking tape back?!" Sandeman roars.

"It's not a tape, it's a video file-"

"- Oh, who the fuck cares?!"

"We came to an arrangement where-"

"- My money?! What about my fucking money?!"

"He's not handing that over because-"

"- Fucking hell! What was the point of you?! You're supposed to help me, but instead you let that fat fuck-"

"- Shut the fuck up!"

"Oh! You're going to tell me-"

"- I'm telling you that you're bad at your job and that if you weren't then you could have avoided all of this!"

"I'm not bad at my job!"

"You recognised the man you met. He was a patient of yours. Why did he stop seeing you?"

"He didn't want to take medication and that was the only way to help him."

"You offered him anti-depressants?"

"No... A diet pill."

"You're such a fucking asshole!"

"Okay! Okay! Look, I'm not bad at my job, alright? I'll prove it... In one session, I'll make you a happier person!"

"You'd have a very hard time doing that."

"Challenge accepted!"

Sandeman guides me over to the couch and encourages me to lie down. I know it's supposed to make people feel more at ease, but the angle leaves me feeling pretty vulnerable and weird.

"Let me just hit record on this thing." He says as he presses a button on a black pad.

I sigh in discomfort.

"Tell me about your childhood." He begins.

"My childhood or my adolescence?"

"Your childhood."

"It was pretty happy. Lots of friends. Things were pretty good back then with my family too. It wasn't until-"

"- Any brothers or sisters?"

"One brother."

"Did you ever fight with him?"

"Yeah."

"Frequently?"

"Yes..."

"Why do you think you did that?"

"Probably because I was mad at other stuff and I was taking it out on him."

Sandeman leans back in his chair and smiles. "That, buddy, is what we call a breakthrough..."

"It's not a breakthrough if I've known it for years – Fuck! Everyone knows about sibling rivalry and misplaced aggression by now!"

"Well, give me more information then!"

"Adolescence. Parents split up. I ran away from home-"

"- Why did you run away from home?"

"I wasn't happy there. I was shackled somewhere I didn't want to be and spent a lot of time trying to shield my brother from the drama between my parents. I felt trapped. I just wanted to get out on my own and start living my life. Be independent. Not rely on anyone. Grow up."

"Grow up?"

"I guess I'm just an impatient person. I saw crow's feet before the egg had hatched. Running to the end when I hadn't even started."

"Interesting... After that?"

"Paris for a year. University back in Ireland. Partying all then time and then, in my final year, I found out I had-"

"- Let's talk about the partying."

"I was in college..."

"Did you ever think your drinking was out of control?"

"Absolutely, yes. Taking a taxi home in your underwear is generally a warning sign."

"Must have been a good night!"

"Probably not for the taxi driver."

"Are you still partying like crazy?"

"I cut down a lot until relatively recently. Didn't really have anyone to go drinking with for a while. I had a pretty major mental breakdown a few weeks after she left because-"

"- She?"

"My ex-girlfriend."

"Ex?"

"She moved back to New York."

"Goddamn love New – Eh – Okay, she dumped you and you went crazy."

"You think I had a mental breakdown just because of her?! There were-"

"- Okay! Easy!" He adjusts his jacket and leans in. "So... This girl, she hurt you badly?"

"It wasn't all bad. I had some of the best moments of my life because of her and the worst moments with her weren't the worst of my life. As I was about to tell you-"

"- Don't change the subject."

"Fine! Yes, she hurt me badly."

"How long were you guys dating?"

"Maybe five or six months?"

"That's nothing! How can you get so screwed up after only six months?!"

"I- Jesus, I don't know... I guess I'd never felt that way about anyone else before. I was addicted to her and to being in love. It was my first relationship where I really connected with someone. I think I'm just stuck in a state of arrested development in that respect... Also, I didn't think I could do better than her. She was the funniest, sexiest, most intelligent girl I'd ever met."

"So, you were insecure about yourself?"

"Yeah – Well – Worse than that. That was the paradoxical thing about my insecurity. I wasn't sure if I was imagining things due to my insecurity or if she was lying to me. If she was lying to me, was it to just deceive me or herself included? It's an impossible frame of mind, to be insecure in your own insecurity."

"What was she lying about?"

"How she felt about me... I reckon if she really loved me she wouldn't have been so selfish all the time, there was never any compromise. She would have given something back, considered my feelings or at least have talked things out with me."

"If she didn't want to talk things out then you don't *know* how she felt."

"But she knew how I felt because I always did my best for her."

"If you did your best then why were you insecure?"

"It didn't seem to be enough."

"Ever think about making sure you were good enough for her? You know, like, working on your appearance?"

"I did that when I was with her."

"You don't do it now?"

"There's no one to do it for."

"Do it for yourself! You need to be a bit more selfish. Focus on you!"

"I don't like being selfish. The world's too big to just be about me."

"Well, you're not going to be happy until you learn how to look out for number one!"

"And I'm number one, am I?" I ask sardonically.

"Yeah!"

"And all the stuff about my ex-girlfriend? She was selfish, I hated that about her, and you don't have-"

"- Well, I don't need to be an expert to-"

"- I'm still not convinced you are!"

"... Diagnose her as a malignant narcissist."

    I give up.

    This guy is absolutely no help whatsoever. I made the right call giving the blackmailer his refund back. I nod my head quietly and close my eyes just so I can roll them to the fucking heavens.

"Feeling better?" He asks.

"Relatively." I reply.

"Everything is relative." He sighs. Sandeman continues while scribbling down on a pad. "Anyway, it sounds like you've been depressed for a pretty long time there, champ! I'm gonna prescribe you some anti-depressants or *happy pills* as you kids call them. Come back to me if you don't feel happier or if you experience any of the ma – few – side-effects."

He tears the paper off and slides it across the desk.

"That's how you plan on making me a happier person? By giving me pills?!"

"Look buddy, we all need help some times. It's just a change in chemistry from being A-Okay to not being A-Okay."

"I'm fine on my own."

"Whatever. Oh! Don't forget to take this guy's file!"

"What file?!"

"The asshole that robbed me?! Blake Thompson?!"

"Why in the name of fuck would I-"

"- Because I just did you a solid by giving you some top notch therapy. *You*, on the other hand, did not help *me* out so much."

"I got him to not send the video to your boss and not blackmail you again!"

"Yeah, well, keep it that way..."

"Two of my favours for one of yours?"

"I'm *very* expensive..."

I snatch the file off the desk and storm out of his office. The ungrateful bastard, I have half a mind to blackmail him myself. I guess I know how Mr. Thompson felt.

I walk past an open office door when Joanna calls out to me.

"Hey there!"

"Hi, Joanna."

"Call me Jo! So... Your session did not go so well, I guess?"

"What makes you say that?"

"Every time he hits record, he actually sends a call through to my office. I must have told him like a gazillion times!"

"And you didn't hang up?!"

"No, I like listening to this stuff!"

This place is a madhouse.

"I'm starting to think therapy isn't for me." I tell her.

"Don't say that! You just haven't gone to the right one!"

"Maybe..."

"How about you give me a try?"

"I'm pretty tired."

"Okidoke! I won't force you anyway."

I feel a little guilty turning her down. She seems to be a little disappointed. I reckon she doesn't get many opportunities to help people here... One last good deed before bed then...

"Maybe just a short session, okay?" I offer.

"Yes! Okay! So! What's up?"

"What's up?"

"Yeah, what's on your mind?"

"Ehm... Work is stressful?"

"How so?"

"My boss is an asshole, he's incompetent and the business is failing."

"Do you like your job?"

"Not really, no."

"Then why are you stressed about it?"

"It pays the bills and I'm comfortable there, relatively."

"Relatively?"

"Uncomfortably comfortable."

"You should change job if you're not happy."

"I need to find an apartment first."

"More stress there."

"Yup."

"What about that mental breakdown you mentioned?"

"I... Basically decided to avoid people for a while... Maybe not so much people but... Connections... Associations... Friendships..."

"Because you've been hurt by people before?"

"Probably."

"Well, you know you're going to get hurt by people no matter who they are."

"I know..."

"So, why avoid people?"

"I guess I'd prefer to be invisible rather than outcast... That way it's me choosing it and not other people."

"Doesn't sound like much of a choice, or a life."

"I grew out of it."

"You didn't crave other people all the time? Intimacy? Companionship?"

"I'm an... Odd person... Despite what I wanted, I didn't feel like I belonged with anyone that I'd met before... Sometimes I feel like I've been alone my entire life..."

"You're not close with your parents?"

"Not really, no. I've put a lot of distance between myself and them."

"Do you love them?"

"I do... I just don't... *Like* them, sometimes."

"Love is supposed to be unconditional, you know?"

"I loved my ex unconditionally... I suppose I needed to."

"Why's that?"

"She screwed me up a little bit."

"No, I mean why did you love her unconditionally?"

"I couldn't help myself."

"You fall in love easily?"

"I guess so... Why is that, I wonder?"

"Well, what do *you* think?"

"Love is a basic human requirement. It's natural to pursue it."

"But you already have your parents' love?"

"You're forgetting the distance I've put between me and them."

"Am I forgetting it?"

"I mean, there's a void there."

"A void you need to fill?"

"Not so much. I have some pretty amazing friends now. People that I really enjoy, that enjoy me."

"So, you love your friends unconditionally?"

"I really do."

"And you don't need to fill the void anymore?"

"Nope..." Finally, I start to understand what she's getting at. "You think I'm trying to fill the void of my parents' love with other people."

"I didn't say that."

"You were going to, though."

"Nope! I'm not driving this conversation, you are!"

"Can we change the subject then?"

"Okay! So! Tell me about this little pet project of yours."

"My what?"

"That thing you did for Sandeman."

"I... I like to help people. Let's put it that way."

"Why?"

"It makes me feel good about myself."

"Do you need to do things to make you feel good about yourself?"

"Usually, yes."

"You don't feel good about yourself as it is?"

"Not exactly. I'm not a very happy person..."

"Happiness is an emotion, not a personality trait."

"Meaning?"

"You can't be a happy person or a depressed person. Only someone who tends to experience more of one emotion than the other. We're so much more than just one thing... You can easily be many things at the same time, you know?"

"Oh, I do know."

"But you struggle with depression a lot?"

"Kind of."

"Don't you have people to help you with your outlook now?"

"I really don't like – I mean I do have people – It's just that I prefer to deal with my own problems by myself. Even emotional problems. I have a couch in my head and the two voices go back and forth."

"Have you dealt with any of your problems lately?"

"I try to... I've just been busy lately..."

"Helping other people?"

"Yeah... Why do I feel like you're trying to get at something?"

"You tell me?"

"Probably because it sounds like I'm fixing other people's problems so I don't have to fix my own."

"Is that what it sounds like to *you*?"

I let out a humorous sigh. "Alright, I see what you're doing. You're saying I should focus on my self, right? Just like Sandeman said."

"I'm really not saying anything. You're the one that's saying all this, and if that's what you think, then go for it!"

I sit back in my chair and mull it all over again. She sits patiently, watching me with her legs crossed and her hands laid professionally on her knees.

"They validate me, I guess... I tend to feel like I'm my own worst enemy when it comes to my self-image... I'm tired of being this miserable... I was a better person when I was with her."

"Sounds like you built your ego around this girl."

"Ego?"

"I mean, it seems like you based who you are and your value in the eyes of others around this one person, then you lost her."

"I guess I just loved her so much she became a part of me. She meant everything to me."

"Aww! That's cute!"

"Thanks, I-"

"- But, yeah, you're wrong! She was bad for you!"

"I know. I was forcing it to keep going even though it wasn't working... She was the sweetest of sociopaths."

"Move on?"

"I try! I do try... I would look around my surroundings and say to myself: *This is my life without her and it's not so bad.* The feeling never lasts too long for some strange reason... I know I can push her out of my mind tonight, but she'll still be there tomorrow. Maybe it just takes practice?"

"It does. But, I also think you need to find someone new."

"You're probably not wrong."

"You also know Sandeman wasn't wrong about everything either? There's not much I can do in only one session. I can't really diagnose you or give you the appropriate advice. I really advise that you come back sometime."

"I'm starting to get an idea... Everyone's got something, right?"

"Right."

On the way out of the clinic, I reflect again on what Jo helped me realise about avoiding my own problems. All this time I've been looking for Mouse, have I really been looking for someone to replace Cat? It's starting to look like I'm chasing a fantasy to replace a memory. I think I need to stop looking for this girl. In the back of my mind, I know I probably would have found her by now if that was what I was really trying to do.

It's been too long a search as it is and I don't think I'm going to do anyone any favours by continuing it. I pull out the flyer with her face on it and crumple up the piece of paper in my hand as I make my way towards the bin.

"Madness, isn't it?" A man in pyjamas states at the door.

"What is?"

"All this! Blocks built up and then fall down. Why bother, eh?!"

"I'm not sure." I reply politely.

"It's a crazy world!"

"It certainly is..." I'm not even humouring him, I completely agree.

"They say I'm doing better, but I don't know what better is..."

"I'm very sorry."

"Yeah... Bushes are funny looking creatures, aren't they?! And trees?!"

I watch the man ramble on, his words muted by my churning mind. I see a man that needs help, but I can't help him. I don't have the skills, or even the time, but I suppose he's getting help here. I can't save everyone, but I don't have to either.

"I'll tell you a secret!" He whispers.

"Sure."

"The world is bi-polar! You're never sure what mood it's going to be in on any given day!"

I leave the madman and walk back down the glittering avenue of the Champs-Élysées. It's a beautiful warm night and in this moment I'm careful to be grateful for my lucidity to enjoy this.

I hear a slight rumbling behind me. Bright lights blaze out in the distance. I can just about make out something bright yellow. I hold my hand up to reduce the glare. It's a digger. That's a pretty odd thing to see in this part of town, usually it's sports cars or taxis. Its long arm and claw lowers slowly down as it moves towards me.

I edge off to the side a little as a precaution. Unnervingly, the digger turns slightly to match my course. I hesitantly veer off in the other direction. Its claws point towards me again. I start to jog nervously as the digger increases its speed. Who the fuck is this lunatic?!

About five metres away from being crushed, I check the street briefly to make sure there's no traffic coming before I sprint across it. I look back to see the digger trundling along.

Either that driver is out of his mind, or I am...

****

I wake up in Charlie's apartment to the sound of him leaving for work. It's my night off and we all have a night out planned for later. Although, with him gone, I have little to do until then.

A text comes through from my mother asking me to Skype her. I leave my phone to the side before the memories of my session with Jo the night before permeate through the silence. I kind of feel like I have something to prove now and oblige.

She's bubbling with excitement. She hasn't seen me since Christmas and seems shocked by how much weight I've lost.

"It's so good to see you! Isn't technology great?!" She exclaims.

"Yeah... It's pretty cool."

I find it hard to match her enthusiasm. I feel guilty in the absence of any other emotion. I reckon she can sense the emotional distance and winds the conversation down, devolving to the usual Irish mother stuff. That is, of course, her spending five minutes trying to convince me that I know someone I don't, and that they are now dead.

"Well, I'll let you go anyway. Take care of yourself, love!" She signs off, affectionately.

"I will!" I can see the disappointment on her face as I hang up.

There's something wrong with me. On the screen, I saw a lonely person who loves me and I can't reciprocate this feeling or tell her the truth. It's the same with my father. They deserve my love. Yet each time I go, not even to say it, but to feel it, the reflex kicks in and pulls it back down. I think I might be broken, and the thought of that is heartbreaking to me.

I pull myself together, clear my mind and look at myself in the mirror. I think it's time to preen the feathers a little bit. I pick out my nicest clothes, shower, shave, and generally doll myself up so I'll look nice at Cole's pub tonight.

****

"Well, don't you look fancy!" Marine smiles.

"Thought I'd put in the extra effort."

"You succeeded!"

"Thank you, miss!"

"What have you been up to?"

"It's been an interesting couple of nights-" I see the rest of the group coming over and I haven't said hello to them yet. "- I'll tell you about it later."

Leona comes down to the table and takes our orders. Aidan waves over in greeting from behind the bar and, after returning the wave, we all start mingling amongst ourselves.

Somewhere in the fray of frothy beers and shouting at each other, I catch the eye and a smile from an attractive girl. I return the smile and, quitting while I'm ahead, I turn back to Aidan at the bar.

"She's cute." He comments.

"She is!"

"Why don't you go talk to her?"

"It's alright... Maybe later?"

"Why are you hesitating?"

"A chronic fear of rejection?"

"What makes you think she'd reject you?"

"I just reckon that she could have anyone here. Why settle for me?"

"You know, for someone as awesome as you are, you've got shit self-esteem. Fix that, then we'll talk." Aidan states before turning to serve some customers.

Throngs of people come and go. Amae shows Marine and Dylan how to perform some risqué dance moves, while Matt and I drink. All around are smiling faces to match my own. Proof that I just need people to think for me sometimes, to lead me to joy and ridiculousness.

Everyone else leaves except for the hotel workers, the doors lock shut, conversations go back and forth until eventually I start to tell everyone about my last few nights. Leona and Aidan are listening this time.

"That is insane." Leona states at the end. "Is that something you do a lot?"

"Yes!" Marine interjects. "He's been off helping people in the middle of the night."

"Not many people would take the time to do that. Fair play!" Aidan adds.

I listen to the crowd talk about me and do my best to respond to them through the achy discomfort of being flattered about something I know to be a strange aspect of myself. These people speak highly of me, higher than I would. They know me better than anyone else, so maybe I have more reasons to feel good about myself?

It seems the best way to really see yourself is through the eyes of other people...

"He once solved a case in Chile! Fucking Chile! And he did it all from Paris!" Amae shouts out.

"I just followed the trail-" I try explain.

"- And tell them about the balloon that you found for the kid!"

Case 16 – No Strings Attached

The early July heat is stifling, even at night, to the point that opening windows only exacerbates the problem. Almost ironically, the temperature has left most of our guests rather cool-headed, each of them chipping in the occasional comment or joke about the heat. The vast majority of our guests at the moment are from the UK and some Scandinavian countries. I'd say the sweltering heat is probably a welcome change to them. Something different. What a holiday is supposed to be.

The temperature rises again as the door opens and Crow marches in. He seems to be a bit highly strung today. His hands are fidgeting amongst themselves and the sweat on his brow seems to be caused by frayed nerves rather than the weather.

"Why are you alwayz juzt sitting?! Clean some-sing!" He snaps.

"Everything is clean!"

"Everysing ees clean, eh?! What ees zees?! Zis corner 'ear?!" He sneers, pointing towards a flower pot.

"No one ever goes near that corner, there's-"

"- Up! You clean zees corner! I do not pay you to seet."

Crow jumps in behind me and extends his hand out in the direction of the flowers. I grab a dustpan and brush, then trudge over to it. I sweep away at the dirt in swift, murderous strokes. Granules of soil from the pot start to slide behind the dustpan.

"No-uh! Slower! Gentell! You make not more of a mess than before, eh?! After, you clean ze – ow do you say - ze wood at ze bottom ov ze wall!"

I'm tired of being this man's puppet. With this rage coursing through me, I swear I could beat him to death with a fucking teaspoon. He starts to berate me in French, speaking too fast for me to really understand. It doesn't matter anyway. I've had enough.

"It's done!" I say, throwing the dustpan down on the ground and accidentally undoing everything I've just swept up.

"Wot deed you say?!"

"I said it's fucking done."

"You wahnt to leave?! I tell you before-"

"- Fire me!"

"Wat?!"

"You want me to leave, you can fucking fire me! Big payout for me! This is France, isn't it?! Of course, *you'd* have to work all of my shifts until you find my replacement!"

I swear to God, I think he just burst a blood vessel in his eye. He's staring at me with an unholy contempt that I've never seen before. Usually he's screaming and shouting at everyone, this silence is something new.

"Zees... Zees ees not over!" He whispers before he thumps his way up the stairs.

My heart returns to a steadier pace and I play back the things that were said. I probably need to be a bit more careful now. Actions have consequences further down the line. Even if I'm not getting fired, I've managed to piss him off pretty good and that's not going to make my life any easier.

I worry about what I've done with every creak in the stairs until my shift ends. I send a few texts out to my friends to see if anyone is free. I need to talk about what happened. Play it out and see where it might end. Crow still hasn't descended by the time Dylan comes in. I whisper the events from earlier to him as he gets settled into his chair.

"So, in other words, you put him in a bad mood for me." Dylan says, rather dryly.

"Sorry, man. In my defence though, he was already in a shitty mood when he came in!"

"Well – Now, don't hold me to this - But I don't think you're going to be fired. He needs people like us more than we need him and you do more for him than anyone else. It might not seem like it, but he likes you more than the rest of us."

"Even his favourite?" I nudge.

"Oh, I stopped being his favourite after I pretended I couldn't hear him over the phone when he asked me to clean the lobby toilets!"

"Ha! Jesus. You got away with that?"

"He never mentioned it to me. I reckon he was too embarrassed... Look, you'll be fine. Try not to worry!"

My phone vibrates. A new message from Matt. He's free to meet up over at Grands Boulevards. I feel better after talking to Dylan, but a night out wouldn't hurt.

"On that note, I'm heading off. Thanks, Dylan. Sorry I put the big man in a bad mood for you!"

"Somehow I'll manage. My hearing hasn't gotten any better, anyway." He laughs.

I reply to Matt to tell him I'm on the way and send a text to Charlie to let him know that I'll be coming back late tonight. There's a slight feeling of guilt lingering about going out when I don't have an apartment to call my own. I know I'll soon be overstaying my welcome, but it's been stressful searching and I really need to blow off some steam tonight. Besides, I know he'll understand. He's just that kind of guy.

I remember searching for an apartment after Cat left. I didn't spend too much time looking. I kept putting off anything that seemed too committed due to my desire to jet off and be with her. We were talking every day online, but the distance gave me a lot of time to think about our relationship, or at least try to. Everything in my head would get tangled up. A twisted mess. Pulling at strings for the knots in your head, and there can be so many strings...

So, we cast that conversation out and reeled it back in repeatedly for weeks. I was stuck in the past. I really wished she never did any of the troubling things she had done because I needed her and couldn't let go of the pain. I needed her to change. On the other hand, she wouldn't budge from the present, and there was nothing to pull us closer or bind us together. She was bobbing and weaving around questions. I was wound up, unravelled and frayed.

I just wanted us to be a real couple before moving over to be with her.

Partners.

Not just the brat and the doormat.

She was a big believer in that no one should have to change themselves for anyone else, especially not if they really loved them.

I believed that she was standing on a principle when we were standing on a precipice...

****

Matt is sitting down on the terrace, smoking a cigarette, when I arrive. A stale pint of blonde beer, the foam long since dissolved, stands across from his own, which is half finished.

"I got you a pint! Bit wrank now though."

"Cheers!"

"So, how's puddin'?"

"I'm doing alright. Had a bit of an argument earlier on with the boss."

"What did that walking haemorrhoid want?"

"The usual. I just got tired of his bullshit so I lost it at him. Told him to fire me, if he wants."

"Good! The bollocks needs someone to shout at him. Fuck him and his hotel!"

"I just really don't need any of this shit right now. I'm stressed enough as it is looking for an apartment."

"Relax. Drink your pint. You're in a safe place now."

"I don't think a pint is going to do it."

"Well, if I pint won't do it, some company might. You getting sexed regularly enough?"

"It's been a while…"

"Why don't you just sleep with someone then? It's not like you have to marry her or anything."

"Easier said than done… Besides, I'm not a huge fan of one night stands."

"When was the last time you had one?"

"Just after my ex left… We were caught up in this vague thing where we were arguing all the time, so we broke up, but we were still talking all the time too…"

"And?"

"Then I met another girl and I slept with her."

"Did you feel better about yourself?"

"A little bit, but… I don't know… I prefer having someone I know. Someone I love…"

"Aren't there any girls on the horizon that you're interested in?"

"Not – Not currently."

"Are you looking for a girlfriend?"

"Yeah."

"Hmm… Do you know anything about psychokinesis?"

I pause for a moment then point at him and say "You realise that this has absolutely nothing whatsoever to do with what I'm talking about."

"Bear with me! Just bear with me!"

I sigh. "Okay, it's about moving things with your mind."

"Correct! So! I was mad into that stuff when I was a teenager and I looked up this site online that said it could train me to develop those kinds of powers..."

"And?"

"And, basically, it said that all you have to do is focus on something really hard then forget about it completely. So, you focus on a pencil, try your hardest to move it, then ignore it. Then the pencil would move."

"Did you move a pencil?"

"Well, no-"

"- Was there a point that you were trying to make?"

"Yes! Yes... Your sex life is the same thing."

"Buddy... I'm not having trouble moving my pencil, I'm having trouble finding women to move my pencil to."

"No, you fucking idiot! You're spending all this time trying to find a new girlfriend..." He laughs, raising his hands for emphasis. "Stop looking for one, then you'll find one!"

"So, I'll find a girlfriend when I stop looking for a girlfriend?"

"Exactly! You can thank me later. Now, it's your turn to buy the next round."

As I get up, I turn to him and say "Sometimes, I can't tell if you're a genius or a complete fucking idiot, but it's definitely one of them and I love you anyway."

"I'll be whatever you want me to be, sweetheart, as long as you're buying me pints." He replies, winking at me.

    Maybe he's right? Maybe it's time to give up on the grand search for love and just go with the flow?

    The conversation takes a lighter tone. Pints are downed and a few hours later he hops on his bike to go home while I saunter towards the metro.

I still have nagging doubts about giving up on my search for Mouse. Every now and then I find myself staring at a girl in the metro or on the street wondering if it's her. There's always something tying them together, either a haircut or the same colour jacket for example. It was the same process after Cat left. I'd think that I saw her on the street until I realised it wasn't possible.

Blindly passing obnoxious groups of drunks and the odd beggar, I notice a young man playing the guitar on the street. A guitar bag made out of cheap canvas lies at his feet with a few coins scattered inside it. People mockingly dance past him or pause for a moment to listen, none of them give him money. One guy even goes so far as to jokingly toss in his credit card, only to take it out and laugh hysterically to himself. I decide to give the poor busker a few Euro in solidarity. After all, we have to look out for our own.

He's a tall, skinny guy with long, curly hair and circular rimmed glasses. His shoulders slouch forward a little when he finishes each song. A few people pass by. I tense up when I see a vagrant woman toss a few coins in. From my experience busking back in the day, I would often have people like her put twenty cents in, only to take one Euro out by slight of hand. She scurries off before I have time to check and is replaced by a man with a red hoody pulled over his face dropping a coin in. The hood is pulled so tight on his head that the strings hang low against his chest.

I'm confused by his appearance until a drop of water lands on my head, followed by a few more. A humid shower then tumbles down. The air is cut to pieces by crystal threads. The busker grabs his guitar bag and drags it in under the archway of a door. With the metro closed for another five minutes, and the only alternative being a booming café with obnoxious suits on the terrace, I seek shelter with him.

"That was pretty good!" I tell him in English.

I can tell that he's an anglophone by the way he sang. Most French buskers let their accent slip through or mix the words up, his was perfect.

"Thanks, man! It's a real shame about the weather though."

"Where're you from?"

"Minnesota, dude. How about you?"

"Ireland."

I know better than to tell people where exactly, or even sometimes generally, in Ireland I'm from. Most people don't know Ireland well enough, unless they're Irish themselves. I assume that's probably why this guy is also giving me a state rather than a town.

"You living here?" I follow up.

"Yeah, I've been here for about three years now on a student visa."

"Ah, grand. My ex did the same thing. There's a cap on how much you can work, right?"

"It's, like, twenty hours a week. Hence, the street-performing." He says apathetically.

"I think you can work more each week, it's just that it's nine-hundred and sixty hours a year or something. I dunno, maybe look it up?"

"Sure, I will! Thanks, man!"

"What's your name?"

"Joel."

"Nice to meet you, Joel. My-" I look behind Joel to see that his guitar bag is missing. "Where's your guitar bag?"

"My guitar bag? Oh, shit!" He zips around the pavement and into the street, frantically looking high and low for it.

"D'you think the rain washed it away?" He asks me.

"A bit heavy for that, isn't it?"

"C'mon! Fuck! Man, I've got fucking bills to pay... Will you help me look for it?"

"Sure. I even have a flashlight."

"Awesome, buddy. Thank you so much!"

A general feeling of anxiety falls over me. A vague sense of guilt for being there when it went missing. Like I'm the only thing connected to the disappearance. I'm lucky that he's nice enough not to accuse me of anything.

"Goddamn it! Where is this stupid fucking guitar bag?!" Joel moans.

"We'll find it... Should be easier than that fucking balloon, at least."

"What about a balloon?" Joel asks, perplexed.

"Nothing, I – Hey! There's a two Euro coin."

"Why does – Oh, yeah! Right! It could have fallen out of the bag!"

"Exactly."

We keep following in the direction of the coin, but don't find any more. It's extremely unlikely that the bag just washed away, but there was no wind to carry it or anyone coming close enough to take it either. The door behind us never opened once. I know it was stolen, I just have no idea how.

We start to look under cars and wind our way backwards until we get to the corner of the street where we took shelter. There, stuffed in a clear, plastic bin, is the guitar bag. Joel breathes a sigh of relief and starts rooting through it.

"Fuck! The bastards took all my money!"

"I'm sorry, buddy." I sympathise.

"Nah, it's okay... At least they left all of my guitar stuff in the bag. Thanks for helping me find it, by the way!"

"No worries... How the fuck did they manage to steal it though?"

"No idea, my friend. No idea."

"Can I see the bag?"

"Why the hell not? Here."

The bag is in pretty good condition so it must be relatively new, considering it's being thrown on the street every day. Aside from a fresh mystery stain caused by its recent adventure in the bin, it's pretty clean too.

I scan over the fabric inside and out. There's nothing really of note, except for one thing. On the inside of the bag, in the bottom right corner, there's a small tear.

"This look familiar to you?" I ask.

"No... Never noticed that before... Damn..."

"Just sow it up?"

"I don't really know how to sow."

There's a story stitching itself together in my mind. I start pulling at the threads, until the mystery unravels itself to me.

"I think I might know what happened, although it's a weird one... D'you do any weight lifting?"

"Look at me... Does it look like I get ripped in my time off? I mean... C'mon..." He shrugs his shoulders. "Buddy?!"

"I guess not, but we're going to need some heavy things for this to work..."

****

I spin out the usual plethora of emails and get a few encouraging responses, but I always wind up short. It's hard enough forcing myself to go visit these places. I find myself pulling tight on my shoelaces in frustration, hoping to strangle my feet dead.

The landlords that don't spurn me seem to favour the more bureaucratically inclined as they have bits of paper linking them to lots of money or fancy jobs. Half the time, I'm sure these people bring fake papers. Documents woven from the expectations of many landlords and fabricated just for them.

After the few pointless viewings, I head into work. I take the metro to give my aching feet a rest from the agitated marching that I often do before a viewing. All this stress has taken it out of me. Rejection after rejection has left me with lead in my heart and a hole in my head. I cheer up a little on the train. The metro occasionally reminds me of the time I went to Disneyland, on a track going to see attractions. Whizzing through dark tunnels, on an adventure. I wish I could see the magic in this city more often...

My stomach knots itself just before the hotel door. I'm still technically homeless and I remind myself that I'm up shit mountain without a rope. I really can't afford to lose my job now.

The night rolls on without a phone call or visit from Crow. I start cleaning early and keep myself busy as a kind of penance, or maybe a silent apology, even I'm not sure. An idle moment is spent checking the reviews of the hotel. There are some newer ones. Most of them are viciously negative. I sigh and close the browser. At two in the morning, my shift ends and I head off to meet Joel.

It's a Friday night and the streets are buzzing. Tight dresses are matched with tight T-shirts. Girls let their hair down and guys tie their hair up in hipster buns. The air is filled with the smell of liquor, pollution, kebabs and cigarette smoke, with the occasional dose of too-much-aftershave.

I arrive at my rendez-vous with Joel at the same place we first met, he's pacing around with his guitar bag on his back.

"So... I am *just* a little bit nervous about all this." He tells me.

"It'll be fine. If you want, I can play the guitar while it goes down?"

"You can play?"

"Yeah, I used to do what you're doing."

"No shit! Yeah, man! Show me what you got!"

"Don't get too excited... It's mostly sad stuff."

"C'mon, buddy! You gotta cheer up a little! I can tell you're feeling a little low. Does that have anything to do with that ex you mentioned?"

"Maybe a little..."

"Did you write songs about this girl?" He asks, deadpan.

"A few?"

"Oh, jeez... No, I mean, I guess that's good, man! You have to express those feelings! Let it all out! Music is like love-making!"

"It's usually over in four minutes or less?"

"Buddy, *c'mon*!" He shrugs with his hands extended. "Music is what ties us together! Connects us! You can let your emotions sail across the sound waves to reach other people feeling the same thing on the other shore! It lets you feel the vibe of this city!"

"In this city, we're all dancing to different tunes."

"Same in every big city! You know anything about String theory?"

"I think I've heard of it."

"Basically, the whole goddamn universe is made up of strings that have length but no width or depth. Everything, buddy, *everything* is made out of this. What makes something the thing that it is, like gravity and shit, is how it resonates-"

"- Resonates?"

"Yeah, I mean... Think of a guitar string resonating? You hit the A string and it plays an A chord. The string resonates and it makes a sound – But tune the same string a bit higher or lower and it becomes something different because it's resonating differently. It makes a different sound, so it becomes an E or a G..."

"So?"

"So the whole universe is made up of strings, resonating at different notes. The whole world! Existence! *Life*! It's all just one big song, man!"

"Is that the meaning of life then?"

"The meaning of life? Well, whose life are we talking about? I mean, it's like I said to this girl I met at a party once. I think her name was

Vic-"

"– I think I might have misunderstood what you were saying."

"Well, okay then... Shall we go stop some crime?"

"We shall."

I'm nervous before I start. I always am. My voice takes a while to warm up before it gets good enough. I'm self-conscious about being laughed at for being bad, even though I know I'm quite a good singer. It only takes three songs and some applause from Joel to put me back into the swing of things. I even start to enjoy myself.

I see the same vagrant woman from the night before walking towards me. I know quite a few of the scams here in Paris. From the ring trick, where they try and sell you a ring they pretend to find on the ground for far more than it's worth, or the simple charity scam, where they ask you to sign a sheet of paper then convince you to give a donation. I brace myself for the rip-off.

The woman hobbles over and drops about fifteen cents in before moving on again. I had already counted how much was in the bag before and everything is still there. I run my finger all through the bag and find nothing out of place. My number one suspect seems to be innocent.

My number two suspect shows up an hour later. A red hood pulled tight around his face, he drops a few Euro in. I try my best to peer in through the pinhole hood and get a good look at him. I can just about see a burn mark creeping out of one corner. Although I feel bad doing it, considering his affliction, I give the bag the same thorough search and come up empty.

"Nothing?!" Joel asks.

"Nope... Maybe they're not coming tonight?"

"Jeez, I guess we're making money at least."

"We?" I tease.

"C'mon man. I gave you my guitar so- Wait, are you fucking with me?! You *are* fucking with me, aren't you? Damn... Look who found his sense of humour!"

I give him a smile and play myself out of the conversation. Another hour goes by and, without anyone suspicious showing up, we decide to take a break. We sit down and I pass the guitar over to Joel to play.

"Dude, I've been jammin' with some friends of mine if you ever want to join?" He offers.

"Maybe, sometime."

"Do, buddy! It's a lot of fun and it-"

A dull, grinding sound interrupts our conversation. As I suspected, someone attached a hook and fishing line into the guitar bag, probably when they put money in, and is trying to drag it away. Unfortunately for this person, the bag has been weighed down with stones to make it heavier. The almost invisible wire is taught under the strain. Around the corner, a pair of eyes peek out.

"Get him! Let's go!" Joel shouts and races forward.

The string goes limp as we give chase. We twist around corners, legs flying furiously. After five minutes of sprinting, he glances over his shoulder back at us. As he does, a car stops in front of the thief and he slams into it. Panicked, he looks back at us. I recognise him now. He's the man from the night before that did the shitty credit card joke.

He bolts off down the street and my lungs give out. I start to slow down. Joel matches my pace until we both end up slumped against a wall, completely spent.

"Goddamn it!" Joel curses.

"At least we know what he looks like..."

"Yeah... *Yeah!* Hey! He must have run past a camera or something! All we have to do is go to the police, tell them-"

"- Can't go to the police." I say panting.

"Why the hell not?"

"Busking is illegal."

"Illegal? I know you need a licence in the metro but-"

"- Can only get a licence for the metro... Busking above ground is... A grey area... But illegal..."

"*C'mon*! There's no winning here! I need a drink..."

"I'm buying I suppose... Fuck! The bag!"

We rush back to find the bag, miraculously, with all the coins still left inside. A stroke of good luck for the night. It probably wouldn't have lasted another ten minutes on the street. A stitch in time, I guess.

We grab a drink in one of the few cafés open at this time, surrounded by empty tables and a few drunks that probably should have gone home hours ago.

"So, what do you do?" Joel asks.

"I work in a hotel."

"Boring, minimum-wage job or fancy hotel?"

"Boring, minimum-wage job. Although, maybe not so boring... It's getting stressful lately... The hotel isn't doing so well, my boss is an asshole, the workload is astronomical-"

"- Woah! Buddy! Take it *easy*! You said yourself that it's a minimum-wage job. This guy isn't paying you enough to worry about this shit! Just take it one day at a time and everything will be fine."

"It's not going to be fine, though. The hotel is spiralling into the ground-"

"- You'll cross that bridge when you come to it. What's the point in worrying about it? Just learn to relax."

"I don't think I've ever been good at that..."

"Well, it takes practice... I mean, it's not like it's a switch that you can turn on or off. Find your calm and own it. It's you making yourself stressed, it's gotta be you making yourself relax."

"I guess I could take a few things less seriously?"

"That's the spirit! You-"

"- Although, I am homeless."

"Homeless?"

"I don't have an apartment. I'm crashing at a friend's place."

"Fuck, dude! Why didn't you say something? One of my buddies is leaving his place soon. It's small and shitty, but the landlady's not picky as long as you pay. You don't even have to sign a contract! Just rent it month by month. I mean, this apartment's a real shit-hole. But you don't have to commit to it or anything."

"I'll definitely look at it!"

****

Tom is leaving Paris to live with his girlfriend back in England. Apparently, notice of his departure had been doing the rounds on Facebook but, me being without an account, I find out the night it happens. I hurriedly pop out to buy him something for his departure. The best I can do is find a key-chain from a tourist shop that's open suspiciously late.

His leaving party is at Cole's and we all wind ourselves around him to honour his departure. I can't help but ask myself what will become of our friendship. Distance tends to weaken relationships, no matter how close they are. It happened with Cat.

After a full week of arguing, we broke up in the middle of August. I had been asking her for a video call so we could sort out the stuff that I had to send back to her, clothing and other things. She had been avoiding the call until that night. I was speed talking at her, pretending that everything was okay. Her answers were short, her face troubled, then she just shook her head.

"Yeah, I know... This isn't working is it?" I said, almost relieved.

"Are you still going to send my stuff back?"

"Of course I will, Cat! Of course... Can I ask you something?"

"What is it?"

"Did you ever cheat on me?"

She paused for a second, then shook her head.

"Well, there's that at least... I want you to be happy, Cat. I really do... I love you..."

"I love you, too... Please don't be sad, babe. You deserve better than me... You're hilarious and kind and your heart is too big for me to watch it break like that."

Tears started streaming from both of us as our conversation was coming to an end

"We can still be friends. I just need about two weeks to get over this and then we can talk again."

"Okay... Take care of yourself, fucker."

"You too, Cat."

My silence only lasted two days. I know I shouldn't have, but it was 3am on a Tuesday, I was alone and I had no one else to talk to, not that I wanted to talk to anyone else anyway.

The end provided a period of relaxation for me. Without the stress strangling me, I was myself again. It didn't take long for us to be chatting every day and reconnecting, but we eventually swung back around to arguing. The same maddening loop, during which I had my one night stand. We severed ties again. This time it was her idea. She wanted to be okay on her own and find herself. I found some comfort in the idea that I was helping her by leaving her. I knew she wouldn't have changed when she was with me. She needed to be alone to grow.

A day after she cut me off, she started sending me messages

again. She told me that she had made a mistake and missed me. I was in a good place, though. I had found my confidence after my one night stand and felt like I wasn't going to be alone for much longer. It was this confidence that made me ignore her until, after a week, I couldn't any more. I had to let her down.

"Hey! How have you been?!" She asked.

"Fine..."

"Only fine?"

"Cat..."

"What?... Oh, you want me to stop talking to you?"

"... It's for the best."

She burst into tears. "What if it's not though?! I miss you so much!"

"I miss you too! But it's over! Whatever *it* was... I wasn't even your boyfriend." The coldness in my voice told her that she couldn't play on my heartstrings any more.

"Of course you were my boyfriend! I never should have left Paris! I never should have left *you*! I just want to come *home* to you! I'm sorry... And I know it's too late... It's all my fault... I don't know what to fucking do! I just want to be with you! I don't know what is best for either of us but I don't know if it is this... All I know is you made me feel differently than any other person I have ever been with. Yeah, we had some issues, but what couple doesn't? I couldn't have been happier laying in bed for hours with anyone else..."

 Two hours passed. She kept at me until I took her back, under the condition that she was going to go a week without talking to me to think about our relationship and what she wanted out of it.

 The vagueness came back about what we were. I have no idea why it dragged out as long as it did. I used to blame her for it. I'd tell myself that she should have cut me loose and left me alone. The truth is, I could have done that myself, it's just that I wasn't strong enough.

Looking back, I know that her begging me back didn't really have anything to do with me. She was just readjusting back to her life in America. It was a scary and lonely process for her. I went through my own changes too. When the owner came back from his holiday in mid-September, I was forced to move out of our apartment and book a hostel.

I sent her back her things in the post, along with a silver necklace that I had bought for her. The package cost quite a bit to post given the weight and distance, but I had to send it at that point. I didn't want to seem like I was holding it hostage when I was really only holding on to pieces of her.

I was sad to leave the place but, despite how disorganised I was about where I was moving to, I left it nice and tidy to honour the experiences it gave me. Strands of her hair were strewn everywhere. After I cleaned our apartment, there wasn't a trace of her left, but there wasn't a trace of me either...

I wonder now if Tom and I will end up simply cutting ties and going our separate ways, or even if there would be a point staying in contact considering he'll no longer be living here? Without the hotel, Paris or co-workers, there'll be nothing keeping us tied together. He seems to read this on my face and approaches me.

"Mate, any time you're ever in London, and it's just a train stop away in the tunnel, you give me a bell, yeah?"

"Yeah, of course."

"We might not stay in contact as much, life goes on, but the lines of communication are ever more sophisticated these days, aren't they?"

"They are, indeed."

"Keep the lines open then. Computer. Phone. String and cup. Whatever it is, I'll be on the other end if you ever fancy a chat."

It's a relief to hear this. The anxiety of losing a friend forever is replaced with a sort of assurance that someday, somewhere and somehow, I'll see this Fox again.

We drunkenly go out for one last mini-tour of Paris so Tom can give the city a farewell. The gang and I venture down to Concorde where Matt scales the fountain, effortlessly skipping across the light fixtures to stay above the water before leaping off to grab a sculpture for grip. I decide to follow suit, resulting in me falling in, soaking myself, just barely saving my phone and then getting one of the most impressionable views of Paris. The Champs-Élysées, the Eiffel tower, Paris itself, is much nicer to look at when you're hanging from a piece of history.

Onwards to the Louvre we go, where we flail about the palace, our group of savages taking it over for ourselves. Every piece of brick starts to come alive for me again.

Another group of friends could turn this city to ash in my eyes. Turn the carvings into dirty rocks. Now, I finally realise what makes this city shine. It's not the cold stone or metal cranes, but warm bodies and pumping blood. These people that make life worth living instead of dreaming. Friends and joy surrounded by beauty that we built.

That people make places...

Case 17 – Out of the Park

We're pushing more people out of the hotel than we are pulling in. I'm not as worried about it as I was before. Seeing as there's nothing I can do about it personally, I figure there's no point wasting energy over it. All I have to do is just work and not worry. Get through another inane shift.

I settle comfortably into the idea of a boring evening when a man wearing a courier jacket walks up to the desk.

"Can I speak to someone in charge?" He asks.

"He's not here. Can I help you with something?"

"Sign here." He says, handing over an electronic pad.

I sign it, my curiosity outweighing my caution. There's no details on what he's bringing in. He takes back the pad and walks out purposefully. It's another five minutes before he rolls a large, wooden crate in on a trolley. He sets the box marked fragile gently down in the middle of the foyer, gives me a side-ways salute and swiftly exits.

I examine the crate. All sides seems to be nailed shut. I tilt it towards me to drag it into a corner. My hand slips and it falls back flat on the floor. Something tinkles inside. What the hell is this thing?

Rooting through the supply closet, I find a small crowbar hidden in a dusty corner. I pry the wood up slowly, careful not to damage the crate in case I have to hammer it back down. The shiny, steel nails are shorter than I expected as they quickly release themselves from the wood.

I peer inside the box to see that it's filled with straw, a pole with ornate engravings protrudes out the top, like a giant needle in a small haystack. I pick up a white envelope lying on the bed of straw.

The envelope is sealed so I can't open it without being able to cover my tracks. Instead, I awkwardly lean over the side of the crate and sift through the straw to get a clearer picture of what's inside.

Perplexed, I press the lid of the crate back down and step away. Footsteps behind me nearly cause me to jump out of my skin.

"What's that, there?" Amae asks.

"It appears to be a crystal chandelier."

"A chandelier?"

"I think so..."

"Why do we have a chandelier?"

"Haven't a clue."

"Fair enough... T'd be better if he just bought diamond necklaces for the maids instead."

"You like your diamonds?"

"I wouldn't say no to them."

"Grand..."

"Strange now, without Tom around."

"Hm? Yeah, I suppose so..."

"You don't notice it so much?"

"Not really. Things change all the time."

"I miss him. Don't you?"

"A bit, but... This is Paris, isn't it? You get used to people leaving."

"But you'd still miss them, wouldn't you?"

"Eh? We'll see him again." I shrug and laugh. "I think I'm just good at watching people go at this point."

Amae looks quite perturbed at what I've just said. "Yeah, but I'd miss you loads if you were gone... You're one of my best friends here."

"And you're one of mine, but it's an eventuality, isn't it?"

Amae's face sours and she turns away. I can feel the burning static in the air. I've upset her more than I thought I could. My logic has come across as a coldness.

"I have cleaning to do." Amae says through gritted teeth. Before I can apologise, she huffs off up the stairs.

I give myself a few moments to feel bad for myself after bearing the brunt of her hostility. I replay what was said by each of us until the blunt thought hits me. I feel like banging my head on the lonely counter in front of me. An attempt to hammer out an apology. I'm a fucking asshole...

I really hate when I screw things up like this. I pissed off Cat to the point of her deleting me on Facebook. It was towards the end of our relationship where I was desperately trying to connect with her again. I kept pushing at her to change things, trying to fix things that weren't mine to fix. To be friends when we could never be friends again.

I just couldn't win. All through August, I kept swinging and missing. It was a sickness where I knew there was no way forward but I didn't want a way out. A malady that I mildly suffer from today. One that clears my system until I expose myself to it again. A radiation level rising and falling. I felt trapped and I couldn't take it. So one night in September, after another one of our arguments, I got drunk and I started casting stones.

"Seriously, you've been so mean to me for two weeks and ignored me and given me a ton of shit every time I talk to you. I'm always doing something wrong to you. It's fucked up!" She replied.

"Says the girl that cheated on me with Jean and Andy! Ooops!"

"I didn't cheat on you with Jean or Andy. Honestly, fuck you! Don't bother calling me if you make it to New York!"

"I'm so glad I believed in our relationship more than you."

"You are being so belligerent. Please go to bed... I'm not speaking to you like this, it's pointless."

"Now who's over exaggerating?"

"Seriously, leave me the fuck alone or I'm deleting you from Facebook like the petty bitch I am."

"Do delete me from Facebook! It's the best thing for you. I want you to be happy in the long run. I can't make you happy."

"You'll never do better than me."

"I'd say the same to you! Find someone pathetic enough to move halfway across the world for you!"

So she deleted me.

And if I listened to my head instead of my heart, that would have been the end of it...

****

I take a walk down to Saint-Michel to clear my head. I know Amae likes to hang out in this area after work and I figure an in-person apology would be nicer if I happen to run into her. If I don't, then I can get a drink and prepare my apology for tomorrow as the walk home to my new apartment isn't a hike from here.

Joel wasn't kidding when he said the apartment was a shit-hole. Mostly because the only toilet is outside the apartment on the landing, shared by other people on the floor, and it's a Turkish toilet. This literally means a hole in the ground. Yet, I can't complain, can I? I'm not exactly a millionaire.

If I had to describe my privileged poverty, it would be like this: My kitchen table is a wobbly stool that can barely support the pasta I can barely afford. My nine metres squared apartment almost ensures that I'll stand on something fallen out of place, often times a plug, sometimes even the adaptor to the plug. "Lunch" has now become Coffee. "Laundry" is now Carpet. I have to stand beside the fusebox when I boil the kettle because the power keeps tripping. My sofa-bed, that blocks the front door when put down, gives me aches all along the back-side of my body, and I mean *all* along. The only sink in my apartment is filled with dirty plates, toothpaste and cigarette ash. The mould on my shower curtain is starting to form some kind of Rorschach test. And even though I don't know what that smell is, I'm just relieved that it isn't me.

When I'm not cooking at home, I'm usually out buying food in fast-food restaurants or boulangeries, not so much to eat quickly as to just simply get out of the apartment and enjoy some space. Spending money I don't have when each night ends with a prayer for pay day.

This contrasts with the recent success I've had with girls. Having a key to an apartment seems to have reopened the door to my sex life. It took some time to brush the dust off my skills, but each failing led to improvement. Of course, none of these relationships are serious. Nothing more than just casual hook-ups.

For the first time in my life, I'm starting to enjoy being single. I can see three girls at one time and none of them will mind, so why should I? I'm no longer as puritanical about sex or feeling guilty about not emotionally attaching myself to them. This past three weeks has undone years of Catholicism.

Anyway, with none of the aforementioned ladies available, I guess I'm not in any hurry to head home tonight...

I pop my head into two bars that are open in the area. One, on the square has formally dressed waiters juxtapositioned against the drowsy drunks slumped against chairs and slurring orders. The next place, a little further down the quay, beams out bright disco lights from a dark room. The music hammering at the windows is almost visible. Being too sober for either, I take a brief roam through the cobblestone alleyways, away from the statue.

I always liked the statue of Saint-Michel. The domineering Archangel, sword held high and a small serpent under his foot. Water cascades over stone shelves and glimmer silver under the lights. I guess it's supposed to represent that evil will always be cast out by the good. It's an ideal, isn't it? The real world is never so simple.

It's an eerily comfortable walk. The narrowness of the alleys both swaddle and constrict me. A Victorian creepiness hangs over me in its well-lit tranquillity. The air is warm, heavy and breathless. I walk slowly around the sharp corners until I get to the main streets again. I'm stopped by a tourist asking for directions who points to their map and taps me on the head repeatedly. I send them on their way, only realising their oddness afterwards.

Still not terribly eager to go home, I venture out a bit more. It's not long before rain starts trickling down. I'm not too bothered by it. It's almost refreshing at this point. I pull the collar of my jacket tight around my neck and continue my walk-about.

I lose track of time and arrive outside a small park. The streets are quiet save for one man walking his dog. The dog potters around the street, his paws plopping around in the mud, dirtying its white coat. It's a Husky, I think. It's unleashed, but seems docile enough so I'm not worried. I like dogs anyway.

A loud, whining sound erupts out of nowhere as something cuts right past me. A striking thud and a yelp follows.

A scooter's tail-lights.

Screeching in the distance.

The man shouts at the scooter then turns to his dog. His face freezes in agony and I follow his gaze to see a limp mound of fur on the ground.

"No! No, no! Please, no!" He cries out, as he falls down beside it. He strokes away at the coat desperately, its chest remains still. I slowly walk towards him and break into a little jog. Drawn by my desire to help, slowed down by the futility of it.

He looks up at me. "Help me! Please! Help him!"

"I- I don't think I can." I stammer out.

"There's a vet near here! By Place Monge!"

I look at the poor mutt's messy skull. Blood is starting to pool around his head, disturbed by droplets of water falling from the sky. Some grey matter...

I shake my head to the tearful man. He moans out, his hands clutching tufts of his dog's hair. I really feel for the guy. I had a dog that died less than a year ago. A Golden Labrador. He was a wonderful animal. A creature of boundless energy and infinite affection. A bit bi-polar, he'd be running around everywhere one minute and then collapsing on the floor the next. Indeed, dogs are like their owners. I was the exact same with Cat. Manic for attention and sulky to be spurned of it. Too much love for the levee to hold.

We had my dog cremated, and that was fitting for him as he was never much for burying things...

I take a step back from the deceased dog and his distraught owner. I extend my hand to signal him to stay there as I walk off slowly in the direction of the scooter.

Visibility was low with the rain. This hit and run could easily have been an accident. Braking wouldn't have been as effective either. Did a bit of precipitation precipitate this?

A single tyre mark is embedded in the tarmac where the scooter turned the corner. I pull out my phone and take a few photos of it. The mark gets me thinking. I scan over the ground from the corner to where the dog was hit. There are no more tyre marks. Just the one at the corner.

My memory is a bit muddled after what happened, probably due to the shock of it all, but the evidence speaks for itself. He never braked after hitting the dog. I would have thought, if it was an accident, that they would have braked automatically, to avoid colliding with something and hurting themselves. This was intentional...

I return to the man to tell him my suspicions. I hesitate as I look at him. He's calmed down considerably. His shoulders rise and fall through laboured breathing as he stares at his dog. I struggle to think of something consolatory to say.

"He was a symbol for me, you know?" He says to me, eyes still cast downwards.

"A symbol?"

"Most of my friends... They made their money, they went back to Senegal, opened up their own businesses. I stayed here, in France. I still support my family back there, but... This place is my home. He was the friend that would stay with me."

"I'm sorry."

"My children, they grew up with him... I don't know what to say to them."

"Do you have any enemies?"

"Enemies?! Of course not! Why would you ask me that?"

"This seems intentional. I just want to find who did this."

"Who did this? What does it matter, when it's done?!"

"To help other people?" I say, weakly.

"Very few people ever do..." He replies.

The Senegalese man picks up his pet and trudges away. His last words leave me thinking. I believe he was referring to the racism he has experienced here. I've overheard people speak vulgar things about Africans, seen the looks people give. It's a strangeness that we could treat something so foreign to us, such as a dog, with complete love and something so close to us, like a fellow human-being, with such disdain.

I return to following the tyre mark trail. I find two more marks guiding me in the killer's direction before losing his tracks. I run up to examine as many scooters as I can find parked on the street but few match the tail-lights that I remember and none have any damage to the front.

I wander around the area a little. I spot a flyer for a cat that's gone missing but, deciding to focus on one animal at a time, I ignore the details. Ten minutes later, I give up and head back home, seething and sore.

****

I swing by the hotel to meet Amae outside and offer my apologies for the previous day.

"I wanted to say I'm sorry for what I said yesterday. I was being a complete dickhead. I would miss you a lot if you left, and I'm sorry if I implied I wouldn't."

"It's okay... I may've over-reacted... It's just because – Well – Me and Dylan are going back to Ireland in four weeks."

"Ye're going back?!"

"We were going to tell everyone! But neither of us were too sure, like. I only made the decision two days ago."

"What made you decide to leave? Don't you like it here?"

"I *do* like it here! It's just that I got accepted into the Masters course that I wanted in Dublin."

"You're going back to college?"

"Yeah. I just don't want to end up working in hotels and stuff for the rest of my life."

"Understandable... And Dylan?"

"He got offered a job back home with his Dad where he can use his degree."

"Right... Wait, what about your boyfriend? Is he going?"

"No, he's staying. We've done long distance before. Neither of us like it, but it's worth it, like."

"Grand..."

"I'm sorry."

"No! Don't be! I'm happy for you! You got the Masters program that you wanted!"

I give her a tight hug to congratulate her, heart sinking and chest compressing. I *am* happy for her and I do want the best for her. And I can't argue that her doing this course wouldn't secure her future in terms of employment.

"I'm going to miss you." She mumbles into my chest.

"I'll miss you too..."

 Amae pulls away and fans her eyes in a mock verge of tears then chuckles before heading back to work. She made making things right easy for me. People that care about each other often do. The transition is smoother, the obstacles less obstructive. It's because we want things to be good again. That what we built is still standing.

 It was harder with Cat. Neither of us were quite sure if we wanted to keep what we had. A week after she deleted me on Facebook, she sent me an innocuous email and we inched back towards speaking again. I got about half of the photos from Croatia from her, with a promise that she'd send the rest later. It was a foot in the right direction, but only a foot...

 The fact that Amae kept her departure a secret from me irked me some, but she's easy to forgive for it. It's strange how this contrasts to the secret that Cat kept from me. Our arguments had finally peaked to a moment of revelations over the phone. We had nothing left to lose.

 I started by telling her that I had been with other girls while I was with her, but I maintained that it was before Andy had come over and that it wasn't cheating. She laughed when I told her. She really didn't care who I slept with.

 But then came her confession. A cruel curveball. That she got drunk and had fucked some guy about a week after my birthday. Another one of her exes. A guy by the name of Hank, her last ex before me. They were together for about a year. She loved him. More than she would ever love me...

 To make matters worse. This guy had a girlfriend at the time, which Cat knew. The thought of her, someone I thought was a perfect form of love, being someone's mistress for a night devastated me.

 After I heard this, my heart and brain was on fire. All the

vague memories and scenarios swirled around in a maelstrom before my closed eyes. Each harsh word snapped at my soul, gnawed at it. The images invaded every tangent I used to escape them. My gut shrank into itself. Agitated hands tore at the bedsheets. All the things I pictured her doing. Things I knew she'd done, but never saw... Was she smiling, I wonder?

I was in a fury. I was going to find him. Tell his girlfriend everything. I wanted to ruin his life. But I stopped myself. I knew that telling his girlfriend would do nothing but embarrass her because she already knew he had cheated. She must have. In the darkest corner of my mind, I knew all along...

We kept talking afterwards, but there wasn't much point. We had reached the end. Our conversations just became a tired effort to stay civil. I knew that I was nothing special, just another in a sea of suitors. I was never going to be enough for her and that there was always going to be someone else. She'd never be mine to keep...

I spent most of the time pleading with her to pay me back for sending her back her things and getting the rest of the photos from Croatia.

I was just trying to grab as much as I could before our time ran out...

****

The chandelier looks quite impressive hanging from the foyer ceiling, albeit just a little bit too low for comfort. The very tip of the base could be slapped if you jumped and extended your arm out. I know this because I've done it already.

As I brush down corners of the foyer for cobwebs, a guest waits awkwardly and silently at the desk.

"Your Wi-Fi isn't working." He says showing me his smartphone.

"That's odd, seeing as my internet works perfectly."

"Well the guest Wi-Fi seems to be down. Can you check the modem?"

"If I can find it." I tell him with a smile. He stares back blankly.

I look around and eventually find where the modems are. To my surprise, I find two. One modem has a flashing red, blinking light that returns to a steady green after it's been reset. The other seems already operational. It dawns on me that we have two so that one is for staff and the other is for the guests. I tell him that the problem has been rectified and he walks off without so much as a thank you.

Something has been bugging me for a while, so I decide to get to the bottom of it. Taking down the details of the two modems. I go back to the horrible online reviews that we had and compare the IP addresses of both modems. The reviews are coming from the staff connection. That can only mean someone working here is trying to sabotage the business...

Wondering who, the list is long...

****

I return to the area where I lost track of the tyre marks and admonish myself for my ignorance the last time I was here. Of course I wouldn't find the scooter on the street, the killer's first move would be to get it out of sight. This time, I'll search the underground car parks in the area.

I search two car parks in the area and can't even find a scooter. The third yields one scooter, but not the one I'm looking for. I trudge around, chain smoking, until another idea pops into my head. A car pulls in to a gated building, its doors just wide enough for the car to fit through. I sprint as fast as I can and just manage to slide in behind it safely. The driver seems worried but I walk past him casually.

Inside, there's a rather large courtyard. Only one car is parked inside, aside from the one parking now. A row of scooters line the wall of the southern building. One of them is covered with a grey sheet. I check the other scooters just in case. All of them are intact. I glance around and wave awkwardly at the man getting out of his car, who nods anxiously back at me. He steps into the building and I give the courtyard one last check.

I roll down my sleeves to cover my hands and lift the sheet off the scooter. The tail-lights, body colour and style is a match to what I remember, but the front is the most damning. The headlight is cracked on one side. Hands in my pocket, I stoop down to get a better look. Inside the crack, I can see the smallest tuft of white hair. A match to our dead dog.

The last thing needed to verify that this is the vehicle in question is to check the tyres. The grooves embedded in the rubber are the exact same as those in the street. I've found his home base.

A chill runs down my spine, despite the humid, night heat. I'm now in the vicinity of an incredibly cruel person. I'll have to tread carefully. There's no telling what he looks like or if he'll be coming around the corner any second. Still, I need to know more about the killer.

With little other options, I'm forced to get my hands dirty. Bins are left out and, even though I don't know what I'm looking for, there might be something to help with my investigation. I'd rather get this one closed as soon as possible anyway.

The smell is horrid. The sticky night air lets it evaporate upwards, burying itself into my skin. Untying a black bin-bag, I use an empty Coke bottle near the top of the pile to root through the rest of the trash. I go through two bags, taking each one out quietly and carefully, without any luck. The third one, as I lift it out, seems heavier than it should be for such a small parcel. It's sealed with a piece of grey string that often comes with the bin-bags, the string wrapped around evenly several times and finished with a near-perfect bow. I pull at one of the strings and unwind it. A putrid odour emanates the second the bag opens. My gag reflex kicks in and I pull my sleeve over my mouth as the bile rises in my throat before I swallow it back down.

Remembering to breathe through my mouth this time, I open the bag and look inside. At first, I'm not sure what it is that I'm seeing. It looks like a mess of butchered meat. Then one of the shapes in the bag begins to make form.

My throat closes around the vomit as it comes up again and I drop down onto my knees. I throw the bag a metre away from me and take a few moments to breathe through my nose this time, not trusting myself to have my mouth open. My stomach cramps as I struggle to regain control of my body. My head begins to ache as the images keep assaulting my brain. I've just seen a cat's head stripped of it's fur.

The courtyard spins and I take deliberate breathes to calm myself down. I need a plan of action. I reluctantly retrieve the cat in the bag and tie it back the way it had been before, careful not to leave any fingerprints. This whole affair is way out of my league.

I'm terrified that this monster is going to find me, and I'm angry that I'm scared of him. This person is pure evil. An abomination. He doesn't belong in the same world as us. Yet he has the power to instil terror in me, control me.

I contemplate giving the details to the Senegalese man if I can find him, but decide against it. Even if he was brave or ferocious enough to take on this animal, revenge would only land him in trouble with the law.

I know what I have to do. I've come to accept it, embrace it even. The idea that the good are never powerless. That we draw our power from our solidarity with others. This killer can only be alone with his secret, but it's time to bring it into the light and show everyone what he is. Take his power away by showing him the strength of what we've spent millennia building. A society that protects us from evil.

I walk into a nearby hotel and ask them if I can use their phone. They oblige me, for five Euro, and I phone the police. I give them the details of what happened in short hand. That a dog was struck and that I followed the aggressor back to his residence. I give them the licence plate of the scooter. From there, I veer off a bit from the truth. I tell them I heard strange noises from his apartment and that after they had stopped, he had come out with a strange bag to put in the bin. When the operator asks me for my name, I hang up and leave.

The police are in no hurry to arrive. Two hours pass before I see a squad car roll up slowly. They sit in the car for a few minutes before three officers get out and enter the building. Half an hour goes by until I see one of the officers come out, checking the street. He's followed by three more figures, two officers and a tall man.

They're quite far away, so I can't really make out much, but the man appears to be handcuffed. He seems quite unassuming. Frightfully thin, poorly shaven. A creature one would almost pity if they didn't know what he had done. I shrink back into the darkness as the killer's eyes roam the street.

I do my best to make sure that fear doesn't get in my way. When I ran away from home, I just picked up the fear and carried it with me. The best thing about doing that is that the further you carry it, the more likely it is that you'll lose it along the way.

Although one could always argue that it was fear that made me run in the first place...

The sense of victory that I thought I would feel isn't there, but rather a relief that it's all over. The world around me feels a little bit safer knowing that he's in custody. I don't understand how there could actually be people like this in the world. So cold and sadistic.

For all the pain Cat unleashed on me, I never wanted to see her upset or in pain. I would always want to take care of her. I suppose I still do, in a way...

Her cacti that she left behind still sit on a shelf in my apartment. I water them once a month. What began as a duty turned into a keepsake. When that memory turned sour and rancid, I told myself that plants create oxygen. It would clean the air of my apartment, which could only be good for a chain smoker like me.

It's a sense of relief that, throughout all my anger, I know I'm not a bad person at heart. All the times my heart broke, my fists crunched against themselves, my mind spiralled out of control, I could never be rid of those prickly bastards. Despite all the rage, when I wished hellfire would rain down on the earth, I couldn't even commit herbicide.

****

I walk home to the only slum in the eighth arrondissement and start to think about Cat again. I hate thinking about her. Where most of my nightly adventures usually do well enough to distract me from thinking of her, tonight I think I need a distraction from this case.

She was an addiction I needed to kick. The thought of being without her wasn't as bad as the thought of being with her. I couldn't keep feeling pathetic about myself and I was vicious to her as a result. Every day a diatribe. Loving her hurt too much. Eventually, I just wanted to be a good person. And maybe that's the only part of me that was left after she was gone...

I gave up on trying to change her. I even stopped trying to get the rest of the photos and my money back for the postage. We ended things over the phone in mid-October.

"You deserve, and can find, better than me..." She told me.

"Take care of yourself, Cat..."

"Good luck..."

So, she had her and I had me...

After the more immediate aftermath of our breakup, only a few minutes, I felt a sense of relief. A promise to myself that I wouldn't let her get inside my head again and muddle things up. That the intense feelings I had, so big and so close to my heart, were finally growing smaller in the distance.

The leaves turned brown as the silence between us settled in.

The greatest love I'd ever known, gone.

A little bit, a piece of my heart, lost forever.

My summer, done...

Case 18 – Return to Sender

It's Marine's birthday and she's decided that she wants to have a fancy dress party at Cole's. Halloween is still about two and a half months away and it's not such a big thing here as it is back home anyway. This is as good a night as any for disguise and debauchery.

I'm glad I decided to go as Indiana Jones. I'm still a little self-conscious about how I'm dressed, but the fedora on my lap and my clothes only make me look pretentious, which isn't an uncommon sight here in Paris. A whip, that I made out of twine and floor polish, along with a toy revolver, lie hidden in a plastic bag. Still, I'm eager to join the other costumed folk.

Standing outside the bar to finish my cigarette, two voices blare out over a microphone singing "Total Eclipse of the Heart". I peer in through the window to see a Zombie and Catwoman, Marine and Amae. The two ladies' voices, normally incredibly talented, are obscured by their insobriety and pure enthusiasm in sounding as obnoxious as possible.

"Who are you supposed to be?" Matt asks through plastic vampire teeth.

"Slutty Indiana Jones."

"How's that outfit slutty?"

"It's not the outfit that's slutty!" I wink at him.

I look him up and down. Slick black hair, a grey cloak and black clothing with a yellow belt.

"You'll never guess who I am!" He taunts me.

"Dracula?"

"Nope! Guess again?"

"I give up."

"I'm the Bat-Man. Half bat – Half man."

"... Right."

"You're just jealous."

"Probably."

"You okay? You seem glum for Indiana Jones." Marine asks, standing between Matt and me.

 Indeed, looking around at couples mingling together, I'm feeling a little left out. None of the hook-ups I've had have panned out to anything else. The few that expressed an interest in something more serious, I turned down. I didn't see a future with them, nor feel any hook of the pheromones, and I didn't want to lead them on to eventually let them down.

 The only girl that I did want a real relationship with didn't reciprocate my feelings, so I walked away from it. It was difficult for me, pulling away from her when I wanted her as badly as I did. But I knew where it would lead if I kept spending time with her. I would just end up angry and possessive. She deserved better than that.

 I abandoned them all. I know it was the right thing to do, for me and for them, but now, in this room, I feel lonely. Maybe even misplaced? Although, I've felt these feelings worse before.

"I'm just having trouble finding the right girl." I tell them.

"You'll find a nice, pretty lady soon enough." Marine reassures me.

Matt wraps his arm around me. "C'mere puddin'. I know your dick's feeling a little lonely, but you're here with some wonderful people who love and care about you. We're all in it together. Although, you'll probably have to wank into your sock for just a little while longer."

"I usually use toilet paper, actually."

"I didn't need to know that, but I'm glad we're at the point of our friendship where we can talk about this... Anyway, grab a drink and catch up with us. Marine isn't getting any younger!"

Perhaps not that eloquent, but Matt has a point. These people have shown me an incredible amount of love and affection over the past few months. Often times, more than I deserved. It's time to return their affection. Give back to them what they've instilled in me. I take it upon myself to buy Marine and Matt drinks for the rest of the night, sending every empty glass back to be refilled. Marine deserves a birthday as good as the one they all gave me.

By the end of the night we slowly start to stumble away. Matt, Marine and I are the last to leave. Matt waves and shouts at me before getting into the taxi.

"Fuck you for ruining us! I love you! Goodbye!"

****

Red, green and brown. A tree on fire. Small enough, but still an eyesore. I can't help but let out an anguished sigh. I know I'm the one that's going to be asked to fix it. I'm usually the one stuck with the shit end of the stick. Paint is so goddamn hard to scrub off. Why would anyone want to graffiti a hotel anyway?

I head back inside, fuming. My blood is boiling, as if it wasn't hot enough. I hurl my jacket up on to the rack and fall into my chair. After calming down a little, I absent-mindedly flick through the calendar on the computer. As predicted, the reservations are even fewer than they had been before. We might not even have any guests for the winter and I doubt Crow is going to pay us to sit in an empty hotel.

Today is proving to be a particularly shit day. None of this seems fair. A guest walks in as my teeth grind against each other. I smile at him with my lips sealed and type in his information with white knuckles, my hand squeezing the computer mouse.

Ten minutes of painful silence go by when I can't take it anymore. I'm going to find out who graffitied the hotel and then I'm going to make them pay.

I walk up to Crow's office on the top floor and knock on the door. My excuse, if he's in there, is to ask him about a week off from work sometime in the next few months. The knock isn't answered and I sneak into the room.

The monitor is off but the computer is left on, as always, and isn't password protected, seeing as Crow is technologically incompetent. I know the name of the software he uses to check the cameras by occasionally having looked over his shoulder. I sit down in the chair and listen intently for any footsteps.

Nothing.

Clicking on the shortcut, I'm greeted with a message in French instead of the camera feed.

"Your subscription to use the online storage and remote viewing that this service provides is no longer available. To continue to use this service, please renew your contract."

I exit out of the message and I'm greeted with another message.

"Storage full. Recording disabled. To delete files, click here."

I look into the saved footage files to find that the last saved recording was from a little over three months ago, back in May. That means Crow hasn't been able to spy on us for all this time. I allow myself a little smirk before I check the real-time footage to find out what's going on now. As luck would have it, none of the cameras are facing out onto the street anyway. I forgot that it's illegal in France for a company to do that. The footage from last night probably would have been useless to me.

I turn off the monitor and slip back out of the room. Crow's kept this one quiet. All this time he's been barking orders at us, he's been doing it blind. The others will be glad to know we're not being spied on anymore.

None of this helps me with finding the graffiti artist though. I step back outside to take a look on the street for any cameras. There's one protruding on top of a shop down the street. Judging by the angle, it should be just about enough to cover the wall that was sprayed. I walk towards the shop to enquire about the camera when I run into Bee.

"Oh, hello! How have you been?" She asks.

"Yeah, I've been good. You?"

"I've been good. Yes... I'm sorry, but I feel bad. I had forgotten your name until I read your badge!"

"I don't think I ever got yours, actually."

"Nina."

"Nice to see you again, Nina."

"Are you working tonight?"

"Unfortunately. Someone graffitied the side of the building. I have to head into the shop over there and ask them for the footage."

"That camera is not from shop. It is from the building. I know the owner. If you like, I can get the video and I will email it to you?"

"Would you mind?"

"Not at all! Hello?! I owe you. I am returning a favour."

"I appreciate it!"

    I receive the email from Nina at around midnight. The recording is about twelve hours long so I fast forward through it. The playback jumps in increments of five minutes. At 1:45am, according to the time stamp, the tag appears.

    I rewind at a slower pace to see the vandal. The picture is quite grainy, but I can make a few things out. He pulls up on a bike, reaches into a white, cloth bag for the spray canisters and a stencil sheet. He's finished after a matter of twenty seconds, then he hops back on his bike and pedals away.

    I get lucky and the vandal rides towards the camera, hunched over the bicycle frame. They're wearing one of those masks people use to guard against breathing in exhaust fumes and a baseball cap, so I can't make out their face.

Just before cycling out of frame, he swerves unsteadily on the bike and the white bag slips forward. There appears to be something written on it. I rewind the footage and press pause. On the bag, I can make out the words: *Yew're It!*

I don't know of any organisation of that name, but it's the closest thing I have to a lead.

A quick search online leads me to an event with the same name, right here in Paris, tomorrow night. Something to do with an ecological-activist group. The only location given as a meeting point is "Notre Dame area. You know where." I guess I'll have to look around on foot.

I return to the blemished wall with a brush and a bucket of soapy water. Crow, unsurprisingly, is too cheap for a power hose. With one eye on the front door for any guests coming in, I start scrubbing away at the paint. Each furious stroke adds a new promise of revenge for the person that's making me do this...

The weather in my head intensifies as I traverse the landscape of my memories. Tempests on both hemispheres when I get to Cat. Dark, dirty clouds in my mind and thunder-strikes in my stomach.

In the wake of Cat leaving and all that I threw at her, I was a fucking mess the night we stopped talking. In a hostel room, drunk as hell. Waving my arms around to the music coming from my phone. The bright light of the screen throwing shadows on the roof. Thinking of her. Replaying everything. After the fact, there was no pacing. The good and the bad rolled one after the other in instants. And I was dying inside.

It came in waves later. A rock placed on my chest after I took a wrong turn in my head. A psychosomatic suffering. I barely slept. All the memories of her raced through my mind. I just wanted to reach out to her, pull her back to me, have everything go back to normal. No voice outside to drag me from the ones inside. Heartbroken and cut-off. Gut-rotted and garotted.

When I look back, I see everything. The whole Atlantic ocean. It's tides pulling me back and forth towards the shores of France then to the shores of America. The waves of why I loved her and why she's gone...

I suffered through losing her in miserable circumstances. I didn't have any reliable accommodation, which led to a few stints sleeping on the streets. I couldn't take being in *our* bar either and left. I had already distanced myself from our co-workers and I needed the holiday-pay owed to me to survive. It was a desperate recovery from a dire path.

I left myself completely vulnerable to her and ended up destroyed, but she came out cleaner. I still can't forgive her. She hurt me more than anyone else ever had. The money she still owes me for sending her stuff back remains a loose thread that keeps hanging me.

I never felt the sincerity in her apologies nor did she do anything to make amends. She owed me a spectacle of her misery to match my own. And maybe she did feel something for me at some point? Maybe there was a love there? A kindness... But I guess none of that matters if it wasn't sure, never shown and it won't be said...

As the bitterness and anger rises in my chest again, the furious buzzing in my temples, I wish to myself that I could push it out. Send it back to the depths that it came from. Replace it with the cool, blue, heavy sadness that I'm more comfortable with than the hot, red, electric hate. I'd rather be drowned in depression than burned out with fury.

Sadness is calmer and closer to peace...

****

It's always a pleasant sight, especially with the sun kissing its sacred stone. The back reminds me of a whale's ribcage, the way the curved pillars spread out and cascade down. The arches over the doorways, and the hundreds of figures carved into the them, leaves me with the impression that they tell a story I never truly cared to hear but can still enjoy its complexity. The Notre Dame Cathedral is quite incredible in its antiquity.

I ask in and around the cafés flanking the northern side of the church. None of the waiters know anything, tourists look back at me cluelessly with an entertained twinkle in their eyes and the locals contort their faces as if I've gone insane.

The church slides into the background as I cross the wide pedestrian bridge, always overrun with rollerbladers, towards Shakespeare and Company. The quaint bookshop is known for being a haven for writers and also for selling English books. Hopefully, someone will know something about what's going on in the area. I squeeze through the door just before they close as people come pouring out, one of them covered head to toe in glitter, and walk up to the cashier, a young, rather well-dressed man.

"Hi. Do you mind if I ask you something?" I ask.

"Nope. Shoot!"

"I'm looking for a *Yew're It!* meeting, spelt like the tree: *Y-E-W*. It's supposed to be somewhere around here."

"Hey, yeah! Someone did actually mention something like that to me recently."

"And?"

"Oh, I wasn't really paying attention though. I think they said something about a squat party?"

"A squat party, where?"

"Beats me."

"Any detail would help."

"Sorry, that's all I got."

"Maybe an area where the squat party is?"

"Look, I gotta close. Good luck finding it!"

I leave with a fake smile and a wave. I'm sure he would have more information if he tried hard enough to think. I could wait outside for him to leave the shop and ask him when he's got a bit more time on his hands. Although, there's no real reason for him to bother, he doesn't owe me anything.

Nina owed me something, I guess. I wonder if there's anyone else I can call in a favour for? A few come to mind. Hummingbird might have made some friends with the Anarchists and they're quite fond of squat parties from what I've heard. I could also ask François to see if there's a drug connection...

Joel! He seems like a pretty bohemian kind of fellah. Very earthy. He's probably been to a few squat parties in his time. He's also a pretty nice guy and I wouldn't mind talking to him again.

The first time dials straight through to voicemail, but the second time I catch him.

"Hello?"

"Hey. Remember that guy who helped you get your guitar bag back?"

"Yeah, man! How you been?"

"I'm good... I kind of need a favour though."

"Sure. Name it."

"Do you know of any squat parties in the Notre Dame area?"

"Squat parties? Why would I know anything about squat parties?"

"Well... I mean..."

"Did you think just because I play music on the streets and dress the way I do that I spend a lot of time in dingy squats?"

"... Yes?"

"... That's kind of insulting."

"I'm sorry! It's just that I'm looking into this thing called *Yew're it!* and they're doing this squat party in the area."

"Well, I don't know of any- How... How do you spell *You're it*?"

"Y-E-W."

"... Goddamn it!... Hang on..."

"What?"

"Ugh... I know where the fucking squat party is. I got invited to it by my friend Millie... I'll send you the address."

"Thank you! I appreciate it!"

"No problemo. So... When are we gonna jam together?"

"Ehm... I'm free Tuesday?"

"Tuesday it is! Ah, shit. I gotta go. I'll text you!"

"Later!"

A moment of exhilaration passes through me for my accomplishment. The text comes through and I'm roaring to go. I finally feel like I'm getting back what I deserve, and now I get to give someone what they deserve too.

****

There's a bouncer at the door, not a licensed one, just a very large man questioning the people walking in. It looks like this place used to be a car dealership before it was closed down and boarded up.

"Is your name on the list?" He asks.

"I'm not too sure."

"If you're not sure, then you aren't."

"I was invited by a friend."

"Who's your friend?"

"It's... Millie..."

"Go ahead."

I step into darkness. The first floor is completely empty, save for a broken office chair. In the centre of the room, there's a large spiral staircase leading down. It's a precarious descent. The dim lighting makes me anxious and the occasional loose tile makes me question the structural integrity of the stairs.

A light below beckons me to go down the corridor, a flood light pointed at the wall. Loud voices chatter from behind a floral patterned curtain. I draw it back.

"Welcome! So glad to have you here!" A woman with dreadlocks welcomes me with a hug. I tense up then relax in her arms. She guides me to the makeshift bar, a counter with plastic cups and boxes of wine. It's two Euro a cup and I figure – why not?

A stage, complete with curtains and spotlights, appears when I turn around. These guys must have worked really hard on this place.

Several different acts come on. Mostly musicians of broadly varying styles, from Caribbean to Country, with some interpretive dance acts and one incredibly mundane mime.

I scan over the room to find someone matching the already vague description that I have, to no avail. They're probably not even here.

I head back to the makeshift bar for another plastic cup of red wine. I might as well get something out of my efforts tonight. It also gives me the courage to start chatting to the random people in here.

"The mime was pretty shit, right?" A girl from the group I'm talking to asks me in a hushed voice. She has a pretty face. Pale skin, her brown hair is cut stylishly short and her brown jacket looks like a military uniform, save for the floral badges on the sleeves.

"Yeah, I wasn't sure if he could see me roll my eyes through the glass wall he made."

"I'm Danni." She says with a smile.

"Are you part of the *Yew're It!* thing?"

"More of a supporter. I'm an artist by trade."

"Cool. What kind of stuff do you do?"

"A bit of everything. Sculptures, paintings, sketches, you know...

How about you?"

"I work in a hotel. It's incredibly boring."

"Well, I bet you meet lots of interesting people?"

"I guess that depends on the night and what you'd define as interesting."

"Ah! I see..."

"I do have some side projects though." I tell her, eager to impress her.

"Like what?"

"Well, right now, I'm trying to track down a graffiti artist that tagged my hotel."

"A graffiti artist that tagged your hotel?"

"Yup!"

"And what are you going to do with this graffiti artist? Turn them in to the police?"

"Not the police... I haven't really thought about what I'm going to do to him."

"Hmm. That's not much of a revenge fantasy!"

"I've had better, I'll admit."

"Ooh! Now that's a story I want to hear! Let me guess... A girl hurt your feelings?"

"More or less. Another American, like you."

"I'm Canadian, actually. Did she study here? I know one or two Americans in my university."

"No, she was working."

"So, what happened?"

I recount the whole story briefly to her about our relationship and my subsequent hardships.

"Long story short, she didn't want to make a commitment and broke my heart." I tell her.

"Why were you with her if she didn't want what you did?"

"Because I loved her."

"That's stupid."

"Why?"

"It doesn't make any sense!"

"I know it doesn't make any sense to you... It doesn't make any sense to me either! But, I reckon love isn't supposed to make sense."

"So, she was definitely the bad guy for not commiting to you."

"In my opinion, yes."

"You're a misogynist, you know that?!"

"No, I'm not!"

"Yes, you are! You're just blaming her for not doing what *you* wanted, for making a choice *you* didn't agree with, and then everything else after she left."

"I-"

"- And this graffiti artist too."

"What about him?"

"Why does it have to be a him?"

"It doesn't *have* to be. But I saw him on CCTV."

"Well... What if I told you that *I* was the one who graffitied the hotel."

    I look at her perplexed and she gazes back at me with a hint of wild thrill, eyes bigger than a cartoon coyote's.

"I wouldn't believe you."

"Even if I told you it was a tree on fire and that I was on a bike?"

I stare back at her in shock. My eyes squint. The plastic cup in my hand starts to gently compact itself under my tightening fist as the wine spills out over my knuckles.

"Express your anger!" She tells me, arms held out towards me.

"What the fuck is wrong with you?!"

"What do you mean?"

"I mean, *darling*, I spent fucking ages scrubbing that fucking wall!"

"Why did you clean it?"

"When you do that, someone has to fucking clean it!"

"I never asked anyone to erase my work. My shit is art."

"You still don't get it, do you? You're making someone else's life difficult because of what you've done. You're just too selfish to realise it! You're just like…"

"Like?"

"*Her…*"

"You've got a lot of anger in you, don't you?"

"I do now."

"I think you should find a better way of expressing it."

"Such as?!"

"Art? Writing? Screaming into a pillow? You have to let that shit out, dude. You're white knuckling it, right now. You can't keep holding it in and pushing it down, wearing yourself out. You're gonna explode! The anger is always there, until it comes back on someone else."

"Like the girl that tagged my hotel?"

"Or your ex?"

"She hurt me too you know?!"

"Sounds like you've been hurting yourself more than she has."

"What do you mean?"

"Well, what can anyone do to you that you can't do to yourself a thousand times worse?"

"You're saying I'm breaking my own heart?"

"I'm saying you have a lot of anger and it seems like you tend to focus all of it on one particular thing at a time."

A feeling starts to flood over me. All this anger over things I could never control. Things I never had the courage to lash out against or express. Every unlucky injustice that's hurt me inside and out.

"I guess I've just had a difficult life..."

"Is that her fault?" Danni asks.

"Huh?"

"She's not here anymore. She hasn't done anything lately to upset you. It's been almost a year since you broke up, so... Is it still her fault?"

I don't have any response for her.

"Think about it?" She shrugs. As someone catches her attention, she pats me on the shoulder. "Good talk!"

With my head aching, I put my crushed cup down, then walk out of the building.

I arrive home and think it all over. Pacing back and forth, which isn't easy to do in a tiny apartment and almost serves to agitate me more. Each of the injustices throw themselves back in my face, taunting me. Waves of rage rise higher and froth.

Jesus, but for a second admit that Danni might be right?!

The scenarios that I keep playing back and forth in my head about Cat never happened, nor will they. Not the ones tearing me to bits on the inside. Scattered and pulled. These torrential torments are my own doing and my suffering is a fiction. I've been having this nightmare for months. I had dreamt of our future, revised by our past and revisited all our best moments, but after it all, the dreams have been watched. It's time I woke up...

I have to let go of her. It's not that I'm ready or it's time to move on, but because *she* is no longer real anymore. This girl in my head that has hurt me for so long is a twisted imagining of the girl that exists. A crooked shadow of the person who moved on from me long ago and left me behind. She's not the girl I fell in love with.

I'm not giving Cat my power any more. She took it and used it against me. My heart in her hands was anguished. She deserves my apathy for it and I deserve my love back. I might have allowed her to be cruel to me, but she was still an asshole for doing it. And with all the memories I have of her, I've had it with her.

By blaming her for everything, I told myself that I didn't have any control over my recent misfortunes. It's time to take it all back...

The power and the fault...

****

I wake up and, after looking at the miserable, end-of-month pile of dirty clothes in the corner, I root through my unpacked rucksack for some clean clothes. I pull out a jacket that I haven't worn in months and idly check the pockets in case there's any money in there. Instead of cash, I pull out a crumpled piece of paper. I unfurl the ball and my gaze is met by Mouse.

I must have forgotten to get rid of it. I turn towards the bin to crumple up the page again but I catch myself looking at her. I guess it wouldn't hurt to keep it around. I grab a pair of scissors and cut around the edges until only the photo is left. Then, I carefully fold the photo and place it in my wallet.

The alarm on my phone goes off to remind me that I have to meet Amae, so I throw on my old jacket and leave.

We go for coffee to say our goodbyes. The clock is ticking down to the time she has to leave as she still has a few things to pack before her flight tomorrow.

We sit on a terrace under the glowing sun as it starts to set. Over warm, paper cups we talk about what the future holds for both of us. Where we'll be. Who we'll be.

"I don't want to leave Paris now." She says nervously.

"Understandable, dear... But Paris isn't going anywhere. You're going to go back, get your Master's Degree and then come back here with a kick-ass job making serious money."

"I know... I'm just going to miss you guy-zez is all."

"Ah, sure, we'll be here waiting for you."

"Not all of ye."

"We'll never be too far away..."

"Yeah..."

I walk her back to the metro in a surreal haze. Partly in denial of the fact that one of my best friends is leaving and my world is changing again. We get to hugging each other goodbye when tears mist her eyes.

"I love you!" She tells me and my heart cracks.

"I love you too! This isn't the end, okay? I'll see you next time I'm home!"

"Oh, you're right! I am gonna miss you though!" She says, regaining control and laughing to herself.

"Same here, miss... I'll see you soon?"

"See you soon!" She assures me.

One final embrace and I walk away from her, waving back until she descends into the metro. I meant what I said to her. Our friendship isn't over and an ocean won't impede us. I won't let it...

I make my rendez-vous with Dylan a few hours later. We sit over a couple of quiet pints, Guinness for me and Blanche for him.

"You mind me asking what makes you want to go back?" I ask him.

"I just feel like it's time to start my life."

"That's funny, I feel like I only started my life here."

"Right... Well, that'd be a new one."

"Yeah?"

"Well, I just think everyone in Paris is running from something."

"From life?"

"Life, family, responsibility. Pick one. This was kind of a break for me."

"I think I need to be away from my family to be who I want to be."

"It depends. I have a good relationship with my family. I know you don't really have much of one with yours."

"Maybe I'm running from them?"

"Maybe... I don't think you need to anymore though. You're your own man now."

"Stronger for my travels?"

"Or for your tribulations! You've been in some right states!" He chuckles.

"Ha! Yeah..."

"I have to go... Early flight. I'll see you at Christmas when you're back home?"

"I suppose you will..." I give him a hug. "Dylan, you're one of the best friends I've ever had."

"Same. God, it's strange to think it's only been a few months."

"You get what you give..."

    Dylan hails a cab and I watch the tail-lights disappear around the corner. Lighting a cigarette, I have a poignant feeling about the whole affair. I'm going to miss them both terribly, but I'm glad they're going back. I want the very best for them. For them to grow even further into the amazing people they already are.

No matter where they are in the world, they'll only ever be twenty-four hours away from me. We'll stay in contact. Even in gaps of silence, the lines of communication will stay open. Even when they're not by my side, they'll always be my friends.

It's the gift that keeps giving back...

Case 19 – Enigma

I don't think I imagined myself being a night porter this long. I guess I thought I'd move along to something better eventually. I'm not sure if it's laziness or apathy stopping me.

I know I could get a more corporate job, I have a degree after all. I reckon I'd be quite good at marketing too, but there's something soulless about it, along with an underlying unfairness. The idea of being paid a lot of money to bullshit people. Working smarter when people are paid much, much less for working harder. It seems like an unjust system that I don't really want to be part of. Life seems more real on the bottom rung.

Maybe I'm just worried that the raw truths of life would get disguised if I was ever successful? That the intricately dressed-up and decorated work would complicate my life more than I need.

Speaking of being pulled into work, I check the reservations for tonight. There are none! For the whole week we're expecting only four couples... But why?

I browse through the online reviews again to see how much worse they've gotten. One-star ratings dominate the board. Further research reveals, to my surprise, that the website which normally facilitates booking rooms with us have taken us off their site.

I check another site, and another. We've been taken off all of them. One cites that, due to dire reviews, they no longer want to represent our hotel. The only way anyone can book a room with us now is to call or walk in... This does not bode well for us...

I look around the empty foyer, then to the clock. Crow has yet to replace Amae and Dylan. There's no company to be had now or when my shift ends. I wish I could talk to them, air my fears about this place, only it would be too expensive for me to call or text them. Maybe it's time to give up on my self-imposed hiatus from

Facebook?

It's not difficult at all to reactivate my account, all I have to do is scratch my head for my old password and log in. Everything is there as it was before. Scary to think that it's been kept that long.

There is, however, one new addition to my old profile. A message from a former friend. Looking at the summary, the message seems innocuous enough. A simple "Hey, How are you?" I'm still hesitant to read it. It lies there like a trap ready to spring. A hole I could get pulled into. Eventually the curiosity gets the best of me and I open it.

"Hey, how are you? I know it's been a while since we've had a talk. How are you dealing with the break up? Me and the guys figured you could do with a bit of space after the whole thing. I know we were her friends too but we're here for you. Anyway, give us a call if you want to hang out."

I stare at the screen, numb. Perhaps I shouldn't have believed my interpretation that their shunned silence was fact, so sure that I knew what was going on behind closed doors that I didn't need to ask. They probably did the same. Read in between the lines and drew conclusions from the blank, white space. We painted our own pictures.

All this time, I thought they had abandoned me. Turns out they were just giving me space. I stare at the profile picture in front of me. A person that I used to call a friend. Used to... I close the tab with some guilt. I'm here to chase Amae and Dylan down. I'm doing this because I care about them and want to know what's going on in their lives. I suppose I shouldn't feel too bad considering this guy didn't chase me.

What I have with these friends of mine, and I know this for a fact because I can feel my heart swelling each time I think of them, is actual love. These people are incredibly special to me. They stand by me.

I track down Amae and Dylan and send a request to add them to my friends list. While I'm at it, I decide to add the rest of my friends. I take a virtual wander on my profile page for nostalgic purposes. I have hundreds of people listed here as my friends and can only really remember about half of them. Most of those I remember, I've since fallen out with. I take a deep breath, start at the beginning, and let the cull begin.

****

It's a rickety ride on Line 8, especially coming into République. You have to get used to the various pulls of the metro until you're able to stand there without holding on to the bars. I call it getting your metro legs.

My friends told me they're drinking by Canal Saint-Martin, a decent place for a few bottles and a guitar. If it gets colder or rains then we can always take shelter in an Irish bar that I know which even has its own book-exchange.

I'm looking forward to chilling out by the water and high, delicate bridges, even if there's no comfortable place to sit. When propping myself up with my hands becomes a little unbearable, I can just lie down on the concrete quay, let my head hang back over the edge and stare at the water. See the lights from the street and the buildings across dance on the calm canal. A world upside down, marvellous and closer to the stars.

I'm almost there now. I've just come into Place de la République. The open space is a relief. Everyone walks quite a distance away from each other, eager to dominate the space denied to us on the narrow streets. A grandiose statue conquers the wide square, plastered with posters and tagged with graffiti. I take a brief glance to see if I recognise any of Danni's work, but nothing stands out.

Homeless people loiter around the area. You can always identify them, not so much by tattered clothing, as most are decently clad, but by the large bags that they carry around, too big to be a late night shopping trip. I notice that they rarely ever carry rucksacks. I imagine it's because a rucksack indicates something valuable inside, or perhaps even the bag itself connotes a type of property, and property is always worth something.

    I hand one a two Euro coin and a cigarette. I know there are a lot of people who are apathetic about giving spare change to the homeless. For one reason, in Paris, it seems incessant. Contributing to their welfare almost seems like you're supporting a problem, feeding a disease.

    I'm a bit more understanding as a person when it comes to alcohol abuse combined with sleeping on the streets, but I can understand the reluctance of others. Yet I can't help but feel that the class system we've built a society on, where those without domiciles are "less" than the bottom rung of our hierarchy, presents itself as a form of acceptable psychopathy. We forget the fact that these people have origins. Their stories, like the people themselves, are varied and numerous. They were children once. Most had homes and families. They had parents.

    It took almost fourteen billion years for that creature to get here. Life rose and fell five times on Earth to create this person. They are amongst the most recent examples of humanity. The very edge of all that is. We share blood and DNA with them. So, if the universe put that much effort into creating them, then I can spare two Euro to keep them here...

    I watch the sheer number of homeless come into focus. They're scattered around everywhere. There are even more out there in the city, I'm sure of that. It's a horrible thing to think, working in an empty hotel, that there are so many empty beds here in Paris and so many people without them. It doesn't seem logical to me.

    I trudge along through the square and make my way down to the canal, eager to lift the burdening thoughts of my head with friendly laughter. I decide to cross over the high-hanging bridges to take a more scenic route and alleviate some of my melancholy. Just as I see over the top step of the bridge, I realise I've made a mistake. There's another homeless man lying down.

    His clothes are filthy and a bottle of Rosé, two thirds of it empty, lies standing upright beside him. His naked, blackened feet stick out from his curled up legs. His tanned brown skin almost highlights how dirty he looks. This time, I'm less inclined to be charitable, much preferring to walk past as quickly as possible and leave him in the background. I briskly stride past only to have an odd feeling slow my steps.

Something's not right here...

I turn my head back to look at the man and then come to a complete stop, staring at him. His hands, his head, his chest... His chest isn't moving... A cool breeze ruffles his hair and the leaves on the tree around us. Still no movement from him. My blood freezes and my stomach churns.

I don't know how long I monitor him, but I know it's longer than I needed to. I put two fingers on his cold neck and let out an anguished sigh. Vainly, I try for his wrist. Rolling up his sleeve, I notice a tattoo. A word and a mathematical equation.

Expiscor

$\underline{150.01952872} - \underline{122.742256}$

3.07   52

I can't find his pulse.

The poor man is definitely dead.

Staring at death leaves you with a grim anxiety. It's a worry, not that life is over, but that there's a cold truth lying in front of you. The harshest lesson to comprehend. The idea that you're nothing special, you never were. Your existence, meaningless. Your destiny, incomplete. Your purpose, unfulfilled...

My hand massages my temples until my brain figures out what I'm supposed to do. I pull out my phone and call the firefighters, oddly the people to call in most circumstances in this country. My phone rings a few minutes later. The caller ID tells me it's Charlie, I had forgotten all about why I'm here. I let it ring out and send him a text telling him I can't make it to them. There's no point in dragging any of my friends into this ugly business.

The firefighters arrive after what feels like an eternity. The dead can wait, I guess. With latex gloves covering her hands, a firewoman checks the deceased man's pulse and massages his chest, listening with a stethoscope, she shakes her head. Her facial expression, as I glimpse it, is that of a weary pity.

Her colleague starts to go through his personal effects, carefully pulling his pockets out and catching the odd bits of loose change before moving along to a canvas bag. As he does so, I start to get questioned about the time I found the body, if he was breathing, if there was anyone else around, if I touched him, if I moved anything or took anything. I answer as calmly as I can.

I overhear them coming to the conclusion that they have no way of identifying the man. I mention the numbers that I found on his wrist, suggesting it could be his social security number. They take one look, tell me it can't be a social security number and conclude that it's probably the work of madness. Mental illness is common with the homeless, after all. It's the age old question of whether lunacy put these people on these streets or if the streets put lunacy into these people.

They tell me that they'll run his fingerprints through the database, but if nothing comes from it then the homeless man will be getting a paupers burial. I ask one of the firefighters if nothing else can be done and he gives me a lazy shrug. I watch them as they pack up their gear and place his body in a bag.

Police officers arrive to ask me questions. I fumble through my wallet for a photocopy of my passport. I pause when I accidentally pull out the paper photo of Mouse, before rooting through the leather again.

I ask the police officer if they're going to find out who he is and he tells me they're going to do all they can. I know he's just humouring me. The officer snaps his notebook shut and tells me he'll be in contact before all parties leave me alone on the bridge again.

There must be something I can do. He's a human being. He *was* a human being... Surely someone out there knows him. Maybe he has friends?

I wander back down along the canal towards République. I peer down every street looking for homeless people to question, and there's no shortage of them. I ask perhaps eleven or so on my way back to the square when I encounter one that's quite mad in the head, his hands are clutched around a filthy teddy bear pressed tightly to his chest. He seems about my age. It's a sad spectacle.

"There's a homeless man that's passed away near here. An older man." I tell him.

"Ah! There's joy in old age! The sculptures are finished! They sneezed a long time ago!"

"Right... You know many other homeless in the area? You hang out here a lot?"

"I've been here for a long time! Since I was little! When I was smaller and the world was bigger..."

"I can see that... You must have suffered a lot."

"We all suffer in life! And the man that didn't? Bless him, he never really lived!"

"This man I'm trying to identify-"

"- You wonder if balance and cycles are really just some unknown third thing? Like, if it's not really one or the other, but one thing. Not tipping scales or coming back around, just maintaining stuff and things."

"What are you talking about?"

"Honestly, I don't even know. I confuse myself sometimes..."

"The deceased. On his arm-"

"- Ah, yes! The dead man! God has him now, doesn't he?"

"I can't say for sure..."

"Oh! One of those new people, eh? You think we're nothing but monkeys clinging on to a dying rock?! A speck of dust in the cosmos?!"

"I don't really know..." My eyes start to wander around him. It's difficult to meet his gaze.

"Well, there's more to this world that meets the eye or the scopes."

"Kinda sounds like platitudes."

"Maybe, but I'm entirely placated, and that's not bad for a speck of dust..."

"The deceased had a tattoo on his arm. It said Expiscor."

The mention of the tattoo lights up the eyes of one man nearby, caught by one of my nervous glances away from this lunatic. I excuse myself and make my way over to him. He's perhaps forty-five or so, it's hard to tell. Fine lines crease the skin on his face, although I'm unsure if this is caused by age, weather or suffering, perhaps all three. His fair, blonde hair is muddled with dirt. The clothes he wears, already quite small, hang off him. His veiny hands pick at themselves. He tells me his name is Navy. An allusion to a past life, he says. His gravelly voice has a smack of someone from Newcastle in England.

"Expiscor... That's 'im alright..." He sighs. "Poor bastard. 'Ow'd 'ee die?"

"Don't know. Maybe just old age? Maybe sickness?"

"Fuck me..."

"What was his name?"

"Don't know 'is real name. Called 'im Numbers, coz of the tatt on 'is arm."

"Do you know what the numbers mean?"

"Not a clue..."

"How about Expiscor. Do you know what that means?"

"'Ee joked once that it'd come in 'andy when 'ee returned to the language. I wuz pissed off me nut an' didn't care much of a shite to ask 'im whatever the fuck that meant."

"Anything else you can tell me about him?"

"Not much. South Americ'n. Old. Liked the drink. Told me 'ee's been travelling in his lifetime. All round the world, 'ee says. Wuz a sailor like me, 'ee says... Said..."

"Were you friends for a long time?"

"Few months, wasn't it?... They say anything about a funeral?"

"Pauper's, basically. Until I find out where he's from."

"You mind me asking why you give a shite?"

"He's a person."

"'Ee was, wasn't 'ee? You know, not many people really see us... People like me, though, we see everythin'. We got time on our hands..."

A sudden thought pops into my head. I rummage through my wallet and Navy looks at me expectantly, only to be disappointed when I pull out the photo of Mouse.

"Have you seen this girl?"

He stares at the photo. "I 'aven't... But leave it with me and I'll see what I can find." He nods at my wallet.

I suppose I can always find another picture of Mouse online. I hand over twenty Euro to him. It's more than the usual amount I'd spare, but it seems like a special circumstance. He looks up at me when I hand it over.

"You expectin' a thank you?! Don't take it personally, mate! I'm not ungrateful, I'm just tired... Tired of begging... Tired of this life..."

"Nothing personal!" I assure him.

I arrange a meeting with Navy for tomorrow night. He tells me he'll still be kicking about the square. In my wake, I look back and see him sitting there alone with his hands held out to strangers. Some give change, others walk by, none stop to talk to him.

I think one of the hardest parts about being human isn't being unique or part of a society. It's trying to reconcile with the fact that, even though this is how you see the world and this is how it *is* for you, there is no one else like you.

At the end of the day, you're alone.

****

Back at home, I do my best to crack the code. I already tried subtracting the larger numbers and get 27.27727272. I start by ringing it like a phone number, to no avail. Searching for its significance online. I even go as far as breaking it down into binary and translating it but that doesn't help either.

I try translating the word Expiscor from Spanish into English but it comes up as the same word. At the bottom of the screen, I see a suggestion to translate it from Latin. "Expiscor = Discover". It's a clue! He's left something behind for me to find. That must have been what he meant about returning to the language. A dead language for a dead man.

But the numbers... What the hell could they possibly mean?! I divide the equation and I'm left with "48.866296 – 2.360428", which doesn't seem to be much use to me... I try the combinations what feels like a million times, using different common cyphers. Nothing helps. This code, and the man himself, remains an enigma to me. Without any context or clue, it's starting to crack me rather than the other way around.

To distract myself from the frustration of this annoying cypher, I let my mind wander. I think about death in its imminency. How I would feel should I ever come to see its face again, what would happen should I be taken from this world prematurely? I think of all my friends and my family, what it would be like for them in my departure.

In my morbid sense of duty, I decide to write a sort of will to have on hand.

"Friends, Family, Loved ones,

I'm sorry I've left you. I know you're all probably hurting right now and I truly wish there was something I could do to help.

Perhaps, in my death, I should show my gratitude for life. It was one that you all have either given me or, at the very least, made worth living.

The love shown to me by you all has been endless, and in that I'm thankful to exist, at least in part, in your loving memories. I feel truly blessed to have known you all.

I don't know what comes next. I can't promise you that I'll see any of you again. But what I can promise you is this:

If there is something after, I will be waiting for you with open arms.

And if there is nothing, then I will share the nothing with you."

With my parting words written, I daydream a little about who would eventually read it. It could be a friend or a stranger. Maybe a loved one? I wonder how Cat would feel if I died? For the briefest moment after our breakup, maybe only a minute, I had considered taking my own life just for the shock it would leave behind. Obviously, I shrugged off the melodrama quickly enough, but the fact that it had crossed my mind was worrying. I was too attached to her. Too dependant. I idolised her.

I loved her randomness. Her jokes and unpredictable behaviour. It made life exciting and hilarious. I felt like I was truly alive with her. And why wouldn't I? Unpredictable elements and random occurrences are how things are created. It's how life is made...

All my anger wasn't caused by her either. She was just a focal point for all the disappointment, hurt and insecurity I've carried with me my whole life. It weighed me down until I broke from it. Her betrayal, for not doing what she was supposed to stand for, was only keener to me because I'd felt it before. I'm terrified it's all I'll ever feel with someone I give my love to. That history will repeat itself until I'm a cold, emotionless coward that will never give so I never lose. I have to let these feelings out, and the courage in.

I can't let people become symbols for me anymore. She can't embody emotions that are a larger part of my life than just one person. As difficult as it is for me, I need to find a way of dealing with how I feel in different ways. Only, I don't know how to start...

It's been almost a year and I'm still trying to figure out life without her.

How to live in the afterlove...

****

I wake up with the laptop beside me. I lazily swipe the touchpad to get it to light up and tell me the time. I have a few more hours before I need to meet Navy and still don't have anything to tell him.

I take a look at the translation for "Expiscor" again. Clicking on the link to additional translations, it tells me that it can also mean "Find out". Does that mean crack the code or find something? I think back to what Navy told me about him. He said he was a sailor too. Maybe it's not a code to crack, but a location to find?

Then it hits me. I divide the numbers again, type them into a search engine and place the word "Paris" beside it. Sure enough, the two numbers turn out to be latitude and longitude. The address given is one not too far from République, the metro is Arts et Métiers. The view on the street reveals it to be an alley beside a church. I grab my coat and rush out the door.

Red clouds hang overhead as the sun sets behind the stone church. It's a stout looking thing, a little dirty from the smog, tarnished with black marks, and not as ornate as many of the other churches in the city.

The exact location is saved on my phone. There's nothing

obvious at first. I look up and around, high and low, with nothing peeking out at me. Whatever the significance of this place, it's not visible to me.

It takes forty minutes of inspecting, poking, prying and trying until I find something. In behind the gate, hidden in the bushes, lies a large rock that seems out of place in the smooth dirt surrounding it. I lift it up and find a small hollow underneath containing a black bin bag.

I pull the bag out and empty its contents into my hands. A passport, an envelope and an aged photo of a young woman tumble out. I flip open the passport eagerly and read it. The photo is recognisable as him, although it shows a much younger and fresher man. Juan Lopez. Born on the third of July, 1952.

The envelope comes to my attention afterwards. An address is written on the back, but there are no stamps on it. I reflect on the ethics and morality of opening it, whether it's just to pry through a dead man's belongings, but I decide that it might help in contacting his family.

Inside is a short letter, dated about a week before his demise. I have to translate it on my phone from Spanish to English. The translation isn't the best and requires a little guess-work using context, but I figure it out. It's easier than the last code, at least...

"My love,

My life has been very hard since you have left me. I have lost most of everything, except for our house, which I cannot bear to live in.

I left the merchant's navy. I blamed my love of the sea and my time away for you leaving. Truly, it was just me not paying attention and thinking I could have both.

I had nightmares of what you were like with him. How you both laughed at my expense while I was at sea. How you loved him more. Nightmares, only in ignorance.

I've been full of hatred for years now. I had blamed you for all my bad luck. You broke my heart by leaving me for him with only a note's explanation. You didn't allow us to talk. But I've learned something out here. I've learned that we're all human and we all make mistakes.

I wanted to tell you that I forgive you.

I hope you are keeping well and are happy.

Love,

Juan"

It's eerie reading the letter of a man I know to be dead, but there's an odd comfort both in the letter and the words inscribed on them.

He describes heartbreak and a masochism that I can relate to. Perhaps we're not as alone as I thought. We follow paths similar to each other. Walk down those long roads together. Maybe we don't walk side by side, but all roads lead to the same place, which we all eventually cross over to.

As for the letter itself, in my hand I hold a tiny fragment of the man's conscious. His story. His life. A paper immortality that will only be extinguished when it crumbles or burns. A moment of him that is alive each time it's read. An afterlife. A form of existence... He may only exist in my mind but I suppose, mostly, we only really exist in the minds of others anyway...

I need to give this back to his former lover, to give her a small piece of eternity. I read the name and address on the envelope. *Rosita Gonzalez*. A quick search online leads me to a phone number. I pause for a few moments in reflection before dialling the number.

"*Si?*"

"*Hola... Ehm... Puedas hablar ingles?*"

"A little. Who are you?"

"I'm- Well- I guess I'm a friend of Juan Lopez."

There's a pause on the other end. "Where is he?"

"That's – I'm in Paris, at the moment – I'm – I'm very sorry to tell you this... Juan has passed on..."

"Passed on?"

I hate myself for saying it this bluntly, but there's no other way to be clear. "He's dead, ma'am... *Esta – Esta muerto?*"

There's another pause on the phone. This one lasts almost a minute. Faint sobbing can be heard trickling through the line until several large exhales come out.

"*Cuan-* When?"

"Last night, ma'am."

"Pain?"

"... None..."

She stays silent.

"Does he have any family members?" I ask.

"A sister... I will call her..."

"I'd appreciate that, ma'am. For- For the body, someone will have to collect it- him!"

"Where is he?"

"I'm not sure... But I can find out?"

"Please."

"I'll call you back when I know."

"Okay... Okay..."

A click and the line is dead. I begin searching the internet on my phone for phone numbers and make a series of calls to hospitals, giving the time and date of his death, until a mortuary gives me the location of the body. I call back Ms. Gonzalez with the news. She thanks me and tells me she'll be in Paris tomorrow with the sister to claim Juan's body. I leave her the number of the mortuary and offer her any assistance she might need. With that done, it's time for me to meet Navy. I'm close enough to walk there and still be on time.

On the way, I wonder what Juan would think of Rosita coming to collect his body. He would probably see it as a strange twist of fate. One of those incalculable uncertainties that occur every now and then. He had seemed to come to terms with them being over. Perhaps I should allow the dead man to give me some advice on life. The man who has nothing is still giving...

I couldn't forgive Cat, so I tried forgetting her and that hasn't worked for me. There's got to be a better way to love her...

I know it wasn't all her fault. When she left I was controlling and overbearing when I could have made her happy instead. I shouldn't have asked her to change nor have expected she would. It wasn't fair to her and love shouldn't work like that.

I thought cowardice had killed us, that she was too afraid to commit to something, to be hurt, when fear was actually what was keeping us together. Neither of us wanted to be alone... And I don't think she ever loved me. Not really... Had she shown me the love I had shown her, I would have followed her to Harlem and back...

Besides, it never would have worked out in the end. We were toxic together. I would have been either doomed without her or damned with her. It's not because I can't forgive her for all the things she did, I'm sure I can in time, but I could never trust her again. How could I be myself and give myself completely to someone I couldn't trust?

I guess it's just me now. The best thing I can do is the best for myself. I can love myself as much as I loved her. Care about my well-being instead of hers. Focus a little more on my happiness instead of others. I can give to myself without taking away from anyone else.

I know I'll fail somewhere along the way. I'll miss her, stare at photos, fall into my maudlin self. I'm okay with that. Any step back is fine as long as I keep walking ahead to a future without her. All this time I was looking for a way out or away when all I needed to do was move with the time that propels me. Just forward.

And I know to do this, I can never see her again. I just can't handle any more heartbreak or disappointment from her and forgive myself. I carry enough painful memories to want any more.

Each memory generated, another ingrained, one more to grieve...

****

Just as I reach République, I get a text from Rosita telling me that there'll be a small gathering for the reclamation of the body before he's repatriated back to his home country. I scan the square until I spot Navy, drinking a can of beer and sitting on the step of the statue.

"I found his family. His real name was Juan Lopez. His sister and his ex-wife are coming to collect his body tomorrow. They're going to have a small service, I think, if you wanted to say your goodbyes?"

"Aye. I will. Numbers was a good lad..."

"Can I ask you something personal?"

"Go on, then."

"What's your plan?"

"My plan?"

"Yeah. I mean, to get off the streets."

"You know what these streets taught me, lad? There's no point in ever 'aving a fucking plan. Didn't plan on ending up on the fucking streets, but 'ere I am! Fuck off, wiv your plan! No point plannin' life when life's got its own little plan for you..."

"Nothing's going to change if you don't do something though. It can't hurt to plan ahead?"

"Let's say we're both right, alright, lad?"

For what it's worth, I can't help but agree with him on that. I nod and he smiles. I write down the time and address for the funeral tomorrow, hand him a few Euro coins and turn to leave.

"Oh, 'ang on! I forgot about your missus!"

"My missus?"

"Yeah. Pretty girl. 'angs out down by Place de l'Opéra a wee birdy tells me. Seen 'er a few times, 'ee has. Took one look at that photo you gave me and knew 'er right off. Tells me she's a good sort. Gives 'im a few bob most times 'ee sees her."

"You found her?! She's by Opéra?!"

"Usually, I'm told." He tells me, handing back the photo of Mouse.

"Well, fuck me... Thank you!"

"Alright, lad. See you tomorrah, I suppose."

"Yeah..."

After all this time, searching and struggling, I finally have a solid lead on Mouse. There are butterflies in my stomach and my mind is racing.

It just took one thing to put everything else into place...

****

The sister holds her sad, shaking face in her hands as the coffin is carried through a hospital courtyard to a van. Navy is accompanied by two other men, all of them wearing ill-fitted, but presentable, suits. I recognise Rosita from the photograph I found along with Juan's belongings. She seems much older now.

We gather behind the van to bid our farewells. Navy was thoughtful enough to bring a candle that he shields nobly against the wind. The well-dressed men whisper one at a time towards the coffin before returning to each other, mumbling.

Rosita stares at the coffin before turning to the rest of us. She speaks slowly in Spanish. I turn to Navy quizzically and he's listening intently. I nudge him and shrug. He leans in and starts translating in my ear. I'm surprised at his ability, but maybe I shouldn't be, him being Juan's friend.

"What we 'ave makes us important, buh what we give makes us great. We can do much in our lifetimes. We can strive fer personal success and merits or titles. Buh what good is all tha' when we're dead?

We can make the world a better place. Be kind. Be good t'all and all will be good t'you. Love freely an' all will love you.

If you do this fer everyone then you will remain with them long after death. When they think of you after you're gone then they will feel loved.

An' tha' is the greatest gift the dead can give the livin'..."

It's strange to hear such eloquence coming from Navy's sombre mouth. He moves forward to speak to the sister. When he comes back, I ask him what he told her.

"I told her, when you can't find justice, seek forgiveness... I reckon those two 'ave a long road ahead together."

He's not wrong. There's every chance that the sister could blame Rosita for Juan's undignified demise, even if they were both missing from his life. Strange to think that they could make such mistakes at that age. I guess I was naïve enough to believe that fallacy was something we eventually shrugged off. That wisdom would set in. I suppose we're never too old to fuck up.

I think maybe I've been too harsh on my parents all this time. I idolised them a little too much for what they were and understood too little about what they are. At the end of the day, we're all only human. Juan is about my father's age. He left his apologies too late and died without seeing his regrets fall behind in the wake. If one of my parents were to pass on before I had the chance to make amends with them, I know I'd harbour that regret for the rest of my life. I can't leave it too late like he did.

I'm sensitive to betrayal. I realise that now. People let me down. They didn't stay true to what they're supposed to stand for, but I'm trying to be a better person.

This experience is also a wake-up call to start taking better care of myself physically. Eat something more substantial for breakfast than three cigarettes. Exercise more. Focus on maintaining my health. Direct my energy into myself rather than squander it.

I watch the van pull off slowly out the gate. Shuffling along with the other people from different walks of life. Complex creatures bound together by a common bond. The thought that we are unquantifiable. There's nothing quite like a funeral to bring people together.

We leave each other on the street. Navy giving me a handshake and a farewell, the others give me casual salutes. Rosita talks to me in Spanish and embraces me. The sister wails. A flurry of activity and then the van drives off.

Alone again, I take a few steps forward before stopping in my tracks. I gather a little courage and summon my forgiveness. It's time to be right again. To be a son of someone.

For the first time in a year and a half, I take out my phone and voluntarily call my parents.

Case 20 – Touching Down

I've been staking out this square for two nights now. Still no sign of her. I'm devoting all my spare time to this, showing up before and after work, right up until I'm too tired to go on. How could I have missed her all this time when she's been so close?

This evening hasn't produced any more results than yesterday. I'm starting to doubt Navy's lead. Maybe he was just telling me for the sake of having something to tell me? Either way, I have to head to work.

Crow has been taking over from Dylan since his departure and I'm not eager to see him. I stand outside and light up a cigarette before my shift starts. I reckon I'll need another one after whatever task Crow has in store for me. I glance in the window and see a large group of hotel workers huddled around the reception desk.

I cautiously finish the rest of my cigarette before walking through the doors. Some of the workers turn to me with perplexed looks then return them back to Crow standing behind the desk. Crow's eyes light up when he sees me.

"Ah, good. We are all 'ere. I will begin..." Some sideways glances are traded amongst us as Crow continues. "As you know, ze 'otel ees not doing so well. I 'ave decided to use zis opportunitay to close ze 'otel for renovations een one week..."

There's a flurry of whispers amongst the staff. I stare hard into Crow's mischievous face, the smirk I know he's holding down. He raises his hands and the murmuring stops.

"Of cowerse, you will all be paid dureeng ze renovations, which will be fower one month."

I feel an elbow in my side as all the staff beam at each other. No one will argue with being paid to do nothing. Why do I feel like we're all being screwed over?

Crow dismisses us and I carry out the rest of my shift racking my brain as to why I'm so distrustful of such good news. Maybe it's my recent disappointment with Mouse? Or maybe it's because Crow has been a curious man to work for? Perhaps it's just my cynical personality? Either way, the ramblings follow me all the way back to my apartment.

I've refined my culinary skills. The routine of cooking every day has somewhat tempered my usual desire to spend impulsively. It's also helped me realise that I'm perfectly capable of cooking food that tastes good. I feel like I have an unlimited choice of what it is that I want to eat.

After dinner, I pull some cherry-flavoured yoghurt out of the fridge and start doing some sit-ups. I've already lost a very noticeable amount of weight in the last year, but I've decided to attain the body I've always wanted.

I take a shower and look at myself in the mirror. I actually like what I see, even with the need for improvement. Maybe it's just a new perception now that I'm starting to take better care of myself, but I suppose feeling good goes a long way towards looking good.

And to think, all this time, I thought taking care of myself was a burden when it was really a pleasure. A pampering, even.

****

Only four more shifts to go until the hotel will be closed. Crow comes in at 4am, grinning, to relieve me. With no guests to check in or any other necessary updates, I give him an awkward goodbye and leave.

I make the short walk down to Opéra and wander around the area aimlessly. Occasionally, I take the creased picture of Mouse out of my pocket to refresh my memory. I've already tried showing it to people on the streets but they tend to either ignore me or give me strange looks, so I've stopped.

Hours go by, delineated by cigarettes and delicate swigs from a plastic bottle of water. The sun begins to rise behind the picturesque buildings. My feet are worn out. The best idea I have is to sit on the steps of the Palais Garnier Opera building to rest and use it as a vantage point to keep a look out for Mouse.

I kick through the scattered leaves, up the steps and sit down at the top. The avenue stretches out in front of me. It's a beautiful view. A lightness comes over me. To gaze upon something this wonderful has taken my mind off all other things.

I've found a moment of peace.

I look towards the few people milling around at this hour and see a girl that reminds me of Cat. It's a mixed feeling, bringing back painful memories, but on the other hand it tells me that there are many people out there just like her. I realise now what I need to look for in a girl. Not someone like Cat, but someone who can make me feel like myself.

There was a lot of pain there. That was the elephant in the room. I could never forget how much Cat hurt me. Now, I feel like I've moved on. I've learned that forgiveness is a muscle you flex. I pushed myself past her. I came to terms a long time ago that Cat was no longer mine, perhaps she never was... But it's only recently I realise that I'm no longer hers either.

Our relationship might have been a mess, but it wasn't a monster. She wasn't bad, just a little broken, in my opinion. And it seems like that's the story of my life. No one to blame, just things gone awry.

She wasn't always wrong too. I do deserve better. Not better *than* her, but better *for* me. I know she'd want me to move on and be happy, she just wanted it sooner than I did. Most of the suffering inflicted on me was done by myself, either through my subconscious masochism or my laziness in looking ahead. She left me alone all this time, knowing she would only hurt me more otherwise. And I can imagine it was probably difficult for her at times.

I'd like to think, after it all, that we both finally landed on the same page. We both deserve our own joy and I hope she finds peace at some point. She deserves it.

And I'm grateful for having been with her. She made me a better person and showed me a part of myself that I couldn't see. That *I* was worth something to myself. By loving myself, I could love her more. For that, wherever she is, whatever she's doing and whoever she's with, she is loved by me. And a part of me will always love her, because that's what love is...

I smile and rest my head in my hands, elbows on my knees. She gave me the chance to rebuild myself, by myself. So, if I had one thing to say to her it would be to thank her.

Thank you for teaching me how to be myself...

****

"Here Kitty-kitty! Here Kit-Kat!"

I pull my head up in a jolt. I must have fallen asleep on the steps. I wipe some stale drool from the side of my mouth and scratch my head, embarrassed by myself. I fumble around in my pockets for my cigarettes and place one in my mouth as I turn to glance at the voice. The cigarette almost falls out. It's Mouse...

Her brown hair is a good bit shorter than it is in the photo, just long enough to be in line with her chin. Her cute, small nose now has a ring pierced in her left nostril. Her round face is lightly freckled. I notice she's quite slim as she leans in, an arm extended through the bars in between the arches of the Palais Garnier. She continues to call out to her invisible friend.

To think I had almost given up. I thought I had accepted that I would never find her, when really I had simply decided it. The distinction between the two can be a tricky one. A fine line between choosing to give up on the improbable or accepting what is impossible. Still, I know I'm lucky to find her.

I have, actually, always considered myself as a lucky person despite the various scrapes I've been through. It just seems that no matter what happens to me, something always comes up and gets me out of it. I've had more than a few bad turns in my life, but all of them have simply put me on the course to here and now. I couldn't be more grateful for that than right this moment...

    I get up slowly and look away, careful to not startle her. I dismiss the idea that she's mentally ill, as she continues her beckoning, simply judging by her clothes. A black leather jacket, white T-shirt, black skinny-jeans and white, high-top shoes, this isn't the usual attire of the delusional or schizophrenic. I steal fleeting glances at her until I make up my mind. It's time to find out what she's doing.

    Time to meet Mouse...

"Hey! Are you looking for something?" I call out.

"Um- Yeah! I'm trying to rescue this kitten." She points to a small, ginger, bleak creature.

"Why?"

"What do you mean, why? Just look at him!"

"But - I mean - Are you capable of taking care of an animal? You seem quite young."

"I'll have you know, I'm studying Veterinary Medicine in university and work in a clinic near where I live, sir. I might only be an intern, but I know some stuff."

"Have you tried offering food?"

"Do you have food to offer?"

"Nope."

"Do you have *anything* to offer?"

"Cigarettes?"

"I sincerely doubt the kitten smokes cigarettes, sir."

"You're right... It's probably too young to be smoking..."

She raises an eyebrow at me. "You sassing me, boy?!"

"No, ma'am! The cigarettes were offered to you, by the way."

"Were they? And why should I take cigarettes from a stranger?"

"Because I'm a nice person?"

"You know, the world is a cruel place to nice people..."

"But it's a better place around them..."

She turns her attention away from the kitten and over to me, smiling a gorgeous smile. I can feel my heart fluttering as she looks into my eyes. I take a slight step back, almost defensively.

"That's true, I suppose... You're still a stranger though..."

"It's strange what people do for strangers."

"I guess that's what make people stranger." She laughs and turns back to the meowing kitten.

"Why are you so adamant about rescuing this kitten?"

"I just believe that it's good to be good."

"Says the girl that believes the world is a cruel place."

"It does not *have* to be. The world's not broken, it's just dirty. It's time to clean it up."

"And how does one do that?"

"By being good."

"Not sure that's for everyone."

"Well maybe I subscribe to a simple belief?"

"Which is?"

"That kindness can be contagious..."

"I've been helping a few people too with some things. Can't say I ever felt like I encouraged them to help anyone else. Most of the time I felt like I was just dealing with problem after problem and there was never going to be an end to it."

"You didn't feel good after helping them?"

"Sure, a few times... But, it seems like the bad outweighs the good most times."

"Well, maybe you're just overly-sensitive?"

"So I should stop being so sensitive?"

"Of course not! How can you stop yourself from being sensitive when the smallest joys become something amazing."

"The smallest slights, something devastating."

"Everything has a cost, sir."

Costs. All the time I spent looking for her and finally I've found her. There's only one more thing I owe her. Every kind of relationship should start with honesty, and the sooner the truth comes out, the better. I need to tell her about my search for her.

"I-"

"Hey, Kitty! *Hi!*" She exclaims as the kitten pounces on her legs. She bundles it up in her arms. "We got him!" She beams at me.

"We did..."

"You want to pet him?"

"Sure."

I stare into the animals eyes and pet him. It glares back at me with what I can only paradoxically describe as an apathetic hatred. As its slitted eyes bore into mine, I grow weary and turn to her.

"There's something I should say... I don't want you to freak out, because you seem like a really nice person. I mean, you really do! I- Well... Basically, I found the missing person's poster of you a long time ago and I've been looking for you for quite some time now... It's- I was trying to help. I wasn't sure if you were hurt or-" She stares back at me dumbly, the arteries on her neck are throbbing. "I'm glad that you're safe, and I'll leave you alone if that's what you want... I just wanted to make sure you were okay..."

She stands perfectly still as the kitten squirms around in her arms. Its claws tear at her jacket, which breaks her silence.

"When did you find that poster?"

"December?"

"And you've been looking for me all this time?"

"Kind of. I mean, on and off, really."

"Damn..."

"You mind me asking who's looking for you?"

"It was, like, my family and probably this guy I used to date, maybe even a few friends..."

"Why haven't you contacted them?"

"I have! I told them I was fine and that they could stop worrying about me. I think I just needed some space from them... From everyone really..."

"So you ran away?"

"I'm *twenty-three years old*, I can't run away from home..."

"A friend of mine told me once that everyone in Paris is running from something."

"What are you running from?"

"My past, probably... Why did you need space?"

"I come from, like, a big family. There's always people coming and going and I guess it's like you're never really... *You*... When there's that many people there... And everyone was trying to decide who I was going to be for me and I had enough... You know?"

"I can imagine... Still, you can't keep running from your problems."

"It's working pretty well for me so far, sir."

"Yeah... But while you're running away from something, you're not running towards anything. You can't live your whole life like that."

"What do you propose, then?"

"That you face your past head on."

"What does the past matter? It's over." She says irately.

"I disagree. The past is important to the present. It shapes you. Lays a foundation. The present you is you as you stand... Looking at the past, painful as it is, also helps us to decide who we want to be, it's a north star..."

"I have confronted my past and I *am* a better person than who I was. I've made huge improvements to myself, I'll have you know. I wasn't always this nice or this charitable, but I worked on it. I help the homeless, animals, I'm always nice to people in the café. I'm a good person now. I feel like a good person."

"Tell that to them?"

"I'm doing fine on my own, you know, *sir*!"

"I do! I can see that! I- I just think that you're probably strong enough to be fine with the people you've been avoiding too. Let them know that you're okay and living your life. That you're happy... Give them some closure..."

"Goddamn... I don't know..."

"Just think about it, okay?"

"Fine... Although, I probably shouldn't be taking advice from some random *weirdo* who's spent almost a year trying to find me!"

"To be fair, it was about nine months... But... I do work in the area, in a hotel. I'm not sure how I managed to miss you all this time..."

"What hours do you work?"

"Mostly nights."

"Right... Well, I'm usually here early in the morning to work in a café on Avenue de l'Opéra and I leave in the evening."

The early bird catches the mouse, it seems...

"So, you're here when I'm asleep or at work?" I ask.

"Usually... I also don't get off at the Opéra metro station, it's usually Pyramides because it's closer. I live on Line 7. I'm like near Place Monge now, in this tiny apartment. It's fine, really, but I think my neighbours hate me because I'm loud. Also, I'm slightly worried because my apartment was broken into before I moved in."

"Anything stolen?"

"No, *dumbass*, I said it was before I moved in. There's just this stupid sticker on the door."

"Grand..."

"Is it *grand*?!"

"An Irish expression. Don't worry about it."

The kitten starts to squirm a little more violently than before.

"Dang. I'm going to have to drop this little fellah off at work."

"Mind if I walk you there?"

"It's a free country! You're welcome, *France*!"

"You're American then?"

"You tell me, stalker..."

"I'm just trying to make this scenario slightly more normal. You didn't tell me your name?"

"You know my name already..."

"I know..."

"Ugh- Fine! – My name is Victoria. Very *pleased* to meet you, sir!" Sarcasm twinges her voice.

"Victoria... Can I call you Vic, or Vicky?"

"No... No, you can't..."

370

Case 21 – No One's Home

It's strange how you can start to get settled in and fed up with an apartment more or less at the same time. The suffocating smallness of the place isn't as unnerving as it once was, but sinks in under my skin with a boredom. It's like the sharp corners of this place have grown dull after being bumped into so many times. A cosy discomfort.

My phone rings out as a text from Victoria comes through. We've been trading texts for about a week and a half now. I can't help but feel happy when I hear from her. I light up brighter than the screen as message after sardonic message comes through. She's inviting me out for coffee tomorrow, to which I eagerly agree. Any excuse to get out of my apartment is welcome. Also, I think I might be more enamoured by her than I'm willing to admit.

I've got a lot of free time now that the hotel has been closed for renovations. It's strange to think I won't be there for another three weeks or so. Despite how much I dislike the place, it's always been a fixed point in my life over the last ten months. The lack of a dutiful destination has left me rambling around somewhat.

My phone lights up again, only it's not Victoria, it's my mother. A twinge of disappointment. She wants me to call her. I don't particularly want to right now, but I know I should. I guess I should have known that making an effort to reconnect with my parents would require some kind of effort...

It's a moment of gravity, talking to my mother again. The flighty feeling of freedom that I've held for so long crumbles away with the burden of responsibility. A duty to simply be there for them as they always have for me. A bound gratitude.

We talk over the phone and she asks me how I am. I'm starting to let my guard down a little and I'm a bit more forthcoming than I have been with previous attempts. I tell her about Victoria, probably in more detail than anything else we talked about before.

As the pauses between sentences grow longer and more pronounced, she lets me go. I'm a little relieved. Still, there's a slight warmth in being in contact with home again. A reminder, maybe, that it was always there, even if the paths were somewhat thorny. I've always known that there's love there, it's just been a long time since I've allowed myself to be exposed to it. To feel it.

Propelled by this emotion, I call my father to catch up with him. He tells me that he went to see a movie with my brother and we end up talking about other movies that he's adding to his BluRay collection. It's a simple conversation, but there's a trace of home bouncing off satellites back to me that's only terminated when I hang up.

I potter around my apartment with some frequent texts from Victoria until about 2am when she tells me she's going to bed and wishes me goodnight.

I cook myself some soup and I can feel myself get giddy at the thought of seeing her tomorrow. Although, there's also a slight anxiety there about whether or not things will work out for us, which I dismiss as quickly as possible. Finding the courage under the web of worries, I assure myself that I'm ready now, regardless, to be vulnerable again. To do the same thing as before with someone new.

I was never a fool to love or trust blindly.

It was worth it.

And I'm no longer more afraid of the light than the dark.

****

Our coffee drags on to drinks. The original shakes of the glass-wielding hand, caused by nerves and caffeine, are now eliminated entirely by the alcohol. As the pints go down, we start to open up.

"So, what is love to you?" She asks me.

"Well... I mean, I don't know... I spent half the time thinking it was the best thing ever and the other half thinking it was some kind of infectious disease of the brain."

"So, you have been in love?"

"Once."

"But you're, like, done with her, right?"

She seems eager to know. "The best thing about meeting Cat was that I finally knew that kind of person existed. That it's not just me, alone in the dark. I got to bloom out instead of keeping myself in."

I analyse her face for a reaction. A flutter of her eyes. "What made you fall in love with her?"

"She was an amazing person."

"You still think that after she broke your feeble heart?"

"Yeah..." I smile. "I'm never going to deny that she was a special person and that I care about her still. I mean, she was smart, funny, sexy-"

"- But?"

"... But often inconsiderate to me. Selfish... She's not the girl I end up with. But, I still got to give my love to someone. Sometimes that's its own reward... I just got stuck on her. Eventually though, the time just came to give up or lose myself."

"Well," she says, staring into her drink as she swirls it "that can't have been easy."

"It wasn't. I think... I guess it's about distracting yourself for as long as you can. I spent a lot of time focusing on other people's problems just because I have a tendency to over-think my own to death."

"Did the distractions help?"

"Kind of... Basically, there were some things that only time could heal and, by distracting myself, I was taking away from the pain. Until I was ready for it... The truth is, you just have to let the pain get tired."

"So you ran from your problems?" She asks smugly.

"*Some* of them. On the other hand, there were some problems that I was avoiding that I shouldn't have and solving other people's problems was a form of escape. And I knew I had problems I was avoiding, but... Sometimes you can have all the answers and still not do anything about it."

"Dang... You've thought a lot about this."

"I have. How about you? Any exes?"

"I have, like, a few. Sort of... I wasn't the best girlfriend ever. There's no one out there lining up to give me awards! But, I don't know. I like to think I'm doing better now and that I'm ready for a commitment. I feel like, now that I look back and see what I did wrong, I can go forward and do right. You know?"

"I do..."

"*Oof.* Heavy topic. You want another pint, sir?"

"Yes, ma'am."

"A pint, coming up. Hick!"

"You have the hiccups?"

"Nope, I, like, only ever hiccup once randomly and then that's it. Like, not even from drinking."

 She crosses her eyes in jest as she stands up and gets us some more drinks. We trade jokes, insults and stories over the next few hours. I torture her into trying some of my Guinness, she tortures me by kicking my shins incessantly. I catch fleeting glances into her dark eyes as they swallow the light around them. The bar closes and we're talked out by the bartender. I'm a little dismayed that the night seems to be over. I offer to walk her home, just for the few more minutes I can share with her.

 We walk down Rue Mouffetard with flocks of drunks trailing down the street and singles slumped against walls. The cobbled stone beneath us challenges our inebriated feet. It's a fifteen minute walk back to her apartment. For each turn, she pulls at my jacket and I reciprocate by placing my hand on her back. The hill leading up is a hike until we get to a large, light-blue door.

"Okay... So I have *a* beer, like a *single* beer, if you want to come up?"

"I'd love to!"

We step into an elevator to get to the sixth floor. I steal glances at her in the mirrors lining the walls. The doors open and she quickly pops the light on for the hallway before leading me to her apartment. I can see the sticker on her door that states it's been broken into and that an investigation is being conducted. It's faded somewhat over time, but is still stuck fast to the wood.

She sticks her foot in the door as her kitten tries to leap out. It takes some food, attention and slight pushing before it settles to curl up, asleep, on a heap of clothes stacked on a chair. She tells me she's named him the imaginative name of *Kit-Kat*.

She pulls out a glass and half fills it with beer from a small bottle. We drink slowly and talk quickly. Almost every conversation ends with the utter confusion as to how we ever ended up on that topic from where we began. The laughter fades out and the fatigue sets in. She checks her phone for the time.

"The metro isn't running... I feel bad seeing as I've dragged you all the way out here..."

"You don't need to feel bad. I had fun!" I shrug.

"Me too... I mean, I *guess* you could crash here for the night. Or at least until the metro is running."

"You don't mind?"

"Not really. I mean, my bed is small, but whatever."

She tells me to turn around while she gets changed for bed. As I take my pants off and clamber into bed with her, I notice she's wearing the ugliest psychedelic-patterned T-shirt that I've ever seen. We roll around awkwardly for two minutes, getting comfortable...

After three minutes we're kissing.

Five minutes and I'm taking the horrid thing off her.

Nine minutes and I'm biting the inside of her thigh.

I lose track of time at this point as I tug her underwear down, push her legs open and bury my mouth into her. My tongue meanders furiously and my hands grasp at her thighs. As her breathing gets heavier and faster, I kiss my way back up, biting on her nipple, using my hand to keep her into it. I kiss her as passionately as I can and slide, hot, into her. She gasps as I thrust in methodically, then starts slapping my back.

"Put on a fucking condom!"

"Yes, ma'am." I smile.

"Alright, then! Stop *Yes, Ma'am*-ing me and put the fucking thing on!"

I leap out of bed and fumble in the dark for my pants. I pull at them as quickly as possible, anxious to get back to it. I grab one leg and my keys spill out. I toss through the fabric looking for my pockets and then riffle through my wallet. Careful to tear at the edges, I pull the latex out and clamber back on top of her as she throws the blanket back over us. I kiss her and roll the condom on.

We get back to it, albeit with less passion than before. I roll over so she's on top, but she's not so much into it and, self-conscious, the sex just gets a bit sloppier. My drunken dick gets a little wobblier and requires some assistance from her hands before it's sailing at full mast again. It's fun though, and I still make her cum before I finish.

I peel the condom off, tying a knot in the middle, and toss it aside. We lie in bed with her head on my chest as I stroke her arm with my thumb. I feel her breath on my skin as I pull the blanket up over her shoulders.

"That was overdue!" She laughs.

"What was?"

"The sex, dummy. I wanted to, like, jump your bones after the fourth day!"

A smugness arises inside me. "Maybe I was playing hard to get?"

"I seem to recall, just a few minutes ago, that *I* had to play to get *you* hard!"

The smugness fades. "Well- I had- When a guy's drunk, sometimes-"

"- Oh, shit!"

"What?"

"I forgot to lock my door!"

"That's an issue?"

"*Duh*! This place got broken into already!"

"You really don't feel safe in your own home?"

"It's a nice area, but you can't be too careful in a city."

She climbs out of bed and my hand slides off her. She locks the door twice with her keys. I wish she could feel safer. Maybe if I track down the guys who robbed this place then I could put her mind at ease a little bit? It's a colder case than I'm used to but, at the very least, I could try. If I succeed, I'd probably win myself some points too.

I slip my underwear back on for comfort while she drinks some water and then open up the covers for her to fall back into bed with me. She grabs my arm and wraps it around herself. I nestle my body against hers.

There it is again... That warmth enveloping my heart. My soul singing electricity throughout my body. The effervescent hope in my head. The promise that something wonderful will be there tomorrow and the day after that. All mixed together with this new joy that I don't have to over-think this. That it's natural, for once.

All we need in life is someone to be fond of.

This girl makes me manic.

Her perfume brings me peace...

And, for the first time in a long time, I fall asleep quickly.

****

Over the last few days, I divided my time between searching for other robberies that are similar to that of Victoria's and spending time with her. I haven't told her anything, I don't want to worry her and she doesn't seem to know much about the break-in anyway. All she could tell me, as I asked with feigned idleness, was that there was no sign of forced entry as the door was still locked, just things gone missing.

I find a site that gives me a list of crimes reported in Paris over the past few years. The burglaries are one thing, but the other statistics are nauseating. Reports of gruesome assaults, rapes, murders. It makes my heart weak to think that such horrible things could be happening in this city, especially with such frequency. Worse still is that I know these are very few of the total number of crimes committed. It's only some of the crimes posted on the site, listed from those actually reported.

No one's safe, it seems. The victims are of all ages, race and gender. Only trauma ties them together. I wish I could be strong enough to protect them from that kind of violation, be more than just one person. It's strange to think that this world, that we all live in, is dangerous. That we haven't made it safe. That often we're the ones making it worse.

Maybe the best we can do is build walls around ourselves. Let the right ones in and hope no unwelcome visitors ever come crashing through our door. The tighter hand on the wallet, the suspicious glancing and the alert stance, the closest thing to a neighbourhood watch.

I put my mind back to the task at hand. I research all the burglaries that have been reported, at least on the site, over the last three years. It takes me hours to go through them all. Scraping for details.

From the limited reports, I find that perhaps forty or so burglaries over the past three years had no sign of forced entry with the doors still locked. It narrows it down from the other hundreds, but it's still a lot of ground to cover. Eight of them occurred near where Victoria lives, which is a pretty good place to start.

****

I've spent over a week asking around, jogging memories, writing it all down, and that was just for the eight in Victoria's area. Most are apathetic about helping me. Their things are long since gone, so why bother? Other's weren't even residents at the times of the robberies, which makes sense given that most would leave to live somewhere they thought was safer. For me, it means I have to track down the original victims too, which is much more difficult.

Back in my apartment, with my notes taped up on the wall like a lunatic, I scan over them looking for a common denominator. Nothing pops out except for the obvious, that there were no signs of forced entry and that the doors were still locked. The apartments themselves vary from flat shares to studio apartments, on different floors and in different areas. The windows are sometimes different, but always secure. The locks are different types and different manufacturers.

The objects taken are mostly cash, jewellery, phones or other small valuables. All very portable. The dates and times of the burglaries are too sporadic to see a pattern. There's no commonality between these people aside from the crime committed against them.

I stare at it for hours. The frustration ebbs away at me until I succumb to tearing the feeble paper off the walls. I know I'm missing something... But what are the odds that I can find it when even the police couldn't? This thief seems to be able to walk through walls.

I scan over the eight reports online again before checking for other robberies in the area. There's a new report of a burglary. My excitement is subdued when I find out that the window was broken in the crime. I click on it anyway out of boredom. Reading through, I start to inch closer to my laptop as the report grabs my attention.

It reads that the window was broken from the inside, as the glass was found outside. The thief jumped from the second floor down. The thing is, the front door was locked by both the bolt and the main lock, as was the window. So, if the burglar couldn't get the window open, and the door was bolted shut, then how the hell did he break in?!

I scribble down the address of the apartment, snatch my coat off the hanger and race down to the scene of the crime. The tenants, a French couple in their late twenties, are reluctant at first. They've already had a stranger in their apartment and that didn't go so well for them the last time, but when I fully explain what I'm doing, they allow me to look around under their careful supervision.

The apartment is a large studio of about 30m². The only other room is the bathroom which is essentially just a toilet, a shower and a sink. A tall dresser stands beside a fold-out couch, the kitchen is located just across from it.

The window, now covered with cardboard and tape, is new, unlike most Parisian windows. Rather than the usual, old, metal handle in the middle of two wooden-framed windows, it's one large pane of glass framed with hard plastic. On the handle, there's a small lock. I look out the window and down to see some crumpled bushes beneath.

"How was the door locked?" I ask them.

"We had locked it when we left. When we came back, I unlocked it only to realise that it was bolted from the inside." The boyfriend says, showing me the broken wood from where he had to kick in the door after hearing the glass breaking.

"What was stolen?"

"Some jewellery mostly. One of the rings stolen belonged to my great-grandmother..." The girlfriend says.

"A smartwatch was also stolen." The boyfriend says and gets a scornful look from his girlfriend.

"Does it have GPS?"

"I kept it turned off. Otherwise the police would have tracked it."

"Shame... Do you still have the lock?"

The boyfriend pulls it out of the drawer and hands it to me. I start writing down the details. At this point, the girlfriend starts to get nervous about my presence and asks me to leave, to which I oblige.

Outside the building, I smoke a cigarette and mull the whole thing over. The intruder could only have had free access to the apartment. He couldn't have hidden somewhere in the studio and waited for them to leave because there's no space or opportunity to do so. He definitely didn't enter through the window, otherwise he wouldn't have had to have broken his way out. The only possible way he could have gotten in was through the front door, but it was bolted and locked... Bolted *and* locked...

Why would the thief lock the door again behind him? Having the door bolted bought him time to escape, but he locked the main lock too. He could have just left the door bolted and that would have been enough. If he had picked the locks, it would just take more time to lock it again. The only thing that makes sense is that he must have already had a key.

It's a clever move. If everything else is left undisturbed, something missing might not immediately cry out that it's been stolen. The victim would have to be sure that whatever it is that's been taken, wasn't just lost somewhere inside the apartment. Think of all the places he might have robbed where no one noticed a thing.

I call the other victims to ask them about the original locksmith that installed their locks and if they had their keys cut. None of them were there when the original locks were installed and only two personally had their keys cut. However, eight out of eight can give me the names, after a few hours, of three different locksmiths: *Clés Inc.*, *Porte Defender* and *La Clé de la Pierre*, all of them located in the fifth arrondissement.

I keep my excitement in check seeing as there can only be a certain amount of locksmiths in a small area and they're not all the same company. Also, the times of the burglaries don't coincide with the locksmiths. Places linked to *Porte Defender* were robbed before and after places linked to *La Clé de la Pierre*. I'm certain there's a connection here somewhere though. I just have to keep digging.

****

I spend four days scoping out the three different locksmiths, finding out who works there and at what time. Standing outside *Porte Defender* again, there doesn't seem to be any connection between the three. No common employees or owners. The only way I'm going to get any answers is by going in and asking.

I have to be careful. I can't just go in and accuse them of robbing the places in question. I need to find a way to uncover who installed the locks or cut the keys without drawing suspicion from anyone. I need a lie that will give me the information I'm looking for. I pull my cigarettes out of my pocket and reach into my back pocket for a lighter when a piece of paper touches my hands. It's a receipt. An idea jumps straight into my head.

Inside, a man steps back from his computer and moves over to the counter as I enter. He seems relieved by the fact that I'm here. I don't imagine cutting keys or installing locks is the most social of jobs.

"Hello." He says, warmly.

"Hi."

"What can I do for you?"

"Ehm, it's kind of embarrassing actually..."

"You've been locked out of your house?" He laughs.

"No! Really... In fact, I'm replacing the locks in my apartment and my landlord is insisting that I get a receipt for the last one so he can "estimate the costs" and I was wondering if you could do that for me? Just details on the installation and the cost."

"The old locks are from us?"

"I believe so, yes."

"And you're not satisfied with the locks?"

The people that got robbed sure aren't. "Oh, I am. I'm just being safety conscious."

"Not a terrible idea. I could just give you the current rates for installation and costs, you know?"

"He's pretty specific and he's usually quite... Adamant... About getting what he wants... Could I get the old receipt and your current rates? It's just that I think he wants to make sure he isn't paying more than he has to."

"Ah, a miser... Well, let me check what we did for you then."

I give him the name of one of the victims from this group and he runs it through the system. The printer whirs as the page comes through. I'm grateful that he's being this helpful, considering I have to ask him for two more.

"There you go. It's an invoice for the locks."

"Thanks." I read over the sheet. "This signature here. Is that who installed the locks?"

"At the bottom of the page? Yes, it should be."

"It's just an *X*?"

"Right." He sighs. "That must have been Max."

"Max?"

"He signed all of them with an *X*. I told him to be more clear."

"You sound fed up with him. Does he still work here?" I pry.

"Not anymore. He quit about five years ago to work for another company."

"Do you know which one?"

"Ehm... Clés something? Why?"

"Just... Shopping around..."

"You should stick with us! The locks haven't failed yet after all this time, have they?"

"The key still fits in the door!"

He snorts at my lame joke while I gather the courage to follow up.

"While I'm here... My friends are worried that their landlords might do the same to them at some point. Drag them down here, I mean. Is there any chance I could ask for their invoices too?"

He eyes me suspiciously. "You know that there's not very much details on these receipts, just information your friends already have. There's no credit card information, not even anything about the keys for the doors."

"I know! I do! And thank god! I mean, it's bad security to hand out those things. It's just that they don't want to have to come down and do it if they ever decide to change their locks. I understand if you don't feel comfortable, though!"

"There's no harm doing it, I suppose." He shrugs.

He prints off the other two invoices. I thank him warmly and walk out as calmly as I can. I wait until I'm two streets away and look back to make sure I'm not being followed before I look at the other pages. Sure enough, both of the other apartments are signed with an X.

Repeating the process in the other two locksmiths, I get the same signature. Chatting briefly with both of the locksmiths, I start to paint a crude picture of the man. His name is Max Wagner and he's a German citizen living in Paris. Quiet but friendly. He's about fifty years old or so. No family or kids to speak of. No friends either. He worked, and subsequently left, all of the locksmiths. The last being *La Clé de la Pierre* about four years ago. His address changes for each place of employment.

He's been a patient man holding on to those keys for so long. He knew by detaching himself from the equation and letting time cover his tracks that no one would come looking for him as the likely suspect. Most of his robberies were probably resolved to be very poorly conducted cases of insurance fraud on the victim's part.

A search online brings me to his Facebook profile. The bastard's been hiding in plain sight all along. He checks in online to state that he's at a bar on Rue Mouffetard.

I wait for a few hours outside the bar. He staggers out and smiles to himself as he rolls up his sleeve, revealing a shiny smartwatch. For a crook as careful as he is, he doesn't know much about security in technology. He thought that leaving no physical trace behind would help him, thinking nothing of the digital trace.

I have what I need to call the police. I follow him back to his apartment, right to his front door. He's too drunk to notice me creeping behind him. I stare at his door smugly and scratch a small X on the door with my keys. He doesn't know he's locked himself in to his own cell. A quick call to the police and-

"Excuse me?" A voice calls out and I freeze.

I spin around to see a short woman. She appears to be quite drunk. Her droopy eyes look at me sadly.

"What- What can I do for you?" I ask.

"I need a Euro."

"A Euro?"

"I *need* a Euro." She sings.

I fumble in my pocket as she continues to talk. "Bless you! Say, what's your name?"

"That's not something I'm really-"

"- My name's Tracey. What's your name?"

I smile back at her and give her a Euro.

"What you up to?" She asks and looks at the door.

"I'm just... On my way out."

"Oh, no you aren't! I can see you! Let me guess. She broke your heart?" She asks pointing at the *X* on the door.

"Broke something..."

"Bet you came here for a little something extra from your ex-girlfriend. A goodbye or something?!"

"Well-"

"- But she wasn't having any of it!" She laughs. "I don't blame you for trying though!"

"I really-"

"- Because you know what they say?!"

"What's that, Tracey?" I sigh.

"Ex marks the spot!" She giggles and walks back to the open door of her apartment, just before I turn to leave she calls back out to me. "What was your name again?"

"Have a nice night, Tracey..." I smile to her, then I exit the building and dial the number for the police.

****

  I'm nervous. More nervous than I should be. I just want everything to go well. There's a lot on the line now that I've build it up in my head. A whole future could be at stake because of this one night. I need a drink to calm me down. It's a good thing I'm going to a bar. I feel my hand being squeezed.

"If your hand keeps sweating I will outright refuse to hold it any longer!" Victoria snaps.

"I'm just anxious. It's the first time you're going to meet my friends and they're pretty important to me. I want you to like them."

"I already like them. They have good taste in the company they keep." She grins.

"Thank you, but-"

"- No *buts*! Everything is going to be fine! Babe, you worry way too much."

"Grand..."

"What is it?"

"Stop!"

"... *Grand*... Hick!"

  We arrive at Cole's and I make the introductions to Charlie, Leah, Aidan, Leona, Matt and Marine. The latter two are the first to warm up to her. Matt being impressed by her ability to parry his dry insults about Americans and Marine after the two ended up chatting in the toilets for twenty-five minutes. After about three pints, the interrogation begins. Victoria tells everyone a bit about herself as each person takes turns asking her questions. It starts out simple, how we met and what she does for a living, before the questioning becomes ridiculous for the sake of levity.

"How many offspring do you wish to have?" Marine asks.

"Oh, dang. I don't know. It used to be five, but now that seems like a lot to handle."

"You wanted *five* kids?!" Charlie asks. "Leah – Ehm – What do you think?"

"That sounds exhausting..." She says, almost to herself.

"I come from a big family! I asked my Mom what she regretted most and she said it was stopping at four." Victoria explains.

Matt slaps me on the back. "Lucky you, dickhead! You've got your work cut out for you!"

  The questioning stops as Victoria starts to ease into the group comfortably. My hand slips into hers and we trade a kiss before her attention is pulled away by Leona who has a question about living in America. As the two talk, my eyes wander around the table.

  I can't say much for ever having a place to call home. It seemed difficult to pinpoint something tangible and state that this is where I am best placed. Even my own body can't be called the safest place for my soul. It can succumb to disease, betray you, expire.

Now, I know I've found a home. Right here, with these people. I'm a better person with them than without them. They make me stronger and I feel safer with them. When I walk into this group, I leave my worries at the door. I'm at peace.

Home is where the heart is and the heart is wherever you build it. Each person a brick in the wall, designed to weather the storms that lie ahead. And for each home knocked down in the past, we learn to build them stronger than before.

We built this home for ourselves because we endear each other...

Case 22 – At The End Of The Tunnel.

"Fuck me in the fucking face." Victoria whines.

"What?" I ask.

"There are no sharks, sir..."

"What do you mean?"

"I mean they've only got the little ones. The big ones must be at the other aquarium."

Indeed, looking around, there doesn't seem to be any tank big enough to hold a large shark. Also, seeing as the most publicised attraction here is a couple of albino baby alligators, it's unlikely that there's a Great White anywhere.

"But I was promised *sharks*!" I whine sarcastically.

"No refunds!" She shouts, grabbing me and shaking me.

We leave the aquarium, slightly disappointed, and make our way to a park across the street. Sitting down on the grass, I stare across the lake at the browning leaves of the trees as the wind gently caresses my face. The sun dancing on the water, a river running on serenity. As Victoria places her head on my lap, there's no other moment I'd rather be in than right now. The two of us, comfortable in the quiet.

"What do you think about getting married?" She asks.

"I think it's a little too soon for us."

"I mean in general, dumbass!"

"I'd like to get married at some point."

"Most marriages don't work though."

"Some do, I hear..."

"You reckon we'll get married?"

"A bit early to say."

"You have doubts?"

"Not doubts..."

"But you're not sure this will last."

I sigh and pull her a little closer. "There's a chance what we have might be temporary, but it's never doomed..."

"... If we do get married, you better buy me a goddamn big ring. I'm talking wrist cramps!"

"How much would that cost me?"

"I don't know. An engagement ring is supposed to be three times your salary though, so I guess we'd have to wait a few years."

"So I can save the money?"

"What?! No! So you can find a job with a bigger salary!"

"Ah..."

I sit up uncomfortably as a small creature scurries across the grass. I fear that it might be a rat until I get a proper look at the size of the thing. It's only a mouse. Victoria turns over to look at it.

"In my café I found a mouse sleeping in the potato bin."

"You did?"

"Yeah... Of course, I wasn't going to just, like, kill him. So I dropped a bucket on him and let him loose in the hotel next door!"

"Why did you release it into the hotel?"

"I dunno... It was close... And warm..." She smiles and sticks her tongue out at me.

"You know... When I was looking for you, that was kind of my nickname for you."

"Mouse? Why?"

"I guess you kind of reminded me of one."

"Because I love cheese?"

"This was before I knew you had a dairy addiction."

"When you were kind of fucked up in the head?"

"Yeah..."

"I'm sorry..."

"It's over now..." I tell her, stroking her cheek, and watch the mouse scurry away.

****

In her apartment, I play the guitar while she puts her feet on my lap and reads a book. I sing a few songs before swapping the guitar for her. We kiss and our hands start roaming. Mine land on her waist and hers land on my face. She looks at me with a grin.

"I'm going to pop those blackheads." She declares, tapping my nose.

"That- That's really not where I thought this was going!"

"We can have sex afterwards! But I have to do it. It's, like, bugging me, sir... Here, lie on the bed."

I sigh and comply. She sits on my chest and her knees hold down my arms.

"Are you serious?!" I ask, incredulously.

"What?"

"I have to be restrained?!"

"I don't want you making any sudden movements!"

She starts pinching and squeezing my nose. I blink back the tears as the sharp pings of pain rise and subside. After about ten minutes, she stops, kissing my nose, my mouth and then travelling further south.

I'm falling fast for her. We just fit perfectly. Comfortable to be completely vulnerable around each other. Disarmed. Naked. A rush every time I get a sweet, familiar taste of her in my mouth.

This girl... Kindness incarnate...

After, lying in bed together, we start talking in the kind of drowsy openness that can only come about after everything else has been said. It's thinking out loud to a new part of yourself. With those you're enamoured with, the companions we choose to keep us company in the dark, it's not about who they are, it's about who they become when they're around you.

"You're not completely correct, you know..." She says.

"About what?"

"About the past being a part of who you are."

"It is a part of who you are, though. It's what got you there."

"Yeah, but people *change*, sir."

"And?"

"*And* to do that they have to look to the future... You can't choose who you are, only who you want to be..."

"So you're saying the future is more important."

"Not more important, but you have to put the past to rest, *mon chou chou*... You can't let that stuff define who you are."

"Why not?"

"Because it doesn't help."

"Looking back helps sometimes when you're looking forward."

"Only to avoid repeating mistakes, not to get trapped by it... You're the one that said we should all be running towards something."

"So?"

"Well, you can't run forwards if you're carrying the past around with you..."

I shift a little uncomfortably in the bed.

"Can I give you some advice?" She asks.

"I'm not great at taking advice from people."

"My advice is that you take some advice... I don't think you trust people enough. I mean, I know you want to be in control of your life. I don't know if that's because you're afraid you're going to be... *Hurt*... At some point... But you need to let people in and point you in the right direction every now and then. There are more right ways to live your life than just one... You need to trust more... Some people have only the best intentions for you..."

"That doesn't always mean they're right."

"It doesn't mean they're *always* wrong either..."

"I guess I'm just trying to get through life with as little misery as possible."

"Well, sometimes life isn't about living it... It's about loving it..."

    I'm starting to realise that she's right. Maybe it's time to trust in people and let myself change without worrying so much as to where that might lead me? All this time, I've been keeping people out of swaying my actions so I can, at the end of the day, say that whatever happens to me is my own fault. Really, it's just given me free reign over my self-destructive behaviour.

    I know I need to move on from the past too. I thought carrying the weight of it was making me stronger. Always taking the hard path because I thought it was the only right path. The suffering building me up. In truth, it's crippling me, causing me to relive and repeat it. I've analysed it enough to know what went wrong. It's already been solved and resolved. It's time to close it.

    So, where to next? Somewhere along the way, I forgot who I really wanted to be. I need to start running towards something. Carry myself forward into the future. Not bury the past, just put it to rest...

I clear my throat. "I'm quitting my job..."

****

I left Victoria's at about 2am. It was a weird compulsion. I just felt like I couldn't wait any longer. I walk down as far as Châtelet to an internet café that's open 24/7 and start typing away. After about twenty minutes or so, I have my letter of resignation drawn up and my CV updated. It occurs to me now that I should have brought a folder to hold these papers.

I click on print and head up to the counter. The letter of resignation comes out first followed by five copies of my CV before the printer makes a crunching sound followed by a bleating, beeping noise. The clerk opens it up and looks inside before turning to me with a shrug. I guess I'll have to print off more later. I pay and walk out briskly to avoid any possible backlash as he starts to tell other customers that the printer is now broken.

There's a pep in my step as I wander through the meandering streets on the way to the hotel. I'm sure I could take the metro by now, but each foot I put forward is a thrill. A march towards a better tomorrow. A new adventure for me to undertake. With the holiday pay that I've accumulated, I could probably travel a little bit. Maybe even take Victoria with me?

This energy is coursing through my veins. I feel born again. High on optimism. I finally realise that there aren't really happy endings in life, no cutaways of the camera, only happy moments and I'm going to seize this one. Stop skulking in the dark just to see what tomorrow brings, but let myself hope for the best.

"Are you following me, dickhead?!" A familiar voice calls out. I turn around to see Matt with his bike.

"Hey! How are you?"

"Good, good. Just on my way home. And yourself? Out late or up early?"

"Both, kind of."

"Been about a few days since I last seen ya. We should hang out soon and make up for lost time, if you fancy a bit of a catch up?"

"Yeah, sure."

"So, what's new with you then?"

"Actually, I have a bit of an announcement to make."

"You're getting back with your ex and moving to New York!"

"What?! No!"

"You said-"

"- I said I have an announcement, not herald the fucking apocalypse, Matt!"

"Alright, calm down! I was only fucking with ya! What's the big announcement then?"

"I'm quitting my job!"

"Nice! You have your CV's printed up?"

"I do."

"Good stuff. Shit, that reminds me. I have to print out CV's too before I get the yearly sack."

"You're getting fired? What happened?"

"Nothing. Season's over. I just have to find something for the winter then I'm back at it again, same as last year."

"I forgot about that."

"Yeah, it's not always easy finding a job. You get nervous too if you don't find one in time."

"True..."

"Anyway, I'm off. Later, porkchop!"

    Matt hops onto his bike and pedals away. The last thing he said made me realise how precarious changing jobs can be. I might find myself in a tight spot if I run out of money before I find somewhere new. It's a short distance to crossing that thin line that separates me from being comfortable to being homeless again.

Maybe I should reconsider quitting my job? It's comfortable enough, knowing the downsides already. Would it be so bad to stay?...

Yes. Yes, it would.

I can't stay in that job forever. I need to move on and it's better to do it on my terms.

I've given myself a month's notice so I can look while I'm working and the holidays will get me another two weeks or so. Although, I would much prefer to use my holiday pay to travel. Get out of Paris for a while, visit different places and explore a new culture. See something new.

The change that's coming, the one that rattled me, isn't as much to fear as I thought. It's one change out of many other things that I have in my life. I'll still have the same friends, the same apartment, the same Victoria. A new job won't spell an end to that, it might even improve the time I get to spend with them.

Walking down Rue de Rivoli, I catch a glance ahead of a woman that looks vaguely familiar. I can't quite place her. She returns the look and eventually I see an awkward smile crawl up on her face. Her arm wrapped around a man, she pulls him in and leans into his ear. I return the awkward smile and give a slight wave.

"Fancy seeing you again!" She exclaims. It's her eyes that make me recognise her. Fresher than I remember them, but still the same ones. It's Mrs. Swan and, to my complete and utter surprise, Mr. Swan.

"Didn't think I would..." I reply. I look inquisitively at Mr. Swan who shuffles on his feet, his reddening face gives me a nod.

"It's alright, love. All in the past." She gives a sympathetic smile to her, what I assume to still be, husband.

"So you two are back together again?"

"We are. Although it wasn't easy... I tried to divorce him! Rather, I filed the papers for divorce and it resulted in a rather... *frank*... Conversation between the two of us. Eventually, we figured out that it was all about fear... And we could either move forward or move on. We decided to move forward. Put the past behind, get over the fear and keep going."

"I met a girl that told me something along those lines."

"What lines are those?"

"Put the past to rest and set a new course."

"Setting yourself goals, are we? It's been six months since we have and, honestly, we haven't been happier! So, who's this girl then?"

"Just someone I kind of... Found..."

"She make you happy?"

"She does..."

"Then that's that, isn't it?"

"That's that."

"I suppose we best be heading off. Lovely to see you again!"

  I watch them stroll away with a strange feeling of contentment. It seems like things worked out for them. The Swans had their fair share of troubles, but they faced them head on and sorted it out. Now, they're happy again. That's the thing about the future, it can always hold promise if you let it. No matter how bad things are right now, there's always a chance that things can be better tomorrow. All one needs to do now is try and sort things out for the next day. It's reassuring to see what the future can hold for me if I follow the same path. That rapture is always within reach.

  I reflect on what she said to me about setting goals. If it wasn't for Mrs. Swan, I would never have set my own and started looking for Victoria. She was the one that started this journey for me. I decided, the day I helped her, to be better than who I was. It was the beginning of a very long road, now that I think of it.

  The different people I've met have all shared a bit of their stories with me. Their pasts and presents, even my possible futures. Each thread, a possibility. None of them connected at all, but all made from the same string. All tiny parts of the same, magnificent story of humanity.

I've helped quite a few of them. Allowed them to overcome those obstacles and continue on their journey to find happiness. I've ran around this city over and over again to make gains for everyone else and for all I've done, I've gotten it back. Some of those I helped turned out to be the most amazing friends. People that pick me up whenever I'm down. They look after me. And for those who aren't so much my friends, they still endowed me with their stories, their cultures and what life has taught them.

Turns out I've been taking people's advice all this time without realising it. Each person I helped had at least one thing to teach me. Over the past year, they've taught me how to be braver and kinder, to not worry so much, to combat cynicism, to care for myself. Overall, I've learnt that happiness is something you make out of what you have...

I arrive at the hotel and try the front doors. Both are locked, which is unsurprising considering the renovations will only be done tomorrow. No one's going to be here until later, I imagine. I go around and get in through the side door. All I need to do now is go upstairs and leave my letter of resignation on Crow's desk.

I take a few steps forward into the hotel when I'm distracted by a light at the end of the corridor. It appears to be coming from the kitchen.

****

Crow stares back at me, frozen. I imagine I look about the same as he does. It's the confusion mostly. I don't think either of us expected to find ourselves in this particular situation. Time passes by at a rate unknown to either of us. He raises his hand up slowly to signal that I stop. I awkwardly look to the exit then return to his anxious gaze to try and figure out what the fuck he's doing.

There's a guilty look in his eye. I feel like I've landed in at the wrong moment. In his other hand, he's holding a loose, exposed wire. This isn't nearly as curious as the dead rat that's lying by his feet. The place looks like a bomb hit it as I turn around. Stained, cloth sheets cover the surfaces and are thrown in bundles on the floor. Sheets of scrap wood are lying in slightly more orderly piles. I look past him. A barrel of white spirits and some other exposed wires are sprawling out of the wall behind Crow.

"What are you doing here?" I ask.

"Nossing!" His eyes start shifting.

"I meant, what are you doing *here*?"

He shrugs back at me. I look back over the other times I've been suspicious of him. A few seconds go by before I connect the threads and figure out what's happening. The dead rat by the loose wire, the white spirits, the cloth.

Shocked annoyance runs through my body. I came here to hand in my letter of resignation, to storm out of this place. My moment of victory has gone up in smoke. He's stolen my fire, this asshole Prometheus.

"You're trying to burn down the fucking hotel!"

He looks at me, red faced and red handed. "Ze 'otel is broke... If I don't burn it down zen zee employees can-not get paid what zey are owed..."

"Fuck me... You could have just sold the place!"

"Een a recession? I sink not."

That lying prick... All this time, he's been planning to burn down the hotel while we've been grinding away. The renovations just an excuse to keep the hotel empty and raise its value. The poor reviews allowing him to reduce staff and hasten its demise. He can just claim that a rat ate some wires and caused an electrical fire that spiralled out of control due to the white spirit soaked sheets. All his money sent back to him by the insurance company. He gets to walk away squeaky clean.

I look back at him and realise my place in this. He can't do anything unless I swear to stay quiet...

On the one hand, people need to get paid. I was going to quit this place anyway, there's nothing holding me here.

On the other hand, insurance fraud is almost as bad as being an accomplice to arson. It's a huge risk to take and I don't know what I'm going to do...

What *am* I going to do?

What would you do?

Case 23 – Sunrise

As we watch the hotel burn, I see all my hard work over the past year go up in smoke. All the polished brass and wiped wood. All the guests I've tolerated. All the time and energy I wasted worrying about the place. All of it for nothing...

Grand...

Crow – or Mr. Corbet, rather – throws an arm around my shoulder, which I gruffly shrug off. Felonies doesn't make us friends. He nods at me awkwardly before walking away, breaking into a jog a few steps in. I follow his direction slowly, careful to avoid the security cameras on the streets, walking away from a mystery that's already been solved.

I ring Victoria until she wakes up and I find her on the tracks of her metro stop, rubbing her eyes, trying to find me in the crowd. I take a moment to just look at her, before she sees me. Clothed in a denim jacket and a white T-shirt, her hair a little bit messy given the time she had to prepare. All I can see is how perfect she is.

A simple kiss leaves me dazzled as she grabs my hand and we jump on the next train. We decide in transit to head to Buttes Chaumont to watch the sun rise. Hands intertwined, she rests her head on my shoulder as I lean in to plant a kiss on her head. Her hair is soft and light on my lips.

"I'm fucking exhausted you know. Thanks for dragging me out of bed." She mumbles.

"I didn't drag you. You met me on the tracks."

"Well, I had about six missed calls from you, sir. You seemed pretty intent on getting me out of bed."

"It's the only way I can get you back into bed."

"Ooh... Yew arre being rromanteec?" She says in a mock Hispanic accent, raising her head.

"Si, mi amore."

"Ai, papi!"

"You are a goof."

"Am not!"

"You are! That's why-"

"Why what?"

"Nothing."

"You were gonna say something!"

"Maybe..."

She smiles back at me, knowingly, and says "You know, I've been thinking..."

"About what?"

"Well, okay... *Serious* topic, but, like... If things go well between us, my um- my lease is up in three months and I was thinking we could move in together... No pressure!"

"I'd love to..." I tell her and lean in for a kiss.

  We alight from the train and blaze up the stairs. A quick walk takes us to the top of a hill. Under some concrete arches, we find ourselves looking out at a red sky framing the whole city. Golden windows shimmer in the distance off of yellow buildings. Brown, autumn leaves are painted orange by the sun.

  We spend hours walking around, enjoying the freedom that the day has given us. I had forgotten what the morning air tasted like. The freshness that other people have at these hours, where the darkness and its grim curtain is at its lowest tide. Eventually, we head down to Place des Vosges, where she steals my phone and starts to take photos of herself.

  Her playful youth reminds me that I can rise above the

cynicism that I've held on to for so long. All the defensive walls I put up before to keep people out have crumbled down even faster in her company. I'm not as guarded against strangers. I've encountered enough to know that each of them possess something in common with me, an interest or an ideology.

I can feel myself leave my body and look down at myself. I see myself amongst everyone in the park, the people on the streets, in their cars. The thronging mass, milling around in different directions. Random and together. An intense feeling of solidarity comes over me, like I've finally found my place in the world.

There are enough things in my life to keep me busy. I can still improve myself in many ways. Some things will take more time than others. Priorities will change. There's a long road ahead until I'll be exactly who I want to be, but I'm used to that by now. It's not as daunting as before.

I have someone to keep me warm for the coming winter. Blessed with a beautiful companion. The chill in the air, a whisper to stay indoors and curl up in bed. Or maybe to take a break?

"What do you think about going on holiday with me?"

"Where?"

"I don't know yet. But there's a whole world out there to explore. Oceans, forests, mountains... We can go anywhere and do anything, even if it's only for a week or so. We can just set out and explore! Go places that most people don't."

"That sounds kinda dangerous, sir."

"Ah, I've survived more than you'd think..."

I'm ready to leave the past behind me. Move forward into the future, braver than ever. To be excited about life. All the cases I solved before only served to prepare me for this.

And now I'm taking on the great case that we all solve eventually.

The future, the biggest mystery yet...

This book is dedicated to:

My family for their constant love and support.

And my friends, the best part of me, who are the most wonderful people I have ever met.

Printed in Great Britain
by Amazon